Surviving THIRTY

NICOLE SHARP

This book has some strong language, smoking, drinking and sex. Enjoy!

The Simply Trouble Series:

Big Trouble in Little Italy
Simply Protocol
Worth The Trouble
A Simple Avalanche

Standalone Books

The Italian Holiday
La Bella Luna
Surviving Thirty

Novellas

Let It Snow
The Museum Guide

For Amy, my ride or die since second grade. Thank you for always having my back as we traverse this wild journey of a life.

Surviving THIRTY

"Dearly beloved,
we are gathered here today
to get through this thing called life."

—Prince, "Let's Go Crazy"

Hello my friend,

I have to tell you, when I wrote this book I was in the mood to write something raucous and amusing; so this book ended up being quite the wild ride. I started joking that I was writing something along the lines of *Bridget Jones's Diary* (without the *Pride and Prejudice* parallel) meets *The Odyssey* (but *The Odyssey* as summarized by a friend who only read the CliffsNotes version and has most of it wrong). I hope you have as much fun reading Ali and TJ's adventure as I had writing it. After all, life is short and we need to remember to allow ourselves to have some fun. Enjoy the adventure! - Nicole

One

I stared down at the Polaroid in my hand and stifled a disappointed groan. There I was, a reluctant smile fixed to my face and a giant sombrero on my head. My grandparents to the left, tritely smiling. My parents on the right, rather grim, enduring the evening. And behind us all, a group of grinning waiters from Poncho's Taco Extravaganza.

The excited shout for everyone to say "queso" came after the waiters waltzed up to our table, firmly placed the giant red, white and green sombrero on my head, set down a flan—that now had its own 'sombrero' of melted wax from the crowded candles on top—all the while singing a raucous, off-key version of "Happy Birthday."

Then, "say queso" was followed by the flash of a retro Polaroid.

And that was it.

This was it.

The moment I officially turned thirty.

The ending of an era. The beginning of a new chapter in my life. I glanced at my supportive but mostly worried-for-my-future parents and set-in-their-ways grandparents.

This was my celebration.

Not the one I'd dreamed of, that's for sure.

It would at least be nice to be out with some friends who could've helped me in my quest to get shit-faced drunk, dance with some sweaty guy and do something wonderfully irresponsible.

Actually, I *yearned* to be with friends who would have happily whisked me away to Vegas for the weekend where we could've gotten accidentally married for twenty-four hours and shoved dirty dollar bills down the front of some greased bodybuilder's thong because we were caught up in the moment.

The *reality* was that most of those friends had moved, married, matured, had kids, had jobs, and had grown up.

I, on the other hand, had been forced to move back in with my parents almost two months ago. My childhood home had become some strange time warp where I was still perceived a teen and rules that applied in another life, were awkwardly reinstated and insisted on being followed by the owners of the house: Call when I was going to be out past eleven, dishes were my daily chore, and my attendance at Sunday dinner was mandatory.

The re-issued rules, a recent-ish breakup, the lack of a real job, and my parents well-meaning; were not mixing well. The last few weeks at home had been an experiment gone bad, and while I was grateful for my parents and loved them, I just couldn't live *with* them.

I handed the sombrero back to our waiter in return for another shot of Tequila, said a little prayer, then threw my head back and attempted to drown out the evening.

But my family continued to negate the effects of the Tequila.

"You know, when I was your age, I had three kids and a good job. And if I lost my job, I had two more lined up before the end of the day." This fairy tale was barked out loudly by my no-nonsense grandfather.

"Don't you know a nice boy you could settle down with?" My grandmother's fix.

"She's just ... dancing to her own drummer," my mother tried, then sighed, "even if it doesn't get me grandchildren." (She already had five grandchildren thanks to my brother and sister.)

"I thought you said you had a few freelance jobs set up this week," my father chimed in.

"I just don't understand this generation. In my day—" My grandfather paused irritatedly to grab the attention of the waitress. "Hey there sweetheart, can we have more chips, and some more of that salsa? I've been waiting ten minutes for another basket."

I caught the waitress' eye, scrunched my face and glanced at my grandfather; hopefully she understood the apology I meant in all of that. She nodded and gave her own eye roll, so since we were on the same page,

I pointed to my shot glass; she winked, acknowledging my need; though as she turned away, I fought the urge to scream 'Hurry! For the love of God, HURRY!'

"What happened between you and Danny? I bet he didn't want a wife who was going to work so much," my grandmother added.

"In my day," my grandfather started again, pulling the attention back to himself, "we knew how to work. We knew that time was precious. You aren't going to live forever."

I had a few soapbox retorts to that statement, but instead turned my eyes upward to the darkened ceiling and prayed to the gods of Tequila to save me.

They did *not* come to my rescue.

My grandmother did, though. "Wilfred, leave her alone."

"I don't want to pressure you, but there was a segment on the *Nightly News*," my mother chimed in, "about how women over thirty have less eggs and the older they get the more difficult it becomes to get pregnant."

"Jesus, I'm trying to eat," my grandfather muttered.

My father attempted a peacemaking bridge. "She's just between jobs right now. I bet there is a lot about the publishing world we don't understand."

My grandmother nodded. "I might not understand the publishing world, but I'm sure there are men in that business. You know," she leaned her upper body across the table toward me, "my hairdresser's son just got divorced and he's living with his mother right now, too. He's looking for a nice girl. I could get you his number."

The waitress returned, placed the chips in front of my grandfather and I desperately grabbed the offered shot out of her hand and threw it back.

Rejuvenated from a few chips, my grandfather recalled the disjointed dissertation he was giving. "I bagged groceries, I worked midnight shifts at the hospital, your own father got a second job every holiday season so he could give you kids nice things."

"A single woman is easy prey for predators, too," my mother was having her own aside. "They had a segment on one of those shows about how single women should be careful with their schedules; you should always change it up a little every day so no one can predict your movements."

My grandfather wasn't about to be waylaid. "I go to the grocery store, the pharmacy and the gas station at least once a week and they always have 'Help Wanted' signs. There's nothing wrong with those jobs, it's honest work and it's a paycheck."

My grandmother tried to placate everyone. "Ali, we're not saying you have to get a job, but you're thirty now. Don't you know a nice boy you can settle down with?" she tried once more, while offering a sad smile. "You're such a pretty girl."

"I thought I had a nice man, Grandma. A few weeks ago he took me out to a fancy dinner and told me he found someone else and has been sleeping with her for the past four months."

That seemed to deter any continued conversation, as well as any attention everyone seemed willing to give. I cleared my throat and nodded to the edge of the booth. "I need to be excused for a minute," I said.

My grandmother pushed at my grandfather. "Wilfred, let her out, she has to make a tinkle."

I didn't hold back my snort of annoyance that accompanied the comment as I scooted out of the large arc booth where our party of five had been placed. "I'll be right back," I muttered to no one in particular.

"Your purse." My grandmother handed it over. "Put on a little lipstick, it will make you feel better."

I swayed a bit on my Tequila-filled legs but managed to keep my head held high as I wobbled my way to the bathroom.

After 'tinkling,' I looked at myself in the mirror and made a face before asking, "What are you doing?"

The answer came when passing the entrance of Poncho's Taco Extravaganza, as I headed back toward the table. I glanced out the front door as invisible gusts of wind challenged my balance; then with a nod of my head, decided I'd had enough family fun and walked out of the restaurant.

I was a few yards past the parking lot when I thought better of leaving without informing *someone*, so I texted my mom that I was very sorry, but I'd had enough and was going to get some air and walk home or call a friend to come get me.

She texted back a winking face and *I don't blame you*.

My mom understands me, even if all those nightly news shows she watches cause her to worry. (And I mean, those are her parents in there with their opinions, so of course she understands.)

Four or five blocks later, I was having a lot more fun. However, the abundance of fresh air was tarnishing my drunken state, so I made my way toward the beckoning glow of a convenience store in the distance. A forty wrapped in a brown paper bag was my goal.

"Happy birthday to me, happy birthday to me," I sang lamely, "Happy birthday Ali Skye..." I trailed off and gave a snort of sad laughter.

Yeah, happy birthday to me.

Two

Fucked.

If there was one thing I could tell about the convenience store clerk from the moment I swung open the door was that he was, one hundred percent, without a doubt, fucked.

"God damnit, tell me the truth!" A woman with rage in her eyes and an inch of brown roots showing through a cheap blonde dye job had a gun pressed to the clerk's head.

They stood in front of the counter, just a few feet from the door.

"I will fucking pull the trigger and kill you Tyler Stone!" she screamed.

I could tell I was still a little drunk, because instead of being scared for my life, I couldn't help but think that the clerk's name was awesome. Though, it didn't seem to fit his lanky frame. Tyler Stone looked like a failed computer science geek christened with a rock star name whose last chance at doing something with his life was choosing the night shift at a convenience store.

"God damnit Tyler! Tell me the truth you asshole, is the bitch pregnant or isn't she?" The screeching voice caused him to pull back from the gun a bit as he opened his mouth; but before he could answer, another woman, facing them in the front of the candy aisle, inserted her own screeching into the situation.

"Of course I'm pregnant!" the alleged pregnant woman shot. "You ain't any good in bed, so he found a *real woman* that won't get all stupid and prissy when he needs a blowjob!"

I kinda thought the moment required some sort of hooting and hollering from an imaginary studio audience; but this was the real world.

I think.

When the supposed pregnant woman, snapping her gum, crossed her arms over her ample chest and raised a badly drawn on eyebrow in defiance of the woman with the gun, I slapped my hand over my mouth to keep the giggle from escaping.

"I'll kill you too!" yelled the girl with the gun.

I watched Tyler flinch as the barrel of the gun pressed harder into his temple.

"Yeah right," the alleged pregnant woman said with a laugh as she put her hands on her hips and jutted her chin, "you ain't been a real woman for him, so I doubt you got any balls to go through with *this* either."

No one had noticed me yet. So in all fairness, I could just back out and leave these three to their 'Jerry Springer Special.' But I couldn't move, partially due to my fading intoxication and partially because it was like staring at a train wreck. And in my state, the 'balls' comment pulled a strangled laugh that couldn't be held back by my hand any longer, causing me to swallow wrong and dissolve into a coughing fit of laughter.

The door shut behind me and I slipped to the floor with an *umph*, which made me laugh even more.

"Who the fuck are you?!" the woman with the gun screamed, turning the barrel toward me.

I held up my hand, the universal request to hold on just one moment as I tried to stop coughing and laughing. When I was finally able to take a deep breath, I asked, "Who is the modern day Jerry Springer? Cuz I can't remember." Okay, it wasn't that funny, but drunkenness and sobriety were playing manic games with my emotions.

"Fuck you!" Gun Girl screamed, but I didn't feel threatened, just more enthralled by her wild, prostitute-blue painted eyes. "I'll fucking kill you too, bitch!"

(I wasn't sure she could say anything without screaming it.)

"Well, my night's been pretty shitty as it is, so ..." I shrugged in reply to her threat.

Her eyes clouded with her frenzied temper and I thought maybe she'd actually shoot me until the clerk moved slightly. I wasn't sure whether it was his movement or the fact that he was wearing a red polo convenience store shirt—which seemed the perfect angering color—that drew back the attention of crazed Gun Girl, but I appreciated it.

"Are there any other customers here?" I asked from where I sat.

It seemed like this had been going on for a while. And for such a busy street corner, there should have been more people in here than the miserable clerk, the trailer trash pointing a gun, and the alleged pregnant, gum chomping, big boobed mistress.

"They all ran out. Someone's called the cops by now. Pretty soon this psycho bitch is gonna have to give up or shoot it out with the po po." The suspected 'pregnant' gum chewer raised her voice while waving her bright pink Press-On nails around and mocked, "That is, if she has any bullets left after she finishes fucking killing us!"

"Ah." It was the only appropriate answer one could give.

"Stop it! I mean it, I'm going to kill you all!" Gun Girl screamed again.

"Then do it already and stop fuckin' around," the alleged pregnant girl said, taking a step toward Gun Girl.

I forced down another strangled nervous laugh, because maybe I shouldn't be laughing. But then again, if I were allegedly pregnant, I don't know that I would be egging on someone with a gun, who had an unhinged look in her eyes, and whose mania was growing with each passing moment.

I thought about pointing out that no matter what anyone thought, Gun Girl did have the upperhand here and probably needed a fraction of respect.

Sure, I didn't care for how my thirtieth year was going so far, but I didn't really want it over so soon.

"You can't kill any of us any more than you can satisfy my man. You're all talk, no action," came another accusation from *Pregnant Girl,*' accompanied by another wave of her poorly manicured hand. "Hell, I bet that gun isn't even loaded."

Then. She snapped her gum.

Looking back now, I'm pretty sure it was that final gum snap that caused Gun Girl to change the trajectory of the gun's barrel and point it in front of her, right at Pregnant Girl, and pull the trigger.

It was slow motion from where I sat. Gum snapped. The gun whooshed through the air. Pregnant Girl raised an eyebrow at the gun now pointed at her. Gun Girl closed her eyes. Convenience store clerk's eyes widened in disbelief. Pregnant Girl had a moment to register fear. Squeeze of the trigger. Then: BANG.

The bullet hit Pregnant Girl in the right shoulder. She stumbled backward, falling into a perfect pyramid of Pennzoil 10W30.

"Oh shit." Gun Girl dropped the gun and covered her mouth.

"Fuck." Tyler stared in awe.

"Wow," I whispered. The reality of the gunshot brought an onset of complete sobriety.

We all stared at Pregnant Girl, lying in a very unladylike position atop the black quarts of oil like some New Age art. She grasped her shoulder, tried to move, and let out a roar of anger.

"You shot me! You whore! You fucking shot me!" she screamed over and over again as she tried to move.

The chant must have given her some sort of adrenaline rush because she was able to stumble to her feet, one hand still holding her shoulder, her eyes taking on a similar wildness that Gun Girl's had moments before. "I'm gonna kill you!"

She was headed for the gun that had been dropped when, for some ridiculous reason, I crawled to where the gun was, picked it up, then stood and took up Gun Girl's position by grabbing the store clerk and pointing the barrel to his head.

Everyone froze.

"Okay, here's the deal. I don't do threats. So, Tyler Stone," I glanced at his name tag, "is your name really Tyler Stone?"

He nodded jerkily.

"Good name." I shook my head and pulled him closer. "Tyler, do you have a car outside?"

He nodded again.

"Where are the keys?"

"In my pocket."

"Ladies, it's been a pleasure. Have a wonderful evening." Pulling Tyler with me, I moved backward toward the door, made him pick up my purse that I'd dropped, and then because we were right next to the stand of plastic, single bottles of liquors; instructed, "Put a few of those in your pocket." Once we were outside I looked around and then shook my head at the black T-Bird with Golden Eagle etched into the hood. "Yours?" I asked.

He nodded.

"Do you mind driving?" As we walked toward the car, I used my shirt to wipe the gun (like they do in all the movies) and threw it in the dumpster.

Tyler started the car. "Where are we going?"

"Away from here seems like a good idea at the moment."

He didn't ask any more questions but screeched out onto the main road as distant sirens began to sound.

After several minutes he asked, "Did you save me?"

"I don't know." I looked out the window and added, "I just didn't want to spend tonight in an interrogation room talking about some moronic woman with a gun," I shook my head, "and no vocabulary."

"She's my girlfriend."

"I don't think she is. Not after the other one showed up pregnant." I snorted.

"Oh God, do you think she'll be okay?" Tyler asked.

"Looked like a flesh wound to me."

"You think?" he asked hopefully.

"Sure." What the hell did I know? I wasn't a doctor. "Can I have those bottles please?"

He handed over the three shots of Tequila. I unscrewed one and tossed it back. When it didn't burn, I glanced at the label, it was a little more 'top-shelf' than I was used to. As the heat warmed me and smoothed the situation I'd just absconded from, I studied the string bean of a man driving. "Two girls at once, huh?" I didn't see the appeal.

"I didn't mean to," he paused, "she just sort of started hanging around the gas station and was always being real nice ..." He shook his head.

"Which one?"

"Bev, the one who got shot."

"Did you know she was pregnant?"

"I just found out tonight."

"How the hell ...?" I let the question trail off, but then decided why not ask what I really wanted to. "No offense, but how does a guy like you get two girls in the first place?"

"I didn't know ..." He sighed. "I could just never figure out who I liked more."

"Well, I don't think that's going to be a problem now." My head began to pound a bit. "As far as breakups go, I'd say that one takes the cake."

"I think I just lost my job too."

"Probably."

"I don't have a lot of money saved, and now both of them are going to make it sound like it was me with the gun and I shot Bev."

"Bev. The pregnant one," I confirmed, though I didn't care too much about his storyline. I was a bit mentally tied up at the moment.

"Yeah. The other one ... with the gun, that's Donna."

"Look, they have cameras in the store, right?"

He nodded.

"I'm sure the police are smart enough to get the video and watch it. It will clear you, clear me, and convict Donna."

"What about Bev? What about the baby?"

"Are you sure she's pregnant?" She didn't look pregnant, though she could have just recently found out herself.

"She said she's six months ... pregnant." He choked on the word.

Another snort. "Tyler Stone, that woman is *not* pregnant. A girl who's six months pregnant doesn't have a stomach as flat as that."

"Are you sure?"

"She probably wanted a commitment," I guessed.

Tyler nodded his head to convince himself that there could be some truth to what I said. Finally, he cleared his throat and asked, "Do you need a ride home?"

"I don't know what I need, Tyler." I sighed and let my head fall back against the headrest then rolled it over to watch him as he nervously pulled at his collar and shifted in his seat.

"Look, we've both had pretty shitty nights. How about we go get a drink, get away from reality for a bit?"

"I don't know." He squeezed his eyes shut for a second and cleared his throat, giving another nervous tug on his polyester collar.

"You must be amazing in bed." I frowned at his shaded face, illuminated by the dashboard lights.

"What?"

My first reaction to Tyler's lanky stature, thinning brown hair and slight haunch of the shoulders wasn't necessarily 'father of my children.' But I guess some women go for convenience store sort of stability.

"Nothing," I said.

He gripped the steering wheel, eyes intent on the road, his lips a small white line.

"Tyler?"

"How am I going to pay rent? I don't think I'm going to get a good reference now."

"You'll be fine."

"How do you know?"

"People say it all the time in tense situations, so it must have some value."

He licked his lips and nodded his head. "So where should I drop you off?"

"Let's have a drink first. Then you can drop me off."

He didn't answer, but after a few nervous ticks seemed to make a decision. "Just one drink?" he asked for confirmation.

I nodded. "One drink."

"Okay." He nodded as he let the idea sink in. "Okay. Where should we go?"'

"I know this really great bar just over the border." I grinned.

"Over the border?"

"Tijuana," I corrected.

"It's so late, and by the time we get there, it'll be ... I don't think—"

"Exactly. Now isn't the time to think about anything." I tilted my head. "Tyler Stone."

"Yeah?" his voice wavered.

"Good name." I sighed.

"What's your name?"

"Ali."

He nodded and continued his nervous steering wheel gripping, but he didn't give any more refusal to drive us south to the border.

Three

"Do I just ... drive in?" Tyler's knuckles were white and his jaw visibly clenched as he slowed the car to the requested fifteen miles per hour. He followed the thin traffic along the secure, high fenced road patrolled by border guards; finally slowing to a stop under the concrete covering with floodlights that lit everything beneath them stadium bright.

"You've been to Tijuana before, haven't you?" I asked.

"Once."

"Drunken night with the boys?"

"I came with my youth group in eighth grade to build a house. For those less fortunate," he muttered as if he were repeating the phrasing used on the permission slip.

I pulled out another single shot of Tequila and swallowed half the liquor before reassuring, "It's no big deal, just follow the car in front of you, stop when the guard tells you and roll down your window so they can talk to you." Another clench of his jaw, so I swallowed the rest of the bottle and with a hiss of a breath added, "And try not to look so uptight."

The border officer motioned for us to stop.

"Do we need passports?" Tyler whispered the thought that had apparently just entered his mind. "I thought we needed passports to get into Mexico."

I leaned across Tyler and smiled up at the guard. "We're just here for tonight, we forgot our passports."

His frown increased and he pulled out a flashlight and shone it into the back seat, then waved to the building off to the right and instructed, "Go in there."

"What's happening?" Tyler asked, following the instructions.

"We're getting some permits and we might have to pay a fine."

"What?"

"And they'll do an inspection of your car."

"What?"

"It's no big deal, they'll ask us a few questions, make sure we're not bringing anything illegal in and they might fingerprint us."

"What about getting back in?"

"I think there's a law that says if we have a US ID, they have to let us in."

He pulled into a parking space, but left the car running.

"You don't have any priors, do you?" I asked.

"No." He pursed his lips and scrunched his nose. "Do you?"

"We'll be fine."

"What if they're looking for us? The cops," he lowered his voice, "from the video at the convenience store."

I met his whisper with my own and leaned toward him. "We didn't do anything wrong. There's a surveillance camera. If anything, on Monday when you go back to work, the cops'll want to hear your side of the story." I brushed a kiss on his cheek then climbed out of the car. After putting my purse strap over my head and across my body, I opened it to study the contents. I don't think I had anything dangerous.

Nope, just a phone, chapstick, mints, a wallet with my ID, a collection of coffee punch cards, two maxed out credit cards, an ATM card (the gateway to my balance: $994.00), and thirty crisp, ten-dollar bills. The cash was a birthday gift from my grandmother who'd opened the envelope between us as everyone was sitting down, to show me the contents, then closed it and shoved it in my purse saying, "Happy Birthday. It's thirty ten-dollar bills, isn't that fun? Put it to good use, to help you get back on your feet."

I was gonna put it to good use, but not to get back on my feet.

Tyler took a moment fighting his own demons before finally getting out of the car and catching up to me.

I pulled out the pack of mints.

"Ali, it's ten thirty," he whispered.

I linked my arm with his and didn't give him another chance to back out of this. I got the feeling Tyler Stone needed a night out on the town.

The uninterested police handed us a form to fill out, took copies of our IDs, and asked us the purpose for our visit.

Tyler stuttered, "She said we should come."

And I reasoned, "It's my birthday and I want real street tacos, booming music to pump through my bloodstream and something to write about."

Both comments received grunts and instructions to follow a guard to the car and open the trunk.

Inspection done, we were off once more.

Ten thirty in Tijuana on a Thursday night. The city was just getting warmed up.

I pointed the direction for Tyler to drive, granted I wasn't exactly sure where we were going. I'd only been to Tijuana three times and the last time was a little over two years ago. I figured we'd stick to the main road, and that would take us somewhere good. "Stick with this current of cars." I pointed.

"Current of cars?"

Sometimes, my drunken state caused me to revert to entertaining myself by having pretentious fun with language. I realized it probably wouldn't go over well with Tyler.

"Go that way." I rolled my window down.

We passed nightclubs with thumping music that shook the car. Street vendors were setting up for the night outside the various clubs; their money makers would be those leaving the clubs after getting properly inebriated.

Strobe lights from inside establishments blinked onto the sidewalk, calling for those walking past to enter.

The colors of the buildings and neon lights created a vibrant candy land. But every now and then, homeless people sitting on curbs, with their livelihood bundled in a bag next to them, offered a sobering reality of this city.

When we stopped at a red light, Tyler nodded toward a group of seedy-looking men who were admiring his T-Bird.

"Isn't it dangerous being American and in this city so late?"

"Loitering makes life worth living," I said, and liked the idea so much, I expanded on it. "Loitering men are the reasons writers write. They're the reason people have adventures. Seedy loiterers are great beginnings to any storyline." The light turned green and Tyler punched the gas.

"We'll be fine." I decided to soothe him rather than continue waxing drunkenly about loitering.

Two cop cars sped past us, their sirens off but lights spinning, adding to the lively landscape.

Tyler turned down another large road and after a moment, I realized I knew where I was.

"Oh! There's a parking lot just up on the right. Park there. They used to have a ... well, a sort of ... attendant."

"A *sort* of attendant?"

I nodded. "Last time, there was a man who lived in the parking lot, and he'd watch out for your car if you tipped him."

"What?"

I sighed. "Just trust me."

"I don't know you," he spouted incredulously.

"I realize that. But maybe the fact that I saved your life reflects on my tender personality?"

"Tender?"

"Jesus Christ, Tyler. Park your fucking car over there so I can get a birthday drink at a dive bar in Tijuana. The quicker that happens, the quicker you can go home."

He pulled into the parking lot and gave a chuckle. "There's the tenderness."

I eyed him through a smirk and wondered if that split-second glimpse I got was what attracted Gun Girl and Allegedly Pregnant.

Out of the car, I scanned the parking lot as I stretched. An older gentleman, maybe the same one from two years ago, stood up from a weathered folding chair that looked as aged as himself; even the creaking of the chair and his bones seemed to match.

"You park. I watch," he said and held out his hand.

I took out twenty dollars and handed it over. He nodded appreciatively and gave me a rotted tooth grin; I swallowed then pulled out another twenty and handed that over as well. "Señor? Hambre?"

"What?" Tyler asked as the man waved us away. "Estoy bien. Go. Be fun."

I linked my arm through Tyler's as he clicked the automatic lock on his car four times. "C'mon Tyler Stone. We're gonna go be fun."

"But what did you ask him?"

"I asked him if he was hungry. He said he's okay, but if either of us is still remotely sober when we come back, let's try to remember to bring him something to eat."

"That's nice of you."

"I'm actually a nice person. I'm just lost." I thought about that personal biography that summed up my entire self thus far and chuckled. "I think I come off bitchy when I'm lost."

Tyler grunted then his head began to scan our surroundings, back and forth, back and forth. As if he were watching the slowest tennis match ever played. Yet with as much tension as the most famous tennis match ever played. (I'm not a tennis person, so I don't know why I made this correlation to begin with.)

"What's wrong?" I asked.

"I feel like I've just traded one life and death situation for another," he muttered as a group of obnoxious, drunk, fraternity-esque young men passed us. When I noticed two of them wearing polo shirts with the collars turned up, I frowned, suspicious that perhaps I'd gone back in time when I crossed the border.

"Actually," I interrupted the ridiculousness, "you're right to be wary of *them*." I hugged his arm. "But we're not going where they're going. No loud, thumping nightclubs with plastic yard cups of frozen margaritas for us."

"You told the guard you needed thumping music."

"I lied."

"Then ... where are we going?"

"A dark, seedy bar. The kind with secrets." Before he could falter we'd turned back onto the safety of a main street and the smells from a crowded taco stand immediately assaulted our senses. "Oh. Are you hungry? I'm hungry. Let's get tacos."

Tyler warily eyed the paper plates of food held by a couple passing in front of us, nodding in agreement.

"I don't have pesos ..." Tyler whispered.

I waved him off, ordered four tacos and handed over my cash. "They'll take dollars and give us pesos back."

We held our paper plates under our chins as we took a bite and let the juices of the magical combination drip. I groaned and rolled my eyes.

"This is good." Tyler seemed surprised.

I nodded and pointed with my plate in the direction we were to continue walking. As we strolled through the brightly lit street, I hoped that the large number of people out and about, the presence of the police, the music, the smells of food, and the vibrant colors would ease Tyler's reluctance.

It didn't.

Especially when I recalled where I was and where I wanted to go. (If it was still there.) We took a right and found ourselves on a street with less light, and people causing Tyler's shoulders to rise higher and higher toward his ears.

In an effort to comfort him, I offered, "Tyler, the trick is to appear like you belong, look like you have no money and you've got something to hide. Like you're riddled with secrets and the kind of guilt that no one's interested in. The kind that most people wanna stay far away from. Do that, and I guarantee, no one'll bother you."

"How are *you* going to do that?" he asked.

I frowned and with a full mouth said, "I'm doing it."

"No you're not." He waved from my head to my feet. "You look like you just stepped out of a book club."

"Oh, so you think I'm good-looking?" I joked and batted my eyelashes. (I mean, I'm as tipsy as I tend to get at my book club meetings.)

He rolled his eyes.

I pointed at him with my plate. "You're no better." I stopped at a trash can, wiped my hands then turned to Tyler so I could unpin his name tag. I slipped it into the pocket of the red polo with the gas station logo on the lapel. "Look, we'll be fine. There are a ton of tourists and enough of a police presence that actually makes Tijuana safer in the middle of the night."

"You should sell used cars," he muttered.

I let a burst of "Ha!" escape. "Actually, I'm a writer, but maybe those two careers go hand in hand. Both are trying to sell lemons to unwitting people."

He shook his head and mumbled, "What are we doing here?"

"That's the existential question that keeps us all chasing our tails." When his frown grew, I offered an easier answer. "We need a drink after the night we've had."

"That simple?" he asked.

"That simple," I reassured.

"Because the way I see it, we ran to another country and the police are probably looking for us and I don't know how my ..." he swallowed whatever he was going to say and instead said, "how Bev or Donna are doing."

"Tyler. Jesus, can we just go get drunk and deal with all of this shit tomorrow?" I begged.

He stopped and glanced around. "I could go home. It's my car."

"Yeah, you could," I gave a game show sweep of my arm and a slight bow, "I thank you for driving me. Have a lovely evening."

He glanced back at the direction we'd come and then in the direction we were heading. "One drink?"

"If I'm being honest, no. There'll be more than one. I need to get shitfaced, but after that we can sober up and head home sometime tomorrow."

He nodded his head once. "I suppose ... we're already here."

I linked my arm through his and nodded. "Exactly. It's fine. You'll see. We're safe and everything will be okay."

Four

As we walked, Tyler cleared his throat several times before finally spitting out, "I don't have time for another girlfriend."

"Two *is* enough. Especially since they know about each other now."

"No, I mean—"

"I know what you mean," I interrupted, pointing for us to take a left at the corner, "and I truly don't mean to hurt your feelings, but you aren't my type."

"Okay." He seemed relieved. "You're sure this isn't dangerous?"

I nodded. "You know, I think the reason you're staying with me is because the situation at the convenience store just proved to you that you're made of pretty strong stuff, and now, on some subconscious level you don't mind a little danger."

"That's you." He pointed at me. "I think *you* are going through something that makes *you* want to figure out what you're made of."

I gave him a double finger gun salute. "You, Tyler Stone, win the hundred-dollar prize. I *am* going through something. And I'm sorry if I've been a little ... much."

"It's fine, I've seen worse. You're not really too unhinged." There was a smile in the statement.

"Good word."

I did feel on the precipice of unhinged, because lately I'd been holding tightly to belligerence. It seemed to be the only thing helping me feel like something in my life was in my control. My other option was to melt into a puddle and cry until I lost myself in a sea of depression. So I called upon an inner bitch to help me ride out all the self-disappointment, lack of creativity and not knowing how to achieve what I really wanted.

But instead of going into all that with Tyler, I settled on an easy explanation. "I turned thirty today and I'm going through some lame crisis. I felt like I needed to shake things up tonight and walking in on you being held at gunpoint felt like the universe giving me an interesting sign."

"What's your name?" he called.

I shot him a frown. "Didn't I tell you?"

"I know it's Ali, what's your last name?"

"Skye. Alicia Skye. Libra. Thirty years old today."

"You're really a writer?"

"I try to be." I started walking again.

"Would I have read anything you wrote?"

"I've written several articles for the *LA Times* and a lot of stories that've been published in literary magazines."

"Oh. I sometimes read the paper so maybe ..." Straightening his shoulders, he pulled at his collar and took a deep breath. "Okay Ali Skye, let's carpe diem."

"Funny."

"When I'm not scared, I am." He shrugged.

I suppose he had a reasonable excuse to be a little off-kilter since we'd met.

We continued our search for the perfect darkened bar, passing tourists already deep in their cups, evident by their crooked line walking.

Neon lights blinked on vagrants cuddled in doorways. Each street corner offered more aromatic smells wafting through the air. The hum of nightlife swirled around us, providing the momentum we needed to continue on.

"Ali Skye sounds like a hippie name," Tyler mused.

"It is. Actually, my whole name is Alicia Skye Locke. My parents liked to joke that they felt like they were old hippies at heart." I thought about the two people who were exhausted from supporting my tireless quest to create a spot for myself in the creative world, which had led to my early midlife crisis shenanigans. "They *were* hippies."

Tyler sighed. "I think my parents were hoping for someone else."

"Yeah, well ... Tyler Stone is a great name."

"You keep saying that."

"Can't help it. I love a good name. Always looking for a good name for my stories." I glanced at him out of the corner of my eye, this boy-man living in the shadow of someone else's idea of what he could be. "You try to live up to it with the car and the girls, don't you?" I asked.

His answer was a shrug and lopsided grin.

"Oh! Here it is." La Malquerida, the bar I recalled from the trip two years ago, stood brooding in front of us. A sagging sun-bleached, red door was propped open by a stool with a frowning man in a tight black T-shirt sitting atop.

Tyler leaned into my side. "Not to sound like a broken record, but are we going to be safe ... in there?"

"I've been here before. I lived. So will you."

I don't think Tyler was invigorated by my crappy pep talk, but I was in need of the rundown, off the beaten track bar, with a lack of tourists and a group of malcontents who needed the shadows while drowning their sorrows.

Tyler was stumbling over what little courage he had, but maybe in an effort to collect himself asked, "What does the bar name mean? Mal ... querida?"

"La Malquerida. The Bad One."

In reply, he took a step toward me and away from the bouncer, who I was pretty sure we could have pushed off his perch for all the interest he had in us.

"Look, I'm not gonna steer you wrong. And let's be honest, anything we do tonight has got to be better than having a gun against your head."

"I don't know ..." he muttered.

I elbowed him. "Just think of me as your deus ex machina. Now come on."

The bar, dimly lit, smelled of stale hope and sour dreams. Outdated music screamed loudly over an old sound system and the cherry on top was the stereotypical looking bartender with a black bushy mustache, frowning at us as we approached.

Three uninterested girls were gyrating in bikinis that had lost as much of their luster as the dancers. Two were bottle blondes that paled somehow to the third dancer, a brunette. A spotlight illuminated her boredom as she entertained from a slightly elevated platform in the middle of the bar.

"I swear she was here the last time I was." What kind of a life must that be? "But I think she's had a boob job since then."

"What?" Tyler's head was back on the swivel, trying to be aware of his surroundings and not scared at the same time.

I waved at the woman in greeting, but her attention was on another life far away from this moment. (Maybe.)

"You didn't say this was a strip club."

"Because it's not," I slipped onto one of the dilapidated stools, "it just has live dancers."

He studied the women with a frown, stepped closer to my stool and the bar but didn't sit down.

I beamed a smile at the bartender. "Dos Cervesas y ..." I counted quietly to myself in Spanish, "diez ... shots of Tequila." Then added, "Cigarillos? Do you have a pack of cigarettes?"

"You smoke?" Tyler asked.

"Tonight, we both do."

The bartender didn't acknowledge anything I said but turned away, which I hoped meant he was seeing to my order. Confirmation came when he slipped a pack of cigarettes and a book of matches in front of me.

Tyler's attention darted everywhere, like a paranoid junkie. "How long do you want to stay here?"

"I believe I've answered this question before. Tomorrow morning, we'll both drunkenly trip down the main street, eat a lot of great food and sober up enough to drive home."

"So we're staying in this bar all night?"

"Tyler," I put a cigarette in my mouth and fumbled with the matchbook, "do me a favor, sit the fuck down and chill out."

He did as told and I took a long, appreciative drag; my lungs burning delightfully. "That's the stuff." I held the smoke in as long as I could before sighing it out and mentioning, "I quit five years ago."

"What's a deus mach ...?" Tyler asked, pulling at his collar.

"Deus ex machina is a literary term that means *god of the machine*, and it was bougie of me to even bring it up. But since we're here, deus ex machina is what an author uses when she can't get her characters out of the quicksand she's written them into. So she creates someone to swoop in out of nowhere and fix everything."

"So you're my god?" Tyler still looked baffled.

I'm not gonna lie, I liked that idea. "I am. You were in the middle of a standoff, but when I walked in, out of the blue, I changed everything."

He grunted as the bartender slid two beers toward us, then lined up ten shot glasses and carelessly poured Tequila into each one.

Tyler looked disbelievingly at the ten shots, then at me. I smiled and picked up the first one, deciding to work my way from the outside inward.

One: To quench my thirst and heat a trail down my throat; slam the glass on the bar.

Two: For forgetting; slam the glass in defiance.

Three: For leaving; slam.

Four: Because it was still my birthday. Slam.

And five: Why the hell not? SLAM.

I licked my lips in thanks to Tequila as the last shot burned its way down my esophagus into my stomach. Then I took another breath of life from the cigarette and closed my eyes. "God, this is what I needed." My bones melted a bit from the sudden rush of alcohol and I felt like I might finally be on the right path to having a good birthday.

I pointed to the other five shots, then to Tyler, wondering how much it would take for him to loosen up.

Five

I t took seven shots and four beers.

As he talked, Tyler continued to look around, his head bobbing, no longer out of fear but more out of curiosity now.

"She was just so sweet when I first met her. She wore a lot of purple, a *lot* of purple." I didn't know which 'she' he was talking about when I finally turned back into the dissertation he was offering regarding his dating life; and it didn't really matter. I'd been lost in my own drunken recollection of the past few years, few weeks, and how I'd poetically ditched my family.

It was poetic, wasn't it? I mean, at least I texted.

A tick in my left eye twitched the opinion that it might have been more cowardly than cool.

"I came here with a poet two years ago," I slurred, changing the subject.

Tyler nodded.

"Not much of a story. Lame poet." I laughed and spittle slipped out; wide-eyed I wiped my mouth as Tyler's fogged over eyes squinted with shared merriment, until he sat up a little straighter and pointed over my shoulder.

I followed the unsteady pointer as a Napoleon-complexed man came into view. He sauntered over to us, his scowl increasing as he puffed himself up. At his full height, his swarthy frame aligned the top of his head with my eyeline. Dark hair with, dare I say, a dashing streak of silver on one side; bloodshot eyes; his cheek scarred by adolescent years of hormones running rampant with acne–the whole of the man a daunting presence.

"This is not a man you fuck with." I attempted to whisper the warning to Tyler, but mesmerized by the character standing in front of me, made the exclamation directly to him instead. Out loud.

A smile thinned his lips as he gave a tilt of his head. "This is true."

"Oh. Shit."

"What do you want?" he asked curiously.

"We just want to drink," I said.

"Two gringos come to this bar just for drinking? I think you come looking for El Zorro Blanco. And you find him." He gave a slight, quick slap on his chest. "So, what business you looking for?"

"Zorro?" Tyler asked excitedly.

"Zorro means fox," I muttered, unable to take my eyes off the man who now had a name befitting *everything* about himself.

"The White Fox!" Tyler declared, impressed; then leaned over me and held out his hand, but only received a suspicious gaze.

Maybe it was good we were drunk.

I tried to explain, "Señor … El Zorro Blanco … god that's great. Or do you prefer Mr. White?" I sucked in an excited breath. "Or El Zorro? Or the Fox?"

He growled low in his throat.

I started again, "We aren't looking for anything. Just drinks." I took Tyler's limp hand and waved it. "This is Tyler, his girlfriend just found out that he was cheating on her and that the … the other girl was pregnant and there was a holdup. And it was *ca–razy—*"

"It was a mess," Tyler took over. "Everyone was yelling at everyone to go fuçk themselves before Donna shot Bev."

"And it's my birthday!" We were on a roll now. "So Tyler and I adiosed out of that situation and decided we needed a drink."

A slight upturn of the White Fox's eyebrow was the only visible reaction. So I continued with my verbal vomit of an introduction.

"Tyler's uptight," I went to pat him on the back, missed, but tried again and came in contact with the side of his face, "don't you think that's weird though? Cuz you'd think a guy who's got a girlfriend and one on the side wouldn't be but I came here two years ago with a poet and that's … that's our story." I glanced at Tyler to see his long nod of corroboration, then beamed a smile back at the Fox. "Yup, that's it." I picked up my almost empty beer glass, saluted him and finished it.

The man continued sizing up our possible bullshit and possible truth while his gaze scanned the length of my body, stopping on the vee in my T-shirt. With a shrug, he pulled a cigarette from my pack, lit it, took a drag and then pointed it at me. "I think maybe you talk too much."

"She *does* talk too much!" Tyler slurred. "She talks and somehow gets you to do whatever she wants you to do and I don't know if it's cute or annoying."

My head swung in Tyler's direction, shocked and impressed. We both jumped when El Zorro Blanco's fist slammed heartily on the bar, announcing his decision, "Okay, we get drunk." Then, looking toward me said, "He is Tyler. Who are you?"

"Ali Skye, like a hippie," Tyler offered before I could open my mouth. "What should we call you?"

"The man who owns this bar." He grinned. "Okay. Let's drink."

Six

The room spun at perfect intervals. When Tyler came into focus, his eyes were half-mast and an adorable, pathetic grin was directed at whatever he was trying to focus on. At the moment I feared it was me; because he had that look men get when beer goggles are firmly in place and all inhibitions (and memories of pregnant or armed girlfriends) have been chased away.

"You're not nervous anymore, huh?" I teased.

"Yer very pretty," he slurred.

I shook my head. "You don't really want me."

He shrugged as El Zorro announced, "If he don't, I take you." He slipped his hand too far up my thigh and gave a squeeze. I was going to have to veto his advances. But you gotta admit, the move was pretty foxy and it's kinda wonderful having to refer to someone as 'El Zorro.'

"I'm flattered," I told his hand, "but I promised Tyler we'd stay together."

He gave another squeeze but didn't remove his hand. So I helped with the removal and 'accidentally' bent two fingers back too far. He just offered an appreciative smile.

"It's a good bar," Tyler declared with a wave.

"It's a good bar," El Zorro parroted happily as he glanced around the darkened corners of La Malquerida.

"It's seedy and colorful," Tyler went on drunkenly.

"Tyler ..."

He closed his eyes and pursed his lips as if I'd misunderstood his compliment. "But in a trendy, rundown way."

"Tyler," I hissed, "don't be inconsequence … don't be unconscious …"
I took a swig of beer, "don't fuck with the Fox's bar."

"I'm not! I like it."

I elbowed the Fox. "It's a good bar." I tried to pacify.

He laughed. "I am good businessman. I find anything you want, anything you need." He elbowed me back. "I am a man who can get things."

"What about the dancing women?" Tyler asked.

"El Zorro Blanco offers them good employment."

"The brunette is *so* pretty." Tyler tried to wink at the woman I recognized from my last visit. He'd *definitely* drank the memory of Bev and Donna away.

"Ahhh," the Fox waved at the brunette, bidding her over. She stopped dancing (if you could call her indifferent gyrations dancing) and came over to where we sat, a mask of boredom firmly in place.

"Did you dance all the life out of yourself?" She snarled at me as I blinked my eyes wide at the fact that I'd asked the question out loud. "I'm drunk!" I attempted to patchwork our meeting. "I love your … bikini."

"This is Yvonne," the Fox introduced. "She is also American, but expat now, right?"

Yvonne nodded and caught the eye of the waiter who poured her a shot in reply.

"Yvonne has a good story, you should tell it." He smiled as he nodded his head toward her. "These stories help make my bar great."

"You were dancing here the last time I was here," I announced at the same time Tyler gave an intensely slurred, "Yer beautiful."

Yvonne tilted her head and looked interested at Tyler as she muttered, "I've been here forever."

After a moment, she took one of my quickly disappearing cigarettes, then pulled up a stool, forcing us to create a semicircle at the bar as she sat next to the White Fox.

"She have good breasts," he began, "I buy them for her." He laughingly added, "They also help make my bar great."

Tyler's head nodded like he was a cartoon and I elbowed him to refocus his eyes elsewhere on her body, and because it looked like he might actually be drooling.

El Zorro continued to list Yvonne's personal details. "She is on run from police in America."

"*I'm* on the run from the police in America!" Tyler supplied, happily finding a commonality.

I absently patted Tyler's knee. "No you're not."

The Fox raised an eyebrow and I shook my head, creating tracers before my eyes. "We're not wanted. Just for questioning. Everything's on video. He's a victim."

"I'm not a victim," Tyler muttered.

"Not a victim in life," I tried to correct, then told Yvonne, "He's not a victim; just this one situation, he was held at gunpoint."

She reached out and touched the pocket of his polo. "Isn't that part of the job when you work at a convenience store?"

"I *do* work at a convenience store." He sounded fascinated at her attention to detail.

"She knows," I tried to explain.

Tyler's befuddled attention ran down Yvonne's arm then back to her chest.

"She was librarian." The Fox added to the dancer's growing credentials.

Tyler gasped, "I've been to a library."

"Jesus Christ, Tyler. Pull yourself together," I garbled, then nodded at Yvonne. "I can see it, though."

Yvonne exhaled a long stream of smoke, still bored. I squinted, trying to clothe her respectfully in my mind. "Did you wear glasses?"

"Oh," Tyler let the word slide out of his mouth, "you're the sexy librarian who lets her hair out of the bun and looks like every man's fantasy."

My inebriated state might have painted the illusion, but I thought I saw her smile prettily at Tyler.

"I let Yvonne tell her story, it is good. Tragic, horrible, wonderful." The White Fox was a ringmaster, giving us a peek behind the curtain, to see what made his bar so good. "First we need drinks. Tequila!" he ordered with a slap on the bar.

Four shot glasses appeared, and the grumpy bartender sloshed Tequila from glass to glass.

"To nuevos amigos!" El Zorro declared.

We messily aimed our glasses together and in impressive succession threw back our heads, draining the liquid. I was so drunk, evident by the fact that the alcohol no longer burned going down.

The Fox patted Yvonne's knee. "Okay, tell your sad story."

Tyler frowned. "Not if it's sad, I don't want to hear a sad story."

Yvonne reached out and touched the side of Tyler's face. "We all have sad stories."

He turned his face into her hand and inhaled.

I wanted to spout something about hygiene or propriety but the words and ideas and my mouth weren't cooperating any more.

Yvonne had been involved in an unrequited love triangle. A fellow librarian, having fallen so in love with her and angry that she didn't return his love, abducted her and his wife, yet somehow the two women overpowered him and escaped. There was a stabbing and gunshot wounds and lives ruined, so Yvonne went south to start over. Apparently, her library science degree either didn't transfer or she wanted something different; the ending of her story was fuzzy.

"You are so strong." Tyler drew out the compliment at the end of her story, reaching for her hand and brushing a kiss on her palm.

Since they seemed to be locked in a moment, I turned my focus to the Fox and asked, "Do you have a sad story?"

He gave a howl of laughter that was so startling, I joined in, understanding how he might have earned his nickname.

Seven

There was a time warp that wrapped itself around storylines, and twisted with branches of neon light tracers and sloshed liquid; all of it swirling together with the wear and tear of the battered bar that held the stories the White Fox wove together in an awful tapestry of tangents.

The bar opened at 2 p.m. every day. They served a simple lunch prepared by one of the nearby street vendors. Happy Hour was from 6 to 6:30 p.m., and from 2:30 to 3 a.m., which was closing time. The Fox only served bottom-shelf shots for half price during that time. He hated the practice, but felt he owed it to his business partner–who mysteriously disappeared seven years ago.

On Mondays, a tall man, who looked to be in his early thirties and always wore a red flannel shirt (even if it was a hundred degrees outside) came in at 1 a.m. and ordered two shots; drank one, stared at the other for thirty minutes, then paid his bill and walked out the door at exactly 1:31 with tears in his eyes. He never engaged in conversation and the one time a dancer tried, he barked at her–like a dog–loudly, and quite aggressively.

The Expat Broken Hearts Club–nine men and women of a certain age–met every Tuesday at 8 p.m. for an hour. They shared bowls of chips and salsa and one beer each as they took turns bemoaning their loneliness. The bartender thought the group thrived on bitter resentment.

The dancers went on stage every night from eleven to close. The Fox employed twenty-four dancers: "The most interesting women in Tijuana" was what he put on the few posters he used for advertising. Another promise he'd made to an absent business partner.

(I was proud that I somehow refrained from asking El Zorro if he'd killed the man.)

Friday nights there was a live band that drew in a crowd of overly made-up women with teased hair and forgotten dreams, all of whom squeezed into tight jeans and flirted the night away in hopes of regaining something they'd lost.

A local bearded bohemian came in Birkenstocks, long board shorts and a sarape, punching his fists slowly into the air to the wrong beats of the drum, his eyes cloudy, as if another lifetime were taking over his body. He ended each session sitting on the floor in the corner, his head in his hands, muttering about how 'it was all over now.'

There were drunken fights a few times a week, thrown glasses and beer bottles more often than not, screeching matches between women and men, and the occasional heart attack.

"That's just what happens in the front of the house," Yvonne muttered after the Fox finished the story of his bar.

The Fox wasn't glaring at Yvonne for any ill prudence she'd caused, but seemed to be interested in how I was taking the information. And my interest was damned piqued.

My finger wobbly pointed into his chest. "The back of the house is where the Great and Powerful Oz conducts his business of getting anyone anything they need."

He winked at me as Tyler loudly announced, "I need something."

We all glanced at him, but his hazy gaze was fixed on Yvonne. "I need to dance. With you."

She took the last drag of her cigarette and in one swift movement, crushed out the butt, blew out the smoke, took Tyler's hand and led him to the area designated as a dance floor.

A few couples were already gyrating against each other in the darkened area as the base of an old '90s R&B song reverberated.

"If love doesn't feel like '90s R&B, I don't want it." I rolled my eyes. "I think I read that on a T-shirt." The Fox pulled two cigarettes out, held them both between his cracked lips, lit them and handed one over to me. I pointed it at Tyler whose hands were splayed against Yvonne's lower back, pressing her against him as he looked down into her eyes.

"He just got out of two bad relationships." The statement made me giggle.

"What do you need, Ali Skye?" The Fox pulled my attention. "What can the Great Oz give you?"

"I thought you were the Great Zorro?"

"Oh, no. I am not *the* Great Zorro. I am ... cómo se dice ... manipulative and cunning, in the way of the fox." He winked. "I can get you anything you want, what you want?"

"Adventure." I gave a snort of laughter, but shook my head to reel it back. "What I probably really should ask for is stability."

His gruff voice declared, "Stability is for later. Take adventure now."

"Sure," I mocked.

"If you want it, I can give you adventure." He leaned forward, closing in on my lips, his hand back where it had tried to start the evening, high up my thigh.

I leaned closer, a breath from his lips and said, "I think this is where I give you the friend speech."

He released me back into my personal space and with his head back added a howl of laughter into the nicotine stained rafters.

"Okay, okay. We are friends. You are friends with El Zorro Blanco now." There was a youthful twinkle in his eyes, but that could have been my drunkenness. "One day, you will tell El Zorro what you need, and maybe I help you." He held out his hand to strike the bargain.

I shook.

He waved to the bartender for another round. "Now, you tell me your sad story."

I gave a drunkenly honest rundown. "I'm a struggling writer who just turned thirty, got dumped by a man I thought I might eventually marry, and because of the breakup I had to move out of the apartment we were sharing. I've barely kept myself afloat financially through odd writing jobs the past few years but it's getting harder each day to do that, my creativity is tapped out and I'm scared I'm gonna end up with a soul-sucking job as a faceless cog in a business machine while my life is stolen from me and that might not matter anyway because I'm stuck and no matter what I try to do, and I can't seem to get any traction cuz my creativity is failing me but I already said that ..."

The Fox shook his head and rolled his eyes; which hurt, because the tough, rough-faced, angry man didn't seem like he was the kind to roll eyes at anything.

"You said to tell you my sad story. That's it." I shrugged. "It might be generic and lame, but it's mine."

He pointed. "No seas ridícula. You say you are thirty? What's thirty? There is still *so* much time." He slid one of the shots that materialized in front of him toward me. "Ali Skye will let stability come later. Tonight El Zorro changes your life." He held his own shot toward me and made a sloshing sign of the cross. "I absolve you of twenty-nine years." Then he repeated the blessing. "I return you to creativity." And with that, he threw back the shot then instructed, "Now, you take adventure with two hands. Claw at it, all of it." He gave a definitive nod. "The rest will come."

I stared into the amber liquid of my shot as my body swayed to an unseen ebb and flow. "Fuck it," I held it up to the Fox and messily mirrored his previous absolution, "to adventure."

*Note: To the best of my recollection, this was pretty much how the evening went. Granted, some of the language might not have been as verbally decipherable as I reported it above, but I'm pretty sure we were all on the same page and always completely understanding of each other.
I think.
Pretty much.
At least, you get the gist.

Eight

The first day of my adventurous thirtieth year began with a sour stomach, sensitivity to light and two bouts of vomiting.

Not the adventure I'd been looking for.

"Sorry." The hoarse apology floated from the doorway of the bathroom.

As I glanced up from where my cheek was resting against the toilet seat–my stomach insistent that we not move too far from this location just yet–foggy out of body experiences and misplaced memories flashed:

Tyler asking me if he can go home with Yvonne.

Checking into the hotel with Tyler, no Yvonne.

Tyler kissing me in the bar.

The Fox kissing me in the bar?

(Not '*in* the *bar*,' on my lips, but we were still in the bar.)

Tyler crying about how much he loves Yvonne and trying to call Bev or Donna as we drunkenly tripped toward a hotel.

A nervous check-in clerk when we dropped the name El Zorro Blanco for a discounted rate.

Throwing my phone across the street to be hit by passing cars.

The Fox whispering in my ear, "Are you sure you don't need a real man? I am a man, not a little boy."

That 'little boy' crying about how his heart was breaking to feel Yvonne in his arms again.

An argument and wrestling match with an ice machine.

An apologetic whisper of 'Happy Birthday.'

A lack of limbs tangled in heat and abandon.

The world spinning so fast, closing my eyes was the only option that brought it to an end.

And then: Groaning awareness. Sunlight dampened from worn, outdated orange curtains.

The blurred red time of the digital clock next to the rented bed declaring it was well into the afternoon.

And a stomach that demanded haste.

"Why are you sorry?" I asked, my throat raw from all the cigarette smoke.

Tyler held up a small white paper bag, the bottom greasy. "Some kind of sugary donut. To help with the hangover." He set it down next to my feet then presented an insulated cup. "Coffee, luke warm." He added it to the stash but it was the glorious small pink bottle of Pepto-Bismol he held up next that won me over.

He opened it as I groaned and righted myself. I took the offering and swallowed as much of the milky, chalky wonder drug I could.

Tyler sat on the floor across from me, cleared his throat and sheepishly said, "We didn't sleep together or anything."

I nodded, delighted that the thick liquid calming its way into the pit of my stomach had done such a bang-up instant job; I indulged in another long slug.

"Just in case you thought we did," he clarified.

I traded the Pepto for the coffee, took a sip of it and closed my eyes with a grateful groan.

"I didn't know how you took your coffee."

"Black, but it doesn't matter. This is good." My throat and head equally rebelled against the simple action of sipping the coffee, but it was so good I ignored the throbbing.

Finally, I was able to force my eyes to focus on Tyler: bloodshot eyes, rough around the edges, but not nearly as hungover as I was. In fact, he'd not only acquired me breakfast, but he'd showered and bought himself a new shirt.

"Why don't you look like I feel?" I croaked.

He touched a finger to the bridge of his nose, nervously swallowed and licked his lips. He didn't need to answer after all that jittery movement.

"Oh, Tyler ... Yvonne?"

"We really hit it off," he muttered.

"Jesus ..." I tried to stand but my head rebelled in full force and I slipped back onto the floor. "Give me a sec. I got you into this, I'll get you out."

"There's nothing to get me out of," he insisted.

I closed my eyes, trying to put the previous evening's flashbacks in chronological order. It wasn't working. "When?"

"After you passed out," he whispered contritely, but a grin still escaped. "I couldn't stop thinking about her. So I went back to the bar."

My hangover began to pound in time with my heartbeat and corrupted my hearing.

Tyler continued, "We talked all night. She's amazing."

"You certainly have a type, don't you?" My stomach growled so I reached over to the bag and fished out the donut.

"We went to breakfast and I figured you'd be feeling pretty bad, so Yvonne went back to her place to freshen up and I came back here to ..." he cleared his throat, "make sure you get home okay."

"Get home okay," I repeated, the prospect sounding as stale as the words and the way they spilled from my mouth.

Tyler explained, "I'm staying. To see what it is. Between us. Me and Yvonne."

Fuck, this was going to be my fault if he ended up in another love triangle. Which technically ... "Tyler, you just got out of two relationships."

He winked at me. "We never really broke up."

I squinted as I took another bite and with a full mouth pondered, "A third woman. Maybe you really are living up to your rock star name."

He blushed. "I was trying to make a joke. Look ..." He cleared his throat. "I'll give you a ride anywhere you want to go," he said quickly, the way a person does when they've been planning something for a while.

"I'm concerned, Tyler."

"I'm fine."

He was aggravating my hangover so I took another slug of Pepto.

"Yesterday I found you with a gun to your head, literally, and you told me you were stringing them both along because you didn't know what you wanted," I tried to reason.

He shot me another puppy dog grin. "And weren't you the one who told me to look at the world from a different perspective?"

I never told him to do that.

I don't think.

"Why would you listen to me? I'm *clearly* going through something."

Why did the little shit listen to me? And when did I give him such advice?

"She might be a murdering librarian hiding as a stripper in Mexico," I packed on.

He shrugged. "Don't care."

I took another drink of coffee and Pepto, then followed with a bite of donut. "I could insist you sober up and go back to deal with Bev and Donna first, but ..." I shook my head, Tyler Stone might be the kind of guy who needed to make the same mistake several times before he learned the lesson he was supposed to glean from said mistakes.

"Fine," I croaked, "I'll leave Odysseus to Circe if I must."

"Is this part of you being my personal god?"

I shot him a soft smile that made my face ache as I declared with a sigh, "Tyler, I'm just the oracle. And no one ever listens to the oracle."

"But I did listen to you, that's why we're here. That's how all this happened."

Rub it in, why don't you?

"Well, I'll wish you the best." What else was I going to say? We didn't really know each other and if I'm being honest, I kinda used him for his car.

Tyler grinned, the grin of a person excited about his shiny new (to him) toy.

Insert deep sigh here.

"What are *you* gonna do?" he asked.

I took another pull on the Pepto. "Well, after the ground under me evens out and I get something more substantial to eat, I might try to keep this momentum going."

Nine

Tyler suggested we go to lunch, and as the world wasn't spinning too badly anymore and my stomach had leveled out, I agreed.

On the way to the restaurant, I bought a pair of sunglasses; white rimmed because they had the darkest frames, and today, with the sun laughing at me, my softly throbbing head needed more darkness. I also bought headache medicine, a pen and notebook paper set (depicting a Tijuana street scene) and a backpack made of soft leather, which I shoved my purse into and found I still had my wallet and a little over two hundred in cash. As far as current worldly possessions, pretty good.

I wasn't surprised when Tyler led me into a restaurant where Yvonne and El Zorro Blanco were waiting for us.

The restaurant showcased the vibrancy of Mexican decor with style and sophistication. Bright maroon walls decorated with large traditional paintings and hand-painted ceramic suns done in various designs and colors. And the perfectly spaced wooden tables with matching chairs, all inlaid with Spanish tiles, were full.

Our lunch dates sat in the dimly lit back of the establishment.

"Is this a setup?" I asked Tyler as we approached the duo who wore matching dour facial expressions. But when Yvonne saw Tyler she lit up like the finale of a firework extravaganza.

(Look, I'm still hung over and shaky, so my metaphors aren't going to be very good. And as I've mentioned, I've lost some of my creative mojo. So you get what you get.)

I watched as Tyler slipped his hands around Yvonne, and with fingers splayed out on her behind he pulled her possessively against him and placed a showy kiss on her lips.

Oh Tyler.

I wasn't shocked when the shadow to the side of me tried to slip his hand on a 'cheek.' I frowned, dislodged it and turned to face El Zorro Blanco in the light of day. (Well, the dim light of a restaurant, but still.) He laughed and reached up with his thumb and forefinger and pinched my chin. "This is what I like about you. Everyone else is scared of El Zorro. You are not. You are not scared to reject El Zorro. It is most intoxicating."

What was I supposed to say to that?!

He gripped my shoulders and stood on his tip toes, pulling my body to him as he brushed a kiss on my (real) cheek this time.

I knew he wasn't tall, but we'd been sitting all night; now his stature was a shock. He stood at least three inches shorter than my five foot seven. Don't get me wrong, I've met shorter men, but I think the Fox's presence, which is larger than life, is what made it a shock in the sober daylight. Maybe he was the kind of guy who grew in stature the drunker you got.

"The sad writer, you look wrinkled."

That was one way of putting it.

He gave my back a resounding slap then motioned for all of us to sit before waving the waiter over. The Fox quickly rambled off an order while I slipped the straps of my backpack over the back of the chair. The waiter gave a quick nod and left without asking any further questions of anyone else.

"I own this restaurant. I know what's the best. You'll be happy with my choice," he explained.

"You own this?" I couldn't hide the surprise in my voice.

He chuckled. "Es moderno y trendy, huh?"

"It's so different than the bar," I verified.

He leaned toward me and admitted, "I am a man of many layers."

Our conversation was interrupted by a patron who came to shake El Zorro's hand and have a whispered conversation with him. As soon as that gentleman was finished, another took his place. So I'm not sure if these were just friends or if they were in need of El Zorro Blanco, the man who could get anything.

(And can we just imagine for a moment if the Zorro we know today had been a White Fox with the tagline: The man who can get you anything.)

Four Bloody Marys with veritable salads on top were placed in front of us. I groaned in surrender at the pepper speckled tomato juice. "Oh, no. I can't ..."

"It will help." The Fox slid his glass toward mine to clink them together then took a swig of his own.

I picked up my glass, held the leafy celery sticks out of the way, as well as my breath, and took a sip. My stomach was still wobbly, but as I waited for the concoction to make its way down into the bowels of *my* hell, and they didn't gurgle in revolt; well, I suppose one could say the added alcohol didn't *not* help.

"So, you have a bar, hotel and a restaurant," was my conversation opener as I watched Tyler pull Yvonne to his side and brush a kiss on her neck. (And hoped the scowl I felt wasn't showing too blatantly on my face.)

"I told you, *this fox* can get you anything."

A grunt of *hmm* was all I was given time for as another 'patron' interrupted us, leaning over El Zorro to have an intense, one-sided whispered conversation meant only for the Fox's ear.

My Spanish being rudimentary and my hangover making concentration difficult, I didn't catch anything that was said. And that was probably fine. I didn't need to be in the middle of anything involving the great and powerful Zorro Blanco.

It gave me time to continue to sober up (or possibly flatline in that world just between sobriety and a little drunk) while I watched the love match across from me blossom in stolen touches and blushes and numerous other 'eses.'

Meanwhile, El Zorro held court. But no one called him El Zorro; in fact, the only thing I heard anyone call him was El jefe.

"El jefe?" I asked after the latest visitor left.

He winked at me. "The boss."

"Can I ask you a question?"

"Of course, corazón, ask me anything."

I grunted. "I guess I've just never met anyone else who called themselves Zorro."

"That is not a question."

"No, it isn't." I took another sip, studying our host.

He offered, "There is a professional Luchador, a wrestler who is called El Zorro."

"That makes sense."

His grin grew. "Do you know, the story of Zorro was written in 1919 by a man in America? He was from Illinois."

"No. Really?"

My exclamation pulled Tyler and Yvonne's attention.

"Sí. He was a writer who made his living writing for pulp magazines. He wrote the story of Zorro. But here is the thing. His story is based on a real man." His eyes twinkled.

I sat forward because this right here, this was the magic of El Zorro Blanco, this was when he began to grow in stature.

"Joaquín Murrieta is the man who gave the writer his story, the man we know as Zorro today. He was a gold miner during the California Gold Rush.

"Joaquín was a good man, but trouble came for him. A group of miners attacked his family and killed his brother. He swore revenge, and as he hunted the men who hurt his family, he began to steal from the rich and give to the poor." He shrugged, his story over, but the layers lively.

"That's cool," Tyler interjected.

I nodded my agreement and said, "I've been thinking, as people've come up to talk to you, how the legendary Zorro was a man of the people and today you seem to enjoy that role. But I think you might be a little more ..."

He leaned toward me, twirled an imaginary mustache and supplied, "¿Malvado? Evil?"

I laughed; it wasn't the word I was looking for, but it worked.

"I don't mean to offend you. I ... your moniker is very cool." I offered a simple retreat in whatever it was my addled, hungover self was trying to say.

I glanced across the table to see if Tyler or Yvonne wanted to jump into this conversation and help me, or turn the tide, or take part.

Nope, no takers.

Thankfully the waiter, weighted down with a tray, was headed our way.

"I am like the Godfather." He winked.

I nodded and offered, "You know, you look so comfortable and Godfather-like, I thought a few times you were going to offer your gold pinky ring for people to kiss."

Really Ali?

I was lucky the correlation gained me a wide, stained-tooth grin.

Still, I thought it was a good idea to attempt an apology. "My mouth gets away from me from time to time."

The waiter began to set down plates of food. Fresh vegetables, perfectly sautéed meat and peppers, fresh tortillas, and house special sauces–a remedy to cure all traces of a lingering hangover.

After several bites, the Fox began to roll up the sleeve of his left arm. "Soy un buen hombre. I am a good man to know. But I'm also the head of the snake." The freed tattoo of a gnarly snake wound its way up his forearm, finishing its slither in an unknown location. "I am a self-made man. From the moment I sell Chiclet gum to tourists waiting in cars to cross the border, I fell in *love* with consumerism and neediness of the American."

Jesus Christ, talk about a man who knew how to entice a writer. Maybe he had restored my creativity.

"And now you have an empire?"

He nodded. "Need a passport? I know a man. Hotel, a good place to eat, a nice bar? I have those. Need your cousin out of jail after a long drunk night? Too easy. Drugs?" He shrugged in reply to that one.

"Sex, drugs, and rock 'n' roll," I supplied.

He slapped the table several times. "¡Claro!"

Because he'd caught Tyler's attention with the noise, I made sure Tyler was looking at me when I made the comment, "But I assume the services of the Fox don't come cheap."

Tyler gave an almost imperceptible shrug as the Fox chuckled before slipping into a bit of his biography.

He was the middle child of seven. His parents were loving and hardworking and retired in an undisclosed location. He didn't keep in touch with any of his siblings but was pretty sure he had over twenty nieces and nephews. He'd been married nine times; went to school until he was fifteen but gave it all up to begin smuggling pot into the states via piñatas. He owned property, a car lot, several businesses, but his favorite was a boba tea shop.

"A boba tea shop?" I asked skeptically.

He laughed. "Gringas love that boba tea!"

"I suppose that is the epitome of stealing from the rich." I was tickled with my analogy but the laugh turned to a cough when hungover phlegm went down the wrong pipe. After as dainty a throat clearing as I could muster, I told the Fox, "You are fascinating, I'll give you that."

"And now you understand why I am a good man to know and why it's a good thing you are my friend."

I tilted my head to the side. "I'm not so sure. Wasn't there a reason the fox and the hound couldn't be friends?"

Ali, you just called yourself a dog. (Shhh, hungover metaphors, remember?)

This unleashed a shocking howl of laughter that at first, froze everyone within earshot before it pulled equal smiles and added laughs.

He gave my back a hearty slap that pushed my ribs into the table. I grunted, but should have been glad that it was a slap on the back rather than one across the face for insulting him.

But that was what he liked about me, wasn't it? My honesty?

So since I was on a roll, and my stomach and head were happily bobbing about on the current of full and finally feeling more human; and because this Napoleonic statured man *was* fascinating; and because I was leaving soon anyway, I indulged. "Is your life often in danger?"

He twisted his lips skeptically as if I should know the answer, but still explained, "Of course. Always, there is someone who might want to kill me, but," he held up a finger and leaned toward me, "*always*, there will be men around to vindicate me too."

"You've built quite the life for yourself."

"Are you calling the Fox viejo?"

"Old? No. No! I—"

"Is okay," he ran a hand through the part of his hair with the white streak, "I am not as young as I used to be. That is why I look to diversify my portfolio. For retiring."

Diversify his portfolio?!

Sure.

"What does a retirement plan look like for a man who can get anything?"

"I have a villa muy bonita en Miami. In a different name of course. But there, I will spend my old years on the beach watching women in bikinis walk by, and listen to the seagulls as I soak up the sun," he said wistfully.

You know those moments you think to yourself: *I might have too much information.*

At least I didn't know the 'different name.'

We were interrupted with dessert; a flan with a candle on top was delivered by several members of the restaurant staff who sang "Feliz cumpleaños," producing déjà vu vibes.

"I do this for you!" the Fox announced loudly after I politely blew out the candle. "Last night, you tell me you had a horrible birthday. I remember this." He pulled out a long rectangular blue velvet box from his pocket and made a show of putting it on the table before sliding it across to me, a wide grin in place.

Now, of course, since I was still thinking about *The Godfather*, and after seeing how many people seemed to think the Fox was important, it did cross my mind that accepting a gift from him was along the lines of: 'I do you a favor, you do me a favor.'

But I'd just come from another birthday celebration where the only gifts were guilt, lectures and deep sighs of confused disappointment.

So I happily opened the damn box.

A silver chain held a freeform stone, a swirl of light reddish orange was held in place by silver prongs. It was the size of a quarter, stunning and unexpected.

"A fire opal." The Fox pulled the box out of my hands and took the necklace out, nodding for me to turn so he could put it on. "It will boost your confidence and promote good fortune."

He patted my shoulder once it was in place and I shook my head. "I can't accept this."

Never take candy from strangers. (Yup, that lesson definitely had a crossover in this situation.)

"It's your birthday. You have to."

"What do I owe you if I accept this gift?" Better to be blunt and safe than sorry.

"This is a boring conversation. We are friends. You owe nothing."

I touched the fire opal.

"It is for your adventure."

I glanced sideways at him. "Adventure?"

"You are not headed home," he said, as if he knew something I didn't.

"I'm not?" I raised an eyebrow.

He gave a tisk of a sound. "Last night, we all agreed now was a good time to start new adventures."

"I'm staying," Tyler interrupted, holding his watered-down Bloody Mary aloft.

Yvonne joined him. "I quit."

El Zorro Blanco shrugged. "I have to get to work."

All eyes were on me then.

What was I going to do with the drunken pact I barely recalled making?

But I'd been thinking about what to do, that's for sure. Earlier, as I'd laid with my cheek on the toilet seat and willed my head to stop spinning I'd decided–

"I have a friend from college who lives in Mexico City." I gave voice to my tentative plan.

The Fox slapped the table. "Adventure. Perfect. Take the bus. I'll buy your ticket."

I sighed as I mentally cobbled together a plan of action and realized I did need something else from the Fox. "Can you get me a new phone? I lost mine last night."

"Of course," he winked at me, "I am the man who can get anything."

Ten

Tyler, possibly due to lingering guilt and seeing the last strands of 'sticking togetherness' through, accompanied me to the bus stop.

Of course, Yvonne came with him and since El Zorro was paying for my ticket, he rounded out our ragtag group.

The Fox handed me my ticket and tried to accompany it with a wad of cash. I glanced at the pesos and asked, "How much is about twenty American dollars?"

He shrugged and pulled out a 500 peso bill from the pile.

I pocketed it and said, "If anyone asks for a bar, hotel or restaurant recommendation, I'll send them your way."

He slipped his arm around my waist and pulled me toward him; his voice low as he warned, "I'm going to kiss you now."

But with the warning I was able to press my hands against his chest and offer him my cheek.

He gave a laughing shrug as he released me. "You can't blame me for trying."

"No, I suppose I can't." I reached into his front pocket to grab his pack of cigarettes, along with the book of matches. I took two out, held them up and said, "For later. Just in case."

"Keep the pack."

I shook my head and replaced it in his pocket. "I quit years ago. Two won't push me over the edge."

He shrugged and patted my cheek before allowing Tyler his turn to say goodbye.

Tyler leveled his gaze on me, asking, "Are you going to be okay?"

I turned the question back on him. "Are *you* going to be okay?"

"I'm going to be okay." He glanced over his shoulder at Yvonne who was clutching his hand. I don't think they'd released bodyparts since they were reunited at the restaurant.

"Tyler Stone," I winked.

He grinned.

I studied the 'couple.' She might be the same age as him. Maybe three or four years older. I thought about asking how old she was, but to be fair, I don't know how old Tyler was. One thing was evident, Yvonne's lifestyle (and maybe too much sun) had aged her a bit more than she probably would have liked.

"Be good to him." It was all the instruction I could think to give for the care and maintenance of Tyler Stone.

"Don't worry." She grinned, her slightly chapped lips cracking around the edges with the effort; which generated images of witches luring children into edible cottages. "This isn't the kind of man you let pass you by."

"I'll keep my fingers crossed for you two." Who knew, maybe this was Tyler and Yvonne's chance, maybe this was the start of their own personal happily ever after. And *maybe* we were all still drunk.

Tyler reached out his free hand and gave my shoulder an awkward pat as he bid me "Carpe Diem."

I refrained from rolling my eyes at the cheesiness and promised, "I'll be fine. Things are looking up for ol' Ali Skye."

I was doing something literary and adventurous. That had to count for something. Right?

After all, what was the saying? No good story ever started with a salad. And so far my story was drenched in Tequila.

Eleven

"Hello?"

I called my mom's cell once the bus began to move. No getting off and going back home now.

"Mom? It's me. This is my new cell number. I lost my phone." Not an auspicious start.

"Alicia," she sighed. "You are certainly going through something, aren't you?" she said in that 'mom voice' that made me want to cry and cuddle up to her so she could fix everything the way she did when I was younger.

"I'm sorry about dinner."

She gave a stale laugh. "I've walked away from my fair share of family dinners. Are you okay?"

I took a deep breath, I'd run through a few different ways to explain my current situation and location but none of them sounded quite right. In the end, I settled on just barreling through. "I needed to do something. So I went out for a drink with a friend last night and we ended up in Tijuana."

"Okay ..." She drew out the word.

"Mom." I was hungover and trying not to be defensive.

"Ali, you're an adult. If you want to go out with friends and go to Tijuana you can."

"Well, I have a plan." I inwardly groaned. I was tired of coming up with 'plans.' Each plan was a means to an end: make enough money to pay for life's essentials so I could keep writing.

And I've had a lot of plans in my life—

Freelance article writing for an adventure bound program in return for free room and board (until the company went under after three months because the owners were embezzling). Living off student loans while I worked for a temp agency and went to school full time. (Even though I *really* used the money to travel to Europe for a month, working remotely for said temp agency until it was time to go home; unsurprisingly, with no funds left. *And,* since I hadn't gone to class, gained no credits toward a degree.) And my favorite, deciding to move in with a man thinking it was the natural progression of a relationship because he declared his love for me ... but now, I live with my parents because the freelance writing I do isn't enough to pay rent on my own.

I shook off my past embarrassments and laid out my 'plan.' "I'm going to see an old friend in Mexico City for a week. I'm also going to call Amy," my most responsible friend who worked for an insurance company that was always hiring, "and apply to work with her company so I can get back on my feet."

There was a long pause.

The pregnant kind.

The kind of pregnant pause that makes you think the doctor originally got the conception date wrong because the pregnancy was going on and on and on ...

"Mom?"

"Life is too short to settle for bullshit."

If I'd been drinking water I would have spit it out. In fact, I was tempted to take a sip of water just so that I could complete the action; even if it was delayed.

But since my bottle of water was in the bottom of my new backpack, all I could do was ask, "What?"

"Last night your father and I were talking, and we don't tell you enough that your writing is good. *Really* good. So I say have some adventure. See the world. You were always happy when you were traveling and writing. So ... write about it all. I don't know how, but I *know* things will work out for you."

"Okay ..." *What* have you done with my mother?

She laughed. "Alicia Skye Locke. Just keep writing until you make something happen."

"I have enough money in my bank to cover my expenses for a few weeks," I whispered.

"We talked about that too. We've never helped you—"

"Mom, I don't want your money, you're already letting me stay with you."

"Alicia. We've helped your brother and sister in the past. It isn't much, but we've got five thousand dollars for you. Who knows, maybe you'll find a little beach city down there where it's cheap to live." She was spitballing and on a roll. "You can do some good writing and freelancing to make ends meet and your things are safe here."

How hungover was I and what parallel world had I woken up in?

"Call or text every day so I don't have to report you as missing."

"Okay ..." It was more of a muttered question than an agreement.

"I'm serious. If I don't hear from you, I'll call the cops."

"Okay ...?"

"Have I met this friend in Mexico City?"

"Yeah, Francisco ..."

"Oh, when you had that fun international food party at the house, he brought me flowers and had such curly hair."

"Yeah, that's Francisco ..."

"Have *fun*."

"Okay." Still a question.

"Your adventurous spirit scares the crap out of me," she admitted.

"I know."

"But what you don't know is that I'm *jealous*. I could never do half the things you do."

I glanced out the window to see if the crack in the matrix was visible. Nothing.

"Now, we'll deposit the money in your account. Should I send your passport and laptop to Francisco's house?"

"Yes, please send the passport. But give me a few days, I'll tell you when you can send my computer."

"I'll light a candle for you; for safe travels." That comment put us back on track and helped me find my voice again.

"Mom ..." my voice cracked and I could barely whisper, "thank you."

"I'm your biggest fan."

"I know."

She blew out a breath. "Okay, I'm not going to look up statistics about women traveling alone in Mexico."

I wiped at my eyes as I cleared my throat. "Probably a good idea."

"I'm glad I made you take so much karate."

"Me too."

"Now hang up before I get too worked up."

"I'm thirty years old, Mom."

"And I'll always be your mom and I'll *always* worry."

"I'll text you tomorrow," I promised.

"Okay. I love you honey."

I sat back and tried to comprehend my parents' support.

The gods were working some magic today.

I glanced out at the soft clouded late afternoon sky. Green bushes dotted the slightly hilly desert. Reds and browns on the empty, calm stretch of road that would deliver me to Mexico City. An excited flutter in my chest vibrated from excitement. It had been far too long since I had purposefully shaken up my life. And if the past few hours were any indication, that's what my life needed.

It was time to take care of the next obstacle. To call my friend Francisco and inform him of my impromptu visit. (Can we take a moment to be grateful for the cloud that stored all my phone numbers and other worldly contacts?!)

Francisco and I didn't start out as friends; ours was a relationship built on a passing attraction and a drunken misunderstanding of a night.

Talk about continually walking the same path.

We met in a history class while working on a project. We enjoyed talking with each other so much that we'd get together often, our conversations lasting well into the midnight hours.

The climax of our attraction took place at a party. Not the stereotypical parties they lazily depict in movies. Sure we were drinking, but it was subdued; I mean, we were in a house filled with people playing board games; some jamming together on various instruments; and others, with poetry books in hand, insisting on proper interpretations.

No one drove home that night. And Francisco and I ended up clutched to each other on a sofa. The only thing of note that happened was a clumsy, brief make out session.

Flash forward to the hungover light of day, I apologized because it was a mistake, but he began a ridiculously awkward admission of having a girlfriend back home. I tried to end the elongated apology by leaving, but my shoes had gone missing amid the other still sleeping 'party animals.' I found one when he loudly whispered, "I think I'm in love with you."

"No, you are in love with the *idea* of lusting after someone," I amended. (Poetry still on the brain.)

He fumbled about verbally– "If this was any other time, if she weren't in my life, I didn't ... I mean, I knew what we were doing ..."

I explained the night was a mistake; he repeated his declaration of love, so I gave up looking for my other shoe and a middle finger was my parting gesture to Francisco.

Two days later, we ran into each other at a campus coffee shop. He gave me a big smile that I returned as we crossed the distance separating us—physically and metaphorically—and mended everything with a hug and apologies. We also agreed we were far better as friends.

We kept in touch on a somewhat regular basis. He was teaching English in the university and coached high school basketball, and according to the Christmas email last year, was engaged. Still, I hoped he would be open to a spontaneous visit. (Because in every email exchange he always invited me to come visit.)

He answered after the fourth ring.

"Francisco, it's Ali."

"Ali?" he asked, surprised. "What are you doing?"

"Well, funny you should ask. I'm on a bus somewhere east-ish of Tijuana. Headed to Mexico City." My voice wavered as I made the announcement.

"Really?!"

"Really and truly."

"That's so crazy. You have to come stay with me and my family."

I let out the breath I'd been holding. "That's what I was hoping you'd say."

"What bus? You said Tijuana?"

"Yes."

"Are you in trouble with the law?" He laughed.

"Not yet."

"Okay, when do you arrive?"

I glanced at the ticket and did quick math. "In twenty-eight hours?"

"Are you sure you're not running from the police?"

"Just wanted to see some country." I guess. Actually, now that I think about it, I bet the reason the Fox insisted on the bus was because *he* wanted me to see some country.

"Okay, send me a picture of your ticket. I can find the itinerary. Call me if you need anything and I'll pick you up at the bus station when you arrive. Then I can finally show you my city!"

"Thanks Francisco. I really appreciate it."

"Of course!" I could feel his smile spread across the distance as he went on, "Oh, I'm going to go ask for a few days off. This will be wonderful. There is so much you need to see."

I said goodbye as instant tears formed; his reaction was exactly what I needed at the moment.

The bus would make several stops on this long overnight express. But as the hours from Tijuana grew, my excitement dwindled into boredom and possibly too much time for contemplation.

The air conditioner on the bus broke eight hours into the ride. The smells of the onboard bathroom and body odor rose and faded as windows were opened and closed. Conversations floated around me; some in soft whispers, some filled with laughter. I spent my time dozing in the warmth as the bus rocked and jerked, and watched through sleep laden eyes the dawning of a new day.

Fifteen hours in, after another stop at a small-town store where I bought chips, chocolate and two more bottles of water, I was getting organized again when I made unexpected eye contact with a very handsome man walking down the aisle. Tall, disheveled sandy blond hair, and built like a Nordic backpacker. (Of course, that could be because he was carrying a travel backpack, and my descriptions aren't on par, remember?) I held my breath as he held my gaze, and I swear, a slight smirk flashed before he sat down, but I couldn't be sure.

Out of curiosity, once we'd been driving awhile, I sat up tall in my seat to see if I could catch a glimpse of him. He was staring out the window and I was both intrigued and slightly jealous. That's what *I* was here for. Couldn't he have waited for another bus?

Adjusting in my seat, I scoffed and rolled my eyes. *It's a big big world, leave the man to his journey, and get back to yours.*

The bus methodically wound its way up into mountainous country. Trees grew thick alongside the road and I thought I even saw a few tropical birds and a monkey, but I couldn't be sure. I was in a surreal state of exhaustion, often being lulled to sleep by the breeze coming through the open window, only to be abruptly woken back to reality by the lurching motion of the bus as it changed gears.

The sound of a gunshot backfire jolted me fully awake in time to experience the breakdown of the bus and the final muscled turning of the behemoth to the side of the road.

There was no announcement, no panic. The driver opened the door and everyone calmly gathered their belongings and filed off the bus. I followed, then watched as the driver opened the luggage compartments; once passengers found their bags, they began to walk. Continuing their journeys as if this sort of thing happened all the time and there were some unspoken rules about how to conduct oneself in this sort of situation.

"I think I've seen this movie," I muttered, standing to the side, trying to figure out what I should do.

I stayed where I was because the air was finally cooler, it was quiet, and I had no idea where the hell I was and surely another bus would be along. Eventually.

Right?

"Right," I reassured out loud.

A misty rain began, a foreshadowing of the coming storm. If anything suggested staying here, *on the bus*, it was this moment.

I would take a nap, eat some chips and then make a decision. That sounded like a great plan. I laid down across the seats while giving an exaggerated yawn, using my backpack as a pillow.

Outside a male voice called, "Excuse me?" (In English.)

Could it be the intruding dreamer? Or maybe the bus driver returned to tell me I was doing it wrong.

"Excuse me?" it came again.

"Yeah?" I answered loudly.

The bus squeaked, giving away the mystery man's boarding.

"Hello?"

So much for a nap. I sat up and glanced over the seatbacks. Yup, it was the intruding dreamer.

"Hello," I called.

Twelve

"Hey," he said, setting his traveling backpack next to him with a heavy thump.

First impression—

Wait ...

Second impression: short, messy hair. Tan, with a sleepy look on his face accompanying a five o'clock shadow. The worn, heather gray T-shirt he wore had a faded Greek god of some sort etched on it in white and the tail end of a tattoo peeked out from under his right sleeve. He was toned and formidable; but the way he casually leaned against the nearest seat—calm, as if he had all the time and not a care in the world—lessened any passing uneasiness.

"Hey yourself," I replied. He held up a spiral bound sketchbook and pointed it to the window. "It started raining," he stated the obvious. "Didn't want my sketches to get too wet."

He was sketching when the bus broke down?

Okay, you have my attention.

"I'm waiting here ... until ..." I shrugged.

"Me too."

"Do you know where we are?" I asked.

"Nope." He amiably drew out the word.

"Me neither." *I* stated the obvious then figured since it was a standoff with a stranger, I'd see to my safety. "Are you dangerous?"

"I don't think so." He narrowed his gaze. "Are *you* dangerous?"

"Maybe," I answered honestly.

We made eye contact until it was uncomfortable until he finally introduced himself, "I'm TJ."

"Alicia." I gave a slight nod.

Another standoff.

Then he straightened and held out his hand, an offering, as he crossed the slight distance between us. I eyed him for a moment before standing, verifying he was a good head taller than me, and taking his hand in mine to make a solid connection.

And a slight shock.

And he didn't let go.

(Well, neither did I.)

We both looked down at our hands, still clasped. Mine looked smaller in his, the veins in his forearms were sculpted masterpiece perfect (and I've never been a 'forearm' girl before). I scanned up the arm to his solid shoulders, a bit broader than they'd looked from farther away. More of a scan and I landed on his face, angular and attractive, the slight beard adding ruggedness that raised my eyebrow as I met his light brown eyes, flecked with amber.

We had passed propriety so many seconds ago that it was as if we were just holding hands now, not shaking anymore. But when he didn't seem interested in pulling away, I forced myself to do it and floundered for small talk, jumping on the most obvious talking point I could find. "So, you're an artist?"

"I try to be." He stepped back a few feet and perched on the arm of a seat, allowing me to get back to a normal breathing cycle and make up fanciful descriptions: Visible self-confidence. Sincere smile. Alluring eyes. A mouth made for kissing.

The throat clearing I did was too loud. "Are you any good?"

He stared at me for a minute.

Actually, he didn't just stare, his eyes penetrated mine and searched my damned soul before he finally broke the connection and walked back to the front of the bus. For a flash of a second, I thought maybe I'd offended him. Or, whatever it was he saw in my soul left him wanting. But he retrieved his sketchbook, returned and handed it over.

I pasted a smile as I accepted the book and mentally scrolled through all the descriptive words I knew when it came to art that I might not like or understand. (Wow, I really love the shading. The way you posed your subject is interesting. What made you choose this composition?)

Thank you freelance writing gigs!

But every clichéd phrase I owned slipped out of my head. I was unprepared to be faced with TJ's sketches.

I was not prepared for the depth and emotion he captured with a few simple strokes of a pencil on a blank page.

I was not prepared for the force felt when coming face to face with true art.

And I was not prepared as I realized I might actually recognize this style.

"You know ..." I'm not an art expert by *any* stretch of the imagination. I had the understanding of a few art movements that I learned about over the years, enough to write a fluff piece. And in truth, I only know, *maybe,* a handful of artists' names. Living and dead.

Still ...

The jolt of recognition sat me down in my seat as I whispered, "Holy shit!"

"What?" He pursed his lips and frowned.

I scanned his whole person once more as I held up his sketchbook, my eyes wide as I softly declared, "You're Theodore Jones."

He groaned before he gave what can only be described as a disappointed shake of his head. "I suppose I am." He took the sketchbook out of my hands. I blinked several times, glanced out the window, then looked back at Theodore Jones (aka TJ), before lowering my gaze down at myself–to make sure I hadn't mistaken any of this for a mad dream.

"I think you should pinch me," I muttered.

He frowned at the request.

I whispered, "You're *never* gonna believe this—"

"You're a fan and you have one of my pieces," he cut in. I'm sure he'd heard that proclamation on more than one occasion.

I shook my head slowly as I tried to focus, but couldn't hide a smile or the bubble of laughter that rose. "No. But you should probably ask me what *I* do for a living."

He cocked his head to the side, interested in this turn of events. After a moment he tentatively asked, "What do you do for a living?"

"I define irony." I let the laugh out (which wrinkled TJ's brow in confusion), then continued, "And I am starting to think there are some strange muses at work here."

"What?"

"Oh my God, I almost don't want to tell you." I shook my head, trying to figure out how to rip this band-aid off. Honestly, I suppose. The simplest way is always the best. "I'm a writer."

His forehead continued to furrow as he asked the leading question, "Would I have read anything you wrote?"

Jesus! I couldn't ask for a more perfect opening.

Seriously, which muse was hard at work in my life right now? Calliope, wasn't that the main one? I should make an offering as soon as this conversation is over. How do you thank a muse? Or did El Zorro really absolve me?

I cleared my throat. "My stories have been in several literary journals. I mainly support myself through freelance work." My face was cracking with a smile as I leaned toward him. "But most recently, Theodore Jones, I had a piece in the *Los Angeles Times* that was so popular *The New Yorker* picked it up."

A few blinks accompanied a shrug; he was still confused so I threw him another clue.

"It was just a little story I made up about a painting I saw."

"Alicia?" He took a step back, his eyebrows raised to the top of his hairline in surprise. "Ali?"

I gave a huge, dramatic nod, grinning as the realization dawned on him.

"Ali Skye?" He growled my name.

I continued nodding as my face stretched with wide eyes and held back laughter.

"Holy shit." His turn to be surprised. After several shakes of his head and several false starts in conversation, he blurted, "Are you following me?"

"*I* got on this bus in Tijuana," I defended myself. "Maybe it's *you* who's following *me!*"

He scoffed at the implication, then his shock turned into a smile and a laugh as he pointed at me. "You horrible person! You ruined my painting."

"I didn't mean to," I joined in his laughter, "I love that painting. Truly."

"Seriously ruined it," he insisted.

"As you explained in your email." I raised an eyebrow.

He waved a hand. "I was really pissed when I wrote that."

"And when you sent it."

"And when I sent it," he agreed.

I stood and crossed the slight distance that separated us and once again offered my hand with a grin. "Theodore Jones, the artist. I'm Ali Skye, the writer. It's really nice to meet you."

He slipped his hand into mine once more. "I stand by my declaration. Fucking writers ruin everything."

"And talented artist or not, you are a pompous asshole for sending that email."

Thirteen

"Why did you write that?" TJ asked.

The rain stopped and we moved to sit outside on a log on the side of the road, using plastic shopping bags we found in the trash can on the bus to sit on. I gazed off into the surrounding foliage, brought to life in shades of vibrant green from the recent precipitation.

"I wrote it for me," I sighed, "I never meant for everything that happened to happen."

"Well, the things we never mean to do make up our lives, don't they?" he responded. Not mad, more curious.

"Very true, Yoda." I picked up a nearby stick and made circles in the wet dirt. "I wasn't supposed to go to that show, you know. I've had to write so many fluff pieces about art shows over the years that I just ... I gave it up two years ago because I wasn't any good and the magazines were just using the work as filler. And I didn't want to grow to hate art. But I swore off shows because of all that. So *your* show, I went because one of my friends didn't want to go alone. I was doing her a favor."

He grunted in reply.

"I feel like you aren't allowed to be all that mad at me," I said.

"Oh, really?"

"I'm pretty sure it didn't hinder your sales or notoriety," I pointed. (Not that he needed my help, his name and work were always on the 'Up and Coming' lists and the prices that were on his paintings at that show ... trust me, he didn't need my help; but it was a good ploy.)

He didn't answer. He didn't need to. We both knew the truth of him being *the* hottest ticket in town at the moment.

You're welcome very much.

"Has *your* notoriety changed since your publication?" he returned the question.

That's the rub. "Actually, no," I muttered.

"No?"

I knew so many writers who'd had doors open wide for them just because one of their pieces was published in *The New Yorker*. I was still waiting. And trying not to focus on the doors, and windows, that seemed to be shutting one after another on my writing.

"I've always hated that when I tell someone I'm a writer, they invariably put me in the 'artist' category," I said instead of going into depth about my career and its current progress. *Or the lack thereof.*

"What's wrong with that? Writing is an art form."

"I'm jealous," I admitted with a smile.

"Jealous."

"It always pissed me off that people who paint can hold up their work and ask, 'what do you think?' and get an instant reply. Meanwhile, when I hand someone a three hundred and fifty-page manuscript and ask 'what do you think?', the answer is often months away."

"It's the nature of the beast," TJ offered.

"It's the nature of the beast," I agreed, sighing.

He rubbed his hands on his worn jeans and sat up straight. "Okay, so who owes who an apology?"

"You do?" I asked, hopefully.

"For writing the email?"

"I did enrich your career ..." I tried.

"You stole the soul of my painting," he volleyed.

"I didn't steal anything." *The gall of some people.* (I thought hypocritically.)

He sighed. "I apologize for writing a rather hate-filled letter." An upturn of his lips and twinkle in his eye accompanied the next level of his apology. "I thought I was safe. I never thought I'd actually meet you in person, much less in the middle of a Mexican jungle."

"Fair enough," I accepted. "And I apologize if you feel like I stole the soul of your painting. I didn't. But I'm sorry you feel that way."

He barked out a laugh. "Fucking writers."

"Artists!" I bit back.

After a few moments of scanning the topiary horizon, he asked again, "Why'd you do it?"

Since we had time on our hands, I suppose the least I could do was explain the course of events months ago that led me to view his work.

"So there I was, Friday night, crying in my carton of Ben & Jerry's, my relationship wasn't going very well, I couldn't write anything, I had just been passed over for an important grant, had been outbid for several freelance jobs and received five rejection letters for a book submission and several short stories. A friend insisted I go out." I mocked, "'Come to this art show with me. I promise it'll make you feel better.'" I glanced sideways at TJ. "So I went. And with my third plastic cup of wine in hand, some overcooked cheesy pastry in the other, pretentious art morons to the left of me, jokers to the right ..." His grin widened. "Let's just say I was done five minutes after we'd arrived."

"Did you hate the show?" His vulnerability was apparent.

"No," I blew out a breath, "I just wan't in the mood. What I hate are the pretentious critics that are always mingling at those shows." I put on my best pompous voice: "Oh *Margo*, I completely disagree with your observations, the subaqueous qualities of the biomorphic forms spatially undermine the larger body of work." I barked out laughter with that mouthful.

TJ elbowed me, laughter in his voice, "I understand what you mean."

"Don't you hate that *those* are the people who buy your work?"

He shrugged. "It's a tricky position. Because of the Margos of the world, I do have conversations like that; but their support allows me to continue to do what I love. And travel, so I can meet writers when buses break down."

"So," he led me back to the original thread of my story, "you are drinking all the free wine at my art show ..."

"Yes, and being finished with all the wine, I wanted to leave so I went to find my friend but then, I saw it ..."

"It."

I pursed my lips. "Don't you kinda know all this?"

He shrugged. "I was angry as I read it. I didn't comprehend it. And I had a problem getting past the degrading remarks about the title of the piece."

"*Tame Me Home*," I said, scrunching my face, "it's awful."

He snarled at me, or tried to, but it ended with a groan. "My agent names a lot of the work. If it were up to me, all my pieces would just have dates. He says people want a name, not a number."

I nodded and pointed. "I *never* wrote that I hated the title. I just said that the name was not representative of the piece."

"You wrote, *great painting, shame about the name.*"

I stopped absently drawing circles and quickly tried to protest by pointing the stick at him, but instead flicked dirt at both of us, some ending up in my eye. Stick dropped, I bolted onto my feet as I began a muttered 'shit' 'damnit' litany while prying my eye open with one hand, and gently, with the pad of another finger, attempted to get the sand out.

"Sand?" TJ asked.

"Yeah."

"Let me help," he said, and since I'd aimed my face toward the sky, it was an unexpected shock when the first glug of water from his bottle hit my eye and most of my face. I let loose with, "What the hell?!"

But it worked.

That, along with the natural tears that formed.

Before I had a chance to thank him, another attempt at 'helping' splashed over my face.

"Shit. Okay. We got it." I backed away from him. My third step back was accompanied by his warning to "stop!" but I didn't and somehow tripped backwards at the same time TJ lunged for me; causing us both to end up sprawled on the ground in a strange tangle.

"Ouch." I blinked up at the sky full of fast-moving gray clouds. My tears soothed my burning eye, verifying that the debris was gone.

"Sorry," TJ muttered as he untangled himself then took my hands in his and helped me up. When we were standing so close, I glanced up into those soft brown eyes and mumbled, "I never said great painting, shame about the name."

He pushed back the stray wet hairs hanging in front of my eyes. "No. You didn't. The way you said it was more literary and therefore hurt more."

I slapped his hands away from my face and smoothed my hair back with a sigh. "Did dumping all your water over my head make you feel better?"

"I was trying to help," he claimed.

I wiped at the corner of my eye that was still watering and he tilted his head as a sly grin formed. "It helped a little bit."

I pulled at the front of my shirt a few times, a lame attempt to quickly dry it.

"Sorry," he said.

"TJ," I stopped trying to placate my clothes and the bit of mud that was on my pants and faced him, "you painted something so gorgeous it brought me out of myself and inspired me."

He shifted from foot to foot and glanced over my shoulder at the compliment; and I kinda liked that it made him uncomfortable, so I continued, "I just stood in that gallery and stared at your work. I even pushed a few people to move when they got in between the painting and my eyes," I admitted.

"I hope it was a few Margos."

The painting was darkness; shades of blue and purple, but mostly black gradients that revealed a disheveled woman standing on a road in front of a haggard truck. She was looking at whatever was down that road, not the man behind her who had his hand outstretched, possible worry on his face. I don't know why I loved it, but it had filled a void. The faces and bodily shapes of the couple were as darkly distorted as the rest of the painting, but there was so much obvious emotion and that alone didn't seem fair. It was wonderful and haunting at the same time.

"I hadn't done any good writing for a very long time. And just standing in front of your work ignited something in me. And I needed to be ignited." He *had* to understand that feeling. "There was a story there," I continued, "a story just for me, by the way."

He sighed and opened his mouth a few times, but when nothing came out he gestured to the log we'd been sitting on. Once again seated, he muttered, "I saw you. Sitting on the floor with all those napkins."

"What?! Then ... you knew who I was ..."

He held up his hands. "No. I remember seeing a woman sitting on the floor writing on napkins. I never saw your face and I didn't have time to talk to you; my agent had me pretty busy."

"I accosted a waiter for a stack of napkins and a pen."

"You didn't have a pen?"

I held up my hands and shrugged.

"Aren't you a writer?" he asked, incredulous.

"A writer who is always searching for a pen and paper–" I gave a dry laugh. If that isn't a metaphor for my life …

"Okay, you were *so* moved, you wrote a story on stacks of napkins while sitting on the floor of my art show."

"Yup. I never met the artist Theodore Jones while I was there that night, so I had no idea what he looked like. Because 'the artist' has anonymity, there wasn't one photo of him anywhere in that gallery."

"It's the one thing I fight for," he responded. "I want the work to speak for me, not some stupid black and white photo of me looking into the distance."

"Hauntingly," I amended, "you would have to be hauntingly looking into the distance."

"Whatever." He elbowed me. "So how did we get to the newspaper?"

"A week later, the same friend who took me to the show bothered me until I let her read what I'd written. The next thing I know, she's pitched the story to a friend at the *LA Times*."

"But you had to okay the piece."

I returned his previous elbow. "According to your angry letter, your agent allowed the *Times* to print a photo of your painting next to the piece without your knowledge."

"I was on a trip," he grumbled.

"Well, I wasn't asked either. Just given a copy and a check from my friend."

"You had to agree to *The New Yorker*, though."

"So did you," I pointed.

Another sigh. "I was still on vacation."

"Don't you take a phone?" I asked.

He nodded and sheepishly admitted, "I just never answer work related calls. And I always let the battery run out."

I sighed. "*The New Yorker* got wind of the story and approached me. I didn't agree to it at first, by the way. But I was in a spot where I needed something to jump-start ... something."

"So you used me."

"And ruined your painting," I finally admitted.

The New Yorker allowed me a quick introduction to why I wrote the short story, then printed my story next to a photo of the painting. No bio pics, no in-depth interviews, no interaction between artist and writer.

We let the rest of the story settle around us. TJ shook his head. "Of all the gin joints in all the towns in all the world ..."

"No kidding."

We sat in companionable silence for a while before TJ stood up and brushed off his pants. "I don't think anyone is coming."

"I get that feeling too."

"I don't know why we're on a dirt road." He pointed. "I didn't want to worry you, but the road to Mexico City is paved and pretty straightforward."

"There were detour signs about an hour ago," I informed him.

He raised an eyebrow. "Welp, that's what I get for taking a nap. How much luggage do you have?"

"Just my backpack."

"Feel like a walk?"

"I don't think we have a choice."

His gaze scanned me from head to foot; probably wondering if it was a good idea for me to walk.

And fair enough.

I was dressed for a nice dinner with family; v-neck black dress shirt, a three-quarter length white sweater (now with a little mud on the sleeve), dark jean capris and black slip-on shoes.

He hesitated. "It's pretty muddy."

I made an attempt to reassure him. "The shoes are comfortable to walk in."

He glanced up at the sky. "It might rain again."

"It'll be a warm rain," I shrugged, "let's walk."

We could have stayed with the bus and waited. But I was on an adventure, and adventures weren't made by waiting around. They were built from movement and action.

With our backpacks on, we decided to follow the direction the passengers had gone.

"I never would have imagined I'd be walking through some unknown forest in Mexico, trying to find the closest town with the man who called me a 'molester of art.'"

"I stand by it," he said, amused.

"Theodore Jones."

"TJ," he corrected.

"TJ Jones? Isn't that redundant?"

"Not really."

I waited a beat for him to expand.

When he didn't I prodded again, "What does the 'J' stand for?"

"Jefferson," he supplied.

"Theodore Jefferson Jones." I mulled the name around.

He tilted his head up toward the sky, then eyed me before saying, "Actually, my name is Theodore Smith." He pursed his lips and asked, "If I tell you my full name and the story behind it, are you going to write it into a story?"

"Maybe?" Might as well be honest. There was a lot of this life that was too interesting not to twist a bit and put in a story. "Of course, I haven't really been writing much lately. So I might not." Maybe that nugget of truth would help.

"I'm reluctant to tell you but I think you'll get a kick out of it."

"Well now you have to tell me."

"It's not like it's a secret," he admitted. "My full name is Theodore Jefferson Lincoln Quincy George Smith."

"Bless you." It was really hard not to laugh, so I had to take some shaky breaths, my head facing away until I was able to ask "really?" and not break into full body laughter.

I didn't do a good job.

He sighed. "My father was convinced he wasn't going to have any other kids. And he wanted to name his son after his favorite presidents."

"In order of ranking?"

One nod was his answer.

"I suppose you should be glad it was a short list." I was still holding back laughter. "So, I'm assuming your father had more children? How many siblings?"

"I'm the oldest of five."

That burst the dam. I laughed, he blushed, and I actually had to stop walking to catch my breath. I held up my hands in an apology before acknowledging, "I really want to write about that."

He grunted. "Just so you know, it wasn't the craziest idea the old man had. My other siblings are all girls."

"Oh ... good story."

He raised an eyebrow, reminding me of my semi-promise. "Okay, so, why Jones?" I asked about the one name that was not a part of his birth certificate assigned nom de plume.

"In high school, my friends called me Jones. They said all I did was 'jones' for art ... things. So it was a simple eventuality that TJ sounded pretty good with 'Jones,' and it stuck."

The greenery that choked the dirt road gave way to a fork.

I took out my phone that had ten percent battery left. "No signal. Do you have one?"

"My phone's dead. Has been for a few days," he replied.

"Part of never having a charged battery?"

He shrugged.

"So one could say—"

"No," he shook his head, "you're not gonna twist my lack of a phone when I travel as the reason my piece was pictured next to your story."

"Can I at least try?"

He winked, maybe to take the edge off his reply. "No."

"Fine. Let's ... look down each road ..." I muttered the words that came so naturally after that phrase: *As far as I could to where it bent in the undergrowth.* I smiled as I explained, "We had to memorize "The Road Not Taken" by Robert Frost in seventh grade. I'll probably have Alzheimer's and still be able to recite it. Along with several overplayed commercials from my childhood," I explained.

"For us it was "Where the Sidewalk Ends," in sixth grade," he supplied, then gestured to the roads dividing before us. "So which one do you want to take?"

I looked in the dirt for footprints, but the recent rain had washed away any signs of travel. "Since we can't even see footprints, I suppose I'm open to either one."

"Well, right is always right," he said, and really, that was as good a reason to go in a direction as any.

"So we keep walking," I stated the obvious.

"Don't think we have much of a choice."

We turned right, which was no different in scenery. Green palm trees, a bright undergrowth of ferns and tall trees with long fingerlike branches that filled in the spaces between bushes—seemed to repeat itself every hundred steps.

TJ broke the contemplative silence, "Ali Skye sounds like a made-up name."

"It isn't. Alicia Skye Locke is my full name."

"That's a nice flashy writer name." The smile in his voice was evident. "You should use the whole thing."

I wasn't offended. "That's actually why I use Ali Skye. Sounds made up and less pretentious than any combination of my full name."

"Did you ever think of using a pen name?"

"I tried, never could find one I liked."

There were so many bird sounds, and gray sky, but no sign of another human for a few hours. I wondered, "Should we be worried? Or scared?"

"I don't think so."

"Are you worried?" I asked.

"Not really."

"Me neither." In fact, it was strange how at ease I felt around TJ. As if I'd known him for years and years. Before this moment. But that could be because I was hungry and tired. And lost in a jungle.

"I think the only thing I should really be scared of," TJ made a broad scan of the area, "is you."

"I am frightening," I agreed.

"You have the ability to maim with your words."

"I didn't maim anything. I didn't write a review about that piece. Nothing about your art, style, medium or... other art things. I just wrote a story."

He grunted.

"You know, it's nice to have an established relationship."

"Even if it is a rocky one?" he asked.

"Is it?"

"Well, it'll be an interesting story to tell our grandkids," he joked.

"Let's get out of the jungle first."

Fourteen

The rain started two hours into our trek.

It wasn't like we could head back to the bus for shelter, we'd come this far ...

At first it was a soft mist that felt good. But then it began to rain in earnest; large, giant, jungle size drops. TJ pulled out a baseball hat and offered it to me.

I pushed my wet hair out of my face, shaking off the offer. "Does it really matter now?"

I gestured to a group of palm trees next to the road, so closely bent together they looked like a decent natural covering to wait out the pouring rain. Only when I stepped off the road to what I thought was a flat area, I slipped, tripped, did a possible somersault (or just a tuck and roll to the side) before finally coming to a sprawled stop; resting on my side amid the mud and muck that comes with a very wet jungle.

"Ali!"

I rolled onto my back, a branch (or twelve) stabbing me. "Ow," I offered sarcastically. I must have lost my backpack in the fall. I closed my eyes to the drops drenching whatever last millimeter of my person might have been left dry.

"You okay?" The sound of careful steps in the underbrush filled my ears, accompanied by a few disjointed missteps.

I thrust my right arm into the air and wiggled my fingers. I was just fine. "I'll get up in a second."

"I got ya," he said, closer than I thought.

When the rain was no longer falling on my face, I blinked open my eyes to find TJ's face above my own. He was straddling my body, his hands reaching for mine. "C'mon."

I reached up and he hoisted me into a standing position which revealed a new set of problems. I used TJ's arms to steady myself as I glanced around.

"What?"

"Do you see my other shoe?"

That and the fact that sludgy, slimy mud was caked into areas of my body that had previously just been damp.

He made sure I'd be okay standing on my own before beginning the search for the other shoe.

Halfway to the road, he held up my backpack, but it wasn't until he was by the side of the road, where I'd taken my first step, that he found my shoe. He held up the muddy artifact, tossed my bag beside his on the road, and returned with my shoe, dropping it next to my bare foot.

"Better than nothing," I said, using him once again to steady myself as I slid my foot in with a squish and suction sound.

He took my hand and I let him help me back to the road. The mud created sounds you wouldn't normally want to make around someone you know well—much less someone you've just met. And added to those awkward noises was me, slipping occasionally on wet muddy leaves, ground, branches ...

When we were once again on solid ground, I looked down at our mud-covered hands and then at TJ. His eyes squinting with laughter, he used the pinky finger on his left hand (the only clean finger) and attempted to move some of the wet, pasted hair out of my eyes.

"So, maybe finding a source of cover isn't really important." I glanced down at myself. Mud was dripping in some areas, squishing in others, and still a few more were simply caked. (That'd be the best descriptive word for it.)

I took a step clear of TJ, held my hands out in front of me and tilted my head back, trying to use the natural resource at my disposal to wash up.

And trying not to laugh, knowing that my open mouth would probably fill with water, causing a spectacular choking scene.

"I have another water bottle," TJ offered.

"You're just itching to pour water on me again, aren't you?"

"Yup."

Several seconds later, he was standing next to me, this time showing me the bottle and his intentions first. "If you'd have told me when I woke up this morning, I'd be helping my nemesis rid herself of a mud bath ..."

"Hands first." I held out my hands as he slowly drizzled the water over them, and while it was nice to have them cleaned it really made no sense. "TJ, stop."

"What?"

I put my arms down for a moment and let the mud hiding up my sleeves drip down onto my hands before presenting them again. "It's not gonna work."

He pursed his lips.

"Does it look as awful as it feels?" I asked.

"You mean, do you look like you rolled around in the mud?"

I nodded while mindlessly trying to use my forearm to brush back the water and mud from my face; only succeeding in smearing a little more on my forehead. When I looked up to get a new wash from the raindrops, TJ's chuckle twisted and grew into a full body guffaw.

I smiled and tried not to verbalize the phrase, 'it could be worse,' then thought it wasn't right that TJ was in better shape than me. So I did the only thing that made sense—lunged at him, throwing my arms around his waist in an attempt to impart as much of my mud onto him as I could.

It seemed like a funny idea in theory, until I was pressed against his surprisingly well-built form; the moment landing quite a bit differently than anticipated.

But when he laughed and tried to stop me, there was no backing down. I nuzzled his neck with my hair and wiped my arms up and down his sides. He bent slightly, trapping my arms with his own. "You are going right back on the ground if you don't stop," he grunted.

I stopped and looked up into his eyes through a screen of wet hair. "I double-dog dare you," I said with a smile, annunciating every single word.

One second I was upright in a perfectly antagonizing stance and the next, I'm in the sludge being rolled around in an impromptu mud wrestling match, complete with laughing grunts of exertion, and squeals (but not from me; there's no way I'm the kind of woman who squeals, but I did overhear them).

After several rolls, once we were properly coated, I was again prone on my back; only this time the drips of muddy water were coming from TJ's face perched above me. A wide smile brightened his face.

"You happy with yourself?" I asked.

"Yup." He beamed.

And because he was a handsome mess and I enjoyed our conversation and I knew what kind of art that mind could produce and because of the strange feeling that I *knew* him continued to tug at me, (and the fact that somehow his lips were free of mud) I leaned up and brushed a quick kiss across them.

When I pulled away, his grin had turned to interest. He tilted his head and slowly licked his lips, grunted a *hmm,* then stood and once again held his hands out for me.

I accepted the help and still slipped twice in the growing mud, but TJ held on until I was steady. I nodded but he didn't let go of my hands. "I don't have a girlfriend," he said. When I raised an eyebrow he shrugged and I couldn't totally tell through the mud on his cheeks, but he might have blushed. "I just thought ..." his eyes rested on my lips for several heartbeats, "in case you worried about kissing me."

"I'm not worried about kissing you."

He narrowed his gaze, looking like he was searching my soul for something, but before I could grow self-conscious from the gaze, he pulled me into his personal bubble and captured my lips in a soft kiss meant to draw sighs and build heat.

When he tried to deepen it, the simple tilt of his head released water and a bit of mud and we both broke off into laughter, separating and turning from each other to spit out the mud.

"Okay, not the day for making out in the rain," he joked.

"Nope." Although, the unexpected heat released with that simple kiss was going to give me plenty to ponder as our day continued.

"So," he nodded down the road in the direction we were headed, "onward?"

"Might as well." I glanced down at my completely pitiful state and wiped my hands on my pants, which was an exercise in futility.

I thought now would be a great moment for a cigarette but those were probably a mashed up wet mess in the bottom of my backpack by now. Which was probably a good thing. It'd been a hard habit to kick the last time around.

We once again hoisted our backpacks on and fell into step, mine being a bit of a struggle as my shoes continued to suction with the weather inside and out.

After a while TJ said, "I feel like I've known you forever. Is that weird?"

"No!" I exclaimed with too much enthusiasm, then tried to dial it back, "I was actually thinking the same thing earlier."

"It probably doesn't hurt that you're funny and smart. And pretty. And you don't mind being in such a precarious situation." He gestured to my whole body.

"Complaining isn't gonna make any of this better."

"It's all part of the adventure?"

"All part of the adventure," I confirmed.

A long hike later, when the rain finally turned from torrents to a soft mist, we found shelter.

Of sorts.

Fifteen

"**Y**ou can't make this shit up," I whispered.

"No, you can't," TJ agreed.

We stood shoulder to shoulder in the light rain, studying the structure in front of us. Eight-foot walls stretched a decent distance in either direction, creating a complex of sorts. And a wooden gate in the center held a large sign. TJ read the sign and translated each word slowly, just in case. "La Orden de las Hermanas de María. The Order of the Sisters of Mary."

"A convent," I whispered; as to not alert anyone of our presence.

TJ met my whispering tone. "So it would seem."

I squinted, as if the action would shift the letters on the sign around and change the situation to something like: The Welcoming Day Spa and Luxurious Inn.

"We could keep walking," TJ offered.

"We could."

"Although, I don't know about you, but I'm pretty tired and covered in mud," he nodded to the gate, "so this *might* be a good option."

"It might be." I looked down the road where we'd come from, then in the direction we'd yet to travel. "Probably not just a group of biological sisters, huh?"

"Probably not," TJ replied.

"There's a good chance though, that if I go in there, the whole place could burn down. Or I'll burn ..."

"So the current expectations of entertainment value of the day would be met."

I elbowed him, and he playfully returned the nudge. "The bus is too far away now." I sighed.

"Yup."

We stood at the edge of the road, silently daring the other to make a decision when the front gate swung open with a loud, protesting creak and out darted a nun dressed in a full black habit, holding an umbrella and a visible frown.

She stood on the other side of the road for a moment before loudly calling, "Come inside. There's no sense standing out here in the rain like idiots," she said in a thick accent, then gave a wave of her hand and turned to go back from where she materialized.

When she reached the gate, she glanced back, realizing we hadn't followed. And while it wasn't audible, we could see her sigh impatiently from where we stood rooted.

"¡Vamonos!" she yelled, making us both jump. And just in case we didn't understand the simple Spanish phrase, repeated it in English, "Let's go!"

We followed slowly; the only form of rebellion at our disposal. Since neither of us had yet decided if going in was a good idea or not.

"I do *not* have all day." Her announcement was more of a command. "And you look awful."

We both grunted audible forms of complaints but followed.

Once inside the gate and covered by an overhang, the nun turned to us, did a full study of our current state as we stood dripping on the concrete walkway, and shook her head in disappointment. "I'm Sister Margaret Mary." Her voice had a no-nonsense edge. "This is a convent. We have been known to help people, and *you people* are obviously in need of assistance."

"The bus we were on broke down," TJ supplied.

"That ridiculous detour," she scoffed, "it's always a bus. Always tourists. They don't have the brains the Lord gave them to follow the locals who *know* what they are doing." She turned and began to walk once more.

We meekly trailed the good nun as she continued her tirade. "If you had followed them, you would have found a village and a new bus in a little less than a forty-five-minute walk. But no, you went the wrong way, got lost, and if we were not here, you'd end up with pneumonia."

"We thought we went the same direction as the other passengers," I tried to defend.

Sister Margaret Mary snorted in reply.

The large courtyard hidden behind the eight-foot wall reminded me of the California missions I had visited on a fifth grade field trip; which stood to reason as the missions were built by Hispanic monks. The trip coincided with a history unit on the missions, that concluded with the building of our own mission model. (Of course, all I learned from that lesson in school was that Carla Moretti's dad was a really good woodworker while my family didn't have enough duct tape in the house and no one was willing to take me to the store to buy more at 11 p.m. the night before my poorly executed project was due. And just in case you're wondering, you can only 'kind of' cut up a dollar store styrofoam cooler and get credit when you declare it's a mission.)

Anyway, this convent had a courtyard filled with organized color. Great care had been taken in the planting and pruning of vibrant flowers that danced around varieties of fruit trees and mingled among vegetables.

I whispered my impression to TJ, "This must be a self-sustaining nunnery."

And another note to self: *Find out if they were still referred to as nunneries.*

At the moment though, I wasn't about to ask our hostess the difference between a convent, mission and nunnery at the moment. We were already unwanted guests.

We walked to a giant door in the back corner of the courtyard; I suppose it was simply the front door, for lack of a better term. Though we didn't follow Sister Margaret Mary through. It was evident we were far from presentable to enter any establishment.

She turned and looked us over with pursed lips, obviously trying to decide what to do with us.

"The nuns here have taken a vow of silence," she told us.

"For their entire lives?!" The idea pulled the unneeded exclamation. "I'm sorry." (This is as good a point as any to explain that I was raised in a Catholic family, so I knew there were clergy who took vows of silence and I knew there was a difference between missions and convents but it had just been so long ...)

The creases in the nun's frown deepened. "Each sister's choice of silence differs in time and scope. *I* am the voice of the convent. For situations that require someone to interact with the public. For instance, *this* situation." Her stern study of us still occuring; you could almost hear her silent question: What am I going to do with you two? She went on, "It's a good thing someone had the foresight to put me here, otherwise where would we be when all you tourists show up?"

"We didn't—" I was cut off by a stern shake of Sister Margaret Mary's head. She took a deep breath and probably gave a silent prayer because as she exhaled all her edges softened a little. "I understand. You are on an adventure to find yourselves."

How many tourists had stumbled into this convent?

I glanced at TJ out of the corner of my eye. Sure, the 'find yourself adventure' was the trek I was on, but I didn't think to ask him what had brought him this way. If I had to guess, I'd assume his driving force was art.

"You need to understand," Sister Margaret Mary continued, "the sisters in this convent are on their own adventure as well. They have made decisions and I help so they can confidently walk their chosen paths." She waited for both of us to nod our heads that we understood.

"Alright. We will let you stay the night, give you some *clean*, dry clothes; a shower, obviously, and a hot meal. By tomorrow we will have all your clothes cleaned and dry and I will find you a ride. In return, I ask that you have no interaction with the other inhabitants, stay in your room and abide by our rules."

"Of course." I nodded my head as TJ uttered, "We will."

"Now, I'm not in the business of taking in murderers. So if you could please tell me your names, ages, occupations and the status of your relationship."

"I'm Theodore Jones, but people call me TJ. I'm thirty-two and I'm an artist. This is my wife—" He gestured to me.

I blinked at him once and then forced a smile. "Ali Skye. I'm a writer and kept my maiden name for my byline. I'm thirty." *And one day.*

Sister Margaret Mary gave a disappointed shake of her head. "Well, what's done is done." She glanced between us, and TJ took my hand in his, possibly to double down on the lie.

And perhaps to reassure me that the silent agreement of marriage we entered was for our safety—since we didn't know what we were getting ourselves into and staying together really did seem like the preferred option.

But now I was in a pickle. We'd lied to a nun and were about to go into the inner workings of a convent.

At least the burst of flames that were about to consume me would be spectacular.

With a sigh and another muttering shake of her head, Sister Margaret Mary motioned for us to follow her.

TJ took a few steps but when I didn't move he looked back at me expectantly. I swallowed, mumbled a "sorry" to the deity inside and crossed the threshold. When I didn't feel any flames licking the side of my face, I took a deep breath and let it out in a rush as TJ pulled us to catch up with Sister Margaret Mary.

She floated and I swear her feet made no sound as she quickly glided across the stone floors. "As I have said before, you will abide by our rules as long as you are under our roof. I always ask this of our drop-in travelers, and yet they just can't seem to stay where I put them. They walk all over the convent like it's their own home and I end up with even more problems on my hands. So we have taken to asking guests to please stay in the room we provide you while you are with us."

"Of course," TJ responded.

She swept us through several long corridors, and after a few right turns she stopped in front of a room. "It's not much."

No truer statement had ever been uttered. I could see why other visitors had left to find something else to do. It was a functional, small space with two twin beds.

"I think the first order of business is a shower. So let's move on."

We continued the bland tour around a corner to another door. "These are the facilities for guests. Inside you'll find a shower, restroom and sink."

It was like she was showing off the indoor plumbing and I wanted to thank her God for his good graces. The promise of the coming cleansing water and soap was a dream. Now, whether it was going to be hot water, well ...

"I'll leave some clean clothes outside. When you are finished, just leave your dirty clothes in the provided hamper near the sink. We'll take care of them. And after your showers, if you could wait for my return to show you back, it would be greatly appreciated."

TJ pushed open the door with his free hand then propelled me into the bathroom as the good sister took her leave.

Inside was a room with a sink (no mirror though, as it most likely promoted vanity) and two doors; one leading to a restroom and one to a shower. A few towels and a bar of soap sat on a small table next to the sink.

"Well." TJ squeezed my hand, then released it.

"Congratulations on your recent nuptials," I said.

"You too."

"Wanna go first?" I pointed to the shower.

"I'll be a gentleman and let you go," he slipped off his backpack, "unless you want company."

I took my backpack off and cringed at the mud and dirt that was already sloughing off of us. "Maybe later."

I opened the door to the room that held an outer area in which to change and the shower itself. When I saw two nozzles and turned on the hot one, it didn't disappoint. I tearfully announced, "TJ. There's hot water."

He handed me a towel and the bar of soap. I closed the door then walked into the shower with all my clothes, because it didn't really matter.

Once the clothes seemed clean of mud, I discarded them and painted the white soap brown again and again until finally, the water rushing over my body was clear. I tried to be quick, because who knew how long the hot water was going to last.

Wrapped in the towel that was large and beige and rough from being dried on a clothesline—but gloriously free of mud—I wadded all my clothes up in my sweater and held the bundle away from my body as I exited to quickly put them in the 'provided hamper.'

"I hope I saved some hot water for you. I tried to be fast."

TJ nodded, took his own towel and disappeared into the shower.

I looked outside the bathroom door, and on the ground were two folded beige garments. I brought them inside, took one and shook it out, revealing a long floor-length night dress. "At least you are dry and free of mud," I said as I slipped it on.

I gave a swish as the air floated up and reminded me what undergarments I was missing. But my underwear and bra were far from salvageable. I glanced down, as thick as this night dress fabric was, two body parts were quite obnoxiously expressing the chill in the air.

"*Jesus* ..." I muttered, rolling my eyes. "Sorry," I announced to the godly presence, pressing my hands over my breasts in the hopes that they'd warm up and 'settle down' before TJ was done. (Have you ever noticed that when you're trying to stop something like that, it never seems like there's enough time?)

When the door to the shower opened, and TJ emerged, towel tucked at his waist, I folded my arms across my chest.

He held his bundled clothes away from his body as he crossed to the hamper. I glanced down and was happy to see that things seemed to have calmed down.

I wasn't allowed too much time to think as a grunt of laughter escaped TJ; I glanced up and my mouth went dry as I took in his chest and toned muscles. Hair washed and mussed, all of it was a revelation.

And now that I had an up close and personal view, I could see his tattoo. Done in black ink, it was a god of some sort—Greek, maybe Roman—the detail so impressive I don't think I was far off assuming he was the creator.

"I like the tattoo."

He angled it toward me. "Apollo, god of the arts."

"Impressive." *Yeah, I was talking about a lot more than the tattoo.*

"Don't write about it, okay?"

I didn't want to write about it, I wanted to trace it with my finger.

I shook myself out of going down that path and instead picked up his nightshirt and said, "I think I'll be more interested in trying to describe how you're gonna look in this." I handed it over.

His gaze scanned my garment clad body and then focused on the fabric in his hand. "At least it's dry."

"That's what I said."

"That's what *she* said," he added with a chuckle as he slipped it over his head. Much to my disappointment. *Because I wasn't done studying him.*

He smoothed the fabric then held out his hands to the side for my approval.

"You look sexy," I offered.

"Really?"

"No."

Holding back our laughter was futile.

TJ slowly twisted from side to side. "This is … ah … a lot of fresh air."

I followed his lead and when a blast of cool air drifted upwards, reminding me what I'd been trying to deter just moments ago, I stopped abruptly.

TJ wiggled off his towel and asked, "What did you do with your shoes?"

"I put them in my towel, I figure we can try to get them to dry in the room."

He did the same just as a knock came to the door.

"Are you decent?" asked a familiar voice.

I gestured between us. "I would argue this *isn't* decent."

"It is, however, formless and lifeless."

That it was.

I answered the door and Sister Margaret Mary assessed us with a nod. "Much better. Are you ready to go back to your room?"

"We left the clothes …" I pointed just as TJ picked up his shoes.

She nodded to leave them, "We'll try to dry the shoes out as well." Then the good sister turned with a decisiveness that caused a person to blindly obey her directions.

She was fascinating, I'll give her that much. I had so many questions about her and her life in a jungle convent and how she spoke English so well. I wonder if she ever had dinner with troublesome tourists; because I got the feeling she'd be very straightforward with her opinions and answers to any questions asked of her.

With backpacks held away from our now clean bodies, we followed her back to the room she'd pointed out previously. The stone floor was cold against bare feet and the chill from the stone walls wafted upward inside my nightdress with each step.

The sister stood aside when we arrived at our room. "I will send someone with a hot meal shortly. And a few more towels so you can wipe your bags. If you need anything, there is a cord in the corner. Please, it is only for use if you need to use the facilities or if there is an emergency. Do not abuse this privilege." She waited for us both to nod in understanding and then offered, "Have a good evening." And with as much briskness as she came into our lives, she turned with a giant swoop of her long dark skirt and was gone.

The definitive slam of our door (and the unmistakable yet surprising sound of our door being locked) cemented our evening plans.

"This is how half of the horror films out there start," I whispered.

"How do the other ones start?" TJ asked.

"With a single girl who takes up with a strange man on an abandoned road in Mexico." I grinned.

We didn't move further into the room, just stood near the door and took in our surroundings.

Sparse was the first word that came to mind. Two single beds separated by a few feet. Each had one pillow, one fitted sheet and one heavy blanket folded at the foot of the bed. Two chairs across from the beds on the opposite wall were tucked into a small table with an oil lamp burning on top. It was utterly functional for the purpose of sleeping.

"Less is more," I muttered.

"How would you write it?" TJ asked.

A simple question, isn't it?

But it hit me dead center in the chest with a large wallop.

Why?

Because no one had ever asked me how I would write something I stood in front of. Even my friends, poets and writers alike, had never stood in a moment and asked me how I'd write it.

Stupid artist.

When I found the wherewithal to voice my opinion, I answered, "Stark." And then, because of the strange feeling that I'd known him longer than half a day, I asked TJ, "How would you paint it?"

"In shades of beige," was his quick response.

We took in the bare bones for another moment until TJ sighed. "Welp, guess we should get our honeymoon under way." Though all he did was put his bag down and begin pulling out the contents. He hung his clothes on the limited furniture, one of the chairs, and one of the hooks on the wall, then put some of his other belongings along the ground.

"Did your sketchbook get ruined?" I asked as I pulled out the few belongings from my pack: a now dead cell phone, the waterlogged contents of a purse, and a notebook that would be functional once it dried out.

He pulled out a waterproof bag and unfurled it to reveal his sketchbook. "I learned the hard way, after a few trips, that it's better to always keep it in a waterproof bag no matter what."

Having spread our worldly belongings out across the room, I sat down at the table. "What time is it?" I nodded toward the watch he wore.

"Six fifteen."

We both did a scan of the room, as if we'd missed something the first time; only when I glanced back at TJ, I found him shaking his head, an eyebrow raised and a slight grin.

"What?"

"A convent in the middle of a Mexican forest with a woman who stole the soul of my work."

We'd both brought it up a few times now. "Because it was as obscene and brilliant as that," I added.

Sixteen

A soft knock was followed by the unlocking of our door.
I was unsure what to do in the situation. I mean, it's not like it was something that was covered in a health class in eighth grade: How to not look guilty as you successfully lie to a nun about a fake marriage while locked in a convent.

They *especially* didn't cover that in Catholic school.

Two nuns, in their late fifties, one sturdy while the other was tall and lanky, floated in. (Maybe everyone here floated.) They didn't wear the traditional habit Sister Margaret Mary wore, but were dressed more modernly in simple dark skirts and white button-up blouses. Neither had a head covering. Other than large crosses worn around their necks, I don't know that there was anything about their dress that screamed 'nun!'

All smiles, they made a confident amount of eye contact as they set a tray of food on the table. The taller of the two touched the sleeve of my nightshirt and shrugged, a very apparent 'what can you do?' sort of sentiment.

I opened my mouth to say thank you but stopped and glanced worriedly at TJ. What protocol was there when faced with someone who took a vow of silence? Should we remain silent too?

They nodded their heads as if they understood then waved to us as they exited the door.

When the click of the lock came again, I breathed out, "Jesus."

"That's the guy." TJ chuckled.

"Are you religious?" I settled myself back in my chair.

"I think in this day and age, I'd say I'm more spiritual. The old, man-made constructs of religion are failing us as a people."

That's one way to put it. "So you've thought about this a bit."

He shrugged and asked, "What about you?"

"I was raised Catholic. Went to Catholic school as a kid. But I'm not practicing." I glanced at the door, as if I could see the nuns and their faith. "I'm not sure what I believe anymore."

"Ah, so that's the reason you were concerned about bursting into flames?"

"It still might happen." I watched as he set a plate in front of each of us and divided the black beans, rice and vegetables between us. It was still steaming and now that I wasn't cold, wet, or in the middle of a jungle mud treatment, my stomach could growl in demand of my attention.

"I don't think I could take a vow of silence," I admitted. "I've been on a silent retreat, and twenty-four hours was nice, but weeks and months?" Definitely not my thing. "But I admire their faith. I'd love to have something I believed in that wholeheartedly."

"Isn't your writing a form of faith?" TJ asked.

"Is your art?"

"Sure. Sometimes."

"I never thought of it that way." And it was something that would require more thinking. In the meantime, I grabbed a fresh, homemade tortilla, filled it, took a bite then rolled my eyes.

TJ mirrored my actions and nodded in agreement. "I didn't realize how hungry I was."

Somewhere bells rang the hour: 7 p.m.

I cleared my throat and asked TJ the one thing I felt needed to be asked to clear the air between us, "Do you forgive me?"

"For getting us locked in a convent?" He grinned before he took another bite.

I squinted, he knew what I was asking.

When he finished chewing, he said, "You were inspired when you wrote what you did. I was an angry asshole when I wrote what I did. So if you forgive me, I'll forgive you."

"Forgiven." I held out my half-eaten tortilla toward him and he nodded, touching his to mine and agreed, "Forgiven."

"So, Theodore Jones. What are you doing here?" I asked; an attempt to drag out our dinner as long as possible. We'd finished most of the food, so TJ sat back in his seat and I rolled the homemade ceramic cup that was almost empty of water back and forth on the table.

"This convent?"

"No, here. Mexico."

"Art," he replied simply before turning the question back on me. "What are *you* doing here?"

"That's what I'm trying to figure out, I'm not quite sure. What do you do on a trip for art?"

"I gather impressions, a lot of sketches. Feelings," he replied. "What do you think you'll figure out on this trip?"

"Well," I watched the cup between my hands as I admitted, "Today is either the first real day of my thirtieth year or it might be the third day ..." I tried to do a quick recap, but waved the math away. "It doesn't matter. I woke up the other morning really hungover, but with enough clarity that deciding to *do* ... something, and explore something, felt like a good plan."

"Then I'd say you're off to a good start."

"Actually, even yesterday was a good start."

"Story time?"

"I don't know if you'd believe me."

He waved his hand to indicate the space around us. "I think I'm willing to go out on a limb. Besides, we kinda know each other."

"We don't *know* know each other."

"We are *aware* of each other."

"True."

"Do you hope you'll find something to write about?"

I shrugged. "I really just meant to get out of the restaurant my family took me to for my birthday and get some fresh air."

"Restaurant?"

"Part of the story, but makes it a little longer."

He glanced around melodramatically. "Do you have somewhere to go?"

A grunt was my reply and I opted for changing the subject. "Are you taking the bus for the inspiration and scenery it provides?"

"I am. Is that why you took the bus?"

"I took the bus because I have limited funds and someone bought me the ticket. I don't think I'd be making some wide assumption if I pointed out that you probably don't have limited funds."

"Is there a question there?"

"Maybe." I rolled my eyes. "No. I don't know."

He smiled. "Well, I *could* fly first class, but you know as well as I do, those stories and scenes aren't real life."

"They're *someone's* life," I pointed.

"They aren't interesting to me."

"Okay, I can understand that." Even if I couldn't afford first class, I understood it. "But sometimes, first class can't be all that bad."

He grinned.

And that sent shivers of awareness throughout my body.

We were going to have to do something about the fact that the only light in this room was an old-fashioned oil lamp, it gave off warm feelings, and I think it was creating a bit more angle to his jawline where his few days beard growth was downright tantalizing in its soft glow.

I shifted and cleared my throat. "So we're both here for inspiration."

"Actually, I wasn't really supposed to be here at all." He stretched his legs out in front of him and crossed his feet. "I was headed to Portland. From San Diego. My flight was canceled and while I was waiting for my new flight to leave, I watched the revolving advertisements on one of the screens near the restaurant I was sitting in. This mural by Diego Rivera popped up; some ad for a retrospective at the San Diego Museum of Art. Well, that got me thinking about his work. Which made me think about Diego's country and surroundings; the kind you can't find in Portland. So I changed my plans, bought a ticket and here we are."

"I thought Diego Rivera's paintings were a lot of modern industrial movement stuff, not landscapes," I said.

"I thought you said you didn't like artists."

"I said I didn't like art *critics*. Some artists are okay."

"Any one in particular?" His voice lowered as he searched for a compliment.

I sat forward and batted my eyes. "Claude Monet."

He winked in reply, trumping my attempt to push him off-kilter.

I cleared my throat. "So you saw Diego Rivera's name and jumped on a bus."

"Yup."

"When did you leave?"

"I've been on the road for four days, before I got on *your* bus this afternoon."

We let the natural lull sweep us away, but there was a weight in the room building between us. (I stand by the fact that dim lighting was the major culprit here.)

TJ gave a soft laugh and asked, "What do you think is making us the most nervous? The fact that we know *of* each other so we aren't really strangers, or that it feels like we've known each other a very long time and it's unsettling?" Here he lowered his voice, "Or is it that the first thing I did when coming face to face with a nun was lie about being married?"

"Why don't you have a photo of yourself on your website?" The quick change of subject was an attempt to shake loose the building tension.

(Would you think less of me if you found out I'd done some 'light' cyberstalking of TJ? I knew as much as a generic bio could tell. He preferred oils, but used whatever medium his moods dictated. I knew he first showed promise when he was nineteen, but came on the art scene strongly when he was twenty-two. I also knew he traveled when he could because a lot of his inspiration came from his travels.)

"You checked up on me?"

"After I received your fan mail." I smiled.

"I like my privacy and I've always thought a picture of my face has nothing to do with my art." He shrugged, then beamed a Cheshire grin my way as he softly admitted, "You have a nice website."

"I knew it!" I slapped the table, sitting forward. "You made a weird reference in your email that could've only come from someone who'd read my blog posts."

"Your bio picture looks nothing like you," he said.

"Of course it doesn't." It was a blurred photo and I loved it that way. "It's a reflection of how I see myself and ..." I shook my head as I shrugged my shoulders before softly parroting, "my face has nothing to do with my art."

"See?" He drew the word out until I nodded in agreement with his feelings. "Well, Ali Skye, I think I can finally admit that I rather liked your writing, what I read."

"Thank you. And your art isn't half bad," I returned.

"Thank you."

After another lull and study of the room, I asked, "Do you have a favorite place you've traveled?"

"You know, these questions feel like you're doing an interview."

I rubbed the back of my neck. "Well, if I'm being honest, I have a headache that's building and I think I'm still ..." *a lot of things, bored, lost, thirty,* "... nervous ...?"

"Do I make you nervous?" His voice lowered, whether he meant it to or not, the octave creating an unexpected reaction in my lower abdomen.

I pressed my hand against my stomach. "I think it's a jumble of things. Exhaustion, lack of caffeine, exertion, shock, your unexpected ... ness."

"My unexpectedness?"

I nodded and searched for a topic to switch to before I told him what I meant by unexpectedness—that he was hella attractive; wet, muddy, or dressed in an old-timey nightshirt.

"I've been to Europe twice," I said quickly. "Once, I did the whole backpack thing with a friend and stayed in hostels. I loved it. Loved the people, the conversations I had. The history we saw. But if I had to pick, I think Rome was my favorite."

"I see what you're doing." He smiled.

"What am I doing?"

"You're making me comfortable so I'll answer your questions. You have nice technique."

"You don't know anything about my technique." I meant for it to be a biting remark, but TJ flipped it; narrowing his gaze, his eyes growing damn near smoky, he softly said, "I'd be lying if I didn't admit I'm pretty interested in your technique."

(See?! It's the lighting.)

"Are you flirting with me Mr. Jones?"

"Maybe?"

We stared at each other for several long seconds until TJ broke the building spell.

"I've always felt the need to see the exact places that inspired other artists. To immerse myself in the surroundings that might have molded them into the artists they became. Not to copy what they were doing, but just ... to see it for myself."

Another commonality that would solidify the feeling that we knew each other. I built on his comment, "You want to stand in the park and see Monet's *Lily Pond*, breathe the same air of Rodin's *Kiss*, and sit on the Spanish Steps where Keats scribbled in a notebook."

"Exactly." He tilted his head. "Have you sat on the steps where Keats scribbled?"

"I have."

He gave the appreciative nod of an artist who understood how cool that was.

"Who is your favorite artist?" I asked.

"I thought you cyberstalked me," he countered.

"Is it a crime to try and get to know you better?"

"Maybe." He cleared his throat. "Victorio Edades."

I shook my head, I had no idea who that was.

"He's a Filipino artist from the thirties. He painted the working class; he used dark colors and I love the way you can see the sweat and dirt and hard years of life on the faces of the people in his work."

A knock at the door interrupted us, followed by the turn of the key as the same two nuns from before materialized. One pointed at our plates; were we finished? While the other set a refilled pitcher of water and a bowl of fruit down in the place of the tray that was now being spirited away.

We offered our thanks, and before they left, the tall nun went to the cord in the corner and pointed to it, reminding us if we needed anything we could just ring.

Another round of thanks given, and we were once again locked in.

"And that ends this evening's entertainment," I muttered.

TJ retrieved his sketchbook and a canvas pencil case, along with a book.

"I noticed you're traveling rather light." He pointed to my few belongings.

"Light is an understatement."

He handed over the book. "I've been reading this. If you wanted to borrow it ..."

I glanced down at the book and laughed.

"I know it's not the most literary thing."

"It's perfect." I accepted Douglas Adams' *Hitchhiker's Guide to the Galaxy* and since he was making space to sketch at the table, I took my cup and moved to claim a bed, sat back against the wall and cracked it open.

I read for a while, letting my breathing smooth out. Letting the day and headache fall away. Another ring of the bells pulled me out of the words and I glanced around, then out the small window, halfway up the wall.

Shadows of clouds were crawling across the sky in the moonlight. Dark blue, almost purple creatures. I loved clouds, they were an ever-changing challenge. I was forever attempting to capture them and put into words the way they worked and twisted. I once spent a rainy spring day coming up with a descriptive word to describe clouds using each letter of the alphabet.

Successfully. (Not to brag.)

I gave myself an eye roll then glanced at TJ, who was staring at me. I raised an eyebrow in question, even though an invisible vice squeezed the breath out of me and a thrill trickled down my spine at the way he was looking at me: hand poised over his paper with a narrowed, intense gaze. He was looking through me or studying some intricate part of me so totally he was no longer seeing the whole.

I thought about the sketch that could result from the study and what he could call it: *Locked in a Convent #12.* I took a deep breath and blew it out slowly to stop the laughter, but didn't hold back the smile. In order to break the spell of being so attentively viewed, I whispered, "Just sketch it already." (Not sure what 'it' would be.)

At last, there was movement as TJ bent over the page and his hand grew frantic, his lower lip between his teeth. I liked the attention and was fearful of it at the same time. I let the feelings fluctuate and tried to settle my breathing as I turned back to the book. Of course, now all I could do was reread the same paragraph over and over. It took a while to finally ease back into the relaxed moment, but TJ pulled me right back out asking, "Why haven't you written much lately?"

"I'm not sure."

"Is it your birthday? It's a big milestone."

"No, I've always been okay with my age, it's just a number."

"Burnt out?" he asked.

"Maybe."

"Do you ...?" He cleared his throat but didn't look up. "Are you seeing anyone?"

"Not any more."

I thought I caught the glimmer of a quick smile pull at the corner of his mouth, but I couldn't be sure.

"We broke up about two months ago." It didn't cause my writing problems, but it didn't help. When someone tells you they were seeing someone else, it adds to the spiral of a word-less existence.

"I'm sorry." He glanced up and I felt once again like he was seeing into the depths of me.

But I wasn't in the mood to have my depths seen to.

"There's nothing to talk about really. He was an asshole. It happens." I shrugged, that was all that needed to be said on the topic.

"We don't have to talk about it."

"I'm not going to talk about it." I turned my attention back to the dark blue-gray clouds. "And just so you know, he didn't deserve me."

"Probably not. Assholes never know the treasure they have, always think the grass is greener on the other side."

That pulled my attention back to TJ. He was sharpening his pencil, glanced at me momentarily, then began sketching once more.

"And just so you know, my creativity wasn't tied up in him. It feels like I've been spiraling for a few years now."

"I understand trying to chase your creativity," he said.

"You can?"

He looked up then and shared a sad smile, "Even though it was tied up in another person, after my last breakup I couldn't paint a thing for two years. It was devastating."

"I keep thinking that if I keep moving ..." I drifted off but TJ nodded, as if he understood what I was trying to say. I asked, "What did you do for two years?"

"Nothing good." He sat back in the chair. "I called her and begged her to take me back for about a month. Slept for another month. Then I ran away and drank. A year into the drinking, I woke up in Spain in the middle of a park with no clue how I got there." He looked contrite but shrugged. "So I sobered up and began to journal and sketch flowers. I figured they were safe. I hated each sketch and each day. But then I woke up one morning, had notebooks filled with flowers and suddenly I wanted to create something once again."

I licked my lips. "I've been filling notebooks with ridiculous drivel."

He nodded. "See, you're still in it. Ridiculous drivel is never a waste of time."

"Part of the process?"

"Yup," he went back to work, "you'll find your way back to it."

So there's that.

"When are you going to let me see that?" I asked.

"How do you know I'm sketching you?"

"You aren't?"

"Maybe I'm sketching the book cover."

Hmph. I went back to the book, and continued to reread the same paragraph again and again; my thoughts were crowded with TJ, El Zorro Blanco, and a tiny little itch of creativity.

Seventeen

When a quick rap at the door was followed by the laborious task of unlocking it, I whispered, "Do you feel like we should be more worried about being locked in?"

"Maybe. But we're also dry and clean."

I shrugged as the opening door revealed Sister Margaret Mary. "I thought I would offer you the use of the facilities once more before I retire for the night."

We followed, because it was the only other form of entertainment.

I didn't realize how much body heat we'd created in our little space. The hallway seemed cooler now and the stones beneath our feet were working on becoming blocks of ice.

Delivered, she squared off with us. "Can I trust you to see your way back to your room when you're finished?"

We nodded mutely.

Then once again she swooped away from us.

"Sweeping," I whispered as we entered. "Just in case you're curious, that's how I'd write her."

"See," he pointed, "you still have that creativity inside. It won't go away, there's just something else that's taking priority at the moment."

The tears that formed were unexpected.

The squeezing of my chest at his reasoning, so nonchalant and hope-filled and sure, was my undoing.

I'd been wondering who I was without the words. I suppose the worry was similar to an athlete who had a career-ending accident and wonders who they are without the thing that defined their life.

I'd also spent many insomnia filled nights wondering if it was society's fault for putting so much pressure on us in the first place to define ourselves, to build boxes to fit ourselves inside. Living to work. Living for the almighty dollar. When just our existence and our *being,* as we spiraled along on this blue rock traveling 67,000 miles per hour, should be impressive enough.

TJ didn't ask why I was crying, nor did he seem put off by it. He did seamlessly cross the slight space between us, slip his arms around me, nudging my arms to drift up and circle his shoulders. Then he pulled me against his warmth and held me while the tears that fell became a sob.

His arms were solid, his heartbeat steady. He didn't shush or try to sooth me with empty 'it's okay' phrases. He was just a lighthouse in the storm.

My crying echoed in the enclosed bathroom space; echoed inside my head and turned into an experimental beat that made sense in that moment. And was allowed for as long as needed.

Finally cried out, I gathered myself but still held tight to TJ. It felt good in his arms, and instinctively I kinda knew he wouldn't let go until I was ready.

When I'd settled down enough, an entirely new set of interesting worries swept the emotional crap off stage and took their place:

He feels really good.

Is it going to be weird when you have to make eye contact with him?

What if he asks what you were crying about?

Why do girls always end up in the bathroom crying?

I think there's a book there.

Now it's been too long and it's getting awkward.

You need to pull away.

But he feels so good.

But each second that passes from the last sob and that deep breath–the one that always signifies a person has gathered themselves and it's okay to let them go–has been way too long now.

To extinguish my internal dialogue, I forced my arms from around his neck and took a slight stepped back. TJ let his arms rest loosely on my hips. He crouched slightly to bring himself to eye level, smiled into my eyes, but there was no searching or narrowing of a gaze. He simply widened his eyes, a silent 'are you okay?' I nodded once and he let go.

"Ladies first." He gestured to the restroom, and I took the escape.

Finished with our 'last call' privileges, we headed back to our room.

"I want to walk slowly, but my feet are freezing," TJ said.

"Mine too."

He glanced over and after a second his pace stuttered; when I turned toward him, I found an eyebrow raised and an amused look as he nodded toward my chest and said, "I see that."

My eyes zoomed down to my chest, once again giving off natural body signals. "Damnit." I crossed my arms over my chest as I began to laugh. "I thought you were an artist."

"I am. And that's my problem. I see the whole picture sometimes."

"Great," I muttered.

"It's human nature," he tried.

"You don't think I don't know that?"

"I'm sorry, I shouldn't have brought it up. It's just ... you're a temptation." His comment coincided with the arrival to our 'room.'

I snorted. "You can't say something like that seconds before we're locked in together again."

He elbowed me as he passed me entering the room. "C'mon Ali, you know how good it felt to be in my arms," halfway across the room he turned, "just like I know how good it felt to kiss you."

I mean, he wasn't wrong but under the circumstances ...

I waved the remark away. "TJ, you can't say ..." But once again his eyes darted down to my chest; I crossed my arms and smirked. "TJ, stop."

He shrugged.

"You can't just tell me I'll find my creativity again and sketch me and be so ..."

"Attractive?" he finished with a wink.

"Congenial," I hissed.

He wrinkled his nose. "Not a great description. But better than asshole."

"Is there a problem?" I jumped at Sister Margaret Mary's voice and appearance.

She might actually be a ghost.

Or maybe when I slipped in the mud, I'd hit my head and I'm actually still on the side of the road, half dead with a head wound.

"Just a lovers' quarrel," TJ supplied.

"Do you need anything else?" the sister asked.

I entered the room, arms still crossed over my chest as we both muttered our thanks, insisting there was nothing else we needed.

She repeated the bell ringing protocol, then closed the door and locked us in once again.

I decided to sit at the table. TJ followed my lead, and I gestured to the sketchbook. "Can I see what you were drawing?"

He flipped to a page then turned it toward me.

It was a close-up detail of hands holding *The Hitchhiker's Guide to the Galaxy*.

I snorted. "You really were sketching the book cover?"

"No." He turned to the previous page and there were my hands. Several sketches of them.

Now, I don't particularly like the look of my hands. To me, they're generic at best, and veiny. Swollen at different times of the day; sometimes they have a length and elegance to them, but more often they are round, hard working things. How they look has never been as important as what they do. My hands are *the* most useful and most *used* part of my body.

I'd never been presented with so many details of my hands and I began to think it would've been better if he were sketching my face.

Because Theodore Jones had just pinpointed the heart of who I was and attempted to imbue his page with my soul.

"It's ... um ... it's—"

"As lovely as the woman they belong to." He softly filled in the critique.

I swallowed and muttered, "I'm tired,"

"It's been a long day," he agreed.

I closed the sketchbook and slid it across the table. "I'm going to bed."

We turned off the oil lamp and arranged ourselves on our beds which left us alone in the dark with our unmatched breathing that seemed so damned loud now.

"This is weird," I whispered.

"Is it?"

"I ran out on a birthday party, made a stranger drive me to Tijuana, befriended what I think is a drug lord, met you and am now sleeping in a convent."

He chuckled, a deep soothing sound. "It's a shame we're exhausted. Because this seems like a missed opportunity."

"What's the missed opportunity?"

"Having forbidden sex in a convent." The bright smile was evident in his voice.

"Jesus, TJ."

"I suppose taking the lord's name in vain will work." He yawned.

"It's not taken in vain, for all I know you're lying about all your names and there's a Jesus thrown in there somewhere."

He laughed in earnest, then ended with a punctuation of: "Fucking writers."

I smiled. "Stupid artists."

It was as good as any 'good night' there was.

Eighteen

T he slam of the front gate behind us was a thrust into a montage
of a very long day.

We were woken with the first bell—5 a.m. according to TJ's
watch—fed, handed our clean, miraculously dry clothes, then
politely kicked out to where our ride was waiting for us.

Sister Margaret Mary sighed. "You are still eight hours from
Mexico City. I have arranged for a ride into town. To the bus station.
You'll find a bus that will take you the rest of the way to Mexico City."
She frowned as she gave us a quick blessing. "You'll have to travel
through a few areas not ideal for tourists, but you'll be with other
locals. So it should be alright." She leaned forward and bored her eyes
into ours. "However, if *anything* should happen, I strongly urge you
to follow the competent actions of the locals you are traveling with.
And all will be well." She considered us once more as she reached in
her pocket and pulled out a rosary for each of us. She gave another
wave of her hand in blessing, a sweeping turn while muttering in
Spanish and then: *Bang!* —the front gate closed and she was gone.

We silently turned to where a once white, now rusted, well-loved
Toyota truck idled, the driver waving for us to get in the back. And
about an hour later, he stopped next to the bus station, slapped the
side of his door and pointed; the only direction we were given to get
out.

We bought tickets, checked the schedule and found we had three
hours before the bus left at noon. So we walked up the road in search of
breakfast, past brightly colored buildings, most shops just opening for
the day, until we found the Restaurant Lupita. A bright peachy orange

building, two stories, the second with a balcony edged with potted palm trees and topped in terracotta shingles.

The smells of hot food wafted out of the open door to greet us, but it was the heightened scent of coffee that had me reacting like a cartoon character: on tiptoes, eyes closed, following a faint airbrushed scent in the direction from whence it came.

After a flavorful breakfast and several cups of coffee realigned my chi, we headed back to the bus station by way of a pharmacy for some phenomenal necessities: A spiral, college ruled notebook. Toothbrush and toothpaste. Deodorant. Hairbrush. Ice cream bar. Gum. And a charger for my phone.

At the station, I charged my phone just enough to send my mom a 'don't call the police' text. And a message of equal importance to Francisco.

Then it was eight hours of shifting in a seat, studying the passing landscape, reading more of the book, and being lulled into calm, twilight thoughts with each rotation of the wheels.

Sitting shoulder to broad, strong shoulder with TJ.

As he became more interesting.

As he became more amiable.

As he became a whole hell of a lot more attractive.

Nineteen

"Alto!" A swarm of police ran past as the air around us erupted with noise: traffic, ambulance sirens, and police accompanied the hysterically loud beat of my heart.

We stopped and held up our hands, all we had done was exit the bus a block over to walk through the artificially lit night to the area Francisco said he'd meet us.

"What the fuck?!" My scream mingled with the noise.

Not one officer stopped to arrest us, so we lowered our hands, but from the other side of the street, out of the door of a restaurant, a herd of men wearing tuxedos and top hats rushed us.

"Jesus Christ," I yelled pressing myself against TJ.

Another onslaught of knights clanging with chainmail and helmets pressed past us.

"What the hell ...?" TJ grabbed my hand as a crowd of teens dressed in neon '80s apparel danced around us. We tried to move out of their way, but were tripped, and as TJ reached for me, we did a strange tumble and rolled into the gutter, our backpacks awkwardly pressing us against each other.

I moaned as my cheek hit the concrete. TJ glanced at me wide-eyed and apologized, but I couldn't hear him above the crowd. And as I clung to him, the ridiculous intensity around us grew, so I didn't have time to comprehend the grime of the city that was seeping into my body parts pressed into the gutter.

We glanced to our side as more police began to scream and blow whistles, but this time it wasn't officers in modern day uniforms but more Keystone Cops (or 'Kops,' for you silent film purists.)

When a parade of drag queens joined in the mayhem, I began to laugh uncontrollably.

Somewhere there were screeching tires and there might have even been a bomb going off, but the playful dancing and laughing surrounding us was one big ball of confusion.

"Do we get up?" I screamed in TJ's ear as I clung to him.

He turned his head, shouting, "we could try!"

We rolled onto our knees, pushing ourselves upright when a line of cancan girls in bright red petticoats came kicking their way along the sidewalk, their high kicks just missing us and forcing us to trip backwards.

"Holy shit!" I screamed.

TJ had my hand and his head was on a swivel but he was grinning in fearful confused delight. The same look I probably had. He raised our joined hands to point in the direction we should run when spotlights beyond the block we were standing on came on and a loud, omniscient voice screamed, "CUT!"

The word floated on a breeze and as the noise around us settled, I undercut it with a snort of laughter.

The cancan girls were still whirling so the voice demanded again, "Cut! Fucking basta! What part of CUT doesn't anyone understand?!"

I moved so I was standing in front of TJ, frozen but looking up at him with wide, excited eyes. He winked in reply as we both pressed our lips together to keep quiet.

"Cut, you assholes!"

Just then a group of clowns twirled out of a store behind us, the first two tossing handfuls of confetti in the air.

I mouthed, 'Oh my god.'

"CUUUUTTTTT!"

There was a soft din of noise, so I whispered to TJ, "Does this mean we're extras now?"

"I can't even comprehend what's happening."

"I thought movie sets were closed."

A speaker began to play some background music but it was drowned out by the amplified voice screaming, "I said CUT! Where the HELL is my translator?!"

TJ nodded to the sidewalk and the way we'd come into this mess, a silent indication we should try to sneak away.

The all-knowing voice exploded again, "Did I or did I not change this scene?! I thought we all understood: police, tuxedos, knights, THEN clowns, retro kids, Keystone Kops, drag queens and cancan girls. And who the HELL decided we would have tourists in this shot?!"

"I don't think we're extras."

We froze.

We both scanned the area where the voice of the omnipresence was coming, shading our eyes from the bright lights. But before we could focus our attention, two strong men grabbed us and began to quickly lead us away from the street.

"So much for a movie career," I mumbled.

"We're sorry ..." TJ began.

The man who had hold of TJ gave one grunt that he'd even heard us speaking.

Once we were escorted to the edge of a group of trailers and tables set up with mass amounts of food, they let go and waved to the direction beyond; their meaning, 'go that way and don't come back' pretty obvious.

We followed their instructions and when we were on the safe side of the street I dropped my bag and bent at the waist trying to catch my breath. TJ did a backbend and gave a slow hiss of breath. "I feel like a teenager getting caught stealing the *Mona Lisa* or something."

We melted into laughing hysterics then, which was the obvious choice after being tackled onto the concrete, surrounded by ... Hell, I'd have to unpack all that later, but after a sober night in a convent, after having met a semi-arch nemesis, now taking in the movie sets of the Centro Histórico in a city of twenty-two million people on the third (*ish*) day of my thirtieth year ... I was allowed a moment of snorting and ugly cry laughing.

Twenty

I squeezed TJ's arm, facing him as I tried to catch my breath and trying to get my ugly laughing under control. TJ's eyes squinted at the edges with his laughter. He slipped an arm around my shoulders, pulling me against his side for a hug. I suppose our unexpected adrenaline spike had to go somewhere, and since we weren't about to take a quick jog around the block to rid ourselves of it, laughing and human contact was much needed.

I wrapped my arms around TJ's waist and nestled against his warm body. The laughter gave way to a long snort of a sigh.

"Your back is wet." TJ smiled into my hair.

"I have no idea what was in those gutters," I told his neck.

"You just like to get dirty." I think he was trying for innuendo.

I pulled away enough to meet his gaze. "That was amazing."

He tilted his head and instead of replying, simply pressed his lips against mine.

The kiss, searing, unexpected, (very much electric), released an entirely new wave of adrenaline.

There was a thoughtfulness to the way he kissed me, but also an underlying demand when his fingers slid through my hair as he swept his tongue inside my mouth. He growled when I met his advances—pressing myself against him, hands winding around his body, attempting to ignite more heat and lose myself in the moment—

"Ali Skye! Why are you accosting that man?"

... and the 'moment' crumbled around our feet.

I pulled away and blinked up at TJ. Maybe he was a ventriloquist and thought this was a good time to show off. But I wasn't done kissing him;

we just got started, for real. But when I met his lips again, the same voice behind me laughed. "Alicia!"

My grin grew as I came back to earth and realized who the voice belonged to. I stopped 'accosting' TJ and looked over my shoulder, "Hola Francisco."

TJ and I released each other as Francisco approached and I was quickly swept up in a long overdue greeting.

"Hola amiga, bienvenido a la ciudad de méxico."

The last time we physically saw each other had been at our college graduation. Keeping in touch via technology wasn't the same.

Francisco crushed me to him in a bear hug and lifted me off the ground slightly as he announced, "I can't believe you're here."

"I forgot how tall you are," I mumbled, my face obstructed by his neck. And I'd forgotten how sturdy he was. He'd played basketball in high school which afforded him a scholarship in college. He let me down with little ceremony and took a step back shaking his head. Both grinning, we studied each other. His green eyes sparkled in the streetlights and the memory of what he used to tell people about his eye color floated past. (He claimed his green eyes were the result of a great-great-great-grandmother and her affair with a Spanish Conquistador.) His black hair was slicked slightly, an attempt at taming the slight curls.

"You look good." I smiled.

He winked playfully before he said, "You look awful *and* you smell. What sort of adventure have you gotten yourself into?"

"Most recently, I was rolling around in the gutter."

He raised an eyebrow and I waved the comment away.

"Francisco, this is TJ. My ... traveling companion."

If TJ had a reaction to the title, I didn't see it as Francisco enveloped him in the same bear hug he'd given me; only this was accompanied by a hearty slap on the back, like he was meeting a long-lost relative.

When the hug was over, Francisco nodded to TJ. "You smell as bad as she does."

"Same gutter." TJ smiled.

Francisco barked out a laugh. "I'm so glad you're here. I want to show you everything. TJ, will you be joining us?"

We hadn't discussed what would happen when we arrived. We probably would have, had we not been experiencing momentary fame.

"We haven't really had a chance to talk about our plans," I offered.

TJ tilted his head slightly and was about to say something when Francisco beamed. "You'll join us! Where do you want to start? A tour? Food? A drink?"

"A drink." TJ and I both fell over the offer at the same time as we picked up our bags.

"I know just the place, great food, cold beer."

Nothing had sounded better in my entire life than the promise of great food and cold beer.

Francisco wrapped his arm around my shoulders and gave a squeeze as he nodded in the direction we should walk. "But maybe we first need to go to my house. I think you need a shower and to change clothes."

"Then we actually need to go shopping first. I don't have any other clothes."

He shrugged as if it wasn't a shock that I showed up wet, dirty, smelly and ill-prepared.

"My sister will have something you can borrow." Another squeeze and he released me.

TJ offered, "I can find a hotel. I don't want to impose—"

"We're friends now," Francisco interrupted, "you'll stay with me and I will keep you safe from Alicia and her mouthy attacks. And if you would like, I can also give you all the dirt I know about her."

I pursed my lips as we arrived at the car and Francisco climbed behind the wheel. TJ climbed in the back seat as he admitted, "I think hearing all the dirt you have on the infamous Ali Skye would be wonderful."

Twenty-One

As Francisco drove us through the city toward his home, he filled me in on what I'd missed since our Christmas email exchange: His girlfriend had broken off their engagement several months ago, so he let one of his sisters and her family move into the house he'd purchased, and moved back in with his parents while he regrouped. He was still teaching college English and high school basketball. And even though we seemed to be in a similar state of breakups and moving back home-ness, there was a calm about him that gave me hope for my own prospects.

Francisco pointed out destinations and neighborhoods as we passed them, places 'we should go,' and places that held some of his personal family history.

I'm not sure what I was expecting from the city. I had something smaller in mind, based on the stories Francisco had shared over the years. I realized he had built a mirage, a close-knit village of family and friends; it was my fault for applying the movies and documentaries I'd viewed into the background of his stories, which created an impression of a small community. But *this* Mexico City, seen with my own eyes, was glorious. The sprawling city and high-rises illuminated the entire horizon.

As Francisco whirled around the traffic of the ever expanding, lively cityscape; the eye candy of it all was almost too much to take in. Night met explosive neon and a vibrant crayon box of primary colors.

He twisted us through suburban streets and when the streetlights allowed, we caught glimpses of colorful walls, trees, and garage doors. He turned onto a narrow street, and pulled to a stop.

After shuffling us out of the car, he opened a large arched door set in the wall, and it was like Alice walking through the looking glass. A cobblestone path led to a brightly lit, two-story stone and white stucco home with a terracotta roof. The living room on the left and kitchen on the right were visible through ceiling to floor windows, their light illuminating the lush yard we were walking through.

The walled-in space was landscaped with trees and flowers. A stone patio was to our right and nestled a table with several oversized wicker seats and a large umbrella.

Reaching the front door where bougainvillea was growing around it, I sighed. "What a beautiful home. This garden is so amazing."

The front door opened with Francisco's mother, as short as her son was tall. Dark eyes with long curly hair, pulled together by a ribbon at the nape of her neck. She wore a housedress of bright blue and yellow, had a towel over her shoulder, and a beaming, welcoming smile.

"Ali, TJ, this is my mom, Doña Elena."

Just like her son, she forwent any handshake; even as I tried to stop her with the warning "I stink." She pushed my hands away, ignored Francisco's translation and hugged me. TJ was next, with the same added long-lost familial back slap her son had given him.

We were ushered through the cozy living room that maintained high ceilings, white wooden beams and so much airy space; it seemed it would give the illusion of being outside during the daylight hours; and followed Francisco upstairs to the room he deemed the guest room.

He glanced between TJ and me, eyebrow raised, a smirk in place as he gestured to the two twin beds the room held. "Will you be okay sleeping separately? Or would you rather a different arrangement?"

"We're just friends." I waved his innuendo away and changed the subject, "Shower first, we'll figure the rest out later."

We asked for a towel to put our backpacks down on, then Francisco gestured across the hall to the bathroom. "There are towels in the cupboard, feel free to use any of the soaps and shampoos. I'll get my sister to find you some clothes."

"Thank you." I glanced at TJ. "Wanna play rock paper scissors to see who goes first?"

"Go ahead, you were the one in the gutter the longest."

"I'll be fast."

"Take your time," he said. "Francisco was going to tell me all about you and I'll tell him about the movie we were just a part of."

Francisco slapped TJ on the back to solidify the deal and with his head gestured for TJ to follow him back the way they'd come.

TJ leaned toward me and whispered, "Does slapping you on the back in this family denote love?"

I pushed him away with a smile before closing the door.

Clad in only a towel, but thoroughly and delightfully clean (more so than I was able to get in the nunnery), I emerged from the bathroom.

I shifted from foot to foot for a moment, trying to decide on appropriate decorum. I heard the laughter rising from downstairs, so went halfway down, waited for a lull in the conversation before politely, but loudly, calling, "Francisco?"

"I'll send my sister up!" he yelled back.

Only, the first person who came up the stairs was TJ.

I tucked the edge of the towel tighter around my chest. "Your turn."

He scanned the length of me with the kind of gaze that can make you feel each droplet of water slipping off your hair, down your shoulders; as if each one was a caress.

Time suspended for the blink of an eye, which was long enough. TJ ironically ended the 'moment' by giving a wink, then passing purposefully close so he could lightly touch my waist to steady himself as he slipped his body past mine.

All of it, unnecessary.

But welcomed.

The door laughingly, solidly, closed and the heat fell to the floor as time began once more. And I was left thinking 'what the hell was that?' as I gripped the towel, not willing to move because I could still feel the weight of his hand on my hip.

"Ali." Francisco made me jump. He was followed by a young woman. "This is my sister, Valentina." She was lithe, only a little taller than her mom. Her long brown hair hung in curls around her shoulders and her skin was deep golden brown and flawless.

We exchanged pleasantries, then Francisco launched into the quick summary of our friendship while I gripped the towel and dabbed with my free hand at the water dripping down my shoulders before wiping it off on the towel.

Valentina took pity on my plight, rolled her eyes, slapped her brother on the shoulder and pushed him out of the way. "When she's dressed you'll tell me everything."

She waved for me to follow her to her room. "I'm a little shorter and smaller than you, but I have something that will work," she offered. Digging through a dresser drawer, she pulled out a pair of black palazzo pants. "They'll look shorter on you, but the waist is elastic so it will help the fit." She then retrieved two blousy tank tops, one beige and one white, both with colorful flower patterns along the neckline. "These should fit and will be the most comfortable."

I licked my lips before admitting, "This was a last-minute trip and I just made the clever decision to wash my bra and underwear in the sink ..."

She tilted her head in thought before giving a snap of her fingers as she began to dig through another drawer. "I think ..." She made an aha noise and pulled out a bikini top. "It'll tie in the back and at least keep some of that ..." she nodded toward my C cups, "up."

"It'll have to do." I accepted the top and she went to retrieve something from another room. She returned with an offering of what can only be described as 'granny' and/or 'old-school period panties.' High-waisted, full upper leg and belly coverage. Clean and faded pink.

"They belonged to my abuela."

I accepted them too, trying not to hold them at their full girth as I knew I needed something. "I'm grateful," I said, because I felt my face making little judgmental scrunches. Then I started to laugh.

"I'm only sad we're not the same size." Valentia sighed. "This is going to give my mother validation as to why we 'cannot' get rid of my grandmother's things." She used a motherly tone, saying, "'Someone might need something.'" She laughed and shook off the problem. "Take your time, we'll be downstairs when you're ready. Mom's cooking for you."

"Oh, I didn't mean—"

She waved my protest away. "You are about to learn your first lesson about madres mexicanas and their love language. But don't worry, she loves having company and loves to cook."

Dressed and feeling a lot better, I stood for a few seconds by the bathroom door, listening to the water, wishing I was one little droplet before I shook myself out of *that* reprieve and joined everyone downstairs where I was introduced to Francisco's father, Don Julio, and handed a beer that turned out to not only be the coldest beer ever, but the singularly best beer I'd had to date.

I took a sip and happily let myself sink into the warmth offered by the kitchen and his family. It was the opening Francisco was waiting for. He leaned forward and asked, "What's going on with TJ?"

"It's a long story. But we're just friends." My hip betrayed me by heating from the phantom memory of TJ's touch, which caused another spark of memory—a kiss Francisco interrupted—so I fought hard to keep from licking my lips as I firmly repeated, "Just friends."

"He wants to be more, I think," Valentina offered.

How do you explain to a lovely young woman you just met that she didn't get to implant butterflies in your stomach with such ridiculous notions? Of course before I could figure that out, her damn brother laughed and inserted, "That kiss you were sharing when I showed up didn't look like just friends."

"So, did you grow up in this house?" I asked abruptly.

He wiggled his eyebrows. "Fine. We will change the subject."

The idea of cleaning up and going to a bar was doused by the comfort of being with Francisco's family, who exuded genuine welcome, and the food his mother set on the table. It was exactly what I needed.

As we joked and eased into the night's ambience, I did my best to ignore the small little voice that was very curiously inquiring, *'Now what?'*

Twenty-Two

Eventually, we convinced ourselves to travel the 'far' distance into the garden with a bottle of Tequila. I tried to politely decline the alcohol, but Francisco handed me a shot glass, tapped his to mine and offered, "Feliz cumpleaños, mi amiga."

So, I was only going to do that one shot; but then that oversized chair engulfed me and the smooth night softened the edges of any lurking worries, and dim music floated around us from a bluetooth speaker, all the while something sweet in the garden filled my nose. All was well. So I gave into my urges to smile and blatantly stare at TJ, his hair on end after his shower, his beard dark in the soft light from the kitchen, a twinkle of mischief in his eyes when he looked my way.

So I did one more shot.

Then it was a new morning and a new hangover.

"Nooo," I croaked as I rolled over onto my side.

The twin bed across from me was empty, but the sun was happy to mock me.

I rolled over to get up, but ended up twisted in the sheets and fell the short distance to the floor.

Grunts accompanied my attempt to crawl to a standing position. The bikini top had wound its way around to the side, so I hitched it back into place, hiked up the granny panties that had slipped down, then smoothed out the rest of the borrowed clothing and muttered, "First stop, clothes."

My phone was charged so I texted my mom: *At Francisco's parents' house, all is well.*

I thought about telling her about TJ, but it was such a long story, and we might be parting ways today anyway. And it didn't really matter. And I was warming to the idea that I would only send proof of life texts for a while until I figured a few concrete things out.

I shuffled in the direction of laughing, my forehead weighted with so much drinking and lack of water. I squinted against the light when I entered the kitchen, but it only seemed to grow more powerful, possibly emanating from the damn walls, all of which forced me back a step as I seethed, "Jesus—" though the silhouette of Francisco's mom near the stove caused me to swallow the rest of the phrase. I replaced it with the word "bright" but the quick change in words and breath made me swallow some spittle wrong and I began to choke cough.

Francisco and TJ tilted their heads in tandem as they watched my entrance. All the coughing caused me to misjudge the distance between standing and the chair I was aiming for, so I heavily slammed my backside onto it which pulled a repeat of, "*Je*-sus."

TJ didn't hold back his laughter as Francisco offered, "Coffee?"

I nodded and began to lay my head on the table, but quickly thought better of the propriety of the action, especially in a home where I was a guest, and straightened with a groan.

As if I were a rabid animal who would bite fingers if they were too close, Francisco pushed a cup of coffee toward me with the tips of his fingers. In my defense it was his actions that made me snarl, not my rabid-ness. That, and I was getting a little too old for these hangovers.

I took a sip, and the glorious heated local treasure was so good I held the cup with both hands and lowered my face to it, an attempt to let caffeinated steam seep into my pores.

"Whatareyoutalkinbout?" I asked groggily.

"We are talking about art," Francisco replied. "Did you know TJ is a pretty good artist?"

"I think I knew that," I muttered to my cup.

"We were talking about what I want to show you today. I want to show you everything! But you will be here for a few days, so I can be calm. But still, there is so much to do."

"Clothes first, please?"

"It is the first stop I put on the itinerary."

I blinked at his excited tour guide agenda, but the headache and exhaustion tried to glue my eyes shut, so it was with one eye open that I tilted a forced smile at Francisco. "Itinerary?"

He gave a giant nod of his head. "After breakfast, we will leave."

We took the metro, a glorious feat in engineering that was efficient, affordable, clean, fast and covered 120 miles of Mexico City. (According to Francisco.) And in reality, was true.

When he stepped aside at a small boutique store for clothes, I had to swallow my pride and admit, "I'm on a fixed budget for this trip."

"Oh, this is my friend's store. And you will find it is very inexpensive."

And it was. The exchange rate of the dollar was doing well. And because we were 'amigos de Francisco,' there was a percentage taken off.

I bought a new bra, and new underwear that were more of a bikini fit, which made me feel good. Along with these most vital garments, I included three shirts, a pair of pants, a wrap dress and a light sweater.

As I paid, I asked Francisco, "You know of a store that sells camping gear or something."

"What do you need there?"

"A waterproof bag."

TJ winked, overhearing.

Dressed in clean clothes that fit, I finally felt liberated and ready to take on the day.

Francisco insisted on stopping at a nearby coffee shop that was owned by another friend. There he introduced us, then waved us away to get a table so he could order. TJ and I walked outside to find a table on the street, directly across from a dreamy, densely overgrown plaza that shaded the whole block.

I eyed the giant fountain in the center as we walked, causing me to bump into TJ. He steadied me, his hand on my hip again, where it felt so comforting and possessive.

"Do you mind that I'm intruding?" he asked.

"I don't know," I answered honestly.

He raised an eyebrow and I tapped his hand, an indication that he could let go, but he didn't.

"I know we didn't talk about it, but if you don't mind, I'd like to hang out with you ... and stay with you," he said,

"I don't know if that's a good idea; together we've gotten ourselves in some pretty spectacular messes." I tried to put a playful spin on the request.

"Ali, I like being with you," he stated as he took advantage of my lack of movement, leaned toward me and brushed a kiss on my cheek. He pulled away only slightly and softly asked, "Do you mind that I intrude for a while longer?"

"No," I let my hands slide up his chest, "I kinda like having you around." It was my turn to brush a kiss on his cheek.

"Just friends, huh?" Francisco loudly laughed as he set down a tray with three small coffees and pastries.

Twenty-Three

Mexico City: A revelation.

That's what it was.

I definitely had preconceived notions regarding the city. I suppose at some point, Mexico City became an extension of what I knew of Tijuana, Francisco's stories, and movies.

I guess that happens, because on my first trip to Italy I was expecting people to be yelling 'mamma mia' while the Pope drove around in his bulletproof car, and I was worried that Tuscany would be overrun with a collection of strong, recently single American women who'd all bought villas in order to find themselves.

In the way movies and society intrude on the truth of reality, I had created a caricature of Mexico City.

But this city was a brightly colored revelation. So many vibrant variations of green in the tree-lined streets. The street art, giant murals that took up the sides of buildings, was a gallery of inspiration that stopped TJ in his tracks almost every other block. So many homes and businesses we drove past punched with color.

The way Francisco talked about his home and the people, the ancestral respect and tie to the land was a harsh contrast to the way my sprawling suburb of Southern California seemed to be tied to 'stuff and things.'

The city of millions that supported the economy humbled the misguided expectations I had.

As we wove our way through traffic and walked from lunch to an afternoon snack, and eventually dinner—with tourist shops and a museum in between—I felt alive in the hectic, creative, and delicious space. The rich heritage on full display churned a yearning inside of me, as if my actual stomach did a twirl and twisted my insides. It was the foreignness; experiencing something completely new that was causing it.

"This is what I love." TJ said as we walked to the next must-see sight, "How trips take on a life of their own."

As we sat in a tarp-covered area eating tacos de pastor, the food Francisco insisted was the most important to try, he informed us of our next stop, "We're going to see my friend Julio."

"How is Julio these days?" I asked my taco.

"Do you know Julio?" Francisco seemed truly surprised.

I glanced up at him and pursed my lips to which he sighed, saying, "I forget how much of a smartass you are." I winked and he continued, "We will go visit Julio. He is a *very* entertaining man."

Twenty-Four

"Ju-li-o! Ju-li-o! Ju-li-o!" The raucous cheer went up again in the arena as lights and music flashed.

Francisco had been right; Julio was a *very* entertaining man.

We'd taken the metro, gotten off, and a few escalators later, we were magically handing over tickets for the evening's main event: Lucha Libre. Aka: wrestling.

We missed the first part of the show where the amateurs warmed up the crowd, but according to Francisco, he'd done this on purpose. We'd come for the main event.

Our seats were in the fourth row, enough space between us and the ring so that 'the illusion would still be complete.'

With cold beers in hand, we watched as the announcer dazzled the crowd and the flamboyance and theatrics engulfed us in absolute spectacle.

There was the expected showboating as masked wrestlers climbed the ropes and tried to one-up each other with flips and jumps. Preening really. There was a lot of unexpected chest slapping of the opponent, accompanied by obvious name calling before the wrestlers got down to business.

The crowd chanted, cheered and booed. Dissipating smoke–from the entrance of various wrestlers–rose into the air, giving an ethereal glow to the crossing spotlights that shone down on the center ring.

There were two teams of three wrestlers, and as Francisco explained, it was a tale as old as time; one of the groups were the good guys, the Técnicos. The other group were the bad guys, the Rudos.

"Julio!" The crowd swelled with the yell of his name, as he seemed to be winning the moment. He was among the good guys.

I joined in the chant but finished by leaning into TJ, loudly admitting, "I don't understand wrestling."

He leaned back. "It's modern-day gladiatorial fights." His breath against my ear sent a shiver down my spine.

"I realize that. I just don't get the appeal."

"Are you having fun?"

"I am." Of course I was, who wouldn't be dazzled by this showmanship?

"Then maybe the point isn't to try and understand it, but to just be here in the middle of it all." He winked.

(Okay, I'm not sure if he winked because he'd been leaning into my side, his warm breath still on my ear, interrupting cognitive thinking. But I feel if I'd looked at him when he made the comment he would have winked. He did it too much. And the stupid little twitch ignited too big a reaction which caused molecules in my body to get all turned around.)

Another cheer rose accompanied by clapping and whistling. Julio pumped his fist in the air from atop a post in the corner, asking the audience to shower him with praise, and to which they did.

I thought I saw him smile beneath his blue and white mask.

Francisco explained the tradition of the mask, how it was a part of the persona and was meant to keep the identity of the wrestler a mystery. The colors were also integral for the spectators as the good guys wore lighter colors and the bad guys, darker ones.

Julio's strong, defined chest was glistening in the light; and his tight pants that matched his mask ... well, they were impressive too.

"How would you write it?" TJ asked.

"Actually, I think Hemingway already did."

"Did he?"

"Well," I shook my head, "I was going to make some parallel between this and bullfights, but I don't think Hemingway would like this. I think he'd hate the level of fiction, even if it is entertaining and they really are working hard."

"I would think it'd be the amount of lycra that would put him off," TJ said. I barked out a laugh.

"So, what do you think of Julio, he's entertaining, no?!" Francisco yelled at us.

We both grinned, giving a thumbs-up in reply, and in celebration, Francisco called over a vendor and ordered three more beers for us.

After a while, the few beers chased me to the restroom. Francisco offered to show me where they were, but I assured him I was a big girl.

Of course, when I finished the stall door wouldn't open. I jiggled, muscled, and slammed the heel of my hand against it. Nope, not budging, and I actually think I just made it worse.

The busy night and large crowd made sure there was a continual cycling through of women accompanied by the sounds of flushing, running water, loud laughter and the distant echo of the announcer; a slight hinderance to my asking for help. Also, the only words I seemed to have in my Spanish language arsenal when it came to the restroom was to ask where it was, so I was at a standstill.

Oh, wait!

"¿Discúlpame?" I knew how to say excuse me. That was a good first step.

After a moment, a hand from either side appeared under the divider offering wads of toilet paper.

"Oh, gracias, but no. I'm stuck?" It wasn't a question of whether I was or not, but a question if anyone understood.

Both hands impatiently waved, so I took the paper and flushed it with a sigh, realizing I was going to have to crawl out.

I measured the options; would it be better to go face first or on my back? Facing the well-used floor after the past few hours of visitors; or facing the ceiling, pretending none of it existed as the wet from the floor soaked into my back.

(Can we take a moment to figure this out? Every concert, every baseball game, basketball game, hockey game ... at every arena event I've ever been to, it seems that about an hour in, the bathroom floors are a wasteland of spilled beer, missed toilet bowls and just other 'wet.' Is it just a thing that naturally happens at these types of gatherings? *Or,* are these microcosms of how, as a human race, we're just a mess?)

I need to stop drinking.

It's an overused construct for writers.

And thirty-year olds.

And it would cut down on my need to use the restroom in public places.

Unfortunately, because there was no way to start the crawl unless my legs were straddling the toilet bowl, face first it was.

No one seemed to care what was happening; I was actually stepped over twice. But finally, having extricated myself, I stood and faced the mirror.

"I just bought these clothes." I sighed and proceeded to wash as much of my hands and forearms as I could, relishing the fact that there'd been enough space between the floor and stall door to keep my head lifted off the wet ground. I used several paper towels and dabbed at the wet spots on my shirt; which was more of a placebo.

I turned to leave just as a woman bent to peek under the stall. I offered, "It's locked. It won't open."

To which she pulled on the handle three times and the door magically opened.

"Fuck ..."

I found the nearest vendor of alcohol, had a shot of something and let the server talk me into ordering the 'Especialidad de la casa,' a Michelada.

I walked slowly back to my seat with the concoction of cold lime juice, sauces, spices and beer in a salt-rimmed cup.

I nodded to TJ and Francisco as I took my seat between them. TJ frowned when he noticed my shirt. "What happened?"

I held the cup up toward him in a 'cheers' motion as I explained, "Just bein' me." I took a sip, nodded appreciatively then handed it over to TJ. "Try this."

Just then, another round of cheering swelled for Julio.

Twenty-Five

You know those times, when you're catching up with a friend who just went on a vacation and they're showing you photos, and at the beginning of the show, you are *in it!* I mean, just immersed, loving the stories, enjoying the local color and even the third video they took in an effort to show off how the birds sounded different.

But then, you're kinda over the novelty of what they're sharing because you just wanted to stop by for a quick coffee and get the *summary* of their trip, not relive the whole thing in real time. And it's already been four hours and you've got places to go and people to see …

So since I don't want to be THAT friend, and so you can make your dinner reservations, the coffee summation of the next two days goes like this:

The air was humid, the clouds rolled through and helped play out several seasons throughout the day. An afternoon rain shower was always expected and left as quickly as it came. I was told the herd of tourists were thin, as this was the off-season.

We barely scratched the surface of things to see in the days Francisco took off from work to show us 'everything.' He pretended we were going at a leisurely pace, but the number of sights and sounds became an exhausting whirlwind.

Art museums and the Zócalo–the main square in central Mexico. The National Palace, where TJ froze in admiration as we viewed the stairwell mural, a chaotic colorful palette created by Diego Rivera called *From the Conquest to 1930*.

("Why murals?"

"Murals could be seen by a large audience. He was a member of the Communist Party; addressing and representing the people in a large space where everyone was allowed, was the culmination of his ideals."

"Cool," I breathed out.

TJ agreed, "Very cool.")

There were open-air markets, plazas, squares, flirting with TJ, another museum, a little more flirting, and food in between it all. Always, our culinary destinations involved Francisco's friends, and food that held symphonies of spices and flavors that wooed our taste buds. But then, there was *always* more to hurry up and see.

Then it was time for Francisco to go back to work, leaving me and TJ to our own devices. And that's how we found ourselves once again in Francisco's parents' garden, with an after-dinner beer, when Francisco asked, "Do you know how much longer you want to stay in Mexico City? Will you go home or maybe continue to explore? Now that you have your passport?"

Sure, things are exciting when you get into the country on a technicality, but once you have your passport and everything" a possibility; shit gets real. And scary.

I had no idea what my plans were, and maybe that's why I'd been okay with the inundation of sightseeing; I didn't have to think about what came next.

"I'm not sure. I suppose I should make some decisions." I eyed TJ and gathered all my courage to say, "We should make some decisions?"

(Of course he winked, you know he did. But at this point do you think it's medical? Or do you think he knows how it's affecting me? Should I tell him? He's laid-back but he also might be the kind of guy who'd use it to his advantage. But would that be so bad?)

I turned my attention to Francisco. "I suppose I can't hide in your family's house forever."

"You've never hidden from anything," Francisco dismissed, "you're just recalibrating."

I raised an eyebrow at that, I didn't hate the idea. I sat forward in my chair and touched my bottle to Francisco's. "To recalibration."

Twenty-Six

I blinked open my eyes, happy that there was no gurgling stomach or blinding headache to accompany the action, and rolled over to find the other twin bed empty and already made. I'm not even sure if TJ, or anyone for that matter, was sleeping in that bed. We never discussed it. Most of the time I went to bed first because TJ ended up spending a bit of quiet time (once everyone went to bed) draped over his sketchbook. Of which, I am woman enough to admit, I was jealous. Though as far as travel companions go, TJ was considerate.

Now, his physical *attributes* and masculinity I got to know better on a daily basis ... *those* were clogging everything up. The way his broad, strong shoulders managed to take up too much of my eyeline. How on the metro he stood close enough to slide his hand around my waist, offering the excuse, "Just lookin' out for you." How his gaze narrowed when he was studying something, so he could maybe pull it from his memory banks later. How tempting it seemed for him to have a tattoo that barely peeked out from under his sleeve, because I'd seen the whole thing and it made my fingers itch to trace it. Not to mention how much I wanted to kiss him again.

"Jeez, Alicia," I scoffed as I forced my body into action to go find coffee. (And TJ.)

"Mornin'," he called from the table where he was bent over a sketchbook and cup of coffee. I grunted a greeting as he continued, "Coffee's fresh on the stove and Francisco's mom left us breakfast. She went to the store, and everyone else is at work."

I shuffled to the life-giving substance, poured a cup and leaned my hip against the counter. "I should write something."

"Who said you have to?"

"I don't know. It just seems like something I should say and something I should do."

"Give yourself time." He sat back and stretched. "You have to fill up the creativity tank again."

"Creativity tank?"

He thought for a moment. "When I had the big breakup, I wanted out fast. She said she didn't love me anymore and I was willing to leave most of my belongings just to get away from the hurt and the memories and ... everything. I think when people like us do something like that, we inadvertently purge ourselves of the creativity as well. So even if it wasn't your breakup that caused problems, something depleted your well."

"So I need to refill the tank."

"You need to refill the tank," he confirmed, then tapped the table. "Okay. Let's eat breakfast and get ready. I know where we should go."

I raised an eyebrow in question but he shook his head. "You'll see."

We packed a few supplies in TJ's backpack and headed out. We took the ever helpful metro to an old mansion with a bronze sign, of which I understood the word 'galería.'

"This gallery has locations in New York, LA and ... here," TJ explained as we climbed the steps.

"Okay," I said slowly, not sure how he wanted me to reply to the shared fact.

When we reached the door, he stopped suddenly. I was about to ask him what was going on until he turned toward me and I watched an obvious barrage of emotions play across his features. His frown grew as he worried his bottom lip with his teeth. He scrunched his nose and glanced behind him before he gave a grunt and shook everything off.

"I have no idea what's happening right now," I said.

With a sigh he reached out and took a strand of my hair, then watched his hand as he twirled it around a finger. The simple, unexpected action did the same to my insides.

After a moment of fighting whatever strange battle I'd witnessed, he let go of my hair, smiled and definitively declared, "Okay, let's go."

We entered the large repurposed mansion and began to walk through the gallery. TJ didn't say anything, but I swear there was a rising tension. A few rooms in, we turned a corner and I understood why.

The unmistakable reason he was so nervous hung before us.

My grin grew and I shook my head in wonder at the canvas that took up most of the wall. TJ leaned in and whispered, "Just don't ruin it, okay?"

"I'll try my best," I whispered back as I stepped closer to one of his original pieces.

This was shockingly light and airy, the polar opposite of the dark colors I'd seen at his show. In the foreground was the back of a woman's head, hair in a messy bun at the nape of her neck. She held up her hand to shade her eyes and the distance she looked into was obscured, obstructed by light and shades of blue and green.

I sighed, "It's gorgeous."

A gentleman in a dark purple suit, with a vibrant blue tie was walking past us. He gave an offhanded glance, but then did a double take. I felt TJ grimace.

"Disculpe, pero ..." He glanced between the painting and TJ several times before continuing, "Yes, you are señor Jones?"

"I am." TJ forced a smile. It was only because I'd studied him so closely for the past few days that I caught the way his jaw clenched in reply.

He truly wasn't an egotistical, self-assured artist. He was just a guy who loved his art.

TJ held out his hand. "We've met a few times before if I'm not mistaken."

The man nodded enthusiastically. "I am head curator, Rafael. It was I who attended your show several years ago and brought your work to the attention of our board. We love having your work as part of our collection," Rafael gushed, his voice sugary complimentary. "And this piece," he stood back with us and put a thoughtful hand under his chin, "the way it speaks to the viewer. About our universal y biológico makeup. It is a landscape that insists on a sense of the sublime." He waved his hands as if he had been caught loving art, then with an elegant and proper poise, said, "I was lucky enough to attend your show earlier this year. We have another painting we are speaking to your agent about obtaining."

TJ lost a bit of his tension. "Oh, that's right, you were at that show. Then this might interest you ..." He turned and tilted his head with a smirk as he said, "This is Ali Skye. She wrote about one of my pieces."

The bus ran over me thoroughly and squarely.

"Pero, no ... the writer who captured the heart of the art piece?"

It was my turn to purse my lips and shift from foot to foot as I shook the hand the curator offered. "Attempted," I smiled and gave a gurgled laugh, "some would say I stole the soul of the painting for my own purposes."

Rafael slapped laughingly at our clasped hands with his free one before letting me go. "No. No, I do not think so."

I aimed a *humph* at TJ. He blew the wind out of my sails by taking my freed hand, bringing it up to his lips and brushing a kiss across the back. Then he turned his attention to Rafael. "We are passing through Mexico City and I just had to take the opportunity to show her your gallery."

The man nodded. "And your beautiful work."

The curator was interrupted by an employee, and after hearing the message, he gave us a look that said, 'a man's work is never done.' He then pulled out a business card and handed it over. "If you are in need of anything, anything at all while you are here, please do not even hesitate one moment to reach me."

We thanked him as he did an awkward slight bow before turning and leaving.

"Oh, Margo ..." I whispered dramatically.

"It's part of the game."

I glanced at the piece and asked, "Is this supposed to be a sublime attempt to capture the biological universe?"

TJ sighed. "I love painting and creating. But there are so many hoops now, so many people who have figured out a niche for themselves, and they can claim that their art is part of a long-term research on social issues or that their work can only be seen in a contemporary political context..."

"Everyone's got an angle."

"This piece ..." he turned and smiled, "my family was on vacation at the beach, my sister said she saw a whale and when we asked her where, she put her hand up and pointed. And I wasn't looking at the ocean or my family, I just saw the color and the laughter and the love that was swirling among us. That's why the lines are swirling. That's why the colors are reminiscent of the ocean."

Yeah, I don't blame you little stomach butterflies, flip away.

"Art for the sake of art?" I asked.

He nodded and pulled me gently to begin walking back the way we'd come.

"Thanks for sharing this with me," I said softly.

"I don't know why I did," he admitted. "It seems ridiculous now."

"I think it's lovely. And it means a lot that you trust me enough to share it with me."

"As long as it doesn't show up in a story," he joked.

(Shhhhh.)

We were outside, back on the street when I held up our still clasped hands and asked, "What is this?"

He shrugged. "Hands?"

"What is this?" I repeated, and this time gestured between the two of us.

"I'm not sure," he angled his head, "but it feels like something, right?"

"Am I keeping you from ... anything?" I know he told me he'd decided to just take this last-minute trip and had no real destination in mind, but still.

"I'm just wandering. Seeing where the day takes me." It wasn't much of a reply. "Am I keeping *you* from anything?"

"I think we've imposed on Francisco and his family long enough," I acknowledged.

"What do you want to do?"

"Keep going?" I cleared my throat. "But I don't know where or how—"

"Ali."

"I'm on a fixed income." That was a larger crux in my current situation.

"So?"

I pulled myself up, and with a ramrod straight spine, met TJ's gaze. "I want to keep traveling. With you," I said a bit too forcefully, but it was the only way to get the honest words out.

"Good. I want to keep traveling with you too." Once again he brought our clasped hands to his lips and brushed a kiss against the back of mine.

"But we need to do it on the cheap." I added the term. He nodded in agreement. "So what do we do now?" I glanced up and down the street as if the answer was there.

"Wanna see some ruins?" he suggested.

Oh, ruins! "I think I do."

"Good." We followed the signs to the metro. "We'll continue our day with seeing some ruins, have some food, work on filling up your creativity tank and figure out what sounds good after that."

Twenty-Seven

"I think I'm impressed," I called to TJ who was a few steps ahead of me.

"I think I am too."

"I also think I've been ... ignorant."

"Why?"

"This is all so amazing ... and huge ... and intricate."

This all comes out in breathy waves while we climb the narrow steps of an Aztec pyramid. And I wasn't sure if I was talking about the archeological site or Mexico itself. Hell, at this point I might be talking about TJ and his art or the capacity of the human spirit.

"Teotihuacán." I repeat the name of the ruins we decided to visit. TJ does the same, "Teotihuacán."

There were only five of us on the hour long bus ride that took us from the city center to the sprawling archeological site. One of the five was Christoph, an undergrad student working on a field survey of the Teotihuacán Valley. He sat across from us and was talkative, informative and fascinating.

He chided us in his thick German accent for deciding to arrive so late at the complex, "You will only have a little more than an hour to explore twenty square kilometers." (Eight square miles according to an internet check.)

During the bus ride, he took it upon himself to imbue us with as much knowledge as he could impart. The ruins were a city built by a people before the Aztecs, but named by the Aztecs: Teotihuacán–'the city where the gods were created.'

He pulled out a printed tourist map, circled exactly what points we needed to explore with our minimal time, then took great care to make sure we knew how to properly pronounce Teotihuacán.

Tay -uh - tee - waa - kaan.

After several rounds and insistence on trying again and again, when Christoph was finally happy with our attempts, he nodded once. "Sehr gut!"

He ushered us quickly off the bus, through the entrance gate, and past the long dirt road that led straight to the Pyramid of the Sun.

And I was inspired. Inspired and motivated and roused; and I don't think I'd be jumping to conclusions if I said TJ felt the exact same way.

Christoph grunted. "You should hurry," he pointed to the gathering gray clouds in the sky, "soon you will have a difficult afternoon rain shower."

"Thank you so much for your help," I said.

TJ stuck out his hand. "Yes. We have the map. We'll hurry."

Christoph nodded and disappeared into the large ancient city.

I looked at TJ and then at the first steps that would take us to the top of the pyramid. He nodded in agreement and that's how we found ourselves halfway up the steepest part of the incline of 248 steps. Which hadn't sounded like *that* much when Christoph rattled off the number earlier. But out of shape and having done nothing more than drink the past week away, it wasn't simple.

On the positive side, at least we weren't as unprepared as we'd been in the middle of the jungle a few days ago. Now we had four bottles of water, a bag of dried coconut, several granola bars, one tube of Chapstick, my cell phone (with a *whole* thirty-four percent of a charge), and one sketchbook and one notebook—all tucked in the dry bag in TJ's backpack.

Of course, we didn't have an umbrella and definitely no emergency rain ponchos. Still we headed up, dissolving into heavy breathing and grunting; those seeming to be the two forces of motivation that encouraged us to keep moving.

We passed a couple on their way down who pointed to the sky and the obvious rain coming our way.

We nodded our thanks and muttered, "we'll hurry," to which I rolled my eyes because there was no way I'd be able to 'hurry' up this Stairmaster.

Only now, there was an end in sight.

"What do you think the difference between a temple and a pyramid is?" TJ breathily asked.

"I think—" I sucked in air. The gathering clouds helped the temperature, but the added humidity caused a heightened sweating that might have been alcohol-filled as much as it was salt-stained, but it proved I was alive, didn't it? "Exertion is good," I offered.

TJ grunted.

"I think," *deep inhale, deep exhale,* "a pyramid is a shape." One leg lifted, foot placed down and glute muscle engaged to propel my body up. "A temple is a place of ..." *suck wind,* "worship?"

"Are these tombs?"

I shook my head and glanced behind me. "Dunno. ShouldveaskedChristoph?"

The last few steps were accompanied by the rush of my breath expanding my skin; burning, stinging my ribs as my lungs pressed against them to gain more air.

"Almost ..." TJ offered.

The tears began then unexpectedly; partially brought on by the exertion, completely brought on by the word 'almost.'

'Almost' has been my mantra for a long while now.

And this was the moment that fact dawned on me.

I had *almost* been proposed to. *Almost* had my shit together. *Almost* able to make a living. *Almost* able to fulfill the requirements of my grants. *Almost* gained some recognition. *Almost* able to find one good sentence.

I pushed myself now for the last ten steps, as the sobs took over while the adrenaline and exertion aided. And with each step, I softly muttered under my breath, "Almost, almost, almost."

But then it was done. We were on the top.

It was no longer 'almost,' it was now 'completed.'

"One. Good. Sentence." I had to breathe out each word separately as I put my arms over my head and felt the dizzying effect of air expanding, exploding into places that had been deprived of it for too long.

"What?" TJ breathed back in response. He'd taken the bent over, hands on his knees, about to vomit pose, and followed his question with spitting on the ground and moaning.

"All. I. Want ..." *slow, breathe, let the tears roll,* "is to ... come away" the tension was lessening, "from this whole," and lessening, "thing," *breathe dammit!* "with one ... good ... sentence." *And there it was.* The ability to finally take a complete breath, so deep my chest lifted to the sky as the first drops of rain began.

In reply, TJ sat down heavily with a *thump*.

At first, the rain fell gently. A refreshment after the exertion.

We spun in a slow circle, taking in the vast landscape before us. The low clouds obliterated some of the mountains in the distance, but the ancient city before us, the straight avenue that ran through the length of the city that once housed over 150,000 people, was stunning.

Suddenly, the refreshing rain became something completely different.

The falling water offered a tangible course in the phrase 'torrential downpour' as pummeling water became an unmistakable insistence that we get the hell off the pyramid.

The trip down was done with less exertion, but a lot more calls over the loud rain of "be careful!" and "oh, shit!"

Two segments of stairs at the top were without anything to stabilize us, but when we got to the center, there was, thankfully, a guide rope that I gripped like it was Jack Dawson and I was Rose declaring I'd 'never let go.'

Somehow we made it onto solid ground and quickly headed somewhere. I don't know where, but I was following TJ, or to clarify, I was following TJ's ankles as I kept my head down, wiping the constant build-up of water out of my eyes.

"There!" TJ yelled. I followed his legs up another set of steps, as safely and quickly as I could, and the rain suddenly stopped. We'd found cover.

I made an animalistic grateful moan as I shook, squeezed and flicked the water off.

When I'd done all I could, I began to take inventory of where we were; just in time for TJ, who was bent at the waist and scrubbing his head, to flick more water at me.

"TJ ..." I stepped away and sucked in a breath.

It wasn't like I was Indiana Jones discovering something no one had ever seen before. The ground beneath was well-worn, this complex had been here since a few hundred B.C.E. But when there is no one around, and you've just come out of a torrential downpour, and you look up to find that you are in a courtyard held up by carved pillars with Aztec patterns—zig-zag bands, spirals, stairstep shapes, and impressive glyphs—and that the walls surrounding those are covered with detailed murals of jaguars and daily past lives done in red ... Well let me tell you, there is a stomach flip that happens and makes you feel as if you truly *are* ol' Indy discovering the unknown.

"TJ." He hadn't seen yet, so I reached out and mindlessly slapped at him while trying to comprehend the view. "TJ. You're gonna freak out."

He stopped his water removal and it was only the quick hiss of a sucked-in breath that alerted me to his first impression.

He dropped his backpack, pulled out the waterproof bag, then took out a borrowed hand towel. (Because according to *The Hitchhiker's Guide to the Galaxy,* a towel 'is the most massively useful thing an interstellar hitchhiker can have.') TJ wiped his face before handing it over, and while I wondered about chivalry, I understood his hurry to get to his sketchbook.

As the rains raged, we sat in the middle of the covered room with just enough dim light to view everything.

I let my gaze wander from angry raindrops bouncing off the uncovered courtyard, to the red paint and worn beiges of the columns, to the way TJ's solid shoulders slouched slightly over his paper. I made note of the humidity and coolness on my cheek, the smell of rain and dirt and my fading deodorant; the sounds of water rattling and tapping and splashing, the way TJ's even breathing sounded next to me as his pencil madly scratched against the paper.

And I let a smile pull at my lips because the whole moment was magical and ... "Damn."

Twenty-Eight

"What are you thinking about?" TJ interrupted my waking dream.

I glanced around, we'd truly lost the light and I was only partially drenched now. There were a few spotlights that had come on, but I don't think they made it easier for him to see his paper.

"Jaguar warriors," I whispered, as if I could offend some ancients. "Serpent gods. Gold. Symbols. History. Time."

"Time." He put his sketchbook back in the waterproof bag, stood and offered me his hand.

"Why hasn't anyone kicked us out yet?" I asked. "It's gotta be well after five." I stretched, my legs sore from the recent exertion. But the rest of my body felt loosened by the expulsion of energy and angst and sweat.

TJ used our proximity to pull me against his body, placing my hands on his waist and slowly slipping his arms around mine, where the weight would become a phantom memory. Then he dipped his head and brushed a kiss across my lips.

And I think I was expecting it.

Hell, I was about to kiss him, if he hadn't kissed me.

In fact it was the seventh or eighth thought I had when we reached the top of the pyramid. (After trying to catch my breath, coming face to face with my imagined shortcomings and figuring out what success would actually look like for me.) *Then* I thought I was going to just take what I wanted, which was a proper make out session and handsy exploration of TJ.

But the rain, and then this place ...

But maybe it was worth the wait. Maybe we needed to come together in a place that hummed with history; surrounded by artwork of ancients, and unwind against each other, releasing the pent-up flirtations. And the simple connection that was binding us together with invisible thread created an instantaneous heat. I tilted my head, rose onto my tiptoes, and gave into the urges that had been simmering under the surface with each flirtatious touch we'd shared since we met.

Fanciful ideas were ghosts brushing past and the faint lingering question: Was it possible for a moment to become a work of art?

"¿Que demonios están haciendo aquí?" The confused echo of a voice pulled us apart.

Even though I tried to separate myself fully, TJ kept his arm around my waist as he turned slowly to the voice that came from behind, where a bright flashlight was shining in our eyes.

"Lo siento," TJ began, "Eramos ..." He cleared his throat and muttered, "I have got to learn more Spanish." He started over, "We got caught in the rain. We ran and found this place. To get out of it."

"Lloviendo," I offered, pulling the word I thought was rain from the depths of my forgotten high school Spanish class.

"That means rainy." The flashlight lowered. "Vámonos. Time for you to leave."

"Muchas gracias," we muttered together. TJ released me, slung his pack on, and we followed the beam of light that would escort us out.

The rain had become a fine mist. We walked in silence but close enough that our arms constantly brushed against each other.

We were relatively close to an entrance. As we arrived at the cobblestone parking lot, which was mostly puddles now, I went ahead and walked through them, an attempt to clean off the mud that had built up on my new shoes during our mad dash from the base of the pyramid to the red jaguar room. (That's what I'm calling that room as an unseasoned tourist archeologist.)

The security guard opened the gate, we offered another sincere thanks, and with a scowl he slammed the gate shut.

The exit was opposite where we'd entered. There were only two street lamps pouring out sad beams of yellowed light, and no buildings in sight.

I sighed. "I think I'm gonna call Francisco."

"Probably a good idea." I motioned TJ to turn around so I could get the phone out of the backpack.

When Francisco answered, I explained the situation and where we were. He insisted I drop a pin in my location and share it with him then gave the instructions "don't move" before he hung up.

Twenty minutes later a small Toyota Camry, announcing its arrival with an impressive thump of bass, screeched in a circle and pulled next to us. The driver leaned a cigarette topped hand out the open window and loudly asked, "Ali?"

I nodded.

"Soy amigo de Francisco." he called, then jerked his head in the direction of the passenger side of the car, the universal sign for 'get in.'

"Um, gracias!" I yelled as we climbed in. He put his cigarette in his mouth and didn't wait for us to buckle, just did another screeching circle back onto the road as he loudly explained, "I can drive you to town, it's close. Francisco made reservacíones de hotel y cena para ustedes."

I frowned at TJ. "Reservations?"

"Hotel and dinner," the friend said through gritted teeth holding the cigarette in place.

"Oh, no," I waved, "we just need to go to the bus station. The ... estacíon de autobús?"

"No, it's too late. You miss the bus. I have work but first I'll drop you off."

And after a wild ride, as if we were unknowingly being chased, Francisco's friend did two screeching turns, throwing us against the doors before he came to a dramatic stop on a busy main street.

"Hotel there." He pointed to a wall painted with oversized bright, colorful flowers. "Dinner there." He pointed across the street.

When we didn't move he repeated the instructions then waved. "Buenas noches." Our indication to leave.

The car took off a breath after we'd shut our doors.

I pulled out my phone and called Francisco.

"Hey, we met your friend. And thanks for the ride, but he said there's no bus now?"

"No bus. And I'm tired, I'm not going to come get you. So instead, I've arranged for you to have dinner at a powerful place, and then you are going to have alone time with that *friend* of yours." He laughed.

"We can pay for an uber—"

"No. I'm locking all the doors to the house. See you tomorrow." He was enjoying this. "Have a good night."

Then he hung up.

My good friend, who set up a ride for me, a hotel, dinner reservations and let me stay with him and his family at a moment's notice, was asshole enough to hang up on me.

Ali! What's the problem? Look at this fine piece of man next to you! I want to lick that damn tattoo that keeps trying to hide from me.

Okay. Fine!

I shifted and glanced around me instead of studying that fine piece of man. Look, I'm adult enough to admit I want TJ.

Hungrily, I might add. That's not a difficult leap. But now that it seemed like it was within my grasp ... my little sabotage monster was cracking her fingers and smacking her lips; she was ready to get in the way.

The first thing she did was parade the word 'rebound' by me with a Vanna White flourish. I frowned and snarled, waved it to keep going.

She wasn't deterred. She knew how to get under my skin.

She tented her fingers and with wide, sad mocking eyes blinked. *'You've slept next to him for so many nights and he hasn't tried anything. He doesn't really want you that way. And you don't really know him. And you are so desperate because you don't have one single idea of how to get your life back on track, so you think you can hitch your wagon to his star.'*

"Food first!" I yelled too loudly, making all three of us jump.

My inner critic gave a Miss Universe pageant wave as she walked away.

"I am pretty hungry." TJ smiled, but looked at me like I had lost a little bit of my mind. "I guess you are too."

My stomach growled in agreement; even the butterflies bumping around thought food sounded good.

We turned our attention across the road to where the restaurant had been pointed out. In the distance the tops of the pyramids were illuminated by fluorescent lights.

We crossed the street and I asked, "Where are the Mayan temples? Or are those pyramids?"

"The Yucatan," he replied, "though I'm not sure if they are temples or pyramids. Why?"

"Well, now that I've seen the Aztec history, I have an urge to see the Mayans."

"Okay."

I raised an eyebrow. "Okay?"

He shrugged. "Why not? We don't have any set plans. So let's go do that next."

"Okay." I nodded and after a few steps stopped and admitted, "I'm overthinking."

He shook his head. "Writers."

I smiled but continued, "Should we ..." I waved between the two of us. "What is this?" I asked and out of the corner of my eye, my little monster self had hiked up her dress and was gleefully running back toward me.

"How about we eat first. Take a shower. Dry out our damn clothes and make plans to get to the Yucatan. *Then* you can overthink this all you want."

"You don't need to overthink this?" I asked.

"I like you. What's to overthink?"

Oh, that's nice.

I grinned at his answer, but that grin was more for the disappointment and angry snarl on my saboteur's face, which caused her to poof into thin air.

TJ stepped closer, which I was really beginning to like; reached out and twirled a strand of my hair, which I was really *really* beginning to like; and asked, "Is that okay?"

"That's completely okay."

Twenty-Nine

Agiant painted wall that read Resturante La Cueva pointed the direction we were to go with a yellow arrow. As we walked, I asked, "You think we look okay for dinner? Do I look like a drowned rat?"

"I think we're fine. It's dark, and hopefully the restaurant will be too."

I chuckled. "So I do look like a drowned rat."

He shrugged. "You look like you got stuck in the rain and are now dry."

Hmph.

"If it helps, you're also beautiful."

Hmph, again. (With a dash of butterflies.)

We followed a dirt road lined on either side by a high wall, eventually entering the restaurant's parking area. Beyond that were trees and a few tables set for dinner, but only one couple was seated. I would've wondered why we needed a reservation had it not been for the number of cars in the parking lot and the faint sounds of music drifting from ... somewhere else.

The walkway led us to the opening of a cave with a large tree growing next to it and just inside the cave, illuminated by warm lights, was a hostess wearing a black button-down shirt that read 'La Cueva' on the pocket.

After I gave my name, she led us into the cave, down three flights of stairs carved into the earth that narrowed as we made our way underground. But the last step brought us out into a wide, grandiose, softly lit cavern.

A romantic, unexpected, dreamy cavern. I turned, wide-eyed, to TJ who was shaking his head with the same shock and surprise I felt.

A large natural opening of the cave that led out of the earth, had been covered with a filmy glass to keep the elements from imposing.

One of the cave walls had been smoothed flat, painted red, and a re-creation of an Aztec mural covered it. Directly in front of the wall, a stage had been set up and spotlights lit the evening's entertainment. A mariachi band, wearing matching white bolero jackets with intricate silver embroidery and red silk ties, but no sombreros, was playing serenade music, rather than the more lively music I expected.

We were led to what I suppose was the 'back' of the cave, and given a secluded carved out spot with room for just our table, which offered a view of the entire space while keeping us secreted away. TJ hid his backpack under the table, pulled out my chair for me, and I smoothed the red tablecloth as he sat across from me.

The hostess produced a small candle and lighter. "¿Ustedes hablan inglés?"

"Sí."

"This candle is your life force," she handed the candle to TJ and the lighter to me "together, you light the candle. Make a wish and when you leave, you can put your candle there ..." She pointed to one of the jagged cave walls crawling with candles and melting wax; what I thought was part of the ambience, was an unexpected, lovely tradition. She winked as she instructed, "Ask God for direction and when you leave our cave, you are reborn."

I glanced at TJ and he nodded encouragingly.

I was a hundred percent on board with this.

I closed my eyes, wished for ... (Well, I can't tell you now, can I? Or it won't come true.)

But with my whole soul, I took a deep breath and let it out to regulate my senses and realign my hope before I lit the candle.

Our hostess took the lighter back, gestured for us to place the candle in the center of the table and left. I stared in wonder at our life force. "Francisco did say he was sending us to a powerful place for dinner."

"Amazing."

I shook my head when we finally made eye contact over the candlelight. I pointed at TJ and instructed, "Don't ask me how I'd write it. I'm not sure."

"Well, romantic for one thing," he offered just as a waiter approached us and began to list the evening's specials.

We fought our way through with our minimal Spanish and the waiter's patience to place our order. And when an iced, blended, pink concoction showed up with a collection of fruit decorating the top, I felt we'd done pretty good.

The music continued to enhance the amour of the atmosphere, and the sounds echoed in the space around us and melted away. Was it any wonder when I finally looked at TJ, really looked at him, his breathing seemed to have grown shallow and his attention on me seemed dangerously intense.

Whoa.

He nodded. "I don't think we've had time, since we met, to just sit across from each other and enjoy the company."

I sat back in my chair and took a sip of my drink, allowing his artistic study as I blatantly began my own.

He'd let his beard grow more; had trimmed the edges, but with the growth and his bedhead, and the candlelight, his jaw was a bit more angular, his shoulders a bit more broad, his hooded gaze definitely sexier. What shocked me the most was how the combination of everything to this point had become a reactionary chorus in my veins.

He smiled, held his drink up to his lips and just before he took a sip, admitted, "I actually liked the story."

"Excuse me?"

He hid a smile behind another sip before he put his drink down and said, "You have a way with words."

I shook my head, unsure how to respond.

"This is where you take the compliment," he instructed.

"Then I take the compliment."

He grunted but continued, "I may have gone online and found a few more of your stories."

"More than the few you read on my website?"

"More than that, I clicked on links and everything."

I tensed a bit, waiting for a review perhaps? (Because that's what we creative types do. We put ourselves out there, happily. And then we freak out because we have this desire to create and exhibit, but we're never ready for our souls to be picked apart … Shit, I needed to apologize to him again.) But before I could get around to saying anything, he interrupted, "You're nothing like I thought you'd be."

"What did you think I'd be like?"

He shrugged, dipped his head and hid a smile before he declared, "Pretentious."

"And now that you've gotten to know me?"

"Well, I think you're accident-prone. Funny. Lost. And sexy as hell."

I cleared my throat. "You know when you throw the sexy compliment in with 'accident-prone' and 'lost,' it loses a little something." I raised my eyebrows.

"You face the odds when things get hard." He was doubling down. "Covered in mud in the middle of the jungle, you never complained. You came on a trip with no belongings and you have this attitude that you'll just figure it out."

I straightened. "I *will* figure it out."

"You have a courageous spirit."

The compliments were that Willy Wonka boat; exhilarating, unexpected … strange.

"Your eyes sparkle when you're excited. You're a good friend, especially if a guy you knew in college is willing to offer you this much hospitality on a moment's notice. You must be a good friend, and a loyal one too."

"It's his culture." I mumbled the excuse.

"You're genuinely interested in people."

"Just their stories."

"You're going to stop downplaying my compliments and accept that you're pretty damn cool, very attractive and each time you walk into a room, you light the whole place up."

His wooing words and the magic glow in a cave just outside some of the oldest ruins in Mexico, an absolution from the Fox, a taco tour of Mexico City and truly being seen a few days into my thirtieth year–felt like a tangible, physical shift in my life.

"Fine. I'm pretty cool. This is romantic. You're handsome. And I'm so glad we met in person."

He winked. "Me too."

Our server arrived with our food, which he set down on a special tray, then made a show of pouring a liquid around the base of the bowl before he proceeded to light it on fire.

The whoosh and large flames produced pushed me back into my seat, and I laughed as he added more liquid to keep the flame rising; all part of the grandeur and display that this cave had become. I glanced at TJ, his eyes alight with the same disbelief. He was a handsome man. And tonight we didn't have anywhere to be and Francisco made sure we had plenty of time on our hands.

As our waiter dished up our food I let my gaze wander TJ's body and rest on his peeking tattoo. I licked my lips hungry for more than food suddenly. As a flush of heat brushed my cheeks, I glanced at my glass and wondered what the hell was in this drink.

Thirty

We wanted each other. It wasn't a secret. And we were adults. (Even if my actions of late seemed a bit repressed and adolescent. I was an adult on my good days. You know, I wish you and I had met then. Not when I'm in the middle of this fluctuation period. Ah, well ... I digress.)

The stage had been set. We were inspired by our afternoon, had appreciatively full stomachs and were lingering over the romantic atmosphere until our waiter explained they would be closing soon.

We placed our candle on an outcropping in the wall of the cave, one you had to go up several makeshift steps to get to. Before I put it down, I gestured for TJ to hold it with me. It only seemed right, it was *our* life force after all.

We walked slowly back to the hotel, where my overthinking saboteur was waiting. She had my thirteen-year-old braces and the dress I wore to Matt O'Rourke's birthday party that same year. As she twirled in the dress, I cringed at the stain on the back that had locked me in the restroom for the entirety of the party; until I convinced Mrs. O'Rourke to call my mom to come pick me up.

'Do you like it?' she asked.

I ground my teeth.

'What is really going on here?' she prodded. *'There's no way someone like him would want anything to do with this.'* She gestured to herself. *'He's fit, seems to have his shit together, and he's doing far better than you'll ever hope to do in the creative world. Give up now.'* She twirled.

"TJ!" I said a little too vigorously. I stopped and waited until he faced me, which he did: handsome, tall, confidence oozing; making me run a gamut of ticks—blinking a few times, clearing my throat, cracking my fingers—before I finally forced out, "You said you like me, right? Like being with me?"

He took a step toward me, reaching again for a strand of hair. "I did say that." He twirled it and out of the corner of my eye, that insecure thirteen-year-old gave me the finger before she stomped off, disappearing into a fine mist.

"You okay?" he asked.

"Much better now." I took his hand and continued into the hotel office.

Our room was pretty standard. The door opened to heavy wooden chairs on either side of a coffee table. Sandy colored walls. Dark tile floors. The bathroom door was to our right and next to that was a small dresser with a coffee maker and ice bucket on top. A large mirror, framed in wood matching the chairs, hung on the wall above the dresser. To our left was a king size bed with a colorful maroon bedspread and towels folded to look like two swans kissing in a heart shape at the foot of the bed.

And fake rose petals.

And a sign that read, '¡Felicidades!'

TJ chuckled, I rolled my eyes.

We stood in the center of the room and before he could say anything, I insisted he shower first.

When he was locked inside with the water turned on, I took out my phone and texted Francisco: *Butthead.*

All I got back was a laughing face emoji and a GIF of a random girl screaming 'Get Some!'

I turned my phone off in retaliation, then stepped up to the mirror and narrowed my gaze. "Okay, listen up Alicia. You *are* pretty cool. You just went through a bit of a rough patch. But you're *almost* done now." I double pointed to make sure I was listening. "Things are looking up every damn second. That man in there likes you. And he's ..." I shook my head as several descriptors rattled off, but settled on, "hot." Which obtained me some mirrored unison head nodding. "Now, this is good." I concluded my pep talk, but then felt something else should be added: "So Go. Be fun."

Pep talk successful!

However, I did continue to pace until he came out.

And when he did, that bastard had the audacity to swagger, the smallish hotel towel hanging loosely off his hips; and that damn tattoo I wanted to lick was still wet with water.

When he motioned it was my turn, mentioning that he'd saved me some hot water, I muttered a "thanks" and quickly shut myself in the bathroom. I pressed my head against the door for a moment, then turned toward *this* mirror; maybe she'd listen.

I whispered, "He likes you, you like him. If the kisses are that intense, can you imagine what the sex is gonna be like? This isn't the rest of your life. This is just a vacation and you know what 'they' say about artists you meet on vacation …" I glared at myself in the mirror with raised eyebrows. "*Nothing*, they don't say anything about it because you're making it up. Now get in the shower so you can feel clean enough to go do some real dirty stuff."

My reflection nodded in agreement. After I'd scrubbed as well as could be expected and let go of the wish for a razor to handle the few days growth of leg hair, I tucked the towel around my chest, fluffed my wet hair as best I could and aggressively pulled open the bathroom door.

TJ was sketching at the small table in the corner, still with only the towel wrapped around his waist.

(I'd call that sketch: *Waiting to Get Some #30.*)

He glanced up at my sudden appearance, and I didn't hold back a grin or the way my voice shakily said, "I think you need to kiss me right now or this whole thing—" He was up after the first few words and had crossed to me by the time I declared 'right now,' as if there was no way he was letting me finish my lame ultimatum. And that's how his lips melted onto mine while I clutched him as if I were drowning.

He grinned when he pulled back for a moment, his hands framing my face as he whispered, "I've wanted you for quite a while now."

"I wasn't sure."

"I thought for sure you knew, the way you took every opportunity to brush up against me all day, every day."

"I brushed up against you?! You put your hands on me …" The idea caught in my throat and he gave me a questioning look. I softly blurted,

"The way you just put your hands on my hips is ..." I grunted, "I really liked it."

Grinning, he kissed me again, lowering his hands to my hips, squeezing when they arrived so they could claim their territory.

We disintegrated into the building heat and yearning. Hands were finally free to search and spread and linger and ignite passion without interruption. It was the beginning of the carnal tangle: lips and mouths, hands and fingertips, arousal and ache.

At some point we made it to the bed. TJ lowered his body on top of mine and I wrapped myself around him; my hands trying to figure out what landmass they wanted to explore the most while moving to deepen the kiss–to grow and become one with every feverish movement.

We traded kisses like we were making up for a lifetime of lost opportunity. Transcoding souls through the action. Devouring the moment.

When mere exploration wasn't enough, and the intense foreplay was no longer sufficient, TJ pulled at the last barricade between us, my towel, and with only the moonlight as our witness, he pushed his way inside me and stopped with a low, appreciative moan. "Damn."

His deep voice, laden with longing, ruptured my eardrums. I wanted more; I relished how he felt too, but there was more I needed. I pushed with my hips to move him into action, but he trapped me with his weight, bruising my neck with his lips.

"TJ, you need to ..." I tried to raise my pelvis and pull his lips toward my mouth. But he stopped the movement and grinned as he whispered, "I want to make you moan and beg," before his lips claimed mine again.

Moaning and begging meant he supplied me with an extended demonstration of his skill in keeping me on the verge, continually threatening my senses until I was lost and reckless and riding the rhythmic moans that came from someone else, because it was no longer me in that body.

My head spun, need became a rock in my gut as my body hovered above the ground and TJ continued his sweet assault.

I begged, spoke in tongues, hated him and longed for more when he finally gave into the imploring that had begun a lifetime ago. He let the last bastions of need wash over us as we moved against each other with wild abandon and the flood gates opened and we became ancient gods fighting old wars of passion with our bodies, scorching the shadows until we rose above it all and drifted into the four winds.

"Oh ..." I breathed as I clung to him, and in my ear he finished, "...my."

Thirty-One

So, here's something interesting.

Did you know, when something devastating is heading your way, like you're about to be hit by a car and you see it coming, you have time to utter one, maybe two words? Most preferable are: "Oh shit."

Did you also know you have time to breathe out one really good expletive when you're shocked and not expecting something: "Fuck!"

And, if you're lucky, when the driver of a nondescript van stops in front of you—as you're walking from your hotel to a restaurant—and two masked men materialize, level guns at you with a menacing "get in the van;" you have just enough time to sputter, "What the fuck?!"

Expletives aside, it's safe to say, the situation completely and utterly doused the 'morning-after' high TJ and I'd been riding as we walked down the street to find breakfast.

My mouth fell open in a silent scream when TJ was quickly knocked out with the butt of one of the men's guns and left where he lay crumpled on the ground.

I inhaled to finally give voice to my scream, but the gun in my face suggested I stop. So I stared wide-eyed and tried to make sense of the situation as my hands were zip-tied behind my back and I was muscled into the van and forced to sit on a bench opposite my kidnappers while a staticky radio station played Right Said Fred's "I'm Too Sexy."

"So this is happening," I muttered, pretty sure that my eyes, still wide as a Big Eye painting, hadn't blinked yet.

But I swear one of the men across from me smiled.

Okay, long bumpy van ride.

It started to rain again.

And since I only had an inkling of where I was in relation to Mexico City when we started this abduction, it's safe to say I was completely turned around and had absolutely no idea which direction we went or where exactly we ended up when the van finally came to a stop.

I *do* know we were well out of the city. Approximately thirty-four songs and as many advertisements out of the city.

The door swung open and revealed a woman standing under a tarp-covered area. She was short in stature, tall in confidence; late thirties, with short curly black hair wrapped in a light green and gold silk bandana, dressed in a tight green tank top and camo pants and wearing large teardrop shaped earrings. And even though she greeted me with a handgun, I still noticed her flawless skin.

"Buenas tardes." She smiled happily.

I nodded as I was unceremoniously escorted out of the van to stand in front of her. "Sure. Why not? Buenas tardes." I cleared my throat and shakily asked, "What's going on?"

"Just a little kidnapping." She smiled wider.

I did a quick survey of the surrounding area; so far just the three men who had done the kidnapping and this jovial woman. The clearing we were in had been covered by several tarps to keep the rain away. There was full tree cover to the left, jungle to the right, foliage behind me and wilds in front.

Here I am, stuck in the middle with you.

Shit, I already used that joke, didn't I?

Do you see *how stressed out I am?!*

"Kidnapping," I repeated.

"¡Sí!" She waved for me to head over to the makeshift campsite in the middle of the wilderness that came complete with a table, crates to sit on, and stacks of plastic totes for storage. There seemed to be homey goods too; like a few buckets, a camp stove, coolers, and a small table set up with water jugs. "Do you want water?"

"Um," I swallowed and shook my head, "no. Gracias. Look, can I say, I am really appreciative of the feminist reality here, a woman guerrilla or ... revolutionary?" It was a question; what did she prefer?

"Oh," she waved, "they are the same thing. But we are not any of those. We are more ..." She pursed her lips as she rocked her head back and forth a few times, looking for the right word. "Outlaws!" she happily yelled.

"Ah, well ... congratulations on being a successful woman outlaw, but, could you let me go? I have no money. I'm really not anyone. And I don't *know* anyone who knows anyone who has money."

"No." She clipped the conversation to an end.

I glanced around, too stunned to lose my shit just yet, nervous sure, but the reality and her happy demeanor were actually keeping my fears at bay. "Well, maybe you could answer another question. What's the difference between a pyramid and a temple?"

She narrowed her gaze and after a moment replied, "Mummies are already dead in pyramids, temples have human sacrifices?"

Good answer, as good as the one I'd given TJ.

TJ.

Who I liked.

Who I'd had the best sex of my life with.

Who I could still smell on my skin.

Who was laying in the gutter unconscious.

(I know it's 'whom' but I'm on the verge of freaking out here and 'who' sounds better and I hate the semantics of this word and I'm not getting into it right now!)

TJ!

Surely someone would help him ...

I needed to focus on my current problems.

Not TJ.

Who had my phone.

(Thank the gods of Teotihuacán I'd texted my mom already today.)

"That's a nice necklace." The lady outlaw interrupted my spiraling.

"Oh," I glanced down and muttered, "it was a birthday present."

"It's a fire opal, no?"

"Yes."

She pulled the pendant (and me) closer to her and studied it for a moment before letting it drop. "That's probably a seven or eight-thousand-dollar necklace."

"What?! No. You mean pesos, right?"

"No. I mean dólares americanos."

I glanced down at the pendant, crossing my eyes to get a really good view; what the hell?!

"Okay," the woman clapped, "you are our prisoner. We know you are important. We know you are running drugs for El Zorro Blanco. So you are going to help us take over his operation."

"I think I'd like that water now," I pleaded as a tidy little package of hyper emotions, wrapped with a ribbon of heart-pounding fear, crashed over me.

I was pointed toward a crate to sit down but reminded my captors, "My hands?" Cut free, I rubbed my wrists as water was delivered and my brain did strange acrobatics with thought processes, and when an idea with great merit flew by, I gripped it tightly.

"So, y'all ready for the World Cup? I gotta admit, you guys have a really good team this year. Great forwards, but your sweeper is pure crap; if you can replace him, I think you've got a chance."

The woman laughed and translated what I'd said. As I was stared down by the men, I forced my hands not to shake. No one said anything for the longest time until a sudden eruption made me drop my cup as views on their country's soccer team exploded around me.

I took a shaky breath as I desperately attempted to recall every last bit of information I'd internalized on the Mexican World Cup team. Thank God for an article and the research I'd done two months ago. The story was shit, but proving to be really, *really* helpful.

The woman tilted her head and with a grin gave a slight nod, an acknowledgement that she liked my attempted stall tactic.

After all soccer debates died down, I held out my hand to the woman who was obviously in charge. It shook, but so what? "I'm scared to death. I don't understand why I'm here. But I'm Ali Skye."

She grinned and took my hand, her shake firm and powerful. She pulled me forward slightly over the table, an intense 'don't fuck with me' vibe firmly in place as she introduced herself, "Rosa."

"Rosa. Nice to meet you."

Having never been kidnapped before, I didn't know what to do next. It did help my tension that the men had spread out and took up sprawled positions around the ... campsite? I'm not really sure what you called a jungle reprieve where you kept your kidnappees. Camp seemed too domestic. Maybe this was a way station and we were headed somewhere else?

"Okay," Rosa clapped even more forcefully, "we know you are running drugs for El Zorro Blanco."

"But that's the thing, I'm not—"

"Do not try to deny it." She smiled. "You were seen with El Zorro in Tijuana. Having drinks with him at his bar."

"Yeah, because that's the bar I went to that night. And I was drinking with him because he was hitting on me."

She tisked as if I'd gotten my information wrong. "He doesn't drink with his patrons."

I spoke slowly, not to offend her, but in a desperate plea to get her to understand, "He was trying to get into my pants." I nodded wide eyed; did she get it? "And he said he was a man who could get anyone anything, so I'm pretty sure he was hitting on me and trying to find out if I was a potential '*customer*.'"

"But you weren't."

"Exactly." Now we were getting somewhere.

"You were drinking with your boss, because you are an employee."

"No. What? No." I shook my head and waved the accusations away. "No. What ... no. Why ...?" How was I going to make her understand? More head shaking did not dislodge the growing fear, so I tried to find some semblance of control. I decided to go with: "Your English is so good." I pointed a finger at her, thought better of it, and turned it toward myself. "*I* wish I'd studied enough to know your language fluently. It's a disgrace that I don't." I jutted my chin at the honest utterance.

"I studied in the states." She shrugged, then winked. "Maybe El Zorro is helping you with your Spanish."

I visibly swallowed in reply.

She continued, "I understand why you think you should claim you are not working for him, but," she pointed to my necklace, "he gives that same pendant, a fire opal, to everyone who works for him."

"What!?"

But it was just supposed to boost my confidence and promote good fortune.

"It is a well-known fact."

Not to me!

"It's not well known to me!" I was losing my mind, or I was having a waking dream.

Wait, yeah, maybe that's what this was.

A hallucinatory state. The sex was so good with TJ, it lulled me into a really deep hallucinatory state with a bizarre ... dream?

I pinched myself really hard and when I didn't 'wake up,' I reached across the table to pinch Rosa, but she slapped my hand away, picked up her gun and leveled it at me.

"So not a dream," I muttered.

"Not a dream," she confirmed. "Be good?" She pointed to my hand and I nodded. She put the gun down as I placed my hand in my lap. "You were at Zorro's bar. You wear his necklace. You were seen eating with him at one of his establishments and you were seen kissing him." She leaned forward. "We know you are working for him."

I mean, when you put it that way ...

She continued, "In Mexico City, you have been so very busy, in and out of businesses, doing errands for your boss I think."

"Okay, now you're the one making things up. I'm a tourist. I was visiting a college friend who lives in Mexico City and we were doing touristy things. Of course we were all over the place."

"The perfect cover. A tourist."

Wait a minute.

Wait one damn minute now.

If this had to do with the Fox, he didn't hate me. He could be the person who could clear my name! Maybe knowing him would easily get me *out* of this situation. A new ray of hope in an otherwise bizarre situation shone down from the heavens for me.

I just needed to get in touch with him.

I started, "Rosa. Can I call you Rosa?"

She shrugged.

"Rosa, let's pretend what you say is true. What do you want from me?"

"We want to know all his routes and the names of all those working for him."

Well, if I gave her any of that it would be a work of fiction. And since I was in the business …

"And we want to know who killed him."

I think my heart stopped. "What's that?"

"Haven't you heard?"

I didn't even want to ask, 'heard what?' And the way my new panic attack was taking over, I didn't want any more information.

But Rosa offered it anyway. "El Zorro Blanco is dead."

Thirty-Two

"I didn't kill him," I insisted.

Rosa shrugged. "You were the last one to see him alive."

Well this is just great.

"Look, I don't work for him. You see, listen. It's just, his bar ... that's just where I ended up. My grandfather wouldn't stop going on and on about how he was a better human when he was my age. It was my birthday dinner with my family, and it was awful. I mean, that's harsh, they love me, but I just ... I wasn't in the mood, you know?" *Engage snowball effect here.* "So I pretended to go to the bathroom but instead I left and walked to this convenience store where this guy was being held up by his girlfriend. *Somehow* we escaped and because we were both having an awful night, we decided to get something to drink in Tijuana, you know? Just to get drunk." I was trying to control the pitch of my voice, but it was turned to runaway speed now. "And we parked his car and had street tacos and walked and finally found a place to get drunk. Which just *happened* to be the Fox's bar, but *I* didn't know it. *I* didn't know *him*. I had never met him before that night."

Rosa raised an eyebrow. "That is a bad story."

"Exactly!" I yelled with a little too much zeal. "It's so bad it *has* to be the truth!"

"If you weren't under the protection of El Zorro, why would you, a gringa, *all alone*, take the bus ride that goes through unsafe places?"

Seriously, the way she kept twisting things had a little whisper in the back of my head making me think the farfetched idea that I might really be working for the Zorro.

"I was having, I *am* having, a ... pre ... mid-life crisis," I offered hysterically. "I thought I would be safe on the bus if I never got off and was just going from Tijuana to see my friend in Mexico City."

"We know you are from Los Angeles, where El Zorro also does business. How do you explain that?"

"There are almost four million people living in Los Angeles? And coincidence?" I licked my lips then clasped my hands together and shook them in a plea. "I swear, before I walked into his bar that night, I had never ... EVER ... in all the days of my life, laid eyes on the White Fox."

Rosa steepled her fingers. "Then it would seem we have a very big problem."

This is where the voice-over in the movie of my life would say something flippant like: 'Things were not looking good for thirty-year-old Ali Skye.'

I was sat in a corner of the campsite, told not to move. And that was it. The rest of my day was spent fluctuating between worry for TJ; wondering if, among Francisco's many friends, he had any unscrupulous ones that might be able to locate me; and trying to plan an escape. An escape where everything would fall into my lap since I didn't know where I was, where I needed to go, or how to get there.

Now, wondering who killed the Fox wasn't on my mind. When you live the kind of life he did–getting 'anyone anything'–even he said his life was in constant danger. *Didn't he?*

Oh, maybe it would help the situation if I could prove I didn't kill him. Or maybe it would help my street cred if I could prove I HAD killed him. *Now there's a thought.*

Two of the men stood up and began making a fire in the portable grill. They pulled out food, then magically, heavenly smells from the barbecue began rising up into the air. I watched this strange scene until

Rosa finally announced, "Time for dinner." She pointed to the crate at the table where I'd been sitting previously.

Mismatched, but real plates and silverware were set on the table with a handful of napkins, followed by a plate of sliced meat, onions and peppers from the grill, a pot of black beans, warmed corn tortillas and a pot of rice.

In the middle of a kidnapping. In an undisclosed location in the jungle.

Sure.

"¿Cervesa?" Rosa inquired.

I mean, beer wasn't gonna hurt the situation.

After the first few bites were comfortably in our stomachs the men relaxed and conversation began to flow easily among them. Low tones, laughter, ribbing and storytelling seemed to be the order of the evening. As I ate I tried to concentrate on the Spanish, but only caught a few words here and there, not enough to build a coherent sentence from. Dinner finished, the sun had set and a lantern was pulled out along with a bottle of Tequila. After everyone took a long swig, Rosa held it out toward me in offering.

"Of course." Getting drunk with kidnappers seemed like a *great* idea.

"It is Mezcal," she explained.

I took a very hefty–help me get drunk and pull me back from the edge of the freak-out I was teetering on–swig before handing the bottle back. I had to suck in a breath as the liquor burned its way down my esophagus. "What's the difference?"

"Technically Mezcal is Tequila, but real Tequila can only be made from a certain type of agave. Which you can only find in five Mexican states."

"Ah," I breathed as the burning finally stopped, "it can only be called champagne if it comes from the Champagne region of France."

"Exactamente." She took another drink and passed the bottle along.

"So Rosa, when you're not trying to break into the drug running game, what do you do?"

"I design jewelry and fabrics."

Of all the things she could have said ... No, that's not true. At this point, I don't think anything was ever going to shock me ever again.

"Did you design the earrings you're wearing?"

"Sí," she took one out and handed it over, "do you like it?"

I gently held the silver teardrop, inlaid with turquoise that resembled an ancient Aztec design. "It looks like the border of one of the columns I saw yesterday at Teotihuacán."

"Good pronunciation."

"I practiced." *Thank you, Christoph.*

"It is based on an ancient design."

I sighed as the bottle was handed to me once again, traded it for the earring, took another swig, then shook my head and passed it along. "So what do we do now?"

"Well," Rosa sat back and crossed her arms over her chest, "you could try to run away, but we'll catch you. And if you somehow manage to get away and we *don't* find you, we are very far from civilization and you will get lost and die in the wild."

Thankfully, my warm stomach kept me neutral as I gained this new tidbit of information that verified my whereabouts.

"I suggest you tell us what you know and tomorrow, we can take you back and drop you where we picked you up."

"How did you find me?" Why hadn't I thought to ask that question sooner?

"Don't you know, señorita? Foxes are cunning. And El Zorro Blanco is no different. He put a tracker in your phone."

The weight of that fact pulled my head down, chin toward my chest. "I threw my old phone away in a drunken stupor," I tiredly explained.

She grunted, probably not believing that fact either. But she changed the subject and asked me the question I'd asked her. "What do you do for a living, when you aren't running drugs?"

I laughed as I told her, "I'm a writer."

"¿Una autora? Really?"

"In my free time," I scoffed, which was followed by a hiccup.

"What do you write?"

"Freelance articles, short stories that steal the soul of famous art pieces, and books that sit in a pile of slush on random agents' desks."

"Fascinating."

"Isn't it?" One of the men pulled out a pack of cigarettes and I asked for one. He glanced at Rosa to see if it was okay and she nodded her approval.

As the lit cigarette was passed to me, Rosa suggested, "You should tell us a story." I held the smoke in my lungs and shook my head 'no thank you.'

But the sudden idea was growing on her. She beamed a smile at me. "If you tell me a good enough story, who knows, maybe I'll let you go."

"I don't tell stories, I write them."

"What's the difference?"

I took another drag and glanced around; how was I going to explain this? Then I saw one of the men's boots untied. I pointed at them with my cigarette. "You could tell me in detail how to tie my shoes, right?"

She shrugged a shoulder in reply.

"But it would be easier if you showed me how to do it, and I just follow your lead, right?"

She pursed her lips. "Maybe."

"There is something about touching things that makes them easier. When I write with my hands, I swear they are the writers, not me. I'm just the ... vessel." I shook my head, I needed a better word.

"What is the name of the lady who had to tell the stories for one hundred and one nights to save her life?"

"Scheherazade?" I asked incredulously.

Rosa winked.

"Am I gonna be here for one hundred and one nights?" Little did Rosa know, my mom was going to call the cops by close of day tomorrow; so my time might be a little shorter than that.

"That's up to you. If you would give us all the information on El Zorro, you'd be home by now."

"But—" I cut myself off.

She raised an eyebrow in question. I shook my head.

But once they had this illusive information, wouldn't they kill me? Because I'd seen their faces and it didn't seem to make sense to return me safe and sound when I could call the cops and report them.

(I mean, that's how I'd write it.)

Fuck.

"My grandfather was a farmer," Rosa said. "He worked hard. Had a simple education. A simple life. But he loved to tell stories, he always told the best stories."

"I think *you* might be a storyteller." It was a blatant attempt to keep all spotlights off me.

"My grandfather started stories badly. He would stop a lot, change little details, but after a while, the story came and he was weaving magic. The story became so good we never wanted it to end."

"The muse took over," I muttered. "They don't come round here much anymore." I tapped my head with a finger.

"I like cowboy stories." She smiled as the bottle had made its way back to her. She took another swig before pushing it toward me. "You should tell us a cowboy story."

"I'm not trying to deceive you, I really don't tell stories aloud very well. Or at all."

"Then tell us a story about how El Zorro runs his operation and give us some names and contacts."

So this was the fanciful rock and a hard place I was now living in. And any way you looked at it, I was going to be telling some sort of story to save my life.

"You know, the first cowboys were Mexican," Rosa said.

"I remember reading about that somewhere."

"Vaqueros, that's the Spanish word for cowboy. And the first cowboys in North America were Indigenous Mexican men."

"So maybe you know better cowboy stories than I do."

"But it's you who needs to tell us a story." She leaned forward with a grin. "I love this for you. Tell me a story and it just might save your life."

If a constant fear of being killed or possibly having appendages cut off at any moment wasn't lingering in the back of my head, I would appreciate how intelligent and formidable Rosa was. And I would laugh at the ridiculous request.

What was I going to do?

Start talking bullshit about a man whose whole legend is based on sitting atop a horse while he watched his food?

A rough-handed, misunderstood, quiet man who would ride a woman as hard as he rode his horse? A man who, no matter how hard he tried, always seemed to be running from something? A man who could be a hero, not good or bad, but definitely exceptional.

"Oh my god," I was buzzed, "a cowboy story is just an American version of *The Odyssey*, isn't it?"

Rosa shrugged and flashed an amused look my way.

"But I'm not Odysseus," I whispered. "I'm the god of the machine who saves him." It was meant to be a joke, but it brought a very sobering idea. A great idea. "Rosa, can I make a phone call? To the Fox's bar? I think I can give you what you need if I can get in touch with Yvonne."

"Who is Yvonne?"

"Tyler's girlfriend."

"Who is Tyler?"

"Nobody. But I think I can fix all of this."

She tilted her head at the thought and after a long while pursed her lips and gave a single nod. "Tomorrow."

Okay. Tomorrow. That was something at least.

"Tonight. We tell stories."

Shit.

Thirty-Three

"Men born in bustling East Coast cities at the dawn of the eighteenth century were christened with names like William James Thatcher. They were expected to be upstanding citizens and hard-working businessmen. For those that didn't like the lay of the land before them, they traveled. Reshaped their souls. Followed the scent of gold and adventure. Some found employment in the cow trade.

"By the time these herders traveled into new western towns, long forgotten was the rumble of the busy city and the need to fill up the silence around them. They became men of few words. And in each new town, since they weren't staying that long, there was no need to introduce themselves. So bartenders and merchants called them 'buddy' or 'pardner.' Sometimes, a man became known for his physical attributes: Shorty, Slim. Or the way they played cards: Lucky, Lefty, Ace.

"As the West envelops a man, he leaves behind the world of his baptism to emerge anew. Billy the Kidd, Wild Bill.

"Cal Hand wasn't any different. Someone started calling him Pal, others Cow Hand. And just the way a river running over rocks smooths the surface over time, all the nicknames smoothed and he became Cal Hand, and that suited him just fine."

Rosa started to laugh and clapped; in return I just stared at her wide-eyed.

Where in the ever-loving name of Louis L'Amour and Mark Twain did that come from?

"That's a good beginning."

I snorted and shook my head.

"Cal Hand." She handed me the bottle of Mezcal. "Good name."

It was my turn to laugh now. Only I was slightly unhinged (and a bit drunk). When Rosa's bemusement morphed into one of concern, I waved it away and tried to settle myself down enough to take another swig off the bottle.

"Now, I'll tell you a story." She repeated her intentions to the men, whom I was beginning to think of as 'her men.' Because they seemed to be seeing to her every whim and other than the actual physical abduction of my bodily self, they only jumped when she pointed and explained how high.

"Did you see the volcanoes when you were in Mexico City?"

"Francisco pointed them out," I said, proud of *not* giving the smartass retort I wanted: 'It was hard to tear my attention away from my various drug dealing activities.'

She nodded. "The volcanoes are called Popocatépetl and Iztaccíhuatl. And theirs is one of the oldest love stories of all time."

You had me at hello.

"In the ancient times, the empire that the Aztecs ruled covered the whole valley of Mexico; and during those days many of the surrounding towns were often heavily taxed. Of course, this was not a beloved practice. The chief of the Tlaxcaltecas decided he'd had enough of the burden and realized it was time to fight for his people's freedom.

"The chief had many children, but his favorite was his daughter, Princess Iztaccíhuatl (ees-tahk-see-waht-l), known far and wide for her beauty and grace. Before all this, before her father decided to go to war, the princess fell deeply in love with a warrior named Popocatépetl (pow-puh-ka-tuh-peh-tl)."

There is something about being in a darkened jungle, the light of a lantern keeping the night at bay, the smell of wet foliage rising up into your nose, with bones relaxed by mezcal, random plumes of cigarette smoke lazily twirling, and the dreamy rich voice of a woman and her story rising into the cool, humid night air.

(The only thing that would make this better would be if it wasn't happening in the middle of a kidnapping scenario.)

"The love between the princess and the warrior was unwavering. Those early days, those were the good days."

TJ.

I shook my head. If I thought about him now, I'd lose the slight grip on the calm rope I had tied a knot in and was desperately holding on to.

She continued, "Those were the times when they walked hand in hand. Shared longing looks and built the foundation of their love."

"Do you believe in love like that?" I didn't realize I'd asked the question, it felt like someone else. I cleared my throat. "I didn't mean to interrupt you."

Rosa was staring beyond my shoulder. "I want to believe that there are those lucky enough in the world to share a timeless love. But I don't know when or how it is possible. For me," she shook her head, "for me perhaps it isn't an option." She stood up then, the spell of the evening shattered with my question.

"I'll show you where you'll sleep." She took a flashlight, said something to her men, then led me farther into the surrounding jungle.

We stopped at an 'outhouse'–which was a modern pop-up shower tent. Rosa pulled the zipper door aside and flashed her light on a bucket with a toilet lid on top of it. "There is a string with liners for the bucket and toilet paper. Line the bucket and then you'll tie the bag when you are finished and put it in this trash." She illuminated another bucket just behind the pop-up.

She pulled a glow stick from her pocket, cracked it and gave it a shake before handing it to me. "You can hang this from a string at the top."

Necessities taken care of, I decided I just might spend my kidnapped days being okay with dehydration, I stumbled out of the makeshift restroom and followed Rosa to a larger tent with two cots.

She followed me in and pointed to the cot on the far side that had a pillow and one blanket, then pulled her cot next to the opening. "Don't try anything, okay? You won't survive and if you don't get shot trying to get away, you could really get hurt."

"What could be worse than a gunshot?" I whispered.

She laughed. "Want to find out?"

I shook my head and laid down, pulling the blanket over my body—more for the comfort it gave than needing warmth—then faced away from Rosa.

She turned off her flashlight and in the darkness, with cries of birds and wildlife I wasn't accustomed to, I finally had time to worry. *Really* worry. Was TJ okay? Did he have a concussion? Was he robbed while he was unconscious? Did he find Francisco? How the *hell* were they ever going to find me?

I had to shake my head several times to dislodge the panic. *Nope, I'm not gonna think about that now. Because I have a plan.*

I was going to call El Zorro's bar and talk to Yvonne and somehow, she'd get me help. Because she owed me. I introduced her to Tyler. God, I hoped their budding relationship was still going.

"What will happen to Cal Hand?" Rosa asked.

"Well, aren't most cowboy stories about longing and loss and unrequited love?"

"I thought you said it was like *The Odyssey*."

"I guess it's a mix of The Odyssey and courtly love."

A quiet laugh rose up from her side of the tent. "That's a lot of pressure to put on a story."

"A story that might save my life probably *should* have a lot of pressure." No truer words ... "I'm not being rude."

She grunted in reply.

"I suppose ..." I cleared my throat. "I suppose Cal probably isn't any different than most cow hands. He would want enough money to buy his own small herd. With that, he'd be able to buy himself some land and build a house and then he'd want to find a woman to love him," I suggested as my mind wrote: *Those were the dreams he'd think on while he watched the prairie grasses blow in the wind, the sky fill with clouds, and the sun work its way through the heavens.*

"What did you put in that Tequila?" I asked.

"Mezcal," she corrected.

"Mezcal," I repeated, and we fell silent. But when the worry tried to grip me again, I asked, "What happens next to the princess and the warrior?"

Rosa was quiet for so long, I didn't think she'd answer.

"The chief went to war. Of course, since Popocatépetl was the fiercest of all warriors, he was expected to go and fight bravely to honor his chief. But before he left, he asked the chief for the princess' hand in marriage. The chief agreed, but there was a catch." She paused for dramatic effect. "Once they all returned home from their triumph in war, *then*, he would happily celebrate the wedding. So the warrior and the princess exchanged all the proper words of love and desperate promises that come with a difficult situation." She gave a yawn and muttered, "Tomorrow. You'll tell me what happens to the cowboy and I'll tell you what happens to the princess and the warrior."

I listened as her breathing became smooth and even. I wondered if I could sneak out and what I'd really do if I made it past her. That curiosity was quickly replaced by a flash of memory—TJ sitting across a candlelit table from me. That caused my throat to ache with threatening tears, but I swallowed them down and forced myself to think about something else. Anything else.

Maybe a damn cowboy.

After years on a lonely prairie, cowboys knew a few things to be true: You knock your boots on the floor before you put them on. You look a man in the eyes when he meets you for the first time. You keep your cattle close and never get involved in another man's business.

Thirty-Four

Talk about strange dreams.

A colorful flying serpent had come down from the sky, grabbed TJ with his talons, and as they flew away, I jumped on a nearby horse and rode as fast as I could, trying to keep up. But I was losing him and I could only watch in horror as he was taken to the highest mountain in the distance that resembled a temple.

I blinked my eyes open and after a moment hoarsely whispered, "Or was it a pyramid."

Headache firmly in place; yet another hangover that made me groan as I tried to right myself, I muttered to Rosa's empty cot, "I'm too old for this shit."

I needed a restroom, coffee, food, a phone, an escape plan and a shower.

In that order.

I unzipped the tent and found one of Rosa's men waiting.

"¿Baño?" I asked.

He walked me the short distance to the bathroom and I didn't care about the morning noises and the fact that he lingered nearby the baño pop-up.

(Eww, you're saying to yourself. Did we need that? Well, I'm stuck in this misery and sharing it helps me feel less alone. So Yes. We needed to hear that.)

Finished, my morning bodyguard wordlessly led me back to the communal area.

"Buenos días, Ali," Rosa happily called.

I grunted but was happy that there was a version of breakfast laid out.

I reached for a tortilla, but she pulled the plate away from me and slid a large, detailed road map of Mexico onto the table.

I blinked down at the lines that were weaving in and out of focus.

"Let's start with a few establishments and connections first."

She took out a paper with something printed out on it and a red marker; then she began circling locations on the map. When she circled the arena where we'd seen Lucha Libre, I realized she was circling everywhere I'd been sightseeing.

I focused on the paper in her hand. The gray logo at the top was clearly a local telephone network, so it must have something to do with the tracker in my cell.

She circled the art gallery and the ruins, then sat back and smiled. "What would you like to tell us about these locations?"

"If you are in section N of the arena to see Lucha Libre, don't use the third stall in the bathroom. The door is broken."

She narrowed her gaze and snarled.

"I had to crawl out." I held up my hands in surrender. "I am not working for El Zorro Blanco. And trust me, I know how this looks. But I swear, I just met him the other day. For the first time."

"Who is at the art gallery? That seems like a strange stop."

I licked my lips and had a moment when I thought maybe I'd throw the pretentious curator under the bus, but he *was* championing TJ's work.

"Can I make a phone call? To the bar?"

Rosa said something to her men; I caught the word phone, but the men, who seemed so docile and bored, were suddenly agitated.

Eventually, Rosa put a hand up and yelled for everyone to stop.

She turned the map and with the red pen traced a road between Tijuana and Mexico City. "Why were you reported walking this road for several hours? Did you have a lot of stops on this route?"

"The bus broke down ..." I whispered.

None of this. Not one bit of it looked good.

I shook my head and tried again, "I really wish I had something to give you. I wish I had names and locations. But I don't. I don't know *anything*."

She translated what I said to her men. One of the men crumpled up the map and yelled, the other two disappeared into the jungle. I started to shake uncontrollably, hoping it was just a lack of caffeine and hangover residue causing it. But until this moment, no one had shown me anger or made any real serious threats; in fact everyone had been so calm, it had been easy to feel like everything was going to be okay.

Nervous about the sudden anger and disappearance of the men, I began to babble and thought I'd start with what was foremost in my mind. "So, for transparency sake, I just thought you'd like to know that my mom is going to call the cops if I don't text her by midnight tonight."

Rosa snorted.

"I'm serious," I sighed, "she's supportive and wants me to see the world, but she also watches too many crime TV shows and too much news."

"But no one knows where you are," Rosa reasoned.

"I realize that."

She pulled out two cigarettes, lit them both and handed one over to me. After a moment of contemplation, she left and returned with an industrial size cell phone, flipped up the solid antenna on the side that made it a satellite phone, punched in a number, then handed it to me. Was this the call to the bar?

I tentatively took the phone and listened to the crackling ring. When Francisco answered, I stood abruptly and dropped the cigarette.

"Francisco!" I screamed as Rosa admonished me for dropping the cigarette and bent to retrieve it.

"Alicia?!"

I heard TJ loudly repeat my name in the background and fought tears.

"I'm okay. Can you tell TJ to text my mom that I'm okay? Otherwise she's gonna call the cops. I have no idea where I am. The people who took me think I'm running drugs for a guy I met in Tijuana called El Zorro Blanco. He owns a bar called La Malquerida. My kidnappers want me to tell them all about his operation but I don't know anything."

Rosa pulled the phone away and ended the call.

"Why did you do that?" I don't know if I was referring to her pulling the phone away or letting me make a call in the first place.

She shrugged. "I just wanted to see what you'd say."

"How do you have Francisco's number?"

"It was one of the numbers you called from your work phone."

"Not a work phone, just a new phone," I mumbled, feeling strange about my proof of life moment. Did I say enough? Would it help anything?

"The curator at the gallery is named Rafael. The reason we went to see Lucha Libre was to root for Julio." Truth. She wanted names, and those were the only two I had, so why not use them and play a round of poker?

Rosa raised an eyebrow and after a moment, gave a slow nod of her head before sliding the food toward me. "It's a start."

I think I was in the middle of a strange game of chicken. Deadlocked in the middle actually. I think Rosa was trying to wait me out and hoping I would give her even more information. The kind of information I was sorely lacking.

Of course, there was an underlying fear that soon, some physical threats were going to begin.

But strangely enough, the day passed with a lot of sitting around as the clouds gathered, emptied themselves, and then passed. And then it was dinner time once again. The men reappeared and began to grill meat and heat up food.

After we'd all eaten, with stomachs full, the same loosening that happened the previous evening took over. They told stories among themselves. The bottle of mezcal and cigarettes were brought out and again passed around. One of the men retrieved a guitar and began to gently strum soft notes.

I mean, it turned into a lovely al fresco dining experience. If you overlooked the kidnapping.

"What kind of woman will the cowboy meet?" Rosa asked.

"Someone solid and sure of herself. Sweet, but made of tough stuff." I nodded. That would be a good woman for Cal.

"So she would already live in the West. Understanding what that life was like."

I nodded. "The daughter of a family who owned a respectable business." I glanced at my empty plate. "Maybe a restaurant." Looming fear aside, it was rather nice to have an idea to mull around. "A restaurant Cal would visit when he was in town. So maybe it was a restaurant and a hotel. Then, Cal could stay there as well. That's how they met. And every time he saw her, she always had a ready smile for him." *That sounded good, didn't it?*

"What's her name?" Rosa asked.

I searched the darkening jungle, running a few names by when I settled on one. "Annabelle."

Rosa nodded. "I am beginning to believe you are a writer."

"Then what's it gonna take to make you believe I'm *not* a drug runner."

A grunt was all the reaction that smartass comment got me. So I took another long drag on my cigarette (promising myself I was gonna quit as soon as I got out of this predicament), and stared into the darkness to figure out where this ridiculous story would go.

Cal would hold back a smile as he walked into the hotel dining room. Met by the usual warm murmur of diners, he'd try not to look for her, but couldn't keep from scanning the room. He'd be disappointed when he didn't see her right away. That's when he'd think he should have bathed before he came, but his excitement to see Annabelle would always win over propriety.

"It's your turn," I said after another shot, supplying Rosa with where she left off, "Popocatépetl had left for war. Iztaccíhuatl stayed behind to worry and long for her soon to be husband."

Rosa raised an eyebrow. "Good pronunciation."

"Good story."

"Well, there are always men who are jealous of true love that is as bright as the sun. And the warrior had a rival who was jealous of his bravery, his stature and the fact that he found true love. And this rival also wanted the princess for himself."

"They always do," I muttered.

"The man came to the princess and told her that her true love had fallen in battle, when in reality he hadn't. The princess was so distraught by heartache, she stopped eating and drinking, embracing her despair until she eventually passed away."

"This is very Shakespearean," I commented.

Rosa winked. "They say this story is the Aztec *Romeo and Juliet*."

"So would I be right to assume our boy comes home safe and sound?"

Rosa nodded. "Of course the warrior was victorious in battle, and as he returned, spirits high and celebrations filling the streets, there was only one celebration he wanted to take part in; his marriage. Instead of joy, he was met with the awful news that his bride had died, thinking he himself had fallen in battle."

A phone rang then.

Rosa paled; I swear she paled and the lounging men righted themselves and all began to scramble.

"Tent, now." She pointed me away and one of the men grabbed me by the arm and led me to the tent.

I could hear the hushed, hurried tones echoing through the surrounding foliage as the phone continued its shrill ring. It was all in Spanish, but there was a lot of swift talking and, in my personal alcohol-infused opinion, defensive conversation happening.

Rosa never returned to the tent.

I heard the van start up and leave.

But as the night wore on, it was filled with agitated, arguing hushed voices.

From where I was sitting in the tent, whoever was on that phone had enough power to upset four people just by calling. And the caller was either angry with the lack of information Rosa was getting; or there were bigger fish to fry and I was going to be let go so they could get to work.

(Maybe that wasn't really going to happen, but my fear needed a second option that ended with me being blindfolded and driven the length of thirty-four songs and roughly the same amount of commercials back from whence I came.)

To help settle myself down, I used all my power of focus as Annabelle sidled up to my cot in the darkness and narrated:

She was never sure when Cal would show up, but she knew when she woke up that particular day that she would see him. She glanced around the dining room, taking note of the customers and then she saw him. Their eyes met, her heart quickened and his soft grin, meant only for her, drew her to his side.

'Cal,' she sighed his name.

Her name on his lips was a bare whisper.

She said, 'I don't mean to be improper, but it's loud in here and I would talk with you for a moment? Outside? Is that alright?' Her voice fluctuated with her nerves.

As Annabelle and Cal dissipated, I rolled onto my back and closed my eyes as I admitted, "She needs help. A good cowboy story comes about because a hero involves himself with a woman's business."

Thirty-Five

"Wake up Ali Skye."

I blinked my eyes open, my headache pounding, but this time I'm pretty sure it was only partially due to a few shots; it was more the lack of caffeine and water that was causing it.

"Coffee?" I asked.

"Aspirin?" she offered

"K."

I followed her to the communal tarp-covered area, accepted a cup of coffee and aspirin and thought I was suffering from Stockholm Syndrome as I'd found myself immersed in a very fucked-up version of adult summer camp with cigarettes and alcohol and the ever-present danger that my life was going to end any moment.

"Where is everyone?"

"They had a few errands to run." She waved, then asked, "Who is Yvonne?"

"A dancer at the Fox's club."

"Is she your informant? Is that who you report to?"

"No, she just works there. And when I was being hit on by the Fox he called her over and introduced her because she had the best story in the club."

Rosa sat back and waved her hands. "We can't do another story. We have too many storylines going as it is."

No shit.

Oh, wait a minute ...

"Do you think *she* killed him?"

That was a real possibility, wasn't it? I mean, what if after I got on the bus, the Fox told her she couldn't quit and she couldn't have Tyler. Would she have killed him? Her 'story' involved a death we never really got to the bottom of. Maybe she'd killed before and she was willing to kill again.

"Anything is possible." Rosa verbalized my thoughts then slapped the table. "I need a bath, want one?"

Obviously.

"Yes?"

She stood, opened a plastic storage tote and pulled out two brown towels. She tossed me one and a bar of soap, then gestured for me to follow her.

Where the hell was a shower in this area? Had we been near a house the whole time? Were we only a few hundred feet from some jungle mountain town and there really were homes nearby, but no one ever told the kidnapped victim in case she ran away? And could I run away if I had a chance and there was a house? Or call someone?

Of course, I only had two numbers memorized. My mom's and my ex's.

Unless, before I ran away, I could find that satellite phone first. Francisco had been called from that.

A janky trail, muddy from all the rain, led to a pool of water and a trickling waterfall on the other side.

So ... no hidden houses.

"Beggars can't be choosers," I muttered under my breath. At least the sun was out, it was warmish in the light and the clouds passing by kept enough distance from each other that we'd stay dry for a little while after we bathed.

Rosa took off her clothes, revealing a bikini, then jumped in the pool; leaving me staring wide-eyed at her grace and beauty. *And craziness maybe, I mean, this wasn't a hot spring.*

I stripped to my bra and underwear and slowly tiptoed into the fresh, cold water. It wasn't that bad. It wasn't a mountain lake in the Sierras cold, but it wasn't a heated spring either.

I hissed my way up to my waist, realized I forgot the soap, then started to retrace my steps when a splash of water arced over my head.

I turned and glared at Rosa, but it wasn't like I could yell at her. Although, the grin on her face and the action alone really did solidify the summer camp feel of my situation.

"What does Annabelle want?" she asked, and I frowned; it took me a few seconds to calibrate the situation I was standing in and figure out who the hell Annabelle was.

"Oh. Well," I cleared my throat, "I suppose her father is well to do, so maybe he has a gambling problem?" Wasn't that usually how these things go? "And he hasn't won in a long time and he owes some really shady men a lot of money."

"One of the shady men sees an opportunity to have the woman he longs for," Rosa filled in.

"That would work. Here's the bad guy, using the debt owed him to get the woman. Of course, Annabelle's in love with Cal and doesn't want any part of the arranged marriage."

Rosa tread water, skimming through the shallow pool, and as I began to wash, Cal and Annabelle swam around me.

Cal listened to Annabelle and watched a dream he hadn't known existed, break into a million little pieces as she explained her predicament. He watched the vision of a small house, with her standing on the porch holding his child in her arms, melt away. Maybe it had been a foolish dream all these years. To think that he could find enough money to take her away and build a life with her.

Rosa asked for the soap and stood waist deep in the water. I didn't mean to stare, I just had never seen someone who looked like they belonged in a magazine in real life. "You know you're gorgeous, right? I don't mean to make less of your power or intelligence, but ... why isn't anything sagging on you?"

She laughed and instead of replying to my strange objectification asked, "Do you want to know what happens when the warrior finds his beloved has passed away?"

Of course I did.

I offered what I assumed would be the next beat of such a story. "He's heartbroken, that's for sure. And angry?"

Rosa nodded. "He demanded to see the princess. When he was shown her lifeless body, he took her into his arms and climbed to the top of the highest mountain before he lay her down to rest. He brushed one last kiss on her lips, lit a torch and knelt next to her, silently promising that he would guard her eternal slumber and that they would remain together for all eternity. When winter came, snow cloaked their bodies and they were transformed into two volcanoes, never to be separated."

"His torch still burns for her, when the volcano erupts?" I asked.

Rosa nodded. "This is the legend, that when the warrior is reminded of what he lost and his heart is broken again, his passion and heartache trembles the land, and his torch smokes high into the skies for everyone to see."

As the end of the story floated around us, Rosa took off for another lap around the pool. I nodded and whispered to myself, "Good story."

Rosa called, "When you are back in Mexico City, you should go where you can see Popocatépetl and Iztaccíhuatl. You can see her laying, and her warrior kneeling nearby."

My mouth dried. *When you are back in Mexico City.* The hope in that phrase illuminated every cell in my body.

Bathed.

Hopeful.

We walked slowly back in the direction of the communal tent. *I think.*

"Cal will want to marry her and help," Rosa said.

Since I was feeling slightly better about the fact I might live, I decided to indulge in this strange international story exchange we'd entered into.

"He doesn't have much money to his name. He has nowhere to take her. But he'll try," I stated as I rolled the ideas around. "She'll have hidden a little money, knowing her father's true nature and the men he's been doing business with. He'd agree to help her."

"If he agrees to help her, he would give her his heart as well," Rosa said, "and she would give him hers."

Their money together might be enough, and this opportunity to be with the woman he loved, to be her hero, to make a life with her was right in front of him. So he reached out with both hands and took what he'd always wanted.

"Cal would make arrangements that night, and no one would miss him when he was gone. But Annabelle would be missed."

Rosa patted me on the back. "You're finding your way through the story now."

We tripped out of the undergrowth and trees onto what looked like a well-traveled dirt road, twisty and wide and graded into the side of a mountain.

The low hum of a coming car stopped me.

Rosa grabbed my arm and tried to push me back into the cover of the foliage, but I didn't want to go back. I turned and watched a small red Ford Festiva drive by, windows down, radio up, and as it passed, the driver smiled and waved.

Not the kind of thing you do if you see two women in the middle of nowhere. The kind of thing you do if you are near civilization or you know one of the women.

I pushed Rosa, my thought to run after the man and beg him to drive me away from here as fast as he could.

Rosa tripped when I pushed her and I heard her call out in pain.

But I ran after the car screaming for it to stop.

"Ali, wait!" Rosa's own loud call desperately mixed with the radio and my running and yelling.

There was no way in hell I was going to wait for anything. This was my chance, I was taking it. I had to try and calm myself as I ran. I had to think fast. What could I do if I couldn't get that car to stop? My heart and lungs and fear were all mingling tightly in my throat.

"Ali! It's not real!" Rosa screamed.

The words didn't make sense.

Until she screamed again, "None of this is real!" Her words echoed around us, a flashbang of ridiculous information.

What?

"I'm sorry!" she screeched.

That stopped me and whipped me around as I screamed back at her, "What the fuck are you talking about?!"

"El Zorro ..." she yelled as she stood and began to limp toward me, "he did have a tracker in your phone. But he's the one who made us kidnap you!"

I took a few steps back; what the fuck? This had to be a trick. A ploy to get me to stop.

She tried to quickly limp toward me, her face scrunched in pain as she yelled, "He said to pretend to kidnap you, make you comfortable, but uncomfortable, you know?" She stopped when she was close enough to be heard, leaning heavily on the foot that wasn't hurt. "He said we were supposed to give you an adventure."

"What?!" I screamed incredulously, shaking my head several times to make sense of her words; I took another step back to make sure I stayed out of arm's reach, but within hearing range.

"It's all a lie. It was all ... pretend. I'm sorry." She held out her hands apologetically. "The Fox doesn't give necklaces out to people who work for him. He just gave it to you because it's your birthstone. It really was just a birthday present."

"So it's just a trinket." I couldn't hold on to any functioning thought.

"Oh, no. I was serious, I think that's really about a seven-thousand-dollar necklace."

"What the hell ..." I squeezed my eyes shut and shook my hands as I gave a frustrated gurgle of anger.

Seemingly contrite, she continued, "El Zorro hired us because he said you were looking for an adventure."

I blinked open my eyes. "Yeah, an *adventure*. Like ziplining or ... or having dinner in a cave. Not *THIS*!" I waved my arms around maniacally.

She took a step toward me again, hands out in offering, in an attempt to calm me down. "Ali."

I took another step away from her, and we both screamed this time.

Because you should probably always look where you're going when you're on a mountainside, even if you're scared of what's happening in front of you.

But I *was* able to prove my thesis. You have time to breathe out one really good expletive when you're shocked and not expecting something: "Fuck!"

Thirty-Six

Consciousness brought pain and another headache. The headaches were not as much a surprise anymore. The pain however, was new.

I tried to roll onto my side and force my eyes open; both options drew shooting pain and moans. I thought I could make out hushed tones and swear I could hear TJ, but that couldn't be right. *Could it?* I didn't remember where I was or where I should be.

All the more reason to finally force my eyelids apart.

As my surroundings came into focus, I saw him.

"TJ?" My voice was hoarse and full of phlegm. I started coughing, which caused random pain points to light up throughout my body, resulting in the coughing being mixed with moans as I tried to push myself upright. Then TJ was sitting on the edge of the bed, his hands framing my face.

And while it was good to see him (so, so very good), I needed something to drink, so I started slapping at his hands.

"Get her some water," another familiar voice demanded, and when the face and flowing robes behind it came swirling into view; I looked wide-eyed at TJ as Sister Margaret Mary handed me a glass of water, all but pushing TJ off the bed.

She stood looming over me, arms crossed, and as I took a sip said, "You've gotten yourself into more trouble and are once again in need of my assistance."

I didn't know I was in need of her assistance.

"Good thing your '*husband*' is a clever man."

Another familiar voice pulled my attention. "Husband?" I glanced over the rim of the cup and saw Francisco grinning from where he stood at the foot of the bed. I shrugged in reply, hoping he'd understand the slight motion meant to convey 'we'll talk later' vibes.

Just behind him was Rosa, worrying her hands, frown lines pinching the bridge of her nose together.

I cleared my throat again and shook my head as I tried to make sense of my surroundings.

Was it another dream?

"I've seen this movie too," I muttered.

TJ nodded. "Just *wait* until you hear the latest turn of events."

I pointed at Rosa. "You lied to me."

She tugged on an earring and shook her head before finally finding her voice enough to softly say, "And I'm truly sorry about that."

I frowned at TJ. "Are you really here?"

His voice was deep and low and lovely when he verified, "I'm really here."

"Is this *the* convent?" I scanned the room. Stark, simple, but not the same as before, this felt a bit more hospital-like.

"Different one," TJ answered. "These nuns are allowed to talk."

Sister Margaret Mary ... (Look, I'm hurting and there's so much going on let's just call the swishy woman Sister M, okay? Okay.)

Sister M huffed, "The nuns at my convent took a vow of silence. They are consenting adults. They can talk if they truly want to."

I nodded as the wash of memories from the past few days swirled and tried to plug themselves in chronologically.

"Oh," as I reached out for TJ, he took my hand, "I need a really good sketch of a cowboy."

"Cal?" Rosa asked.

"Who's Cal?" Francisco asked, as he pushed past TJ so he could brush a kiss on my cheek. "We were worried."

"I was worried too ..." I said mindlessly and then sucked in a breath. "TJ, is your head okay?"

TJ gave a dry laugh. "Mine's been fine for a while. How's *your* head, you're the one who fell down a mountain."

"I fell down a mountain." That's right.

"You slipped, really," Rosa muttered.

"Is that better?" I frowned.

She shrugged. "If you'd fallen and tumbled, you would have been more badly hurt."

I let my head drop, it felt so hard to hold it up and make sense of what was happening. I forced it back up into a righted position. "What is going on? Am I really in a convent? If I fell, why aren't we in a hospital? What time is it?"

Rosa started, "El Zorro ..." (Oh yeah, that asshole.) She cleared her throat. "He told us to come here. Not as many questions."

"So, he's not dead."

She shook her head a few times, glancing all around the room until she'd gathered enough courage to look me in the eye and admit, "He isn't dead."

"And you brought me here because the Fox said you should?"

"In a hospital, you might accuse me of kidnapping you before I had a chance to explain ... everything."

"You *did* kidnap me." My raised voice accusation hurt my throat and head.

She shifted from foot to foot, cringing as she did, reminding me about her fall moments before mine. She crossed her arms over her chest and defended, "It was a light kidnapping."

"Rosa, you're not helping," TJ said. I glanced wide-eyed at him; he gave me a smile. "Ali, we'll explain everything."

"Rosa?" It was an accusation of his friendliness when he said her name. "You know her?"

He scrubbed his face with his hands. "I do now."

Francisco laughed. "Ali, we'll explain everything. And it's crazy."

What was I supposed to do with that? I sighed; moaned because I even felt *that* slight expansion in my ribcage. I was aching in places I didn't know existed in my body. "Don't I need a doctor?"

Rosa answered, "You've been seen by the doctors who work here, and they did X-rays."

Okay, that's good. There were doctors nearby.

"You're just banged up," Francisco added.

"Just banged up," I repeated dryly.

"It's like you fell down a mountain." TJ winked as he attempted the joke.

The tears welled up then, from the fear I refused to allow myself to feel over the past few days, and from the pain that came with every slight movement. And because I missed that stupid wink. Because we never got to have a morning after or another night. Which we were on our way to doing, I think. I took a deep breath to give in to being a sobbing mess when Sister M tisked, pulled a Kleenex out of her sleeve, handed it over, then clapped her hands and demanded, "Okay, everyone sit."

Four chairs were pulled around my bed; TJ next to me, Sister M next to him, Francisco and Rosa near the foot.

Rosa spoke up with another attempted apology, "I really am sorry. But it wasn't all bad, was it?"

"I don't know what it was, Rosa." I tried to shake my head, but when that caused tracers, I looked at TJ and asked, "What did the doctors say? What's really wrong with me?"

"You've got some great scratches on your arms and legs," he lightly touched the side of my face, "a bunch of bruises; but nothing is broken or fractured."

"And that's what the X-rays showed?" I narrowed my gaze on his face, ready to read it for any lies.

He nodded. "That's what the X-rays and CT scan showed." Then he took a deep breath, and as he let it rush unhurried out of his lungs, his smile grew and he admitted, "I feel like I haven't been able to do that since I was knocked out."

"Are you okay?" I asked.

"I don't think I've ever been so worried about someone in my life."

I slid my hand into his when my stomach gave a loud gurgle. Sister M stood and picked up the receiver of an old phone hanging on the wall of the room.

"That's different," I whispered to TJ.

"This is more a hospital than a convent; it has unlocked doors, visitors and doctor nuns."

I took a deep breath, causing another shot of pain, but I squeezed TJ's hand because it didn't matter how I was feeling; 'Camp Kidnapped' was over.

"How long have I been here?"

TJ answered, "Fourteen-ish hours. It's about four in the morning."

"So I'm fresh from the fall."

He frowned at my turn of phrase.

"Too soon?" I asked.

"Way too soon."

Sister M took her seat again and a few seconds later a nun carrying a tray of food arrived. She set it across my lap and I gotta admit; applesauce, water, pudding, and soup never looked so good.

"Why did you not tell me upon our first meeting you knew El Zorro Blanco?" Sister M asked.

"I *just* met him at a bar. I'm not running drugs for him," I defended; because the way Rosa had spun the facts, I was still concerned I might be (unknowingly) working for him.

"Of course you aren't." She frowned.

"He tried to hit on me at his bar, I rejected him. He bought me and my friend drinks. That's all. That's everything that happened."

That fact received an indignant eye roll. "Of course he hit on you."

A swallowed laugh from TJ made me frown in question. He gently implored, "Sister?"

She gave a *humph* and pulled herself up. "That idiot, El Zorro Blanco," she snarled the moniker, "is my brother."

My eyes hurt as they tried to bug out of my head. And my neck screamed as I quickly glanced between everyone in the room.

And it hurt my vocal chords when I loudly demanded, "What?!"

"The Fox is Sister M's brother. Not the religious kind, the one in a million coincidence, fraternal brother kind," TJ supplied.

Another neck pain whip of my head. "What?!"

Francisco chuckled. "It's quite the story."

"It's true." Sister M sighed heavily.

"Holy ..." I swallowed the rest of that sentiment.

"I'm not really sure how to start this part of the story," TJ said.

I was having trouble pulling back from the most recent fact shared, so it took me a moment to explain where I thought he should start. "You woke up with a big bump on your head ..." I offered as I picked up the bowl of soup (tried to ignore that even that brought muscle pain), held it close to my mouth, and with eyes focused on TJ, began to eat.

"Those guys jumped out of the van and I didn't even have a chance to fight for you before I was hit on the head."

Thirty-Seven

TJ cleared his throat a few times. "When I woke up, I was laying on the side of the road, and paramedics were just starting to transfer me onto a stretcher, asking me questions while shining a light in my eyes. The headache was instant. My awful Spanish was limited to art, not medical emergencies, and it took me several belligerent moments to figure out what to do because the image of you being ripped away from me was still so vivid."

My throat began to constrict with the feelings I'd developed for TJ, for the danger we'd been in (fictional or not) and because, other than my parents, I'm not sure anyone else had ever 'worried' about me.

"You have been given a shot for pain," Sister M interjected. "In case you're wondering about feeling some above average emotional responses."

I blinked back the building tears and out of the corner of my mouth mumbled, "Thanks for explaining that." The woman had a way about her, that's for sure.

She waved for TJ to continue.

"They calmed me down, I called Francisco and put him on speaker as I explained what had happened and he helped me translate. He arrived just as I was released from the hospital, and took me back to his parents' house." TJ shook his head. "Your friend has some very interesting friends and family members. I walked in the door and his mom shoved a plate of food at me, then sat me down at the table where there were about six other people, each one on their phone."

Francisco grinned. "I have friends who are part of an intelligence agency in town."

"You have friends in intelligence ...?" *Sure, why not?*

TJ continued, "First they tried to track the van that was used in your..." He cleared his throat, trying to soften the wording but Francisco railroaded him by supplying, "Abduction."

TJ nodded. "Yeah, so they hacked into a few surveillance cameras and were able to follow the van, but only for a short distance."

"Francisco, you have friends who can hack into surveillance cameras?"

"Ali," Francisco chided, "if you keep interrupting, we are never going to get through this story."

"Okay, but we need to keep in touch better."

"Okay," he repeated and took up the story. "The problem was that east of Teotihuacán—"

TJ and I both parroted the word after he said it, "Teotihuacán," then grinned at each other.

"Yes, east of there, cameras are limited and the van that was being used was stolen, so the trail went cold very quickly."

I glanced at Rosa as she sighed, "I apologized."

I pointed my spoon at her. "Oh, we'll get around to you."

"We didn't have anything to go on until you called us and gave us a name," TJ said.

"It was easy to find El Zorro's bar, but more difficult to find the actual man," Francisco added.

"But lucky for us," TJ went on, "*another* friend of Francisco's had a plane, so he took us to Tijuana."

"You went to Tijuana?" I asked.

"That was the lead we had." Francisco shrugged and TJ grinned as he said, "And that's how we met Tyler Stone."

"You met Tyler Stone ..."

"Yup, he and his *wife* are the new owners of La Malquerida."

"What the fu ..." I remembered Sister M who raised an eyebrow and corrected, "heck?"

She rolled her eyes.

"He looked like that actor from that movie," Francisco informed me. I frowned at TJ for an interpretation.

"Wild patterned shirt unbuttoned too much, a shell necklace, aviator sunglasses pushed on his forehead and a sunburn."

I still didn't know what movie that might be but I could only imagine. "Jesus, Tyler." I sighed. "Sorry, Sister."

Francisco continued, "My favorite part was when he thought TJ and I were the police. He freaked out and said, "'I didn't shoot her, I didn't have the gun, you've got the tapes.'" Both Francisco and TJ chuckled.

"So we settled him down," TJ said, "told him about you and that you'd been kidnapped and that we needed to talk to the Fox guy; but that's when we found out it was a difficult task because—"

"He really is dead?" I sucked in a breath. "No, wait. Rosa said he was alive."

TJ nodded. "Yup, he's really alive but was on his yacht off the Florida coast, having left no way to get in touch with him. So Tyler tells us this story about how he met his wife, and the Fox paid for the wedding and set them up in a condo and is turning a few of his holdings over to Yvonne."

"Yvonne." I just stared at TJ. We still hadn't gotten to the part where the Fox turns out to be Sister M's brother, and my headache was having a difficult time keeping up with all this.

"So we finally tell him that you've been kidnapped and about the call you made. He got his wife and told her the story, and she started making phone calls. Turns out, this isn't the first time the Fox has tried to 'help' someone like this."

"He's had other people kidnapped?"

"No ..." Rosa said, but didn't continue.

Francisco sat forward. "El Zorro Blanco is a chameleon. He is a paragon for his people."

TJ interjected, "A lot of people think of him as a sort of, modern-day Robin Hood ... mercenary."

Sister M scoffed, "A mercenary doesn't care which side he fights for. Robin Hood was a martyr for the people."

"Depends on who he's helping, Sister," Francisco replied. "Some see his actions as those of a mercenary, those he helps see him another way."

I finished the soup and moved on to the applesauce. "Who did Yvonne call? I thought you said the Fox was on vacation."

"She called ...." TJ gesture to his right.

"Me," Sister M sighed, "I have a way to reach my brother when it's important."

Francisco smiled. "And it was pretty important."

"Yvonne explained that she had gotten in touch with the Fox's sister who was going to call him and have him call us at the bar," TJ said.

"It took a few hours but then the Fox called Yvonne and told her everything had been taken care of."

I glanced at Rosa and she admitted, "That was the phone call we got. I was going to tell you, I swear. He said everything went further than anticipated. You were supposed to be alone. No one was supposed to hurt anyone. And he just wanted to help ... jump-start your ..." her voice faded before she muttered the word "creativity."

"That idiot," Sister M supplied.

"No shit," I agreed then followed with an apology that she waved away this time.

"The plan was to tell you the truth and drive you back to Mexico City," Francisco stated.

"Tyler promised you were safe and would continue to be safe," TJ said. "So he put us up for the night in a hotel."

"I bet I know which one," I mumbled under my breath but when TJ raised his eyebrows in question, I shook it off. "It's not important."

Rosa started again, "The problem was that we'd been a little too convincing."

"Where were we?" I don't know why it mattered, sure my broad sense of place regarding Mexico had gotten better, but I wasn't fluent in the geography of the land.

An unexpected laugh escaped Rosa, and after that she couldn't hold back; it took her several tries before she was finally able to say, "We were renting a glamping site."

I blinked. A hundred times as I soaked up this new layer of information.

"That wasn't glamping."

"We made some adjustments." She dissolved once again.

And everyone else followed suit.

"I'm sorry," TJ offered, trying to stop. Sister M hid her mouth behind her hand, Francisco slapped Rosa on the back.

It hurt too much for me to laugh, and there were parts of this 'adventure' I was still trying to figure out.

"So you were going to tell me; when exactly?"

"After our swim. I thought you'd be refreshed and it was beautiful at the pool and I was going to tell you when we got back to the campsite. I sent the boys to get you a change of clothes and gas up the van ..."

"But then I fell."

I almost couldn't make out her softly whispered, "Slid."

That put a damper on the laughter.

TJ picked up the story again. "We were headed to the airport when Tyler called us and told us you'd been in an accident. That you were being taken to a special hospital that was run by the Sisters of Mercy."

"Déjà vu?" I asked.

He nodded. "I still didn't know about Sister Margaret Mary, though. Just that the Fox's sister had gotten in touch with him."

Francisco leaned forward. "So we changed our flight plan and came directly here."

Sister M went on, "Yvonne called me and told me what happened. That my ridiculous brother had tried to help and it backfired. I felt responsible, because I am the eldest and feel the need to fix my family's mistakes." She pursed her lips as if this was something she would have to think on more later, or get therapy for. "She did tell me the young woman's friend and boyfriend were headed to the hospital as well. I drove here to see if there was any way I could help. So you can imagine my surprise when I arrived and came face to face with TJ and then saw you with my own eyes."

I slowly shook my head in wonder, "Sister ... there are millions of people—"

"The Lord works in mysterious ways," she excused with a wave of her hand.

We all fell silent as the story floated around us. "Rosa," I asked, "who are you?"

She shifted her gaze around the room and swallowed while she gathered her courage. "I really do design jewelry and fabric, but I'm an actress."

It was my turn to start laughing.

Uproariously.

Moaning with the pain.

Sister M stood up. "Okay, I'll show everyone to their rooms. It's been a long day. Later this morning we'll have breakfast, finish answering all the unanswered questions and then I will, once again, send you on your way."

I put the last empty bowl down and Sister M picked up the tray, pausing to allow her gaze to take me in. Satisfied with whatever she was looking for, she gave a nod and turned, instructing everyone else to "Come along."

Francisco kissed me on the cheek, Rosa offered another apology, then they both left.

I looked at TJ. Just the two of us. The tears finally fell then.

He moved to the edge of the bed, pulled me into his arms, and I didn't care how much it hurt, I needed to be held.

"I need to talk to the Fox," I whispered into his neck.

"Okay."

"I think I need reparations." I cried and laughed and melted into TJ and the safety of his arms.

Thirty-Eight

A trip to the restroom helped boost my confidence that no one was lying about my current state. I was a mess of sore muscles and bruises and it was exhausting just walking the short distance. It felt like I'd just finished an introductory bootcamp training session that some misguided friend took me to once the day after New Year's. (Needless to say, I never took the company up on their ninety percent off New Year's introductory rate.) So even though I was that sore, I was able to move. And being able to walk myself down the hallway went a long way in centering me.

Not that there'd been a lot of 'centering' since I'd run away from a Southern California restaurant.

But the whole point of the moment was that I was willing to believe everyone when they said I'd be okay.

(Okay or not, I was once again parading through nunnery halls in a handsome night dress.)

TJ helped me get organized sitting once more and this time, he sat next to me on the bed and handed me my cell phone. "I texted your mom."

I read the bland back and forth. *Just checking in. All is okay.*

To which she wrote: *Thank you. I love you. Have fun. Send more pictures.*

"That's a relief."

He picked up the sketchbook sitting near him on the bedside table. "As much as I hate lying to your mom and having that be my first interaction with her, even though she didn't know it, I figured I'd give our current situation forty-eight hours before I called and told her the truth."

"Thank you."

He began to turn through the pages; I watched as pages filled with pencil and ink became a flip-book diary of TJs life. "Ah," he stopped and tilted the page toward me, "is this your cowboy?"

It was Cal, sitting atop his horse, overlooking the prairie at sunset, with the form and function of TJ's art. The sketch might be done in gray pencil, but color filled my sight.

"That's him," I whispered and tentatively touched the page. "It's perfect."

"Why a cowboy?"

"I may have found a story while I was glampingly kidnapped."

"Did you?" He smiled.

I yawned. "Of all the things, a damn cowboy ... and I don't really care for westerns, and it's never crossed my mind to write one." But I *didn't* write any of it. I cleared my throat and said, "I found some words, TJ."

He elbowed me—a familiar, loving, weird amalgamation of our entire relationship to this point.

"Are you going to tell me the story?" he asked just as I said, "We never had a chance to have the morning-after talk."

We answered each other. "I'll tell you the story when my throat stops hurting and my headache goes away," I said, as TJ asked, "Do you want to have the morning-after talk right now?"

It was my turn to elbow him. We'd talk later.

He held out the sketch for us to study once more then turned to an empty page and picked up a pencil he'd put on the nightstand.

I rested my head on his shoulder and watched as his sketch of the table and chair from across the room formed. Such a normal thing to do. Such normal objects to sketch. So comforting.

No Adherance to Silence Here #15.

I giggled and TJ asked what was funny. I told him what I named the sketch, which rewarded me an eye roll and the comment, "Writers."

The sound of his pencil against paper steadily became a form of white noise. My eyes grew heavy and I lay down on my side, put to sleep by TJ's even breathing and pencil scratches.

Thirty-Nine

I woke up with a start. Alone. Facing the bedside table. The lamp was on and propped up by a glass of water was TJ's sketch, which he'd ripped out and left.

Good ol' Cal Hand, maybe he wasn't looking over his cattle astride his horse this time. This time he was watching to see if someone was going to be following them.

Annabelle's father would wait a few days, out of fear and uncertainty; or maybe to give his daughter a fighting chance at happiness.

But in most stories, when an evil man is promised a pretty bride, he's not going to look so 'kindly' on the circumstances if someone else takes her. He'd receive the news about her running off and there would be no distressed speeches or emotion. He'd just gather up a few men and tell them they were going for a ride.

A man like that would be named Daniel, after my ex, with some long, highbrow last name.

(Talk about woman scorned and the power a writer could wield.) I smiled as I wiggled into an awkward sitting position just as a phantom floated into my doorway.

"Let me help you."

"You move like a ghost," I told Sister M, "like a regal ghost."

She grunted at the comment and strong-armed me into an upright position, handed me the glass of water and scowled down at me for a moment before pulling up a chair to the side of the bed.

"How are you?" she asked.

"Not as bad as I thought I was," I admitted.

"You're young and in good shape, that helps when you take a fall like that."

"The story is still ridiculous."

She frowned. "Of course it is. My brother is ridiculous." She mocked, "'I am a man who can get anyone anything.'" She snarled, "El Zorro Blanco. Such a ridiculous name. And one we gave him, by the way. Did he tell you how he got the white stripe in his hair?" She didn't give me time to respond. "When he was a kid, he sun-bleached it with lemon juice and told everyone he'd faced down death himself, leaving him with the streak." She scoffed but there was a hint of pride under it. "He's kept up the ruse his whole life, only now I suppose he pays someone to color it."

"He said he doesn't talk to any of his family anymore."

She raised an eyebrow, as if she couldn't believe after all this I was still buying his stories. "We have a family reunion every other year in Miami. *He* is the one who organizes the whole thing."

I shook my head in wonder. "You and your brother definitely went in two different life directions."

"We did. That we did." She waved a hand. "Which direction are you headed?"

"Me?"

"I know enough about human nature to know that you are searching for something. Have you found a direction yet?"

Now that was a question.

I took my time putting the glass back in an attempt to put the answer off as long as I could. Which wasn't very long because the distance was short. And it wasn't like I was going to find something I'd been searching for over the past few years in the slight distance and time Sister M allowed.

As I righted myself I thought about 'accidentally' rolling off the bed to get out of this existential conversation, but that was ridiculous.

So I went with the truth, "I haven't found anything yet. I'm not sure about anything lately ..."

"Purpose is an interesting thing, isn't it. We think it will be a large thunderclap and sometimes, it is just a quiet breeze."

"Well, I'd love even a quiet breeze at this point, but this ship I've been on has been in the middle of the ocean for a very long time without a hint of one."

She gave a *humph.* "That's just life. Some days are good, some are bad. Some months and years are seamless, some are difficult. You have good friends, a new relationship that seems to be quite interesting, and you are talented."

I raised an eyebrow in question at that comment.

"We have internet at the convent," she raised an eyebrow, "I checked up on you and TJ Jones. *Not* husband and wife, by the way. But two very talented artists."

"Thank you." I sighed. "You know what I really want, Sister? I'd like a huge, bright neon sign with an arrow that is so big I can't miss the obvious 'go this way!' message, with a description of what my purpose is below the destination."

"Well, as you know, it doesn't work that way." The good nun's edges softened. "But that also isn't very fun."

I gave a slow nod; sure, but some days it would be really helpful.

Sister M continued, "If we had all the answers and never had to struggle or face our fears and find out what we're made of, then when we reach where we *are* going, it wouldn't mean anything."

"You are the epitome of the sage nun."

"I have a lot of time to think where I live. And not a lot of conversation, so I find myself doing plenty of journaling and I've figured out a few things over the years."

"So, it sounds like what you are saying is that the journey is the most important part."

She grinned. "That's what Homer would have us believe."

"What does the Bible say?"

Her grin grew. "To have *faith* in the journey."

I took a deep breath and let it out slowly, "Well then, it would seem that since I am lost and still searching, I can't go home just yet."

"Can't you?"

"You know, your brother asked me what I wanted. My instant answer was adventure ..."

She gave an exaggerated eye roll.

I nodded in agreement. "He obviously didn't quite understand that part. But I told him what I probably *should* want is stability. Then he said I should go have an adventure, that stability will come later."

"My brother will always be on the side of the irresponsible."

"I don't know ..." I thought for a moment. "Look, I'm in no way defending what he does or how he goes about it. But he seems to be taking care of people too, and someone irresponsible wouldn't care about a stranger's worries."

Frown lines were deepening as her eyes narrowed, so I stepped away from any defense of El Zorro Blanco. "What I'm trying to say, I think, is that when it comes to advice, you're both pretty similar. The execution, however, is worlds apart ..."

"So, what will you do?" She turned the conversation away from her brother.

"I feel like I need to keep moving forward. To see what happens."

She nodded. "And with my brother out of your affairs, it should be a little more docile."

Docile. Even without the minor setback of an adventurous kidnapping, a docile trip was open to interpretation.

"What's his real name? Your brother?"

She raised an eyebrow at the question, her smile growing, "Alejandro."

I nodded.

"Did you know that in the stories written of the Zorro you've probably heard of, that character's real name is Alejandro?"

"This just keeps getting better and better."

She chuckled. "Did you know the name Alejandro means 'defender of man'?"

"Of course it does." I laughed, which caused another round of moaning. Bells rang the hour and I asked, "What time is it?"

"Seven. In the morning. If you'd like, you could meet your friends in the common area, they will be serving breakfast now."

I nodded and began to move, but it still hurt like hell. Sister M helped me into a standing position, tucked my arm in hers and slowly led me in the direction of a common nunnery room.

"Do they still refer to convents as nunneries?"

"Miss Skye, do you know what Shakespeare meant when he said, 'get thee to a nunnery'?"

My college English class came slamming into me like an unseen wave. The nunnery of the Dark Ages was a brothel. "Oh, Sister. I didn't mean—"

Her laughter interrupted me, and I glanced sideways to find a cheeky smile in place. "I'm not a completely dull person." She gently patted my arm. "I think these days, nunnery is used in a mocking way. People mostly say convent now."

"You know, certain things have a way of twisting with the passage of time; if Shakespeare were alive today, I feel like he'd use 'get thee to a nunnery' as an insistence that the character needed to put down all technical devices and go be quiet for a while."

"Well then, Ali Skye, it seems that it was quite time for you to have gotten yourself into a nunnery."

(I mean, she wasn't wrong.)

"Do you know where my clothes are?"

"They are pretty much ruined, but I could find them if you'd like," she offered.

"I had the rosary you gave me in my pocket. I'd like it back," I admitted.

She squeezed my arm. "I'll find it."

We turned a corner, where a desk with a nurse in scrubs smiled up at us. The long hallway had a few closed doors and those opened had hospital beds and patients sleeping, some hooked up to IVs and a few with beeping monitors.

"It really is a hospital."

"Why would we lie?"

"Why wasn't I in one of these rooms?" I asked. "Not that I'm not grateful."

She cleared her throat, and with the no-nonsense attitude she gave during our first meeting, said, "I wanted you closer to my room just in case there was anything I could do for you. I feel responsible for you."

"Oh." I squeezed her arm, because I didn't know what to say.

Down another hallway and after another turn, I told her, "Your brother absolved me of my sins from the past twenty-nine years."

"Now you're just trying to get a rise out of me." She grunted then scoffed, "I'm assuming the idiot did it with a shot of Tequila."

I nodded.

"Idiot," she repeated.

Forty

A large room, with different size tables spread out, all covered with light blue tablecloths, a wall of windows on one side, and a cafeteria buffet on the other, was a welcome vision.

There were a few people eating already. I noticed three women in scrubs, with stethoscopes around their necks, and another table of women who might be nuns. Then there was a table that looked so *very* good. TJ and Francisco were sitting across from each other, lounging with cups of coffee in hand. Beside Francisco, Rosa sat over her cup, attention on the contents, holding it with both hands and a frown in place. (Okay, *she* didn't look so good.)

"Buenos días," Sister M called, capturing their attention.

TJ smiled up at us, standing to help me into the chair next to his.

"I have work to attend to. Have a good breakfast. The doctor would like to see Ali in an hour. I believe she can be released this afternoon."

"I can?" She hadn't mentioned that.

Sister M nodded. "I said you're young and healthy, just a little bruised and banged up from the fall. You'll get through this."

It was a good thing I was sitting down, as I was hit with yet another offhand comment that landed so powerfully in its metaphoric mastery.

"What would you like to eat?" TJ asked.

I watched Sister M's retreating form, and it wasn't until she swished her way around the corner, that I was able to focus on what TJ had asked. But instead of answering him, I said, "I think she practices that."

"Who practices what?" Francisco asked.

I adjusted myself in the chair and told TJ, "Eggs and coffee. If they don't have any of that, whatever you think sounds good."

He winked. (Of course.)

I took a deep breath and sat forward, figuring since I'd been seated across from Rosa, it was time to finish this piece of the current storyline. I narrowed my gaze until she met my eyes. "Enough. Stop feeling bad," I demanded. She visibly swallowed, and I thought her eyes grew glassy. "I'm okay. You're okay. Everything's okay."

"Can you forgive me?" she asked.

"I think so."

"You think so?"

I slid my hands across the table, then took her coffee cup. "If you give me your coffee right now."

Rosa relinquished her hold and I took a sip of the warm, life-giving substance, then nodded. "All is forgiven."

She actually looked as if the weight of the world had slipped off her entire being. Francisco slapped her on the back, happily declaring, "See? I told you everything would be okay." Then he turned his attention to me. "Did you know, my friend Carlos' girlfriend's cousin is Rosa's hairdresser?"

"It's a small world, isn't it Francisco?" I replied.

Rosa reached into her pocket and pulled out the fire opal necklace. "They took it off to do your exams." She limped over and put it on. I nodded my thanks as I touched it and chuckled.

"The Fox said this would bring me good fortune. I suppose the fact that I'm still in one piece means it's working."

TJ returned with breakfast; chilaquiles—deep-fried corn tortillas soaked in a red sauce, then topped with cream, onion, cheese, two fried eggs, avocado, cilantro and slices of radish. Not to mention another hot cup of coffee and a pastry.

Rosa and Francisco went to get their own food but I wasn't going to wait for them.

"Oh my GOD," I moaned, unaware the sound would echo and draw one or two disapproving gazes my way.

With a full mouth I muttered, "Really, it's not a name taken in vain, if anything I'm kinda giving thanks."

TJ leaned over, and with his mouth very close to my ear, his breath sending shivers down the side of my body, said, "I recall a night, not too long ago, when we both gave *a lot* of thanks."

He pulled away slightly, so I could glance sideways to get a better look at him; his provocative grin and those brown eyes that were always looking at angles and light and the world a little differently. Eyes that I'd missed.

"It's nice to be able to flirt now that I know you're okay."

I had a few lines that came to mind; one to heat up the moment, one to knock it down, and even one to keep him on his toes. In the end, I just leaned forward, brushed a kiss on his lips, then went back to my breakfast.

"Why did the nun call TJ your husband?" Francisco asked as he sat down with a tray of food.

"We lied to her when we first met her so we wouldn't be separated," TJ explained.

"Really? She does not seem like the kind of woman you should lie to." He shook his head as he filled his fork.

"How did you get to me? After I *slipped* down the mountain?" I asked Rosa.

"The road winds back and forth, you were polite enough to stop your fall just off the road, about a hundred meters down."

I nodded. "I am ignorant enough to not do well with the metric system, and in this case, I don't think I want to know how far that is."

Rosa continued, "We got you in the van, then called Yvonne. She told us to bring you here and that she'd inform everyone else."

We fell silent as we ate and I accidentally dropped my fork with a disturbing clatter against my plate. "Even lifting the fork to my mouth hurts," I apologized as I placed the offensive tool to the side and sat back.

"Do you need help?" TJ asked.

I waved him off. "No, I'm full."

"Then maybe you could continue your little story," Rosa said.

I shook my head while Francisco asked, "What story?"

"Rosa told me the story of the star-crossed lovers forever immortalized in the volcanoes," I quickly announced, hoping it would push everyone off the scent of my story.

"And Ali told me a cowboy story," Rosa snitched.

Francisco looked at TJ. "Did she ever tell you I translated several of her short stories for a local literary magazine in Mexico City?" he asked.

TJ shook his head as I gave the excuse, "*That* was a long time ago."

"So, will you tell me what happens next?" Rosa asked.

"I think I'm still hungover and my throat is raw from all the smoking you made me do." Which I needed to stop because I'm pretty sure I was one more pack away from a total relapse.

"No one forced you to smoke and drink," she mumbled.

I was incredulous, defending, "I was attempting to soothe myself with what was on hand during a difficult situation." My voice raised slightly and when several throats surrounding us cleared themselves to quiet me, I waved. "Lo siento, lo siento."

"I'll tell it then," Rosa offered, as if I'd be offended. I wasn't and gestured with my hand for her to 'please, be my guest.' As I sipped my coffee, Rosa's voice—smooth like silk with just the right depth and a fabulous twirl of an accent—lulled us all into different states of contemplation. I stared into the distance, not seeing what was there, but rather something else I hadn't seen in a long time. A little hope.

When she stopped, I felt like I'd come out of a trance. "You have a voice for telling stories."

"That's why I'm an actress," she said. "So what happens next?"

"I don't know," was my excuse to not pick up the narrative.

"That's a lie." Francisco pointed his fork at me. "We don't see each other a lot, but I remember how you lie."

I snorted and shrugged. "Fine. I was thinking Cal would try to put as much distance, and possibly weather, between himself and what was coming. He'd push the limits of his horses as well as himself and Annabelle. But she wouldn't ever complain. And at night, when Annabelle fell asleep from exhaustion, Cal would worry about who was coming and the future he held within his grasp."

"You don't think they would be able to get away?" Francisco asked.

I shrugged. "This is the tension. The part that ruins perfectly good love stories. The bad guy never really cares about love. He likes making people pay when they take what he thinks belongs to him."

Francisco grunted, knowing that was usually the truth.

"They could still get married," Rosa offered.

"They could," I pondered, "but before that, there would be quiet, lovely declarations in the middle of the cool evenings as they lay across from each other, the flames of the fire the only thing between them."

"Fine," Rosa sighed.

"What?" I asked.

"When two lovers have nights of low conversations and declarations of love, it means things are never going to end well," Rosa surmised.

"A good cowboy story ends with the man riding off into the sunset alone on his horse." I yawned, bringing a close to the day's story time.

And bringing a close to the visit with Rosa and Francisco, who both declared they needed to get back to their lives.

Francisco tackled me and TJ with bear hugs and back slaps and made us promise to at least text once a day so he knew we were okay.

"I'll add you to the list," I told him.

Rosa gave me her phone number and said if we needed anything, we should call. "And if you ever finish that story, even a little bit ... Maybe you could email it to me."

I was back in the room near Sister M's, TJ sitting with his legs propped up on a chair sketching. I watched his steady movements as my eyelids grew heavy with sleep once again. Now that I knew we were going to move forward, that this adventure wasn't finished and TJ was with me, I gave over to letting my body do what it needed to do the most to heal, and slept.

Forty-One

"We will not miss you." Sister M raised her head so she could look down her nose at us as she made the declaration.

This is the goodbye we're given at the front entrance of the hospital-convent complex. And because we're in the middle of an actual city, an Uber was easy to arrange. Granted, the whole thing was being funded by El Zorro Blanco.

The doctor did not release me yesterday. So I had time to call the Fox and tell him he was not to insert himself into women having pre-midlife crises ever again. He apologized profusely and I asked him for a ride to the Yucatán Peninsula and for him to put me up in a hotel that had a beach but wasn't too far from Chichén Itzá. TJ and I wanted to see the Mayan ruins now.

The Fox readily agreed and a few hours later, when TJ and I had sat down to have dinner in the communal area, a bouquet of flowers and a bottle of champagne were delivered, along with an intense ticket situation. Apparently, an Uber would pick us up in the morning and take us to a helicopter, that would take us to a private jet, that would take us to Mérida, Yucatán where another driver would be waiting to take us to 'Robbie's' for a few nights.

I showed the itinerary to Sister M, who read through it, bristled, but confirmed, "There is no ill will at work here. Take him up on the offer. And I will make sure you have plenty of Acetaminophen and aloe vera to help the bruises heal faster."

TJ and I had another sappy conversation about how we wanted to continue to travel together and worked ourselves up into a lovely, uncomfortable, make out session that was interrupted by Sister M walking by the room and clearing her throat, *comically*-loud. But the pain I was still in and her subtle 'stop it' did douse the flames.

Which brings us up to date. This moment: Sister M, hiding her feelings behind the lie that she wouldn't miss us.

"I don't like all the talking." She cocked an eyebrow at me and my throat began to ache, I was going to miss her too.

"We appreciate everything you've done for us," TJ said.

"Yes. *Everything*," I added.

She scrunched her nose as she scanned the length of me; gone was the handsome night dress, long gone were my original 'new' clothes I'd been wearing when I was 'kidnapped.' I did get the rosary back however. TJ had a few of his belongings, but Francisco was mailing the rest of our things to 'Robbie's' in the Yucatán. (I was making the Fox flip the bill for that too.)

Today I was fashionably dressed in items of clothing retrieved from the lost and found: Hello Kitty flip-flops (adult size), a black and white checkered skirt (knee-length), an orange tank top (with the Denver Broncos logo), and a butter yellow button-down sweater (that smelled of men's aftershave and tobacco), just in case I got cold.

I pulled at the arms of the sweater tied around my waist and shrugged. "I'll go clothes shopping on your brother's dime when we get to our final destination." I had visions of a bathing suit with a matching cover-up and bright T-shirts with sayings about the beach and Tequila.

"That sounds like a good idea."

TJ pulled out a paper from his sketchbook, something he'd shown me earlier, and I was excited to watch the exchange when he handed the page to Sister M. She frowned as she accepted it, then whispered, "Oh ... my." Her eyes blinked in disbelief at the sketch; TJ had drawn her standing in the courtyard of the silent convent, a contemplative, peaceful look on her face.

She touched the edge of the sketch and once again whispered, "Oh my."

TJ nodded. "You are a wonder."

She still hadn't been able to take her eyes off the page, so silently told it, "You know, vanity is a sin."

"So is wasting one's God-given talent," TJ argued.

"True," her smile grew, "true." She cleared her throat. "I did see online that your works sell for impressive prices. Maybe I'll just hold onto it. If we ever fall on hard times, who knows, perhaps we can sell it."

"If it helps, you should," TJ agreed.

She cleared her throat again and I thought she might be fighting back a few tears. She looked down at the picture again and shook her head. I knew how she was feeling. When you saw a picture of yourself sketched by TJ, it was as if you were looking at your soul on display. It was a giddy and terrifying experience balled together. Granted, to date, I'd only seen my hands sketched, but to date, that was quite enough.

"Listen my wildlings ..." she took a deep breath and shook her head, "I don't know what advice to give you. Other than keep safe so that I don't see you again."

"We'll try." I actually meant it.

She opened the back door of the waiting Uber, then hugged us before pushing us in. After closing the door, I watched her mouth move in what I suspected was a silent prayer.

The driver looked at us expectantly; were we ready?

I held up my hand. "Un momento, por favor." I turned and watched Sister M, quietly telling TJ, "I just want to watch her—" and she made a grand sweep of her skirt as she walked through the front door of the hospital.

I sat back in the seat with a grin and nodded. "Now we can go."

Forty-Two

We tripped out of the last taxi ride after a whirlwind of scenery: jungle green, vibrant cityscapes; and first-class treatment: 'Would el señor y la señora care for some refreshments, breakfast, lunch, coffee, a drink, a hot towel or a shower?' (I'm not kidding, the private plane we took had a shower and a small bedroom. But I didn't use it. Typical, here I was amidst first class treatment that I would probably never experience again and I was so sore, all I could do was shift from side to side, give grimacing smiles and pop another Acetaminophen in the hopes it would kick in any second. I did take the flight attendant up on a glass of champagne halfway through our flight. I would try *anything* to ease any muscle or joint of my body.)

We arrived in Mérida in the late afternoon, and the driver taking us to our final destination glanced at me nervously throughout the first twenty minutes of the hour-long ride.

My face, with a large bruise on my cheek and several abrasions that were scabbed over, had been declared by the doctor to be 'healing quite nicely.'

I sat forward. "Lo siento, pero ¿hablas inglés?"

The man nodded. "Un poco."

"I look like this," I gestured to my face, "because ... estoy practicando to be a luchadora. A female wrestler."

As he gazed back at me in the rearview mirror, his frown broke and he started to laugh.

"No creo que seas muy buena," he said, "I think you are no good."

I sat back, glad I could help him feel more comfortable. His worry dissipated and he turned up the radio and offered us water bottles.

(Okay, so look, 'Robbie's' isn't someone's rundown house in the middle of nowhere. Turns out, 'Robbie's' is a resort.)

Wondering who Robbie was exactly was a thought that dissipated as the driver pulled through a gate and up a long drive surrounded by lush shrubs and trees that led to the front of an impressive reception building hidden among the vegetation.

He gave a low impressed whistle as TJ and I became two stereotypical cartoon orphans from the '30s who'd never seen such elegance in our lives: pressing our faces to the window of the car as if that would help us get a better view.

A woman dressed in a simple skirt and white shirt was waiting for us.

We thanked the driver, tried to tip him but he waved us away saying, "Already paid."

"Ali Skye and Theodore Jones?" The woman pulled our attention. We nodded, but I was unable to focus on her; being surrounded by so many palm trees and other manicured jungle greenery. The pathways leading in several different directions from where we stood were perfectly made circles of grass among white sand.

"Welcome to Playa de Sueños." She smiled.

"Beach of Dreams." TJ whispered the translation to himself.

"If you'll follow me."

We followed one of the magical paths tucked among the beautifully groomed landscape, passing arrowed signage every now and then that pointed out the beach and various named places.

"You will be in La Villa del Sol for three days and two nights."

We followed a turn in the path that brought us to a sign that read 'del Sol' where a small detached room lay before us; a modern, square façade of off-white concrete with dark wood doors and detailing. She opened the double doors with a flourish and stood aside.

Presented was a living room with modern amenities, clean and elegant. Behind the living room, large sliding doors had been left open so we had a perfect view of the early sunset colors against the covered patio with a table that had been set with glasses, a bowl of fruit and some sort of iced bottle. Beyond that was the pool, half the size of a normal pool, but still.

"The pool ..." I choked out.

"It is your private pool. This villa is very private and you will have no visitors or anyone who can see you." I think that was her way of saying skinny-dip to your heart's content.

But beyond the pool was a path with hedges on either side, that led to the beach and softly breaking waves.

"The beach area is also your own, no one is allowed access."

TJ had taken a step further into the front room and as I joined him, he blindly reached for my hand to tug my attention to the right where large double doors were open on a giant bed. One that looked soft and downy and plush.

I let my gaze wander over to the left where another set of doors were open revealing more foliage and a hammock hanging on a side patio. This too, secluded and private.

"The bar is complimentary," the woman continued as she walked into the room and pointed out a bar with three short shelves, backlit and full. "The fridge contains a wide array of non-alcoholic beverages and water." She opened and closed the fridge next to the bar.

"Dinner can be brought to the villa; we have a full kitchen staff on hand and the menu can be found on the desk next to the phone. We also have a dining room. And if you would rather dine in town, I can assist you in reservations and arranging transportation."

Numbly, we nodded. I had never been faced with such extravagance before and I'm not sure I was built for it. I mean, *we are*, we all deserve it. But in my experience, I haven't had a massage to date that wasn't gifted to me. As most of my money was spent on luxuries like water, power, food, a phone and internet. Sometimes getting nails done and a cheap haircut. But this ...

Well ...

"It was worth being kidnapped."

TJ coughed to hide his laugh but whispered, "Too soon."

"Is there anything else I can help you with?" our assistant asked.

We gave more wordless shakes of our heads. She nodded with a smile, as if she was quite used to this reaction. "Have a wonderful stay. My number is next to the phone should you need anything."

"Gracias," we mumbled, but didn't watched her leave; we were both frozen in place trying to make sense of the opulent setting before us.

(I'd love to say we jumped right into that big ol' comfy bed and teased each other and took part in the 'privacy' of the room and swam naked and lounged, but I was still in some uncomfortable pain.)

So I soaked as long as I could in a full bathtub. I then sat and watched the last of the light disappear as TJ swam in the pool. We ate dinner by candlelight on the back patio of our villa, talking about nothing important until my yawning was too much. Then we fell asleep without spooning or anything, because in order to be rewarded with this romantic getaway, I had to fall down a mountain.

Forty-Three

Okay, the next day I was feeling more human.

I woke up and shuffled around the villa in my underwear and Denver Broncos tank top and found a fresh pot of coffee and a shirtless TJ sitting on the patio table, as the sun, fading in and out of various colorations, rose beyond the gathering clouds.

It was warm and muggy and the ocean looked so inviting. I grinned at TJ and winked (my turn!) as I continued past him, down the personal path, onto the soft white sand (which I'm pretty sure had been 'groomed' and cleared of any overnight debris before the sun rose).

And as the morning sea breeze blew back my hair, I thought about my fall that could have truly cost me my life. And the kidnapping, that felt pretty real. And every other moment of mortality I'd faced in the past few days. And I felt so damn lucky and alive. And since this was the one time I would have a beach all to myself, I took off my tank top and bottoms. (Granted it was not done in a sexy way like they do in the movies, where it's one swift motion. My body was still sore, so bending at the waist was accompanied by an awful bout of grunting and moaning first.)

So there I was, and with the soft sea mist baptizing my body, I confidently waded into that lukewarm, heavenly, slightly rippling water. But by the time I was waist deep, the salt had found every abrasion that hadn't completely healed.

"Damnit!"

"What?"

Shocked, I glanced to find TJ next to me.

"It stings," I said then waited out the pinpricks of pain until they all subsided.

TJ's eyes were focused above my waist, but below my chin. I put my hands on my lower back and pressed my chest forward proudly, hoping it looked a little sexy, because in my peripheral, I could still make out the faded yellow and purple bruise on my cheek.

Instead, I focused on the seeming lack of boxers on TJ.

And the next thing I knew, he slid an arm around my waist, pulled himself against me so I didn't have to move, and used his free arm to help my sore muscled arms rest around his neck. Then he brushed a kiss against my lips. And then I wanted more. We let the gentle undulation of the waves set the pace for the kiss. Slow, deep, steady and heated.

That feeling, that I'd been kissing this man for a lifetime before this and still wasn't able to get enough, washed over me. I slipped my fingers into his thick hair, and his hands splayed against my back. We twisted together, and when we came up for breath, he bit my earlobe and began to nuzzle my neck.

"TJ ..." I sighed.

That was all the hint he needed, so we turned to make our way out of the ocean.

(Now here's a little public service announcement for ya. If your pool is surrounded by hedges and palm trees and overgrown foliage, *that* will be a private pool. But if someone declares you have a private beach, all that means is that no one is gonna roll up with a cooler, umbrella, and blanket to set up in that general vicinity.)

It also means we started laughing when we discovered that there were two other villas who had a nice view of our 'private' shenanigans, as well as our beach.

Thankfully, only one couple was on their patio enjoying the morning show. And they were polite enough to slowly look the other direction when they realized we saw them seeing us.

I hid behind TJ as we made our way back out of view. I made him pick up my discarded clothing knowing in my current state it would take me too long to pick them up; which made me recall my recent artless striptease.

Oh man ...

(Also, you might be interested to find out that you still get sand kicked up into places you'd rather not have it being, just by walking through dry sand, hurriedly, while you're wet and naked.)

But at least it was an excuse to use the large, double-sided shower made from earth tone rock and indulge in the complimentary, full size, five-star spa products.

And as the shower heated up, so did the attraction. But this time there were no Olympic-style theatrics. (Not that I have ANYTHING against Olympic-style theatrics.) Sore is sore, even when you're turned on. So we slowly and sweetly rode our way to heightened passions.

Breakfast was delivered and I finally had an entire pot of coffee to myself, so I was feeling properly jittery and happy. We arranged a ride into the nearby town, then found a clothing shop with a colorful woman who upsold everything we touched.

I bought new bras and underwear, a bathing suit with matching sarong, a light green sundress, a T-shirt that read "ONE TEQUILA TWO TEQUILA THREE TEQUILA FLOOR" (super appropriate), and a light blue shirt that had a flying quetzal bird and read Yucatán. I found tennis shoes, a pad of paper that had a faded photo of the main temple (or pyramid) from Chichén Itzá in the background, sunglasses and a cotton backpack to put it all in.

While TJ picked out a few T-shirts and shorts, I found a section that made me giddy: personal hygiene.

Face wash, face cream, deodorant, a makeup bag to take the 'free' spa items from the villa's bathroom, a razor, and mascara.

After we were rung up and I had all the items in my new bag, the woman smiled and said, "Now, go hurry and eat. Then get home. Viene el huracán."

"Excuse me?" TJ asked for clarification. "Huracán. Hurricane?"

"Sí," she said happily, and produced our receipt.

We walked out, stood on the sidewalk and glanced at the sky, which did seem to be filling up with rather ominous, gray clouds.

"Hurricane?" I asked TJ.

"But she said to eat first, so maybe ... let's have a little something and we'll get some clarification," TJ suggested.

The waiter at the outdoor restaurant, the gentleman we'd bought a coconut from, and the driver who took us back to the villa all shrugged and said the hurricane was coming. But we'd be fine.

So the first thing we did was find our personal assistant (whose name we never caught, but now wasn't the time for semantics). Because: HURRICANE!!!

She gave us our bags that had arrived from Francisco and handed over a hurricane preparedness pamphlet with the instructions, "There will be an alarm if there is a problem. We are only at an orange level at the moment."

We didn't move, just stared at her dumbfounded. That wasn't enough to answer all the questions that were multiplying. For example: What does orange level mean? How quick did hurricanes come in? How long did they last? Did the Fox know when he sent me here that a hurricane was a possibility? Wasn't it me who asked to be sent here in the first place? Could I really blame anyone but myself? Our villa was right on the ocean; would we be washed away?

But the most important question of them all I asked aloud to TJ, "Now what?"

PREPARATION:
YOUR FIRST LINE OF DEFENSE

Here at Playa de Sueños, hurricane preparedness is of utmost importance to us. Our establishment has hurricane-resistant structures, backup generators, and ample provisions to address the needs of our guests during weather-related emergencies.

EVACUATION IS RARE

However, if it is required, you will be informed in plenty of time and a shuttle will take you from the resort to a local school downtown.

FACTS

We provide a 72-hour emergency kit in the front closet of your villa. It has essentials like a first-aid kit, flashlight, batteries, whistle, dust mask, and hygiene items. We suggest you add your own supplies, such as medications, passports and cash.

BE SAFE

Close all windows, shutters and doors. We recommend you keep your belongings in the bedroom closet and shelter in the bedrooms during the height of the storm. The bedrooms of each villa have been designed to be interior rooms with no windows and an extra layer of surrounding walls.

THE NATIONAL MEXICAN WARNING SYSTEM

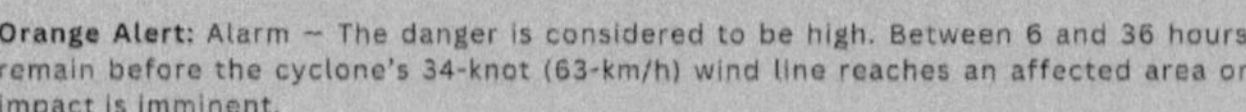

Blue Alert: Watch — Danger is considered minimal. The presence of a tropical cyclone has been detected and no more than 72 hours remain before the cyclone's 34-knot (63-km/h) wind line reaches an affected area.

Green Alert: Prevention — Danger is considered low. Between 24 and 72 hours remain before the cyclone's 34-knot (63-km/h) wind line reaches an affected area.

Yellow Alert: Preparation — Danger is considered moderate. Between 12 and 60 hours remain before the cyclone's 34-knot (63-km/h) wind line reaches an affected area.

Orange Alert: Alarm — The danger is considered to be high. Between 6 and 36 hours remain before the cyclone's 34-knot (63-km/h) wind line reaches an affected area or impact is imminent.

Red Alert: Effects Present — Seek immediate shelter and obey authorities. A tropical cyclone is impacting an area.

Forty-Four

We walked and read the preparedness pamphlet together but by the time we reached the front door of our villa, we still had more questions than answers. "I do believe I'm going to act a little overly hysterical right now. I've got a few questions this doesn't answer. Wanna join me?"

"I'm way ahead of you," TJ assured.

We turned around, trying to ignore how the clouds were gathering and darkening the sky, and how the breeze seemed to have a little more gumption now.

We returned to the reception area where our assistant was just finishing with other guests. I held up the pamphlet but first asked, "I'm so sorry, we should have done this yesterday. What's your name?"

"Daniela."

I shook her hand, and TJ followed as we muttered how it was nice to meet her. Then I held up the pamphlet and shook it while trying to sound calm. "What do we do now?"

She smiled, as if she were soothing a child about to get hysterical, (which was fair and what I needed). Then she started, "The storm is imminent." It was a shit beginning.

"Imminent ..."

She reached out and gave a gentle squeeze of my forearm, calmly saying, "It just means that it will make landfall. But right now, with the trajectory it's on, it is headed inland. The eye of the storm will miss us."

I sagged.

"However, we will still encounter high winds and rain. The storm is predicted to make landfall in the next two hours. So I would suggest organizing yourself. If you would like a puzzle or some games or a book to read, we have many items to choose from in our community hall."

I glanced at TJ, a silent question of what he wanted to do and should we try and run for it. (You really gonna outrun a storm, Ali?)

Maybe.

TJ gave an encouraging nod. "Sure, let's see what they have to offer."

She led us down a hallway then pointed through an open door to our right. It was a community hall; exactly like it sounds. Before us was a large room decorated in the same earthen tones found throughout our villa. Chairs and tables were set up in various groupings and one portion of the wall was decorated with various bookshelves and knickknacks.

She gestured to the collection of books, DVDs, puzzles and games, and asked, "Is there anything else?"

"What do we do?" My repeat of the question was a mix of begging and distress.

She smiled. "When you get back to your room, there is a radio in your seventy-two hour preparedness bag; turn it on. The information about where the storm is and where it is heading will be continually announced." She crossed to the books, pulled out a guide on the Yucatán Peninsula and handed it to me. "This has a map so you can follow along. Right now, the forecast is declaring the storm will only last about twelve hours. When you are finished here, I suggest you go to the restaurant." She pointed to the door that would lead us there. "They have prepared snacks and meals you can take to your room."

We thanked her and as she left, I wrapped my arm around TJ because I needed a hug. He brushed a kiss on my head and said, "Okay Ali Skye, how should we entertain ourselves during our first hurricane?"

We took a deck of cards and the game Sorry. (Although we debated this choice for a moment, the macabre of the name and all, which TJ suggested should be seen only as a game, not an omen. Then he helped to calm me down when he playfully muttered 'fucking writers' under his breath.) We took a puzzle, even though I told TJ I didn't like puzzles; and I grabbed a book by Louis L'amour and a guide to card games.

The restaurant actually had several people sitting and eating at tables. That helped make me feel better, to watch people in the same situation doing something so normal.

"Do we want to eat here?" TJ asked.

"Are you hungry?" I asked.

"Not really."

"Me neither." We perused the buffet of wrapped food and snacks and took several items that looked good.

We were handed a paper bag to put all our goods in and headed back to our villa which was way, *way* too close to a natural water source.

TJ broke the silence. "This is so weird."

"But on brand," I replied. My statement caught us both off guard and we chuckled, which helped to alleviate some of the building stress.

After taking a few steps inside the villa, I slowed and asked, "TJ, do you think I might be unlucky?"

"No."

"Think about everything that's happened since we met."

He tilted his head. "Okay. If it's all happened since we met, then how do you know *I'm* not the one who's unlucky?"

"You weren't with me when I met the Fox or was kidnapped."

"I kinda was. I was in Mexico when you met the Fox and I was standing next to you when you were kidnapped."

I made a face and tried to make my point again. "I feel unlucky. Is thirty going to be an unlucky year?" I thought about the things that had happened to me so far in my thirtieth year and wondered, "At this rate, am I going to survive my thirtieth year?"

"It's just a bad day, not a bad life," he said.

"That's so fortune cookie of you."

He picked up a nearby pillow and tossed it at me. "C'mon. We have our next adventure to prepare for."

Adventure. I huffed and tossed the pillow back at him.

I need to define adventure, print it out and laminate it so the universe understood: Adventure=ziplining, dinner in a cave, a walk to the top of a pyramid (or temple).

With nothing much to do, we organized the bedroom. That meant we pulled out the emergency preparedness goodies from the seventy-two-hour bag, turned on the radio, and turned to the page of the guide book with a map of the Yucatán. We plugged our cell phones in (for once) to get charged. And tried to understand the rules for gin rummy.

"This book was published in 1964," I said when we were two hands into the game and confused. To be fair, the rules read like *The Handbook for the Recently Deceased* from *Beetlejuice*.

I handed it to TJ for a few rounds and eventually we figured it out.

Then the announcements began in earnest, but it just became noise as the wind picked up speed and howled through small cracks in and around the villa. It felt like 'a bad storm' and being from Southern California, I was no stranger to high winds. Plenty of Santa Ana wind storms in my youth had me hiding beneath the covers.

But there was an eeriness to this. We both repeated the information when the announcement came that the eye of the storm would miss this town.

"We're not in the eye of the storm." TJ leveled his gaze at me and nodded.

"Not in the eye of the storm."

But the storm we *were* in the middle of, slapped various debris against the roof and the metal shutter-covered glass doors.

"Are you scared?"

"I'm nervous," he admitted. He'd been sitting across from me on the bed, but now he moved to my side and slipped an arm around my shoulders. "But we'll get through this. So far we've gotten through everything we've come up against. So any way you look at it, we're battin' a thousand, babe."

A large thud against the roof and a high-pitched whistle made me jump. And then, because all the nervous energy has to go somewhere, I began to laugh at myself.

And the laughter got louder and more ridiculous, accompanied by snorts and wheezing. And tears formed as the amusement built into something slightly manic. TJ's smile fluctuated between entertainment and wondering if he needed to slap me to calm me down.

So I tried to explain in large gasps of breath, "Of course ... we're in *the* most ... luxurious place ... I have *ever* been." Cough, laugh. "I am bruised; sore as hell ... in the middle of a hurricane ... and you're right Theodore Jones, we've got this! Because what the hell?" I stood up and proclaimed, "I'm at that Lieutenant Dan point, when he's on Forrest Gump's boat in the middle of that storm screaming at the gods to 'bring it on!'" I leaned back and yelled at the ceiling, "What else you got?!"

Then when the laughter buckled my knees, I lay down and wiped the tears away, but before the emotions could get the best of me, TJ pulled me under his body and began provocatively kissing me; in that way you kiss someone you are trying to calm down, only the shock of passion twisted into something heightened and full of yearning.

A surge in the storm paralleled the swell of need growing between us.

He released his own pent-up emotions on me and I used him in return. He wasn't soft and careful with my body, but demanding as he forced the desire between us to rise into a swirl of a storm inside to keep my mind off the one outside.

"I think we made the power go out," I whispered as I tried to catch my breath.

TJ squeezed my hip where his hand was still possessively lingering. "Not the hurricane?" he joked.

I had taken the storm as a challenge and the howling of wind as a motivator, attempting to cover the sounds with the ones we were making.

"It's gonna get humid in here," I whispered.

The air had already grown heavy. There was no light, which made where our bodies were touching even more sensual and comforting.

"Will there be a surge in the ocean or anything?" I asked a little anxiously. "Is the next worry that a giant wave is going to wash over us and drown us?"

"I think there would be something about that on the radio and we would've been evacuated if that were a possibility."

"But—"

He squeezed my hip hard. "Stop writing this. We just had mind-blowing sex. You were amazing. *I* was amazing. Just let me have this."

I trailed my hand down and found that he was once again growing interested in showing me his amazingness.

TJ laughed and began to trail kisses along my neck, then tried to roll me onto my back. But I fought him and pressed his shoulders against the bed as I straddled him.

"My turn."

I cleared my throat, preparing for another attempt to drown out the sounds of the storm.

Forty-Five

We rode out the storm.

(Hint, hint, wink, wink.)

The generators started up sometime in the middle of the night, along with the air conditioning, taking the edge off the heavy, humid air. According to the news, the hurricane did minimal damage where it made landfall. We fell asleep eventually. I woke late the next morning and we took our time enjoying the amenities of the villa. We swam in the pool, even though it was filled with debris, and drank coffee on the patio in the muggy morning.

Eventually, Daniela came to check on us; she was glad we were safe, but it was time to check out.

"Alejandro has arranged a ride to Chichén Itzá."

I blinked a few times, then glanced at TJ. Who the hell was ...? *Oh yeah.* Alejandro. 'Defender of man.'

"Did you know when we checked in that there was going to be a hurricane?" I asked her.

She shrugged. "It's the end of hurricane season." As if that explained everything.

"A driver will be waiting for you in one hour at the exact location you were dropped off." She smiled and turned to leave when TJ caught her attention.

"Daniela?"

She turned back with a raised eyebrow.

"Why did Alejandro call this Robbie's place?"

"Ah, the gentleman who owns this resort is Señor Alejandro's brother. Roberto."

She walked away as I muttered, "Of course it is."

I consolidated all my worldly possessions into my new backpack then we left to find our next driver waiting for us.

A taxi this time. He got out of the car to open our doors and waved us in as if he were on a schedule.

Once in, the driver turned and studied us for a minute. "¿Americanos?"

"Sí?" We both answered in the form of a question.

"¿Chichén Itzá?"

"¿Sí?"

He made a low guttural sound.

"We can take un autobús," TJ offered, "if it's easier?"

"El autobús dura cuatro horas. Bus takes four hours," he responded.

"Okay?" I aimed this agreeable question at TJ.

"Chichén Itzá, it's no good," he said, still a little dour, but quickly asked, "Hungry?"

I shrugged at TJ who offered, "We could eat."

"We eat first, en el restaurante de mí familía."

"Sure," TJ agreed as I nodded along with him.

The driver gave us another study then reached a hand over the back seat. "Me llamo Diego." We exchanged introductions, sat back, bid farewell to the Beach of Dreams, and drove an hour to a small restaurant. The kind we'd never find on our own. The kind that ended with us being wrapped in the warm embrace of family, with cheeks getting pinched by Diego's abuela, and fed to our hearts' content.

Then, a few more hours in the car and it was four in the evening. A light rain started as Diego drove through the streets of a small town lined with palm trees, past a lake and through the gates of a Zona Arqueológica, toward several small buildings where vendors sold their goods. Only two of them were still open, but each small building had palm frond roofs and the whole scene was backed by thick forest. The parking lot only had five cars, and when Diego pulled to a stop in the back corner, where a square concrete building was fronted with a covered ticketing area and a large sign that read "Cobá," he pointed. "*This* is a good place. Better from Chichén Itzá."

"So ..." A lot of questions followed that statement. Not sure which one to ask first, I deferred to TJ.

"How far are we from Chichén Itzá now?" he asked.

"Noventa minutos."

... pause for high school Spanish to translate ...

"Ninety minutes?!" I asked.

He pointed to the entrance. "This is better." He pulled a pin from the pocket of his shirt, a notepad from a holder sitting along the dash, and wrote a number. He ripped the sheet off and said, "After you finish, después o mañana, call this number." Then he handed the paper over.

I stared at the note as TJ took it.

Diego got out, opened our door and smiled. "Okay," he said as he gestured for us to get out.

"How much do we owe you?" I sputtered, still in a state of shock at this turn of events.

"I'm paid already for the day."

I said to TJ, "The last of my reparations?"

Diego shooed us toward the entrance, frowning at our sluggishness. "They close soon."

TJ put the small piece of paper in his pocket and nodded. "That's normally how we like to visit archaeological sites." Then we shrugged on our backpacks.

We said goodbye to Diego and walked over to the ticket booth. As we bought our tickets we were asked if we'd like to walk, rent bikes or hire a guide. The young woman pointed at the map of the massive archeological site and then motioned off to the side where we spied a lineup of actual bicycles waiting in the shade of the trees; and across from that, a line of empty tricycles, each with a seat in front so the guide could convey tourists through the jungle.

"We'll rent a guide? Does that mean we ride in the tricycle?" I glanced at TJ. "A guide probably knows where they're going ..."

We paid for that convenience as well. She radioed and a gentleman appeared, greeted us and walked us over to a bike. He took out a bright blue patio umbrella, and put it in a cylinder in the middle so it would cover both himself and us from the soft rain. He used a towel that had been around his neck to wipe down the yellow seat.

The seat was in front so we had a perfect view of what was coming. The driver would sit behind and power the tricycle.

"You're late today," the man said, finishing his work.

"We are," I said, because the other option was to admit that we were redirected from our original destination because we'd put our trust in a man who'd had me kidnapped because I'd acknowledged I needed an adventure.

"We will make a little time," he assured and gestured for us to climb on as he said, "Bienvenídos a Cobá."

There wasn't a lot of room, but it was good to be cuddled next to TJ, our bags between our legs to keep them dry. As we settled ourselves, TJ held out his hand in introduction to the young man, "I'm TJ, this is Ali," he offered.

"Carlos," our driver replied, then nodded. "Okay, let's go."

He climbed on the bike behind us and began to pedal us down a well-packed dirt road. He didn't seem to be struggling through any mud, but there were puddles here and there. It was humid, not too warm, and the rain amplified on the umbrella added to a surprisingly peaceful yet expeditious feel.

"Thank you for taking the time to show us some sights," I said, turning in the seat so he'd hear me.

"Of course, but because we do not have very much time, I will take you directly to the ruins of Nohoch Mul. Nohoch means big, Mul means hill or mountain. So we will go to the big mountain. It is the highest point in the peninsula." He wasn't even winded as he spoke and powered the bike with the added weight.

The ride was slightly bumpy, but expected when traveling on a packed dirt path on a bike. Occasionally we'd see a small triangular thatched roof over an artifact, or other ruins peeking out from densely packed trees, palms and ferns.

Carlos launched into his practiced tour. "This area was first settled around 50 BC and has a very rich history. It was an important trading center and we have found eighty kilometers of man-made roads called sacbeob that connected many settlements. Some of the goods traded were pottery, obsidian, jade and other textiles."

The ride before us yawned out, the rain tickling the top of the umbrella soothing, the heat and humidity tempered by the shade.

Carlos spoke up again, "You are lucky; next month, they will close Nohoch Mal. No more climbing will be allowed so they can preserve the integrity of the stones." Carlos went on, "You can't climb the temple at Chichén Itzá, and soon we will follow."

An eyebrow raised, I glanced at TJ and whispered, "Diego might have been right, these are better."

A slight bend in the road and the last hundred yards brought into view Nohoch Mal, a temple that rose out of the jungle. The steps were still intact with the new addition of a guide rope laying directly in the center; however, the sides were deteriorating, holding the shape of a pyramid but the old girl was definitely showing her age. No wonder the archaeological folks here were making moves to stop the wear and tear.

Carlos stopped a slight distance from the base, so we could crane our necks and look up from under the cover of the umbrella.

There was a palpable excitement in Carlos' voice as he introduced us to the ruins. "This is Nohoch Mul, it has one hundred and twenty-seven steps and is the second tallest temple in the Maya world. It is a temple, even though it looks like a pyramid; those are from Egyptian culture, our temples are religious buildings of the Maya."

I glanced excitedly at TJ, and we spoke at the same time. "Finally it's all clear," he said as I announced, "We have a final answer."

I turned to Carlos and explained our reaction, "That was a question we had when we climbed the temple in Teotihuacán."

He shook his head. "Oh, those are Aztecs. It might be a pyramid."

It was difficult not to laugh.

Carlos pointed to the high mountain looming in the drizzling rain with three people slowly making their way down, on their behinds, hugging the rope and going one step at a time. "It is believed that after the working class built the temples, only the priest was allowed to climb to the top."

"Carlos, do you think it's sacreligious to see so many tourists climbing the steps? Is anyone offended by it?"

He glanced at me before looking up at the temple; not answering right away. In fact, his furrowed brow was the only sign that he was thinking about how to answer me or maybe if he even should answer .

When I was just about ready to apologize, he said, "Tourism is what keeps Cobá alive. If we are to live, we must have the economy that tourists bring." He shrugged. "And there are good tourists and frustrating tourists, but I think the peace here; the trees, the shade, the calm helps ease the frustrations."

"Thank you." I truly meant it.

"Now, you will find some calm and peace in your climb." He pedaled closer to the base of the temple. "You can leave your bags here, it's dry and you can trust me."

I glanced at TJ. "Should we ...?"

"That was our plan when we stood at the top of the Pyramid of the Sun." He climbed off the seat then held out his hand for me to follow.

We stood hand in hand at the bottom and glanced up through the misty rain. "Up?" TJ asked.

"Up," I verified, and that's how we found ourselves panting; again.

Exerting ourselves and ascending. Again.

And how I ended up feeling that I'm an archeologist, discovering something new and needing to figure out how to describe the whole experience in order to write it for *National Geographic* in the '20s.

When we got to the top, the rain stopped. Clouds parted slightly, and we stood shoulder to shoulder as our breath came at jagged angles and the sunlight shone spotlight rays on the lush, green forest sea that spread out before us.

I'm pretty sure I could speak for us both when I say we found ourselves, once again; fully, completely inspired.

Forty-Six

"It's so peaceful." TJ's observation echoed around us; off the clouds, the single entrance of the small four-walled temple behind us, and possibly down the stairs and back up again.

I glanced down, from this angle the stairs looked creepily steep. No wonder the three tourists we encountered were scooting down on their behinds so slowly.

Getting down was going to be interesting, but that wasn't a problem for right now.

Right now, I couldn't move. I was still held in the resplendent grasp of the sight before me. The wind from the hurricane had cleaned the air and the rain seemed to have brought out a vibrancy of green tones—all the jungle shades were present. The light from the sun that was dipping down on the horizon, shone through the clouds, illuminating various sections here and there with ethereal rays. It was gorgeous, the sea of ruffled green treetops stretching into the distance was made more superb because they were set against a stark cloud-filled sky, where other billowy shapes curled around each other in countless tones of gray.

"Incas," I whispered, which brought a chuckle from TJ and a quick reply, "I was *just* gonna say the same thing."

"It only seems fair," a breeze blew my hair back and I lifted my head toward the sky as the weight of humidity lifted, "to give all the ancients of this land a chance to pass along some of their wisdom."

"What wisdom are the Maya passing along to you?" he asked. I glanced down at Carlos, sitting on the seat of the tricycle reading a book.

"I'm not sure yet."

We could have stayed for hours, but we wanted to be courteous of Carlos' time and kindness.

(Look, since they are closing the steps, I don't need to pass along yet another 'public service message' but we've been in this together for a while now, so for your information: I tried something.)

I went backwards, holding onto the rope that was bolted into the top, bottom and middle of the route. But the second time my foot slipped, I cursed under my breath and decided I'd sit and slip down the stairs like the other tourists had been doing. Like a little kid would come down the stairs. Only I'm not sure kids have their stomachs in their throats as they slowly descend something so steep and I'm pretty sure they don't care overly much when their clean shorts get waterlogged and dirty. And I'm really pretty sure the few steps they slip down in a normal house don't cause their new shorts to split.

(Did you know that if you scrape your ass along 127 steps, give or take a few—and if you're me—you can rip the seam of your shorts and end up with your new pink, lace underwear taking the brunt of the final steps?)

Or, I suppose my other option could have been to turn around and give Carlos a good show, but even though the guy had probably seen it all, I had *JUST* been talking to him about being respectful; and aiming my lacy ass at him didn't seem very respectful.

(Oh yeah, and TJ's height and long legs seemed to help him take the steps standing while holding onto the rope. He's that guy that makes things look easy.)

When I arrived at the bottom, I looked up to find Carlos and the bike back where he'd dropped us off.

"What did you think?" he asked.

"Glorious." I slipped onto the final step as TJ was climbing back onto the seat we shared; but when he turned and saw I hadn't moved, he asked, "You okay?"

"Could you bring me my bag?"

He did as asked and watched me pull out my sarong. I stood, tied it around my waist and nodded. "Now I'm ready to go."

A raised eyebrow in question was directed at me but a wave, I hoped he took as 'we'll talk later,' was all I gave him.

Once more, we were bouncing along the wet road. The clouds assumed position over the areas the sun worked so hard to penetrate and a new drizzle began again.

"Do you have any charge on your phone?" TJ asked.

"No, do you?"

"Nope."

He turned slightly in his seat. "Carlos, we need a place to stay tonight and don't have a car. Do you have any suggestions?"

"Sure," he said but didn't offer a location, so we figured he'd probably tell us back at the front gate.

This time on the road, we were passed by a group of ten on bikes of their own, all wearing plastic rain ponchos; a reminder that we weren't always alone on these adventures. But it also meant we weren't going to be the 'last tourists' out of the park.

And that was something.

Only when we arrived at the entrance, Carlos waved and called out to a colleague then continued to drive us out the front gate, through the parking lot, then down the roads of the small town of Cobá.

"So Odysseus and his company of men were once again thrust into unanticipated adventures."

"Fucking writers."

We passed brightly colored buildings, many with palm frond thatched roofs and others with corrugated tin. Carlos pulled to a stop next to a mound of bricks overgrown with weeds and pointed. "This is an example of a mound that has not been excavated yet. It looks like possible trash, but it is actually part of the ancient city. There are over six thousand buildings in the park and the surrounding area. But only two percent of them have been excavated."

"That is *a lot* of work," TJ said as I shook my head in wonder.

"The jungle is very dense, and it would take a lot of people and money; but slowly we will continue," Carlos predicted before he pushed off again.

There was a fight against poverty at work in this small town; evident by advertisement banners that had been repurposed across front entrances of homes to be used to create shade. Trash lined the front of several establishments and empty, crumbling buildings made of concrete bricks were commonplace every now and then. But there were also the well-kept homes, landscaped areas of the city, and small businesses with their colorful dream catchers and clothing proudly displayed in front.

The telephone lines that ran through the streets spoke of modernization, and pruned palm trees in the center of the road spoke of current regentrification. This city, probably one of the largest Mayan cities at one time, was now dependent on tourism and whatever support the archeological site could get from the government.

My questions were stifled by our arrival at a small business with two red tables and matching chairs under a covered overhang with soft lights spilling outside, and a sign that read 'TAQUERÍA.'

"Ohh," TJ said appreciatively.

We followed Carlos inside where we were introduced to a cousin, and lovingly assaulted by the glorious scent of meat cooking on the vertical rotisserie.

It was my turn to give a groan of delight and after pleasantries were exchanged, we were asked what we would like. I said, "Whatever the specialty is," as TJ declared, "One of everything."

We were ushered back to one of the tables in front, a strand of twinkle lights were turned on and a colorful tablecloth was proudly draped over the table; along with salt, pepper, napkins, and two bottles of hot sauce. The woman who set the table smiled as she added a citronella candle and said, "Just in case."

Carlos brought us two ice cold Pacifico cervezas before returning to chat with his cousin while our meals were prepared.

TJ held his beer toward me as a smile played on his lips, but his eyes pierced me with that soul-searching study that upended all the butterflies.

"Yes?" I breathed.

"I don't think I've ever had quite the range of adventures with anyone that I've had with you."

I wanted to say so much to him. How I hadn't had this much fun just sitting next to someone. How alive I felt. How excited I was to see the world through his eyes. But I simply settled for touching the neck of my bottle to his and whispered, "Salud, amigo."

We slipped into the night as the stagnant air cooled and the last light of day faded away. Our food was delivered, a mix of tacos for TJ and for me a torta with avocado and some kind of magic applied that made it so wonderfully delicious.

When Carlos was done talking with his cousin and about to sit with his own plate at a table inside, we waved him over to join us.

"Thank you so much for your time today," I said.

He shrugged. "I love what I do."

"There must be a lot of studying that goes into becoming a tour guide?" TJ led the question.

Carlos nodded. "In school I studied English and then continued in university with a focus on archeology. When you are born and raised in this place," he waved a hand and glanced around, seeing a life and history play out before him, "I decided it would be helpful. I did training to become certified by the Instituto Nacional de Antropología e Historia. I took courses in Mexican history, archaeology, anthropology, and customer service." He smiled. "There were other courses as well, but I have my certification and I am able to work all across the Yucatán. Sometimes there is an opportunity to assist with a dig. I enjoy that very much."

"With such a limited amount of time, we missed a lot today on our tour, didn't we?" It really wasn't a question.

"You'll come back one day and make up for it," he reassured.

Would I?

I glanced at TJ through lowered lashes as I took a bite. What I'd do 'one day' seemed so far-fetched at the moment.

"I want to ask you a question," I aimed at Carlos, "and I hate that it might sound offensive or stupid, and I'm not sure the proper way to ask, so ..." I cleared my throat, an act of gathering courage. "Are you of Mayan descent?"

His grin grew. "This is a very large conversation."

"Is it?"

He nodded, sat back and wiped his mouth; taking his time to think through his answer.

"I am Maya. However, what visitors do not understand is that there are many different groups of Maya and they never went extinct, we continue today."

(You know that moment you feel like you are learning something so very interesting and at the same time ashamed for what you were too ignorant to understand previously? Yeah, me too.)

He continued, "The ancient civilizations never referred to themselves as Maya. The easiest way to explain it I suppose, is that the Maya identified by the languages they spoke. And there were over thirty Mayan languages. So this means there were at one time, over thirty distinct groups of Maya. And we were found in Guatemala, Belize, Honduras, El Salvador and Mexico. Today there are twenty-two different Mayan languages still spoken by more than six million people."

"Wow." I shook my head in wonder, and out of the corner of my eye saw TJ beginning to dig through his backpack.

He pulled out his sketchbook and flipped to some sketches he'd done so far of people he'd met on the road. "Carlos, I'm an artist. And I sketch people who are interesting and just catch my attention. Would you be offended if I sketched you?"

He let Carlos look at his work and I muttered, "You never asked if you could sketch me."

"Because I just sketched your hands," he whispered back.

"Yeah, my very *soul*," I said, then pointed, adding, "and don't you dare wink at me."

(He winked at me.)

Carlos returned the book and I think he was blushing. "I don't think I am interesting, but okay."

"How did the languages survive?" I asked as TJ sat back, crossed his ankle across his knee to prop the book up and began to work.

Carlos waited for TJ to look at him or do something, but when all he did was keep his attention on the page, he relaxed and answered, "I think the better question is how did the *Maya* survive?"

I gave a deep nod; okay, that *was* an interesting question.

"Our ability to adapt is how the Maya survived."

Yeah, we're all thinking it: I might have just found the lesson I learned from the Maya people.

He continued, "The Maya were not interested in creating empires. There were many different imperialistic peoples who tried to conquer them. But the ability to reject what didn't work for our culture, absorb that which did, and rework new ideas into our belief system ... that was how we thrived." His explanation was so easily given but ripe with depth.

"Fascinating. I never thought ... the Maya culture has been painted as this dead entity, hasn't it? I never thought ..." I shook my head, "but that's the ignorance of it. I never thought of the descendants and the continuation."

He thought again before adding, "There are these famous books of Chilam Balam. A chilam is a priest who tells prophecies and balam means jaguar. The books were written in the seventeenth century in the Yucatec Maya language and they are a gathering of history, religion, literature, astronomy and prophecy." His face took on a far away look as a warm smile formed. "In those books there is one entry that says: 'those who try to take over the Maya people are plagues that will have to be endured, but always, despite such evils, the Maya will persist.'"

Goosebumps.

When you are faced with a person's respect and love for their life and what they do and it is almost tangible the way they talk about it all – you are overcome with goosebumps.

"I'm so glad you are a guide and work here," I said, "it's important."

"It is," he agreed, with the amiable grin that he'd given us when we first met him.

"I ... thank you," I repeated.

With an incline of his head, Carlos looked like he was about to say something more, but was interrupted by his cousin who was bringing out more food for us to try.

We encouraged his cousin and wife to pull chairs up to the table as we ate. We talked about the restaurant as the man shared with us how he prepared his food and how he and his wife had met. And we continued to fall into companionable conversations as bird and night sounds surrounded us.

Forty-Seven

A friend of Carlos arrived at the end of dinner, parking a small blue car next to the tricycle. "This is María," he stood to introduce us, "she has a room she rents on vacation rental sites and said it was free tonight."

"Oh, that's great," I said, "thank you."

"She will drive you," Carlos added.

As we said our goodbyes, TJ showed the sketch to Carlos who studied it. After a moment he nodded. "If you ever make copies, my mother would love that."

TJ carefully tore the page out and handed it over. Carlos shook his head and held his hands up, stuttering that he couldn't take it. "You can," TJ insisted and after a moment, Carlos carefully took the sketch and held it gently in his hands, then gravely nodded his thanks.

"Please, call if you need anything while you're here," he told us. "María has my phone number and there is a phone in the room where you'll be staying."

I handed a folded amount of pesos to Carlos, which he tried to wave away but I gently took his hand and wrapped it around the money. "This is the tip we were going to give you anyway. And it's also the only way we know how to thank you for your kindness, for finding us dinner and a room for the night. Please."

He accepted it and with another round of "gracias" and "buenas noches," we climbed in María's car; me in the front, TJ and our bags in the back.

"María, thank you so much for this," I said.

"De nada. I understand Carlos showed you around Cobá today?"

"Yes, and it was amazing."

"Are you on your honeymoon?" She grinned as she turned off the paved road and the dirt road crunched under her tires.

"Oh no, we're just ..." I glanced over my shoulder at TJ, with his slight beard, that ease firmly in place, and his shoulders taking up more space in the small car than I thought they would.

What were we just?

"On vacation," he offered.

María pulled up to a small, bright blue house. It was surrounded by trees and a hip high concrete wall. She pulled into an opening in the wall, and the trees and shrubs had been cut to allow for a small circular driveway.

We climbed out when she brought the car to a stop and followed her to the back of the property where there were more trees and a small building, all still within the walled space. It had a thatched roof, walls made from smallish tree trunks—fitted together perfectly to create solid walls—and a door with faded dark red paint. There was a rock lined walkway leading to the door, and an edging across the front where pink, burgundy and purple flowers bloomed.

María opened the door and we followed her inside as she flipped on a light switch. There was a cozy-looking full size bed with a green sage comforter in the middle of the room; it was covered with a hanging ceiling to floor mosquito net. Opposite the bed was a three drawer dresser topped with two towels, several bottles of water and washcloths, along with a phone and a small box fan.

The light for the room hung over a bench space next to the entrance to a restroom. The restroom was a concrete room within the room. Made with three sides and no ceiling, as that was taken care of by the vaulted thatched roof. But a look inside and there was a shower, sink and toilet.

"Is there anything else you might need?" María asked.

"No, this is perfect," TJ replied.

She nodded. "Whenever you wake up, come over to mi casa azul, the blue house, I will have breakfast for you."

"Oh, we don't want to put you out," I said, "this is already so kind of you."

"Breakfast is usually included. It is no trouble." She smiled. "There is no key or lock. Cobá is safe."

After another glance around, as if she was forgetting something, she gave a decisive nod. "Buenas noches."

She left and we stood across the room from each other, taking it all in.

"Everything keeps working out for us, huh?" I asked.

TJ raised an eyebrow. "Only a few bumps along the way."

"Well," I waved, "that was so long ago who can even remember what the bumps were."

He pointed to the lower half of my body. "Why are you wearing that?"

As my grin grew, I untied it, then turned, looking over my shoulder as I demonstrated the split in my shorts. "I didn't think Carlos was ready for all this lace to be pointed his way as I slipped down another mountain."

He gave a grunt. "I think I can take the view, though."

"Shower?" I asked.

"Oh, yeah."

We made sure the water pressure and shower worked well: very decent hot water tank.

We tested the bench just outside the restroom: sturdy.

And for all around quality sake, we made sure the bed was up to snuff: made from that new technology–no springs or squeaks–but a bit difficult to get a good 'groove' going. (And a slight setback as we tried to get onto the bed through the mosquito net, both trying to help, which just ended up getting us ridiculously tangled.)

The soundproofing of the room, however ... well, we were on vacation and we tried to be as quiet as possible, which only made us laugh, which caused more moans to be released than we anticipated.

Five stars all around.

Forty-Eight

The night around us came alive with so many sounds. Birds, crickets, maybe a monkey, and insects put on a symphony.

We aimed the fan at the bed, as our exertions had warmed us up, and the humidity was not helping, nor was our cuddling. But neither of us seemed to want to untangle just yet.

TJ lay on his back, his arm around me. I lay on my side, my leg wrapped around his and my fingers lazily making abstract designs across his chest. My eyes rested at half-mast.

TJ's deep voice was a whisper. "Do you know, this will be the first room we've paid for since we met?"

"Is it?" I ran through the past few days that felt like months; it *was* the first place we'd paid for. "I've saved you a lot of money then." *Hell, I'd saved myself a lot of money.*

"Then you'll let me pay for the plane to Peru?" It wasn't really a question.

"Plane?"

"We could take a bus ..." he tempted.

"I'll let you pay for a plane ticket if you let me pay for the hotel," I bartered.

"Done," he agreed.

I wanted to sleep but at the same time I wanted to drift around in this dreamy moment. There were no storms on the horizon. There was no schedule. I was safe. My bruises, with the help of the aloe vera, were fading quickly. We had been driven well off the beaten path. And my body hummed with the exertion of climbing ancient ruins and keeping up with TJ's stimulating exuberance.

"When you paint, do you do it without a shirt on?" I asked.

"Where did that question come from?"

I splayed my hand on his chest. "Just curious."

He flipped the question. "When you write, do *you* do it without a shirt?" But before I could answer he groaned, "Because if you do, I'd love to watch that."

I laughed. "I don't, and that would be pretty boring to watch."

"I don't think so. I'd get to stare at you, watch the rise and fall of your chest, listen to the sound of your fingers flying across the keyboard, and know that you'd blush from my attention ..."

I creeped my knee closer to his 'goods' to stop him and he chuckled as he squeezed his thighs together to prevent the possible assault.

"What's your favorite food?" I asked next.

"Are you getting to know me better?"

I brushed a kiss on his shoulder.

"There is a little hole-in-the-wall restaurant in a small town in Oregon, they have a Bolognese lasagna that rivals the authentic ones I've had in Italy." Again, he turned the question around. "What's your favorite food?"

"I'm a sucker for brunch. Waffles, fried eggs with a little melted cheese maybe, and bacon. That's the good stuff right there."

"Favorite color?" he asked.

"Blue, *sky* blue." He chuckled at the joke I'd made many times in my life. "What about you?"

"Lately, my favorite color seems to be your eyes." The unexpected answer given with the deep timbre of his voice sent lovely shockwaves through my body.

"The guy who took my senior school picture called them blue-gray and said they were unique. I never gave them much thought before that," I admitted.

He smiled. "I'll probably try to recreate the color one day."

"If you ever do a painting of me, can you make sure it's small?"

"Why?"

"I don't know ... it just seems like it would be shocking to see yourself bigger than life, caught on a canvas. I don't know how I'd feel about it."

"What if that's how I feel about you? That you're bigger than life?" Another round of goosebumps and fluctuations of butterflies rippled and I let the comment float around for a few moments.

"You said you're the oldest of five?"

"The only boy, four younger sisters."

"Is that why you're so laid-back?"

"I don't think I'm that laid-back."

"Mr. Jones, you're so laid-back you're almost horizontal," I teased.

"Writers." He gave a *humph*, then asked, "Have you thought about your cowboy again?"

I sighed. "Not really."

"I think you have. And I think you should tell me what happens next."

I gave an exaggerated sigh before I admitted, "I have an inkling."

"Of course you do."

"It's weird, I see the story in sepia tones. Like it's a silent black and white that needs a narrator and an organ player."

"See, bigger than life," he whispered, then prodded, "When last we left the fated duo, they had decided to find a man who would marry them."

I let the ideas that had slipped in here and there come through.

I really did see it in sepia tones.

"Cal wouldn't want to spend their wedding night on old bedrolls and he'd insist on a hotel. Annabelle would ask for the stars far from the small town."

She would gather her courage to admit to Cal that she always thought of him when she was finished with her work. At night, she would open her curtains and stare up at the night sky, watch the stars and think of him sleeping under them.

I continued, "Cal would abide by her wishes and over the next few days they'd wrap themselves in a false sense of security and revel in the newness of each other."

TJ pulled me closer against him.

"Yeah, something like that."

He matched my tone when he spoke, "There's a 'but' coming."

I nodded. "They can't run forever. And one day, maybe they think it's safe enough to go to town but a good samaritan or clerk at a mercantile will tell them that some men had been by with descriptions of them, offering a reward for any information.

"Annabelle would do the unthinkable. One night, once they were exhausted and Cal was asleep, she'd leave him. She'd leave the marriage certificate where he could find it, and she'd write on the back of it why she left: He would be her husband for all time, but they would never be safe. She'd love him forever and cherish each moment they'd shared all the days of her life. But it was because she loved him, she wouldn't put his life in danger."

That was as far as I'd gotten really. I wasn't sure what came next.

"Would she go back and marry the bad guy?" TJ asked.

"Either that or Cal will go and call him out and we'll have a good ol' fashioned shootout."

There was nothing left and we were tired. The night sounds worked their way into my bones, easing everything and allowing sleep to claim me.

Forty-Nine

The next morning I woke with a vigor I hadn't felt in a long time. A very long time. We're talking a heady, hopeful, heroic kind of vigor.

TJ was gone, probably outside sketching something. So I grabbed my moment with both hands (or in reality, by one hand), retrieved the razor I'd yet to use and finally shaved my legs.

(Look, TJ hadn't said a word about it. He continued to whisper about all the things he did like and prove it with actionable movements ...

... please hold ...

A few memories just fluttered by and I rather like standing here under the running water, staring into nothing as I relive them for a moment.

*insert sigh here.

Okay, so I shaved my legs and as I was saying, TJ hadn't said one word about it and *I* know it's natural and all that blah blah blah, but *I* feel better when they are shaved. *I* feel sexier and more confident and I don't care how that's interpreted.)

There's something about feeling like your life is just beginning, as opposed to swirling the drain, that can put a little giddy-up in your step. And it doesn't hurt having clean, smooth parts, and unsoiled shorts.

I was ready to take on the world. I nodded at my reflection as I smoothed down the butter yellow shirt with a flying quetzal. "Let's see where this day takes us."

TJ wasn't outside, so I assumed he'd be in the casa azul; and he was, sitting at a table talking to María over a cup of coffee.

When I walked in the back door, he looked up at me and his face brightened. *Seriously brightened,* and a smile formed, just for me. I don't know if his reaction was new, but this morning it was so evident and inviting and wonderful it warmed me all over.

Oh, did it warm me all *over.*

I couldn't breathe as I took him in. TJ Jones was a handsome man. Solid, easygoing. I think his hair would always have that tousled, just woke up look. I'd watched him try to comb it once, after he got out of the shower at Francisco's, but I got the feeling it seldom cooperated. His peeking tattoo teased me, but less now that the Greek god and I were well acquainted.

I stood still as I took stock of the moment, and TJ—besides the feeling that I'd known him for a very long time, the initial attraction and lust were morphing now, turning into something more. Something that scared and excited me.

I watched him watching me, those dusty brown eyes hooded slightly as he pursed his lips a bit; in return I bit my lower lip as I thought about what his sexy mouth had—

"Buenos días," María called.

"Morning!" I declared; then rubbed my stomach as if that would erase the memories forming and María waved me over to the table as she stood. "I have coffee and breakfast."

As I passed his side of the table, TJ slid his chair back, caught my arm and pulled me between his legs. His hands spread out on my hips then he looked up from where he sat, as I rested my hands on his shoulders and smiled down at him.

"Morning," he said softly.

I bent and brushed a kiss across his lips in greeting, and when I pulled away, he took his hand and brushed his thumb against my bottom lip. "Chapped?"

"Worth it," I whispered.

"Definitely worth it," he agreed and let his hands drop as María set a dark brown ceramic cup on the table.

I pulled up a chair next to TJ and offered my thanks as she returned to the stove.

"What time do you normally wake up?" I asked, curious.

"Four-ish. Five if I'm sleeping in."

I raised an eyebrow as I held the magic elixir of warmth against my chest. "What if you stay up late?"

"That's when I wake up at five." He shrugged. "I've always been that way. It's like I'm worried there won't be enough time to see or do everything I want. I might miss something."

"You did miss something," I muttered into my cup, and when he looked at me questioningly, I flirted, "you missed waking up with me."

He slipped his arm around the back of my chair as María placed a plate of fried eggs and a bowl of various fruits in front of me before sitting back down.

"Oh this looks good. Muchas gracias." After a few bites I sat back and sighed. "Okay, what's the plan?"

"Well, María was telling me that there are several buses we can take to Cancún today, they are tourist buses ..." he trailed off.

"Is that the nearest airport? Cancún?"

"There are better available flights to Lima there," María replied.

"How long is a flight from Cancún to Peru?"

"Five and a half hours," she answered.

So the question was whether we wanted to leisurely make our way to Cancún today and stay the night there, or hurry and try to find a flight out today and deal with a hotel whenever we finally arrived in Peru.

I didn't answer. I knew Peru was the next stop, but something was off. TJ squinted after several seconds. "What are you thinking?"

"That it doesn't feel right to follow tourists."

"Honey, we are tourists."

"Not normal ones," I defended. "I don't know exactly how to explain it, but being on a bus with tourists. I think ... We haven't really planned anything since we met. We've had a direction but something always gets in the way to make sure we get where we're supposed to go instead."

His gaze scanned my face before he asked, "So what are you thinking?"

I glanced around at the colorful, comfortable kitchen, then thought about asking Maríawhat she thought we should do when I recalled Diego.

"Let's call the number Diego gave us."

With a chuckle, TJ patted me on the shoulder before leaving to retrieve the number.

We asked María to make the call for us (made another comment to each other about how we really, truly needed to up our Spanish language skills), and after a quick conversation she hung up and said, "You have a ride that will be here in thirty minutes. His name is Antonio. All he said was that he is a friend of Diego and was waiting for you to call."

I nodded at TJ. "Doesn't this sound about right?"

Once we'd finished our breakfast, paid María for the hospitality and reorganized our backpacks, we were sitting on a bench in the shaded driveway when two motorcycles pulled up in front of the casa azul.

Two men of short stature, wearing well-loved jeans and T-shirts, climbed off the shining black bikes and pushed their sunglasses up on their heads.

"Oh." I blinked rapidly.

TJ laughed. "Yeah, this definitely seems right."

And because I needed a moment to comprehend the fact that I was going to be riding on the back of a motorcycle (a prospect that had never been availed to me before), I whispered to TJ, "How would you paint it?"

"Cool." He grinned at me. "How would you write it?"

"Quickly," I muttered, pulling an unexpected laugh from him which I liked hearing so much I added, "with lots of 'z' sounds and the word vroom."

We were introduced and told our destination was an airport nearby.

"But not Cancún?" I asked.

They shook their heads, but no one gave us the name of the airport we *were* headed to.

So because it was what we did–meet people and do what they tell us to–we climbed on the back of the motorcycles. We were handed helmets (which the drivers did not wear) and given a quick hand signal guide to being a passenger on a motorcycle, the gist of which was: hold on, but not too tight, and don't lean from side to side.

And we were off with a wave of thanks to María.

And it was glorious.

They sped down long straight stretches of road hugged by encroaching jungle on either side. They wove around cars going too slow and when we came to small towns, they crawled along, letting the vibration and hum of the bikes shake the air, but allowing us to see the small towns we might never drive through again. Then it was a twist of the throttle and we were flying again.

It was a little over an hour later when we pulled into the private entrance at an airport, and delivered to a jet that looked suspiciously familiar.

A flight attendant was waiting for us by the stairs and I gave my name twice to make sure it was really for us. And after we climbed aboard and got settled, I was handed a telephone.

"Hello?"

"My sweet Ali, how are you? Was the hurricane horrible?" (We all knew it was going to be Alejandro, El Zorro Blanco.)

"No, it was fine. We survived it." *I mean, what else was I gonna say?* "I appreciate the use of the jet again." I shrugged my shoulders looking at TJ; did that sound okay? Too stupid? "How did you know?"

"Antonio is Diego's cousin," was all the excuse I was given.

"Where in the world would the writer like to go next?" the Fox asked.

"Peru?" It was as if I were seeing how far I could get with my requests. "And that's really all we need. We can figure it all out from there."

"It's my pleasure, no problem at all. I will let the crew know where you would like to go. If you need anything else—"

"No, no. Thank you so much, but this is the last thing we need. And I don't want to offend you, but I hope I don't really need anything else from you after this."

He let loose his Fox laugh then said, "But we are friends now. All you need to do is call if you need something." Then he hung up before I could turn down future help.

Our flight was quickly arranged and with two glasses of champagne, we were buckled in and the plane was taking off into the bright blue horizon.

The flight attendant came to tell us the elevation and cruising speed of the jet, and how much time until our arrival. Then she asked if we needed anything.

I pointed to the back of the plane where the bedroom was. "I think we'll just take a nap. If that's okay?"

"Of course," she gave a little nod, "there is a call button on the bedside table."

TJ unbuckled as I did and followed me to the back of the plane. He wrapped his arms around me and pulled me against him when I stopped to open the door. "Are you tired?"

I patted his hand, waited until the thin door was closed and locked before turning and saying, "I'm not tired, I just figure we should make the most of this trip."

"Oh?"

I pulled my shirt off and grinned up at TJ. "Do you think there's some kind of documentation we fill out or signature needed, or do they just give us a pin or a patch once we explain we've joined the mile high club?"

Fifty

Turns out, eventually you do need a nap on a plane if you take advantage of the amenities.

(You get it.)

We landed in Lima as the sun just reached the horizon. Our flight attendant accompanied us to the bottom of the stairs of the plane and pointed. "This time you must go through customs. It is easy. Follow this yellow line and it will come to a stop where you wait for a transfer bus."

Easy enough. We thanked her (and I might have tried not to make too much eye contact because she had to know what was happening on the jet, but I'm sure we weren't the first and probably wouldn't be the last ...), said goodbye and began to walk.

Surrounded by the sound of large whirling engines, we followed the single painted yellow strip created to save us from certain death if we deviated from its path. (Isn't that just what Dorothy had found out in *The Wizard of Oz*?) Apparently, it works for modern-day airports too. And no doubt about it, these flying monkeys would crush us if we came in contact with them.

We found the bus and began a subdued migration from bus; to sliding doors; then into the Jorge Chávez International Airport, where we were bombarded by bright welcome signs and thorough fluorescent lighting.

We were divided into groups: foreigners, Peruvians, and those requiring preferential service.

After handing over our documentation, it was a scan, click of a stamp, then, "Bienvenido a Perú."

We were next herded through the duty-free store, through a penetrable wall of mixed perfumes, and into the center of bright, shiny consumerism. It had been a while since I was presented with so much eye candy. It was a shock, even though we were just treated like superstars on a private jet, but to come from the jungles of the Yucatán–where there was a definitive slowness to life–to this hurried, incandescent, materialistic world was jarring.

"I feel like we just did some strange, unexpected time travel," I commented.

"That's what it is." He nodded as his own head was on a swivel.

We bought converters for our phones, but didn't linger in the store. We followed signs to the baggage claim; a vast, wide space with echoes of voices and movement swirling all around us.

With nothing to declare, we continued our hiking shuffle to the far end, sent our backpacks through an X-ray machine and were deposited into the international arrivals area.

Only this space was far more chaotic. So much commotion–people being greeted; families at the end of their vacation ropes; and a sea of well-dressed men and women, wearing various colored lanyards, asking if anyone needed a taxi.

While TJ politely shook off one offer, I took a deep breath then frowned. "TJ, do you smell McDonald's?" I tested another deep inhale and muttered, "That's weird, I could swear I smell McDonald's."

"You staying in Lima?" A smiling young man in his early twenties, or possibly just twelve years old (he looked so young and I was not getting any better at telling the ages of the next generation), kept his distance but raised an eyebrow with the question.

"If you stay here, I know a good hotel. If you need Cusco, we can take my helicopter." He pointed to his lanyard and the photo, declaring, "I am certified." Then he handed us a glossy pamphlet that he'd been holding.

Gorgeous Jorge Helicopter Adventures, it said. There was a picture of the Andes, city skylines and other natural wonders Peru had to offer.

"It's big fun, no matter where you need to go," he said.

I looked at TJ, then back at the youth. "Are you Gorgeous Jorge?" I asked.

He struck a pose, one that men on runways do at the end of their catwalk and I swear he was attempting to smolder. (And not doing too bad a job, he was a handsome little thing.)

"How old are you?" I asked.

"Twenty-five. How old are you?"

I grunted at the question.

"So, you will come with Gorgeous Jorge?"

I turned to TJ and whispered, "I mean, we already took a helicopter, so it won't be a disappointment if we don't get on this one."

He matched my tone, "But he found us and it just seems in keeping with the theme of the trip. Very unexpected."

"This is true." I glanced over at Jorge who was scanning the crowd, looking for his next customer if we turned him down. I continued my aside with TJ, "So, we're gonna go have some big fun?"

"Big fun." He winked.

Gorgeous Jorge heard us and clapped his hand. "Big fun. My helicoptor is shiny and new and I can give you good pricing." He jerked his head in the direction we were to go.

"We need to exchange money. We don't have any ..." What was the name of the currency here?

"Sol," he said.

"Sol. We don't have any sol."

"Okay, the ATM is just there and my company takes credit."

With a little sol in our pockets (everyone should have a little soul in their pockets) we headed back where we had just come, but this time went through a different set of doors where Jorge showed his credentials to the agents guarding it.

That had to be a good sign, right? No one glanced at his badge then at us with a face that seemed to imply, 'you poor stupid tourist.' So that *must* be good.

Another side door led to stairs and we were back on the tarmac and another lifesaving yellow line that led to Gorgeous Jorge's helicopter. Gorgeous was right. It was shiny and new; we climbed in the back to find comfortable seats, and adjusted our headphones as he stowed our bags.

Then I began to worry. Was 'new' a good thing when it came to helicopters? Didn't you want something a little more worn in? Then again, we were about to be flown by a man-child so did it really matter?

"TJ ..." I was about to ask him if we'd made a big mistake, but he took my hand and gave it a squeeze.

The confidence Jorge exuded as he began his preflight check helped.

The abundant gas fumes swirled, matching the swirl in my stomach as the whir of the helicopter started.

Jorge turned in his seat and adjusted his microphone. "We are ready. Are you ready?"

We nodded and that was all he needed.

Our chariot rose into the sky, away from the crowded airport, on a path toward the ocean and the smoky pink sunset.

Jorge turned the helicopter, heading south and giving me a perfect view out my window of the setting sun.

"It's good, no?"

I sighed, squeezed TJ's hand and cuddled closer to him without taking my eyes off the horizon as I agreed, "*So* good."

We floated noisily over small villages, big cities and everything green until we lost all natural light, leaving only city lights to gaze down upon.

"How long is it to Cusco?" TJ asked.

"One hour, thirty minutes," Jorge answered. "You will go to Machu Picchu, yes?"

"That's the plan," TJ replied.

Jorge pointed to his chest. "I am descended from the Inca kings. My great-great-great-great ..." he paused to think then shrugged, "I am of the Inca."

I leaned over to TJ and even though Jorge would hear the comment, said, "That's *exactly* how I would write it."

Fifty-One

"Where will you stay tonight?" Jorge asked.

I got a downright excited feeling as TJ replied, "We're not sure yet."

"Oh, then I know what we can do." He made an unexpected dramatic correction, throwing me against TJ and causing us both to scramble to hold on to something, "We can have dinner and stay with Tía Camila tonight."

TJ caught my attention and winked as Jorge laid out our evening festivities. "She likes visitors. Her house has a good view. Tomorrow we can go to Cusco. It's better to arrive when there's light."

"We don't want to impose." It was the polite thing to say but we were waved off.

"Tía will be happy to meet you. And it's good to be at a low altitude. It will build your lungs for Machu Picchu."

And that's how we settled the unanswered question of 'what next?' It took care of itself.

Jorge brought the helicopter down a fair distance from the back door of a square, two-story house lit up by the landing lights enough to see it was painted yellow and the stucco was crumbling in a few places.

The back door opened and the light spilling out created a shadow of an older woman, apparent by the slight hunch of her shoulders. She was waving what looked like a rag at us, whether in anger or surrender was yet to be determined.

"Tía doesn't like my helicopter." There was a smile in Jorge's voice.

I wonder if it's the helicopter or the fact that he landed in her backyard; (and while we're wondering things, how did the neighbors, a few houses down the road on either side, feel about the surprising intrusion?)

When the propellers stopped and the final electrical whir of the beast came to a grinding halt, Jorge turned everything off. We took off our headphones as he was opening our door to help us out.

His aunt had made quick progress across the yard and was yelling at her nephew, but it might have been all bravado because she laughed a few times in between her scolding.

Jorge tisked at her antics and spoke quickly, gesturing toward us as he met his aunt; then he picked her up so her feet were off the ground and hugged her tightly.

She giggled and when Jorge released her she slapped at his arm with the towel.

He continued to talk and gesture at us as he spoke.

TJ slipped his arm around me, and I realized as I watched the interaction, I had been shivering. We were no longer in the lower humid jungle, these were the Andes. (At least, I think they were. This would be one of those good times when having a charged phone ... nope, I have a feeling there weren't any cell towers close by.)

The woman shook our hands, her brown hawk eyes studying our faces as her light shake lingered. Then after we'd been inspected, she clapped and gestured to the house. "Bienvenidos a mi casa." She pressed a hand against her chest and instructed, "Me pueden llamar Tía. Tía Camila."

"Gracias, Tía" we both called as she linked her arm through her nephews and energetically chatted. Jorge translated when he could.

"She made dinner for us. She had a feeling today she should make a lot. Until she heard us land, she didn't know why."

We followed them into the kitchen which was right off the back door, and were instantly enveloped by the warm scent of waiting dinner in a warm kitchen.

A table that could easily seat twelve took up most of the space in the kitchen. It was covered with a woven yellow tablecloth with stripes of blue, purple, red and orange running down the center. The walls were stucco, whitewashed, and natural wood beams were exposed along the ceiling.

She ushered us to sit and urged Jorge to set places for dinner.

"Does she have a big family?" I asked.

Jorge shook his head. "No, Tía's children have moved far away and Tío passed many years ago. She has a big table because she likes company. When you buy a big table, someone always shows up," he explained with a knowing grin.

The actual kitchen was rather sparse.

There was a small two burner stove with shelving on the left side that held all her dishes. To the right of the stove was a thin sink matched by a thin fridge (think half-sized Kenmore), and next to the fridge, more shelving that held dried goods. There were bunches of dried chilis and other herbs hanging from twine near the food shelves. One thing was for certain, Tía Camila was magic. With one counter for prep work to be accomplished, she presented a meal that was unbelievable

She proudly positioned full plates in front of us. Chicken in a creamy yellow sauce was topped with a few chopped pecans, half a hard-boiled egg and a few dark olives, along with a side portion of rice.

Jorge groaned in delight, sitting across from us next to his aunt. "This is named Ají de Gallina. Tía uses a Peruvian pepper, it adds the yellow color."

I didn't realize how hungry I was until I took a tentative bite; the spice and cream was stew-like and created an immediate comfort. I gave a moan in appreciation which was quickly followed by TJ's and when he was finally able to speak, he said, "Muchas gracias señora. Esto es muy bueno."

"Lo sé," she responded and then laughed at her confidence.

I smiled and took another bite, torn between savoring it or inhaling it. The rice was garlic in flavor and helped smooth out the spice, but under the chicken was an unexpected surprise of peeled, boiled potatoes.

When I'd eaten enough to slow down and find some decorum, Tía Camila took our plates and filled them once more. I sat up straight with an excitement I hadn't had in a while from food.

Camila asked a question and Jorge had to finish his bite to translate. "She asked how you like my helicopter?"

"Oh, it's very nice."

She frowned and shook her head.

"Tía doesn't like it. She never goes with me for a ride."

"Really?"

"She likes her feet on the ground," he said.

Through Jorge, Tía continued to ask us questions.

Were we here to see Machu Picchu? Where were we from? Where are our families? Where had we been?

(Of course, I left several integral parts out of that answer.)

"You two are lovers?" Jorge repeated her question and I swallowed wrong at the shock of it. Not that I minded the question, but she was so cute and short and we put these stereotypes on older, hunched women that they've never been in love, never had a lover, never had sex … but that is ridiculous; still, it caught me off guard.

She enjoyed my reaction and since I was trying to clear my throat, TJ motioned between us and in his nonchalant way, answered, "We are, but it's changing. There's more here now."

She shifted forward in her seat, eyes narrowing as her gaze traveled between us. Then she held her hands across the table, motioning for each of us to take one, then she nodded. This woman—who cooked so much food because she had a feeling there would be visitors and had a big table in a very 'if-you-build-it-they-will-come' way—nodded.

And Jorge translated for her. "Tía says you have known each other before. She says the woman needs to find more of her self, but the man will help."

Tía squeezed our hands and joined them together.

Jorge continued her translation. "She says you should not leave each other. It's important."

Goosebumps and a dry throat and tears sprung and I think I began to shake and I was scared to look at TJ.

(What do you say to that?)

Nothing, because TJ, in his ever-present even tone, assured Tía, "Then that's what we'll do." He gave my hand a squeeze then went back to eating.

"That's what we'll do," I repeated, just to hear my voice; and when I finally glanced over at TJ, he winked. (Of course he did; you know it's coming just like I do; coming to 'release those kracken-y butterflies.')

Then he repeated the phrase to solidify it between us, "That's what we'll do."

Comfort food, a long day, some great sex on a plane, and a substantial altitude change can exhaust a person.

Dinner finished, I listened to the quiet conversation between Jorge, Tía Camila, and TJ. I yawned at regular intervals and when it was too much, Tía stood and declared it was time for sleep.

"I'll show you where to sleep," Jorge offered.

We thanked Tía and asked once more if we were putting her out before she waved us away.

"Tía and I have rooms downstairs. You two will sleep up," Jorge said as he led us upstairs. "The bathroom is here, and here is your room." He opened one of the bedroom doors, flipped on the light then stood aside.

TJ was first in and delightedly said, "That's about right."

I was right behind him to take in the twin size bunk beds that helped make the most of the space in the room.

Jorge shrugged. "Or you can use the other room, it has only one small bed. I think you want to be together?"

"Tía did say we shouldn't leave each other," TJ reasoned.

Jorge yawned. "Buenas noches. If you need any drinks or food, it's in the kitchen."

"We'll be fine," TJ said.

"Please tell your Tía again, we are grateful for the room and the wonderful dinner."

He wiggled his eyebrows. "I told you Gorgeous Jorge can take care of you." He struck his runway pose before leaving us to revel in the small room with a skinny three drawer dresser, a wooden chair and a bedside table.

"So, this is happening." I grinned.

"We can either try to squeeze into that," TJ pointed to the bottom bunk meant for someone about five-five at the most, "or we divide and conquer."

"Your feet are going to hang over the edge," I observed.

"Probably."

"Then I'll take the top."

Teeth brushed, nighttime routines finished, we crawled into the (thankfully) well-built and structurally sound bed.

It was eerily dark in the room. "I think we're on the outskirts of a town." I reasoned the lack of outside light.

"It's so quiet," TJ whispered.

I rolled on my side and stared into nothing. "We've only slept together in the same bed a few times."

"You miss me?" TJ asked.

"Maybe. You miss *me*?"

A grunt was my non-answer.

"This is where I'm tempted to overthink and analyze and try to ruin this or force it into a box," I admitted.

"What sort of box?"

"A boyfriend girlfriend box, a friends with benefits box, a something at first sight box ..."

The bed gave a little wobble; he must have rolled over. "You're a writer, you want defined terms and solid definitions."

"I do?"

"I'm not sure. It just sounded like a good excuse."

"I don't hate it." I smiled.

"Do you want me to tell you what I think we are?"

"No." That was a lie. "Yes." That was a lie too, because with his truth came great vulnerability that I may or may not be in the right headspace for. "Maybe."

"I think we're Ali and TJ, two people who feel as if we've known each other forever and met under strange circumstances. We like being together. The sex is pretty good—"

"Pretty good?"

"*Damn* good," he corrected. "We're on a cool path and about two years from now we'll find ourselves on a Sunday afternoon at a coffee shop somewhere in the world, arguing over whether the jungles of the Yucatán were more majestic or imposing."

I wasn't going to need an extra blanket to keep me warm tonight; that declaration would do the trick.

"I like it," I whispered.

We traded a few stories then, in the safety of the darkness. We talked about first pets, broken hearts, and family traditions. I yawned through most of it and several times woke up halfway through a strange sentence.

"I'm falling asleep, TJ."

"I know." His smile was evident in his voice and I knew what that looked like.

My eyes fluttered shut and in a very soft whisper, TJ's deep voice penetrated my final awake moments, "Buenas noches mi cielo lindo."

My beautiful Sky.

The endearment followed me into my dreams.

Fifty-Two

I woke with a start—the kind they say is part of our evolution kicking in to make sure we don't fall out of a tree.

Since there was daylight flooding into the room, I stretched and gave a loud yawn, knowing I wasn't going to bother TJ.

I heard the scratch of his pencil on paper and thought whatever he was drawing, I'd name this one: *Lovers' Bunk Beds in Gray #9*. I chuckled at my cleverness then whispered, "Good morning."

"You probably need to scramble out of that bed and see this," was his reply.

It wasn't so much a scramble, because I'm a grown ass woman and getting down from a bunk bed was a lot less coordinated than getting up.

Down, I pulled the blanket on top of TJ's bed around my body, against the cool morning, and turned toward the window where he sat in the chair by the ledge.

And no wonder he'd told me to hurry.

Tía Camila's house faced a lake with a lush green backdrop of mountains rising into the distance.

Jarringly steep, large mountains with puffy white clouds painted across the soft blue morning sky.

"Wow ..." I blew out a breath, such beauty. I glanced down at TJ's sketchbook. When he saw I was looking, he flipped back showing me three other sketches he'd already made.

"Wow," I repeated, touching the edge of the page.

"How would you write it?"

I laughed, "Well, as a matter of fact I was going to call it Lovers Bunk Bed number nine, and for a second I thought it might not work, but this is art and you people tend to name things whatever you want. So I'm gonna hold fast to that. 'Lovers' Bunk Bed #9.' That's how I'd write it."

He tossed his sketchbook aside and pulled me onto his lap so I had to wrap my arms around his neck to hold myself in place.

I looked into TJ's dreamy, brown eyes as he whispered, "I'd write this as the beginning."

I brushed a kiss on his cheek. "Get out of my head." Then because the moment was so raw, I changed the subject. "What time is it?"

He checked his watch. "Seven thirty."

"Ready to see where this day takes us?"

I dressed in my shorts, T-shirt, and sweater that smelled like mothballs and Old Spice. Then we packed up our few belongings once more.

"We need to go shopping again." I glanced at TJ, in the same situation as me. "We're not dressed for cool mornings and nights."

We went downstairs to see what Jorge and Tía were up to.

The curtains of the kitchen were open, allowing the light and the view in. Jorge sat at the table with a cup of coffee as Tía Camila stood at the stove, one hand holding the pan she was using, the other stirring the contents as she sang quietly to herself.

It was warmer in here and smelled wonderful. If I were to put a name to it, after just the slight conversation I'd had with the woman the previous evening, I'd say it smelled like love and comfort.

The reasons for her big table were as clear as the majestic (if not imposing) scenery beyond the window. Tía Camila was apt at imparting feelings of love and comfort and wanted to share it with others as much as she could.

Jorge handed each of us a half full cup of hot water, then a glass pitcher holding what looked like a rich brew of coffee. He watched us closely as we added the heady concoction to our water, nodded, then retrieved another clay pitcher with steam rising out of it. "Crema caliente. A little sweet."

I added a dab of sweet cream and took a sip, then hugged my cup to my chest.

(Oh yeah, I was moving in with Tía Camila so she could spoil me through cooking, *this* coffee and her sage advice.)

As if she'd heard my silent plan, she turned from the stove with two steaming plates and placed them in front of TJ and me. Steak, onions and tomatoes had been cooked together and were served with a side of rice and a slice of bread and jam.

"Muchas gracias." I grinned up at her and she gave my shoulder a pat before dishing up a plate for herself and Jorge.

We ate in companionable silence, my gaze never drifting too far from the window and the view beyond.

When we were done, Tía Camila put on a large pot of water and poured more cream into a pan, added sugar and slowly stirred until it was warm.

I didn't have to wait too long to find out what she was up to. People who lived nearby began to arrive; as if a bat signal had gone up and Camila was having a party.

Which it kind of had. Everyone heard Jorge's helicopter land last night, so came over this morning with mail and packages for him to take to bigger towns to be posted; I wondered if a few were going to be hand delivered.

Camila kissed everyone on the cheek as they entered and ushered them to the table for coffee. She introduced us, then we found ourselves sitting in the middle of the happy growing crowd. There were several people who spoke a little English, and we had lovely conversations with them through our limited Spanish. As we all drank coffee in the warm living room and around the kitchen table, a flood of unexpected emotion washed over me.

How in the world could I ever repay this stranger, whose nephew forced two tourists into her life, but who still allowed us into her home and treated us so kindly?

Jorge packed all the parcels and our packs in the helicopter, and all too soon, it was time to go.

We asked Jorge if Tía would accept money from us for the stay and he shook his head and said she would be offended. So we told him we'd like to give him money and perhaps the next time he visited, he could bring some groceries from us. This he agreed to.

Tía Camila walked us to the helicopter, pointed back and forth between TJ and me several times. "She says you must remember to stick together," Jorge said.

A hug and memory, that I hoped to do justice one day if I decided to write it, was all I ended up taking with me.

We realized quickly there was no time for maudlin feelings, though, as Jorge opened the door of the helicopter explaining that we had new passengers.

Two chickens were sitting in a large woven basket in the middle of the back seat. They were for his sister and he didn't have the heart to argue with his aunt.

"If you are calm, they will be calm," Jorge reassured us.

That safety announcement over, he waited for us to climb in so he could follow and begin his preflight check.

I put the headphones on quickly. "Hey Jorge, what happens if they get ... worked up?"

"They won't."

I glanced at TJ who had reached out a finger and was petting the bridge of one of the chicken's noses.

"Have you been around chickens before?" I asked.

"Nope."

The helicopter came to life with a giant whir of sound, followed by a shiver of the aircraft. The chickens ruffled slightly, and I hoped that was a good omen; if that didn't distress them, maybe they really would be okay on the flight.

"Ready?" Jorge asked.

I was too busy staring at the chickens and trying not to picture all that could go wrong, so only TJ answered.

"Jorge ..." I wasn't sure which scenarios to run past him but a glance at TJ, who happily declared "chickens," washed all my worrisome storylines.

At different moments each chicken placed a gnarly talon on the side of the basket in an attempt to hoist themselves up, but TJ was quick both times to give them a small pat and demand, "Just stay where you are."

Eventually I was able to stop my hypervigilant babysitting and look out the window as the views shifted and changed.

The sun and clouds created shadows and light, changing the color of the world beneath into shades of green that hadn't even been named yet. Lush greens that looked like velvet, rolling and dipping as far as the eye could see. Occasionally we'd fly over tiered farms, cut into the side of small hills which would give way to jungles of deep cover. Jorge pointed out cacao farms and a village where his second cousin (twice removed) lived and another where his grandmother was born.

Our flight path dipped and turned as if Gorgeous Jorge, enamored by our questions and sincere interest, thought of another place he should show us since we were in the area.

Which I'm sure is why we made a pass at a glorious waterfall that cascaded and disappeared into the covering of trees.

There were plenty of mountains for the helicopter to play in, and Jorge was doing just that. He never stopped grinning, and I figured flying must feed his soul. And why not, he came from a people that liked to live life on the edge, literally. I read enough to know many famous Incan trails were perched high on the ledges of mountains with long drops; probably the closest they were to feeling bird-like. It must be ingrained in their heritage somehow—it was a nice idea at least.

"Are you going to Cusco just to go to Machu Picchu?" Jorge asked.

"Well, yeah," TJ said.

"I can take you closer, you can skip Cusco."

"Thank you, Jorge. But I need to get some clothes that are warmer first," I called.

"Ah, okay. So you have time today. See the city center, find clothes, but take the train to Aguas Calientes before the sun sets," he instructed. "If you take train in the dark, you will miss all the good sights. It's easy to find a hotel at Aguas Calientes."

I glanced over at TJ. "And now we know where the day wants to take us."

Suddenly, the city rose around us, terracotta roofs gathered in numbers, and the mountains closed in on every side as the helicopter touched down on the far end of the airport runway. Gorgeous Jorge left the rotors running, and with his head down, jumped out and opened our door for us.

We followed his lead past the area where we were free of danger, TJ paid him through a reader on his cell phone, then Jorge pointed the direction we were to go, shook our hands and wished us well before giving us one more 'gorgeous' pose. Then he and the chickens were off.

"What is this made of?" I pulled up the tag on the lightweight jacket I was trying on. "It says here it can keep you warm in a blizzard, fend off a bear attack, and help you do your taxes."

"Then let's buy two."

We purchased train tickets for Aguas Calientes at a kiosk at the airport and with four hours to waste, took a taxi to a clothing store.

"Very good," the clerk said, ringing up our pants and jackets.

"We have a little bit of time before we take a train, what should we see here in Cusco?" I asked.

He pulled out a tourist map and circled a market. "Go have a fresh juice and explore Mercado Central de San Pedro."

So we walked slowly, feeling slightly winded, through the streets of Cusco—lined with massive Incan built walls, limestone rocks so perfect in their symmetry that when it came time to fit them all together, no mortar was needed.

As we crossed a street I asked, "Are you lightheaded?"

"No, are you?" He stopped when we'd crossed, pulled me closer to him gently by the elbow and frowned into my face, searching.

"No, I'm fine. Out of breath, but I know the lightheadedness is a thing. I was ... just ..." But the thought didn't get finished because TJ kissed me.

When I was competently kissed, he whispered, "Okay, *now* I'm lightheaded."

"Good, cuz kissing you continues to take my breath away."

Surrounded by the sounds of squealing brakes and occasional honking and traffic, the streets of Cusco were clean and filled with life. Roads closed to traffic had women sitting by wheelbarrows filled with colorful seasonal fruits and long sticks of what must be sugar cane for sale.

We caught glimpses of Spanish Colonial influence, turned a corner and found the open-air market of San Pedro, which was an explosion of stimulation on the senses. Each color was represented and the smells vacillated between sweetness, spices, citrus and bread.

So many stalls. So much to see. There were bags of dried fruits and nuts; purses, scarves, hats and belts. Blankets and table runners hung on display next to vendors of oils, cheese, tea, fruits, candies and gorgeous smelling loaves of flat, round bread. We purchased a loaf because it was too good to pass up, then found four aisles of vendors with white stools in front, the sound of whirling blenders filling the air as various fruit juices were created. I don't even know what we got, but it was fresh and delicious.

Next were the vibrant souvenirs, magnets, shot glasses and miniature llamas, made from real llama hair, wearing traditional Peruvian hats in bright blue, pink and red. However it was a small square of Peruvian textile that looked like the tablecloth on Tía Camila's table (in keychain form) that I immediately purchased.

We left the giant market of bustling energy and continued our meandering. TJ stopped often to touch various goods laid out on tables for sale. Eventually, we came to a square with women dressed in traditional Peruvian attire—dark green and blue calf-length skirts, bright sweaters, tall hats, their long black hair worn in braids left down or twisted up. All had colorful striped bags slung on their backs, and a few held a baby sheep or llama in their arms.

Knowing what he needed, I motioned to a bench nearby.

As TJ sketched, I let my gaze wander among the clouds; thick and gray but never releasing any rain. When the blue canvas of the sky presented itself and the sun shone, it was warm and comfortable.

After a while, TJ sat back and glanced at me. "Are you okay?"

"Of course."

"I ... just had to." He nodded back at the women and held up the sketches.

"I love this part," I admitted.

"Which part is that?"

"When I get to see the world the way you see it. Thanks for sharing this with me." I reached out and touched the page as he asked, "And how do you see it?"

I pursed my lips for a moment. "A vibrant kalidescopic prism."

"Writers," he mumbled laughingly.

Fifty-Three

M achu Picchu.
(Okay, look—

I don't know how to break this to you …

So …

Okay ….

Look.

If you get the chance, take the train into the Andes from Cusco. One hundred percent, do it. Chug along the edge of the river on the PeruRail in the Vistadome with full windows on the side and on the top of the car, and gaze in wonder at the spectacle of jagged mountain peaks rising up into the clouds.

Soak in the farming terraces, the peaks and the dreamy greenery that is from from another planet.

Have a cup of coffee when the train takes off and beverage service begins. But then try to ignore the fact that the continual recorded announcements over the speakers—which explain the things you're seeing—are in English and you feel like you're back in the states because every part of this adventure has been built for the tourist.

And there are just so many tourists.

But you know what I think the real problem is?

Somehow, the idea of Machu Picchu had too much pressure on it. As if the ancient stop off would be the final chapter on the strange road a disillusioned writer and easygoing artist found themselves.

But it wasn't.

Did you know that 2,500 tourists ascended into the ancient city of Machu Picchu on a daily basis? There is a restaurant where the buses drop you off that sells ice cream by the way. And a kiosk where you can buy postcards.)

It was dusk when we tripped off the train into the city of the Hot Waters: Aguas Calientes.

The exit funneled everyone from the station through an open-air market; vendors and restaurants swallowed up passengers, thinning out the herd as we walked.

Aguas Calientes was a small, thin village. Even the buildings were narrow with all the streets and stairs that went up rather than branching out. There wasn't room for much in this long thin valley at the base of Machu Picchu.

I wondered what had come first, the village or the tourist. With the number of pizza places, cafés and souvenir shops we passed, I had a clear idea of the answer.

We had headaches, but that could be altitude, hunger, lack of water or the fact that this wasn't feeling right.

We found a food stand with no line, asked for four large bottles of water and then ordered the specialty–a sandwich of fried pork, topped with some sort of compote along with a few things slathered on the bun, and wrapped in parchment paper. While we waited, we drank as much water as we could and listened to Peruvian flute music that came crackling out of a sound system. I turned a big circle to take in the hanging Pepsi signs, the chalkboard menus written in English, and the tourists filling the sidewalk café tables on the road leading to hotels.

We walked and ate in silence, then wandered into the first pharmacy we found where we were greeted by a tower of altitude sickness medicine and Aspirin; so we stocked up. Then when TJ shrugged and pointed to the hotel next door to the pharmacy I nodded in agreement. We got a room and fell asleep, waiting for headaches and exhaustion to dissipate.

The thing is, we woke up the next morning feeling better, ready to figure out how to get a bus that would take us to Machu Picchu. It was a crisp, clear morning so the ancient ruins weren't crawling with mist or ethereal whispers.

Instead, they were crawling with so damn many tourists in sensible hiking shoes, most of whom had their arms extended with a smartphone attached to the end, tripping over each other to get the perfect shot.

"I just never thought I'd feel the encroaching population of the world on top of Machu Picchu," I said to TJ.

It felt like tourism might have wiped out anything spiritually gratifying about this place. *But what was the answer?*

(Look, it is *impressive*. It is *insanely* masterful. It drove the point home that the Incas were sophisticated architects who conceived of terraces to farm and road systems to travel news from one place to another.)

But I may have put too much on the shoulders of the Incas. I guess I thought that this third archeological sight would be the pinnacle of a life-changing moment.

Neither of us found something hidden deep within ourselves; just tourists who asked if we would take their pictures, while overhearing numerous complaints about the air and several disgruntled grievances aimed at tour guides, who'd supposedly given maps that lacked detailed explanation.

We stood shoulder to shoulder, waiting for something as we studied the majestic sight, trying to see it without the clutter of people.

When TJ shook his head no to the next person that came and asked if we could take their picture, I turned slowly to look at him. He sighed. "I'm done. I think I hit a wall."

I scrunched my face. "I'm kinda glad, I was beginning to wonder if you were human."

He shrugged and I slipped my arm around his waist to offer some sort of comfort. We'd brought my backpack this time with my notebooks and his sketchpad but neither of us felt like liberating them.

"It *is* gorgeous." I gave voice to the appreciation I had even as I tried to come to terms with the strange feelings of disappointment.

"Stunning," TJ agreed.

"I'm glad we came." And I meant that.

"Me too."

"How would you draw it?"

"Misty, shrouded," he answered. "How would you write it?"

"Primal."

But those were dreams of the place. Not our current reality. So we took the earliest bus back to Aguas Calientes.

(And trust me, I feel like an ass even admitting this to you. But there it is. The truth of what I found. Sometimes expectations fall short. And that life lesson is just as valuable as all the others.)

Fifty-Four

I nteresting fact: Bars at the base of 600-year-old ancient mountain towns sing, vibrate, pulsate and *thrive* with spirits.

Okay, to be fair, most of them are liquid. But once you get a few of those spirits in your system, the whole world becomes quite poetic.

"TJ, it's like ... it's like everything is poetry," I announced with a wave of my hand around the bar.

"You're drunk." his eyes are hooded, he has a slight blush rising up his neck to his cheeks, and a perma-smile fixed on his face.

"*You're* drunk too," I pointed.

"I am," TJ admitted. The altitude, our lack of food and proper water, made the spirits very potent.

We didn't mean to get drunk, it wasn't what we were after. We thought, let's have a beer, in a very '60s Hemingway and Picasso artistic sense. We could take a moment to wallow in our disappointments.

The first beer tasted so good, and the bartender was quite an affable character, so when he suggested a shot, that too seemed like a good idea.

The third and fourth ... well ... I forget who suggested those.

"You," a scratchy, thick accented voice boomed over the music and liveliness of the bar, "you are two halves, part of a whole. You are in the wrong place." It was as if it were in my head, or right next to me, but when I glanced to my side, no one was there.

TJ was doing the same thing, looking around confused. "Did you hear...?"

It took a moment to will my eyes to focus and when they finally did I was surprised to find a crone of a woman pointing at me from the entrance of the bar.

"You two." She pointed more forcefully.

"Me?" I gestured to myself with the shot glass I was holding and spilled some of it down the front of my shirt. "Shit." I dabbed at my shirt, but the voice was once again a whisper in my ear; "You must leave now." It was so jarring I thought I felt the heat of her breath against my ear, but when I glanced up, she was still across the room, limping toward us.

"TJ ...?" I called.

She crept toward us; ancient as the dirt under the ruins, her shoulders hunched with age and malnutrition, and when she raised her head like a turtle, I couldn't tear my gaze from her dark black eyes; I couldn't see where the pupil ended and her black eyes began, they simply formed one dark orb. Her hair was soiled into a greasy matted mess. She wore a dirty robe of faded rags and completed her ensemble with a stench as aged as she was. I gagged when she was a few feet away. If ever the word 'Witch' was ever to be used properly, it would be for this woman.

"Who ...?" TJ asked.

"I don't ..." We were simply speaking in ellipses now.

"Ali ..."

"Yeah ..."

The smelly Witch snarled, stepped closer and I gagged again. She jabbed a finger into my chest, her voice echoing in my head as she demanded, "Come, we go now."

Since I'd sidled up as close as I could get to TJ, I knew we were both shaking our heads at the offer.

"Destiny put artists together for a reason. Not to get drunk." She took the shot glass from my hand and threw it on the floor.

I stared in awe and fear and drunken wonder. She spoke again, "We leave now!" The sound was so loud we bumped elbows in our attempt to cover our ears.

It resonated in my chest as well as my head and strangely, helped sober me up.

The small Witch raised herself to her full height as best she could and began waving her hands and cursing us in Spanish.

At least the hands she waved in our general direction and the eye contact made me assume it was a curse.

(Yet again, another reason to learn the damn language of the land you visit, so you know exactly how bad the curse is when it's coming at you.)

As her animated movement grew in intensity, so did our sobriety. I glanced around the bar, no one seemed to notice her or what was happening. We'd ceased to exist.

I grabbed a few bills from my pocket and tossed them on the bar as I took TJ's hand, to make sure of him.

"Come now!" This time I'm sure her mouth didn't move when she screeched the words. I tilted my ear to my shoulder and cringed, squeezing TJ's hand as he squeezed back.

She turned and walked out the door, and we followed as if attached to her by an invisible string.

"Is this real?" I asked.

"I don't know," he said softly.

"Come." She turned, a few feet ahead of us. The urge to follow her was a physical compulsion.

I found enough temperance to ask, "Who are you?"

"No time, hurry." She waved us to follow her.

"No time for what?" TJ asked.

"You must get to sacred ground," she insisted and waved a hand for us to continue following.

"Should we ...?" TJ asked.

She turned again and wheezed, "You can trust me. But we must go now."

I tugged on TJ's arm. He leaned his head down toward me but didn't take his eyes off the old woman. Neither did I for that matter as we continued to follow her.

"Did you ever see that movie *Midnight in the Garden of Good and Evil*?" I asked him quietly.

"It's been a while."

"Remember when the voodoo woman led the writer into the graveyard? The friends I was watching the movie with laughed and said no normal person would ever follow the woman except me. They predicted this. They said if I ever had the opportunity to follow a stranger at midnight, I would."

"The difference is that we're in this together," TJ whispered.

(I must admit, it felt pretty good to be in the thick of something so damn strange with someone.)

"So, we're gonna follow a Witch into sacred ground?" He sounded willing.

"We're gonna follow a Witch into sacred ground," I verified.

Even though we were following, we weren't complete idiots. We made sure we stayed at a safe distance. I mean, I was enthralled and curious, but there was also the very plausible scenario that 'sacred ground' was a back alley where someone was going to steal all our money.

We didn't end up in an alley, but instead got onto a bus with several other tourists; an old yellow school bus that had been decorated completely in a bright mural.

"This is different," I mumbled as we sat down in the seats she pointed to.

(Never, I repeat, NEVER go with a stranger to a second location. Unless you go by bus that is full of other passengers. Then again, maybe don't do that either.)

The Witch stood by the driver, who gave her a large bag before his bus hissed the door closed and began to chug.

After several minutes of the bus making its way uphill, I leaned over to TJ. "Are we going back to Machu Picchu?"

"Maybe that's the sacred ground?" he wondered.

Something strange was happening. It felt like each time I blinked, large gaps of time had passed. In the blink of (four) eye(s) the bus came to a calamitous stop. The door hissed open and our 'guide' turned and waved to us. "Let's go."

So we went and I can't say we were at the 'front entrance' of the ruins. Because I'm not sure where we were. But that was the least of my concern as the bus turned and drove back the way it'd come.

"Now," she insisted again.

Now it was dark, with only a slight glow from a waxing (or waning) moon. And of course we followed. I don't know about TJ, but an urge I hadn't had in a very long time was coming back to life: to see how the story would play out.

We blindly climbed over ruins, up and down rocks, feeling our way with our hands and feet as the old woman lithely floated in front of us.

When we came to an open space in the middle of what seemed to be an overgrown courtyard, she stopped and sat down, pulling items from the bag the bus driver had given her.

"Sit," she ordered.

No sooner had I arranged myself, then the clouds parted, allowing the moon, which was now quite full and not so much a sliver, to shine down, an eerie spotlight for our unexpected (most likely illegal) presence; causing the hair on my forearms to instantaneously stand on end.

Our midnight guide busied herself laying out small bowls, a few jars that looked like oil, several shaped rocks, and a bundle of sage.

She took out two pieces of paper, handed one to each of us along with a pen and instructed, "Write your name three times, then fold that page three times."

When we were finished she pointed to the bowl we were to put the papers in, stood and lit the bundle of sage and began to circle us chanting in Spanish until a cough caught in her throat. She tried to clear her throat several times and the moonlight played tricks on my eyesight as the Witch straightened to a very full height that cured her aged osteoporosis.

"Bloody hell!" she yelled in an English accent before giving a final cough.

"What happened to your accent?" I whispered, pointing. "What's happening to your back?"

Still trying to get her cough under control, she managed to say, "I'm British."

"No shit ..." I glanced at TJ who was shaking his head in wonder.

The moonlight changed her before our eyes. She still stank to high heaven, but her rounded malnutritioned shoulders had righted into a straight spine. She stretched her arms in front of her and shook her shoulders out. Her age, which I had thought to be over sixty, was wiped off with a sly smile and she looked to be in her late thirties. Even her fingers straightened themselves.

"What the hell?!" I stood, took a step back and reached for TJ who was still seated, whispering, "Changeling?"

"Oh, we do *not* have time for this," she pointed to the moon, "you wanted an ethereal experience, well, we only have a certain amount of time, you see."

"Are you really a Witch?" I asked so quietly, I wasn't sure she really heard.

"Yes," she said and bent to pick up one of the vials of oil. She opened it and walked over to where I stood; I backed up.

"Alicia, we are on a schedule here." Her impatience was palpable.

"How do you know my name?"

She glowered at me with one eyebrow rasied. "I believe we've just covered that."

"Are you a good Witch or a bad Witch?" TJ asked, having finally found his voice.

"Now that would be telling." She smiled at him, and since he'd stayed seated, she quickly anointed his forehead with her thumb that she'd dipped in the oil.

She turned to me with an expectant look, and since TJ hadn't dissolved into a puddle, I bent my head toward her. What could it hurt being anointed with oil in the middle of the night, half-drunk, bathed in moonlight, among the humming of ancient ruins?

"You still smell really bad," I said after she finished.

"Sit."

I did as told.

She continued chanting under her breath, took palm sized rocks and held one on either side of TJ's cheeks. She chanted as she gently traced his face with the rocks. She turned and did the same to me.

"What are you doing?" I asked and she hissed the words she was chanting at me with an obvious 'shut up' vibe.

When she was finished, she took out two carnations and handed one to each of us. Pointing to the bowl that held our folded papers, she instructed, "Rip them up and put them in there."

"Should we be concentrating on something while we do it, or making a wish?" I asked.

"Don't be daft," she replied.

Me? Daft?

After the carnations were done, she held the bowl up toward the moon, then walked around us three times.

She came to stand in front of us, dipped her hand into the bowl (which now had water in it, or I missed when she put it in), pulled out her fingers and flicked it at our heads, making us flinch slightly. She repeated the action three times for each of us, chanting as she did.

Finally, she sat down across from us, took another bowl (this time metal), set the rest of the sage bundle inside and lit it. It eventually glowed red, and earth and musky scented smoke rose up into the night sky and filled our lungs.

I didn't feel any different, no wave of overwhelming enlightenment. No prickly ghosts rising out of the old stones came to dance with us in the moonlight. I looked at TJ to see if he looked different. Same gorgeous man I was more and more attracted to each day. I wonder what he'd draw after this. I wonder what I'd write.

"Will you please cease, Alicia?" the Witch bit, annoyed.

"I'm not doing anything." I blinked.

"Your endless careening..." She tapped her head with her finger. "Your thoughts are as noisy as a jaybird that has misplaced her young."

My eyes bulged. "Are you telepathic?"

"No." She ruffled and in a mutter amended, "And a little yes."

I opened my mouth to ask her what that meant but she held up a hand. "Just try to settle your mind, please?"

"I'll try," I mumbled. But it's going to be hard because of the little information I *do* have about you now, and the information I *want* to have. *There are so many questions.*

She glared at me again and I cleared my throat. "I'll really try this time."

"Close your eyes," she instructed us.

That helped, because once I did, I was finally able to start breathing in and out deeply and steadily.

My mind cleared, the air that was chilly now had grown warmer; as if the clouds hanging around the mountain had parted to allow the moon to shine down, blanketing us in warmth.

TJ's rhythmic breathing so close to me helped ease my nerves, and the night sounds of the wind along with various nocturnal creatures calling their greetings to each other, took up space.

My body began to float, and it felt so good to be this light, I gave into it.

If ever there was a moment the earth stopped and took a deep inhalation, and peace prevailed for the briefest of moments, it was now.

I soared on the midnight breeze, the moon warmed my skin, and a hum began to vibrate in my bones. I felt everything; a leaf falling in the woods, a ship in the middle of a squall, the morning mist on the Blue Ridge Mountains, the rough stone of Nohoch Mul. I was everything and nothing.

"Ali."

The voice drifted across parched deserts and vast jungles to arrive.

"Ali," it called again, fingers of sound searching for me.

I blinked my eyes open. I was laying down, TJ propped up on his elbow next to me. "Hey," his deep voice called as he reached out and twirled a strand of my hair around his finger.

"You okay?" I asked.

"I don't know what I am," he whispered.

I glimpsed up at the sky, the moon had been eclipsed by the clouds. I sat up and glanced around, no sign of our Witch guide.

"Was that real?"

"I'm not sure."

But it had to be something, because we were surrounded by ruins and the sun was coming up.

Fifty-Five

"I think we were really drunk," TJ offered by way of explanation as we rode an empty bus down the hill. It was the bus for those who wanted to see the sunrise over the ruins.

The driver didn't ask us where we'd come from, though I suppose he could have figured we were from the hotel that had been built near the entrance of Machu Picchu.

"TJ, do you think that bus was real?"

He scrubbed his face. "Honey, I'm at the point where I think maybe we were roofied."

"That's one explanation."

He said, "I have to admit, I haven't felt this rested or relaxed in a very long time."

"Me too." I gave the muttered agreement. "Were you cold?" I asked and he shook his head as a frown of wonder crossed his face. "Me neither." I offered, "though it could have been our new magic jackets."

We watched the scenery pass for several seconds before TJ whispered, "She must have been real."

Dropped off and halfway back to our hotel, TJ grabbed my forearm and pulled me to a stop.

"What?"

"Look!" he whispered excitedly.

"Where?"

"There!" I followed his finger and saw the ghost of our Witch. She was cleaner and taller, but it was her.

"No way!"

His hand slipped into mine and an unspoken agreement had been made as we hurried toward the restaurant she'd entered.

We mamboed awkwardly with a couple trying to get out as we tried to get in, too excited in our quest.

"Oh my god," I whispered when I saw her sitting in the back of the quaint restaurant. Her hair was washed, a neat brown braid hanging over her shoulder. She wore a white billowy, long sleeve peasant shirt and a simple black skirt.

Her face was tanned from the sun and weathered from the wind and a possible lack of moisturizer. When we came to stand in front of her table, she stared at us for several moments before giving a heavy sigh and dramatically throwing her hands up. "You got me."

We didn't say anything. I still wasn't convinced she was real, so I reached out and tentatively touched her shoulder. She frowned. "I am real." She gestured to the seats at the table. "You might as well join me."

A tall, handsome man in a clean apron approached our table, eyeing us suspiciously and gazing at the woman, a silent question on whether or not she was okay.

"The bus driver," TJ muttered.

He wiggled his eyebrows then asked, "Hungry?"

Spices and the wonderful aromas of food registered and I inhaled appreciatively, adding my nod to TJ's already agreeing head bobs.

The bus driver left as the sounds of the restaurant registered: dishes rattling together, the sizzle of a grill and the music coming from a tinny radio station.

"I suppose you have questions," she said.

"Just a few," I sputtered.

She rolled her eyes and smiled. "I normally don't spend this much time with those I am inclined to ... help. Normally, they have the decency to run screaming from an old crone after several seconds," she sighed, "but the two of you ..."

TJ laughed. "Writers, am I right?"

I glanced at him out of the corner of my eye and retaliated with, "More like artists ..."

"Yes, well, you two needed a bit more attention," she said.

"What did you do to us last night?" TJ asked.

She shrugged. "Cleansed your spirits."

"So, not drugs?" I asked. She tisked at the very idea.

The driver/cook came back to our table with three plates. As he placed them before us, our Witch touched his arm. "Thank you, my love."

"They find out your secret fast." He winked at her before he disappeared back into the kitchen.

"Lomo saltado," she said waving to the plates of beef with onions, tomatoes, peppers, potatoes and rice, "Sergio makes the best lomo saltado in Aguas Calientes. The best in Peru really."

I took an obliging bite and moaned in appreciation, I didn't realize how hungry I was.

After another bite, I sat back and admitted, "I'm not sure what to ask."

"I suppose we should start with introductions. I am Elizabeth Rule." She gave a regal incline of her head.

"The Witch."

She winked. "I'm English, grew up in an upper-class, stuffy home; but I never fit in. Children who have knowledge of mysterious things never quite do. So I was sent to the best boarding schools and struggled through the awkward years." She stopped and leaned across the table. "And no, Miss Skye, you may not write my story."

(By the way, writing someone's story and writing 'about' someone are two completely different things and I refuse to argue semantics with you.)

She grunted and shook her head. (Remember that telepathic thing that may or may not be?)

Elizabeth continued, "When I attended university, I began studying the occult along with anthropology. The two seemed to go together. I found insight to what I could do, and was happily cuddled safely in the bosom of a research role in England's prestigious British Museum when I had a vision of Peruvian graves." She looked beyond our shoulders as memories floated past, then shook them off. "But you cannot just show up and tell some well-educated archeologists, please sir, dig here, would you? I've had a vision." She laughed. "Eventually I found academic proof and moments after I handed it over, I was drawn to Aguas Calientes. Here I found a little more ... direction. And Sergio. And now, I go to those who need me the most and put them back on the proper path." She picked up her cup and toasted the air with it.

"Why the ... costume?" I asked.

"Oh, at first I didn't, but do you know how many people laughed at me? A proper British woman trying to tell them their future? I decided to dress up. At first I just dressed as a Gypsy and tried to speak with a Peruvian accent. There were still so many questions. People wanted more, it's this instant gratification society we live in." She shook her head. "So I started to ..." she pursed her lips as if looking for the right words, "mar my appearance. But still there were questions."

"So you added the smelly clothes?" TJ asked.

"Yes, when a person smells that bad, *no one* will stick around and ask questions. I can pass on the little piece of information they need and then they are on their way."

"Smart," I said. "Wait, do most people you help speak English?"

A shrug was all the non-answer she was willing to impart.

"Why Aguas Calientes?" TJ asked.

"Most people who come to see Machu Picchu are tourists, but there are many who come to this place in search of something; they come in the hopes that the ancient stones will hold some powerful answer to the mystery of their lives." She leveled an obvious gaze at me. "They can't find it on top of the mountain."

"It's too crowded," I supplied.

"Isn't it just?"

"So you help," TJ whispered.

"I *try*," she corrected, then cleared her throat and sat up straight. "That is my story. You will have to be satisfied with it as it is."

"Elizabeth, last night ... what was that?" I asked. "Because I felt like a lot of it was for show."

She blushed and gave a dainty shrug. "Maybe it was, a bit. But all I did was relax you enough so you could expel all the bullshit." She shot us a cheeky grin. "And realign your life force."

"But—" I started and she held up her hand to stop me.

"Let it be," she said softly. "So now, you'll take the bus to Iquitos."

"Iquitos," (E - key - towz) I repeated.

She nodded. "I have your tickets. Once you are there, find a boatman by the name of Bob. He will take you down the Amazon."

"And that's our path?"

"Maybe." She smiled.

"What?" we asked at the same time.

She gave a shrug. "I only know that you need to go to Iquitos, find Bob, and see the Amazon. And stop worrying."

"About what?" I asked.

"*Everything*." She elongated the word.

"It's all very cryptic, isn't it?" I asked.

She raised an eyebrow as if I didn't know the half of it. Then she got a damn twinkle in her eye. "If we had road maps and neon signs, we wouldn't learn what we're supposed to, or become who we are meant to be."

"But I could argue that you are a bit of a road map arrow."

"A swift kick in the ass every now and again doesn't hurt." She stood up and handed over two tickets that were sitting under her plate.

"Where ...?" TJ asked.

"Go." She pointed to the entrance. When TJ reached for his wallet she waved that away and politely, but forcefully repeated, "*Go.*"

I stood, opened and closed my mouth several times, weighted down by the sheer amount of questions I had.

Her whole demeanor eased as she said, "Alicia, I only get glimpses, no one ever gets to know the whole of it, not even me." She shook our hands, then offered a "bon voyage my friends" that suggested this interaction was completely finished.

So we did what we were told. Got our bags, checked out of the hotel and boarded a bus with glorious cushioned seats, immense windows and a small footrest.

"So, an English Witch in Peru." TJ squared himself toward me once we were settled.

"You can't make this shit up," I whispered.

Fifty-Six

The bus didn't break down.
Not the first one.
The second one.
Or even the fourth one.

There is no bus that goes directly from Aguas Calientes to Iquitos. Turns out Iquitos is north of Agua Calientes, about 650 miles as the bird flies.

In the human realm, using available transportation and viable roads (aka: the bus tickets Elizabeth bought us), Iquitos was four bus rides away. That equates many hours of sleeping, flopping back and forth uncomfortably, stretching when we were able, getting off the bus at every roadside stop to have food and snacks, and fighting claustrophobia and boredom. I finished *The Hitchhiker's Guide to the Galaxy*. TJ did a sketch of a blur of trees out our window that I named: *The Blur of Progression #3*.

This time he wrote it and laughed asking, "But does the number signify the number of studies done on a subject or the print run?"

"The number of times you sharpened your pencil."

"Writers," he mumbled but I saw his grin.

I was expecting something different after our time with Elizabeth. I thought things would be ... easier. (Better maybe?) But the reality was that she 'spiritually' dosed us and all we got was a really great night's sleep.

Time became a strange thing on the bus. Moments were divided, expanding until they reached end to end and circled the earth several times over; then like a rubber band being pulled to its breaking point, was propelled back into something paper-thin, pressing my very existence into a speck.

There were other moments of the arduous drive when it rained, and surrounded by the various jungle foliage, time hung in the air, paused for a moment. No big life decisions needed to be made.

"I think I'm better here," I said. Only when I glanced over at TJ, he was asleep. I turned to the window to finish my confession, "Elizabeth was right, when I let go of overthinking everything, all the expectations I put on myself, away from the relentless screaming of society in all its technological forms ... I'm better here."

The fourth bus pulled into a sleepy town called Yurimaguas. We passed small houses and businesses, a lot of corrugated metal roofing. There was a mix of red brickwork, concrete and stucco-covered walls patched with palm trees, bushes, and vibrant blossoming flowers.

A tangle of power lines paralleled our path along the street. As we drove deeper into the city, I assumed we were in a high tourist area because we passed bright signs advertising buses and boats, their routes and timelines.

Our bus came to a stop in the large parking lot of a gas station at one in the afternoon. (According to TJ's watch.) I don't know how many days it'd been since Aguas Calientes. But I was happy to get off the bus. I was shocked, however, by the humidity and heat that seemed to violently kiss me full force on the mouth as I stepped onto the ground. Bienvenidos a Yurigamas.

"Whoa!" TJ exclaimed behind me.

In a daze we followed several locals to the street where a line of taxi drivers were waiting in open air, three wheeled vehicles.

I nodded in the direction of a driver who was trying to catch our attention and said to TJ, "When in Rome?"

"When in Rome." He followed.

The three wheeled vehicle was a converted motorcycle with a covered bench seat in the rear and behind that, a rack for luggage. We climbed into the bright canvas-covered seat and the driver, a young man wearing flip-flops, shorts and a teal green shirt of a local sports team, glanced between us for a moment before saying, "¿De Estados Unidos ?"

"¿Sí?" I answered his question with a question.

"Okay," he grinned, "do you go to Iquitos?"

"Sí."

"Okay." He started the motor taxi and off we went down the street. He pulled onto the road littered with motorcycles and motor taxis; no seeming rhyme or reason to the traffic coming toward us or that we were ensconced in. Either side of the street held parked taxis with drivers lounging in the seats waiting for a fare.

The heat was oppressive, after being so cool atop high peaks just a few days ago.

"Take a fast boat to Iquitos," our driver said loudly. "I'll take you to buy tickets. Take a fast boat to Nauta, then get a taxi to Iquitos."

And as with all things that had been accomplished this trip, we nodded, agreeing to the suggestion.

"Elizabeth said Bob would take us on a boat." I shrugged.

"I suppose we're about to meet Bob."

Yurimaguas was an interesting place, that possessed a palpable peaceful and slow pace. (Of course, that could be me projecting my own lack of enthusiasm at moving at any hurried speed through this humidity.)

But I was grateful when a small coat of rain began to patter against the top of the canvas roof. I was less grateful when it didn't cool anything off.

The driver stopped in front of a building with a large banner that had a picture of a boat. He pointed toward it and exclaimed. "Tickets."

When we climbed out he pointed to himself. "I can wait here."

We entered a building without a door and were greeted by two women wearing matching dark blue polo shirts standing behind a desk. Behind them was a bookcase topped with a large model of the boat from the banner outside.

I pointed out the obvious, "That must be the boat." It looked sound. Kind of cool. Of course it was only a reproduction.

TJ called out a greeting and the women brought out a map of the river. It turned out, Yurimaguas was the end of the road; *literally*. A port town where the only way to continue anywhere north was by river. Thus the need for a boat.

The women laid out our few options. I asked if any of the boat drivers were named Bob. When they shook their heads TJ said, "Then we really do have several choices."

We ended up purchasing a ticket that would take us from Yurimaguas to another town and then by taxi into Iquitos. A trip that would be 'doce horas en barco,' twelve hours by boat, and another hour and a half by taxi.

We headed back to where the motor taxi was still waiting and our driver asked to see the ticket, then pulled out his phone and nodded. "You have two hours. First get food before you take the boat."

He took us to an outdoor market but before he parted ways, he pointed to the wide brown tinged river a few hundred yards away and a green building. "Go there for food. Over there, find the boat."

And thus began another whirlwind of colors and sights and sounds. But at least we were walking now, no longer in a cramped bus, and I allowed visions of The Rock and the *Jungle Cruise* to waft about.

There were tarps and umbrellas covering a variety of vendors selling fish, pork, snails and turtles (but not only as pets.) There were fruits, T-shirts, shoes, watches, and baskets piled high with small rolls and fresh baked bread.

We bought large water bottles, bread, fruits, nuts and chips, figuring it would all be enough for the next fourteen hours.

Right?

But as the boat left at 4 p.m. and was an overnight excursion, sleep would take up some of the time.

(Maybe.)

With a new bag bought to carry our food, we headed to the boat dock nearby, which consisted of a rundown open-air room with benches for waiting; although, they were already boarding when we arrived.

We formed a line on a dirt path that led to the water's edge. After handing over our tickets, we were helped down several man-made steps carved into the earth, then a quick jaunt across a loose piece of wood connecting land to the front of the boat. A small hull was open to enter, then down three steps and we were on the boat. (The inside of which had the same damn layout as a bus.)

We groaned in unison and my legs cramped at the idea of another twelve hours in the same position.

The rows had two seats on either side of the aisle; fans were placed at various intervals; and orange life vests were strapped to the ceiling, one above each seat. Side flaps, made of waterproof tarp, were tied up to allow in what little breeze there was.

Across the top were open overhead areas for bags. Once we were seated in the full boat, the more substantial luggage and goods strapped to the outside roof of the boat, we were unceremoniously pushed off into the water and set sail.

And as we floated downriver, with the remote jungle keeping up pace alongside us while the sun set, I took TJ's hand in mine. "This isn't such a bad bus ride," I said, eyes wide. This wasn't something I got to do every day. This was far better than the bus. TJ, having offered me the window seat, I stuck my head slightly over the edge of the boat, letting the wind whip my hair.

"Beautiful." The change in TJ's timbre caught my attention, so I turned my grin toward him, he wasn't looking out at the river.

I leaned my head back and met his gaze, gently touched the side of his face and agreed, "Yeah, this view isn't so bad either."

Fifty-Seven

I was uncomfortable and tired of being in a bus seat. So was TJ, apparent by the way we both wiggled constantly, taking turns standing in the aisle and stretching. My legs had that bit of restless leg syndrome you get from not walking or moving. We took catnaps amid the low conversations and snoring of others and the hum of the boat. At some point we stopped by the side of the river where a group of locals came aboard to sell some food and fruit. I bought several plantains in the hope that the potassium would help ... something.

TJ tried to distract me, "Do you know how your cowboy story will end?"

"I've been thinking about it."

"You have to tell me what happens."

"I have to?" I questioned.

"I've shared everything I've sketched. It's only fair."

I tried to snarl in reply but gave into his request with a grin. "What Annabelle didn't understand was that Cal had no life without her. He wasn't gonna be kept warm with just memories. He'd try to give her a few months, but he'd go back to her. Drawn to her light the way a moth is."

"Nice," TJ offered.

I smiled. "Cal would see her on the street, coming out of a store or something. She'd see him and not be able to move or breathe. When Cal got close enough to her, he'd see that her eyes were ringed with lack of sleep and red as if she'd been crying. She'd start to shake because she had done the unthinkable."

"The unthinkable?" TJ asked.

I nodded. "Cal is willing to die for her, she is willing to give anything for him to live. So she married the bad guy."

"Whoa," TJ whispered, "didn't see that coming."

I gave a snuff of a laugh. "Me neither." I nodded several times as the ideas swirled. "She pulls money out of her purse and gives Cal everything she has and tells him to go build a life for them. The bad guy has so many enemies, he can't live forever. But Cal doesn't hear anything because he finally takes in her whole body and realizes that something was different, then it falls into place; she's pregnant."

"Dun, dun, dun." TJ added the soundtrack.

"Cal will feel betrayed. But she'll tell him she made sure she was pregnant before she married. And maybe she made an agreement with the man her father forced her to marry; that she would only lie with him once for the duration of their marriage. The baby is Cal's. He doesn't hear anything else, just walks over to the bar owned by Annabelle's new 'husband,' calmly takes out his gun and aims for the man's heart."

I blinked and shook my head, not sure. TJ waited out my silence as long as he could before he finally asked, "And?"

"I think ... in trying to save each other, they killed what they had."

"So Cal's going to die?"

I shrugged. "I don't know. I think so. If he lives, he'll never be the same again." I frowned as I thought about it. "I think if he lives, Cal Hand will die an old man on a horse, watching over a herd of cows. In his possession will be a marriage certificate, a picture of a young boy that looks exactly like him and a few mournful, beautiful love letters filled with regret."

TJ gave a low whistle, his voice appreciative when he softly drew out, "Fucking writers."

Soon after the story ended, the tarps that covered the side were raised and the sun was rising over the river.

The woman behind me tapped on my shoulder to politely explain the river we were on wasn't the Amazon. Not yet.

(But I'll tell you what; even if this wide, vast river was a tributary of the Amazon, it was glorious in the sunrise.) Deep orange stretched from just beyond the trees, into the smooth morning waters. Thin clouds pulled like taffy across the sky, an attempt to mimic the morning light.

We arrived in a small town, shuffled off the boat and were greeted by a wide array of helpful men in our personal space asking if we needed a ride; and we did, but my legs were sore from doing nothing and I was exhausted and hungry for a real meal and the added humidity was making me punchy. And when the taxis turned out to be more motor taxis, I sucked it up as I watched TJ negotiate with a driver that we were headed to Iquitos.

So it was back in a cramped space, bumping along a rough road while the sounds of the surrounding vast jungle serenaded us and the occasional modest structures with thatched huts and open sides blurred past.

Iquitos was not an island, but a city so remote and surrounded by so much jungle it was only accessible by boat. (And this one road that connected two cities and cut off a few hours of river travel time.) It was also a thriving metropolis of half a million people and somehow we became one in a sea of motor taxis. The sound and trash built up on the divider of the streets mingled with smells that fluctuated between body odor and humid garbage and occasional sweetness.

The driver turned in his seat and asked, "¿A dónde vas?"

His question pulled an unexpected laugh from my chest, and turned out to be my breaking point. Because tears were very, very quick to follow.

Where are you going? ¿A dónde vas?

Wasn't that the existential question I'd been asking myself for a while now? The reason I walked out of that restaurant and continued to move forward?

And the answer is: I don't know. I have absolutely no idea.

TJ frowned and bent to look at my downcast face. "Ali?"

"I'm done." I declared my defeat as the tears fell.

(And look, don't act like you've never been on vacation and haven't reached the end of your proverbial rope before. It comes about from any number of things. Exhaustion. Weather. The mixture of different personalities of those you're vacationing with. The overwhelming sights and sounds. Strangers in your personal space, babies crying, kids whining, headaches, queasy stomachs ... Vacation burnout comes for us all and pushes us up against our wall.)

My wall was born of ultimate exhaustion, being in confined seats for too many days on end, and being asked where I was going. I let my head fall onto TJ's shoulder.

"What do you need?" he asked as he wound an arm around me.

"A break," I said.

"I'm right there with you," he brushed a kiss on my head, "so I have an idea."

I nodded, definitely open to ideas.

"I'm gonna find a great hotel with air conditioning and room service and we're gonna spend the next two days sleeping." It was a question at the same time it wasn't.

Because in answer to his idea, I gave in to full-body sobs. Nothing has ever sounded so amazing in my entire life. I'd argue about money and where I was going and all that crap later. Right now, finding a bed and a shower and food and air conditioning was the exact soul food I needed.

(And we're all going to agree that I am merely human for wanting to give into such things at this moment in time.)

Fifty-Eight

When I woke up on the third morning of my air-conditioned hotel stay, I had officially become well-adjusted.

(I present you with a theory: Two days of sleep in a soft king size bed; on the sixth floor of a decadent hotel overlooking a plaza of well-landscaped greenery, fountains and a backdrop of a terracotta and earthen colored church; where food was delivered three times a day to our door; including several showers and air conditioning; can realign your entire nervous system, chi, energy grid and life in a way not much else can. And yeah, when you feel clean and rested and a sexy ass man reaches for you in the middle of the night, that's gonna help too.)

TJ was back on his schedule; he'd left a note on his pillow that he'd bring me breakfast; under the note he sketched a cup of coffee and a croissant. (An easy one to name: *About Last Night #4.*)

I padded out of the dreamy bed, across the maroon carpet with a modern swirl pattern, pulled open the floor-length curtains, then went in search of my notebook. It was wrinkled, stained, and looked as travel weary as I had felt a few days ago. But finally, after so many buses, trains, ancient ruins, new friends, dirt, sweat, and confessions, I was *inspired.*

We stole the journeys of others. We ripped off the adventures of explorers. We borrowed scenes from movies and walked in the footsteps of those that came before us; we tread politely at times, and at others, we left slash marks and prints, frustrations and fatigue, our problems and our solutions.□ We burned, we loved and found new worlds. We found glimpses here and there of our souls, glimpses that reinforced who we thought we were all along.

"I like that smile," TJ said as he entered the room.

I was wearing a huge grin when I glanced up at him, but it twisted into a mouthed 'wow' when he came into view. He was holding two cups of coffee and a bag, but he'd showered and shaved and looked ... delectable in a navy blue, boatneck, short sleeve linen shirt; the flimsy buttons along the vee of the neckline were undone, which caused a dryness in my mouth. He had a pair of off-white, lightweight pants and flip flops.

"I like that." I gestured at him from head to foot with my pen.

A blush rushed up his neck as he glanced down at himself, "It looks okay?"

"Oh, yeah."

He put the coffees and bag down, reached into his pocked and pulled out a silver bracelet, took my hand and slipped it onto my wrist.

It was a sweet silver chain design, stiff with a silver cuff that was inlaid with different blue shaded stones.

"TJ ..."

He twisted my wrist slightly back and forth to watch the stones catch the sun. "It reminded me of your eyes."

I glanced up and watched this artist, this man who looked at the world and saw more than most; who stood solid, his self-confidence visible; his kindness understated; and felt my continual racing heart everytime his attention turned to me.

"So Theodore Jones, I'm gonna go out on a limb here."

There were those eyes turning toward me.

"I like you a lot. Even though I don't know everything there is to know, I'm falling for you. Pretty damn hard."

He flashed a smile and winked. "I know."

"Oh," I twisted my lips and muttered, "good."

He leaned forward, making sure he had all my undivided attention before his deep voice softly confessed, "Mi cielo lindo, you solidified a place in my heart quite some time ago."

"Oh," butterflies took flight, "good."

He sat next to me on the sofa, pressed a kiss on my cheek then opened the bag and pulled out something that looked like an empanada. He took an appreciative bite, then nodded to my notebook. "You were writing?"

I took the empanada out of his hand. "I was."

"Read it to me?"

"No."

"Okay," he yawned, "then how about I tell you a story."

I raised an eyebrow as a smile pulled at the corner of his mouth. "I was ordering breakfast, and wouldn't you know it, I overheard this couple speaking English. Then because it felt right, I just kind of introduced myself and asked where they'd been and where they were headed. They'd just come from an excursion that they claimed was a do-not-miss-expedition. A three-day stay in the jungle. And then they handed me a flier." He pulled it out of his pocket and handed it over.

A yellow glossy photo of the Amazon and monkeys and toucans were surrounded by the arched English phrase, "Bob's Authentic Jungle Tours."

"So we found Bob?"

"I think we found Bob," TJ agreed.

I read through the pamphlet and handed it back as he asked, "Am I calling Bob?"

"Has a pamphlet steered us wrong yet?"

Whatever the hell it meant, we were headed for an authentic jungle adventure.

We repacked our bags, checked out of the hotel and took a taxi to a boat dock.

Walking down several awkward steps dug out of the side of the river, we stepped onto a dock where a small man, wearing a dirty long sleeve shirt and no shoes, and a tattered baseball hat, stood on the bow of an open-sided boat and waved. In a thick New York accent, he asked, "Hey there, are you twos lookin' for Bob?"

"We are," TJ replied.

"Well, ya found him."

Once docked, he slid a wood plank out. TJ climbed aboard and reached out for my hand.

And as I took his hand, I knew he was mine. TJ Jones belonged to me in the same way I belonged to him. My heartbeat pounded heavily in my chest with the realization, but there were no other elementals that helped to put an exclamation on the moment. No lightning bolts. The sky didn't open up. There was no dramatic whirl of wind, no earth-jarring recognition of my revelation or even a shocking flight of birds taking off.

Just simple ease.

Because Tía Camila had told us to stick together. Because an English Witch in Peru told us we were two halves of the same whole. Because Francisco knew we were more than friends from day one. Because Sister M had faith in us.

Without any warning, Bob pushed off from the dock and I stood on the side of the small boat watching the brown water flow past.

TJ stood beside me and I whispered, "There's a lot of literature here."

"Peru, the Amazon or Iquitos?"

"This moment. It's the boatman on the River Styx taking us to our final destination. It's another leg of Odysseus' journey. It's *The African Queen*. It's … *Romancing the Stone*; without the danger." We both chuckled, then I asked, "When did this trip become steeped in so much Greek Mythology?"

TJ playfully elbowed me. "Honey, all life is steeped in Greek mythology, they were the ones who put it on paper."

Unsure of where we were going, how long it was going to take or what we'd find next; we sat down to wait and see what would come.

Bob found the current and he too sat, a content smile in place as he rested his arm on the rudder, his eyes focused on the horizon.

And that seemed like the best place to focus one's eyes and energy, on the horizon.

The End

Notes from the author

-I hope you enjoyed the time you spent with Ali and TJ. I know I did, and I added so many items to my Bucket List!

-This book was inspired by my real-life 30th birthday dinner with my family. There were numerous questions as to what I was doing with my life at said dinner. However, I did not get as drunk as Ali and stayed seated for the duration. (My imagination, however, *did* walk out the front door.)

-On many many occasions, I find myself with an idea, but no pen or paper (and sometimes no phone). I have joked often that I am a writer without a pen or paper.

-Getting into Tijuana: Have your passport or equivalent ID with you. I truly haven't been for several years. Side Note: Yes, when I was in 8th grade, our class went to help build a house for a community service project.

-You cannot magically be locked into the Teotihuacán archeological site after they close. But from November-July, you *can* go at night for a guided tour and a light show. (*Adding to Bucket List right now.)

-The restaurant La Cueva is real. In fact, surrounding the archeological area of Teotihuacán are three restaurants located in caves. I mixed a few things I liked from each to make the one TJ and Ali visit. Also, the restaurants all close at 6 p.m. But still, isn't that cool?!

-So, let's talk for a moment about fiction. The reason I love writing it so much is because fiction has a malleability that real life doesn't have. And my imaginary friends can stay late in archeological sites, meet Witches who take them to Machu Picchu and befriend some shady characters without any real consequences.

Fiction aside, I have a deep respect for all things Archeological, Museum and Library. So in real life, let's all be respectful and follow guidelines when visiting important sites and stay out of the roped off areas.

-Sadly, you can't go willy-nilly in the middle of the night to Machu Picchu alone (even if you are with a Witch.) Machu Picchu is open every day of the year, including Sundays and holidays. Visiting hours are from 6 a.m. to 5:30 p.m. The closest you can get to Machu Picchu at night is a hotel they've built near the entrance. At the time of writing this book, the prices to stay there were quite expensive.

-I have no idea what the significance is of the ritual done by Elizabeth. It was made up. But I suppose … Carnation petals work especially well in healing spells; sage has been used by many different cultures to purify the spirit; and Machu Picchu Stone is a "mystical and powerful gemstone known for its enigmatic properties and gentle energy. Mined from the base of Machu Picchu in Peru, this stone is said to be capable of healing even the soul's deepest wounds".

But really, I just make it all up.

-The Jorge Chávez International Airport in Lima, Peru has a food court open 24/7 with a McDonald's, Papa Johns, Subway, Starbucks and Dunkin' Donuts. When Ali says she smells McDonald's as they walk through the airport, this is why. I added that bit because I find it fascinating and intrusive and I'm not sure how I feel about it all …

-Yup, that's the real National Mexican Warning System that's used in case of a hurricane.

-As I worked on the final edits for this book, I started taking notes of all the lessons that were inadvertently passed along to Ali. This is what I thought she would jot down in her notebook:

* WALK OUT OF THE RESTAURANT WHEN YOU KNOW IT'S NOT WHERE YOU SHOULD BE.

* CHOOSE THE ADVENTURE. STABILITY IS FOR LATER.

* RECALIBRATION IS GOOD WORK IF YOU CAN GET IT.

* SOMETIMES THE CREATIVITY TANKS NEEDS A REFILL.

* 'ALMOST' ISN'T A WASTE OF ENERGY.

* HAVE FAITH.

* IF YOU WANT COMPANY, BUY A BIG TABLE—THEY WILL SHOW UP.

* BE OPEN TO ADAPTATION BUT ALSO HAVE THE COURAGE TO REJECT WHAT DOESN'T WORK.

* SOMETIMES EXPECTATIONS FALL SHORT.

* THE DESTINATION IS OFTEN LESS IMPORTANT THAN THE JOURNEY ITSELF.

* GO, 'BE FUN.'

* IF LOVE DOESN'T FEEL LIKE '90S R&B, DON'T ACCEPT IT.

* ACCEPT ADVENTURE WITH TWO HANDS. CLAW AT IT. ALL OF IT. THE REST WILL COME.

* A SWIFT KICK IN THE ASS EVERY NOW AND AGAIN DOESN'T HURT.

Acknowledgements

-First, I'd like to thank **YOU**! I know how much your time is worth in this day and age and I appreciate that you chose to spend it with my imaginary friends. With all my heart, thank you.

-I edited the bulk of this book at my public library; at the very time when the libraries in my state are under attack. It has been a pleasure watching them rise above the misconstrued hatred, and continue to work to the best of their abilities to educate, inform, and provide unrelenting services and support to our community. With everything in my being, I'd like to send a heartfelt thanks to each staff member in the **Boise Public Library system;** for ALL the good they continue to do and their fight to allow humans to connect to information.

-A few moons ago, the book club I belonged to read the original version of this book. Let me tell you, it has changed A LOT since then! Thank you for your support!!: Lori Reading, Cindy Ray, Danielle Wallner, Monika Hatfield, Jamie Delavan, Alison Monasterio, Angie Elliott, Dani Porritt, Ronna Parish, Erika Molchan(Evans), Mary Rossiter(Zrubek) and Pam Twilegar.

-Support your local indie authors and the indie bookstores that support them!!! I'd especially like to thank all the wonderful people at **Barn Owl Books** in McCall for their continued support. You are amazing!

-My friends and family who love and support me and take me to coffee and give me sage advice or just listen when I need to talk, you are the reason I have the confidence to attempt what I do, and the courage to fail.

This book needed a fierce team to bring it the final few miles home, so a huge thanks to:

-**Rocio Guillen**, for the help with the Spanish.

-**Kristy Labardee,** who did an intensive sensitivity reading for me; her feedback was vital and amazing! Thank you so much!

-**Michele Tomlinson**, the alpha reader among alpha readers! She is the last read through and makes sure I can shine and sparkle to the best of my ability. Thank you for your support and work and friendship.

-Do you love this cover?! I love all my covers. This one is glorious! A huge hug of thanks to **A. M. Rasmussen**, my friend who moves temples (and pyramids) for me. You're a rock star! (If you are reading this, go check out the cover; my artist placed a Quetzal bird and the shadow of a Jaguar as little Easter eggs for us!)

-**Ariane Kimlinger** at Owl Focus Editing is the best human. We spend hours talking through plot, syntax, grammar and character motivations. And we have so much fun doing it. She is a tireless editor and fabulous friend. She is my grammatical guru and she makes my books the very best version of themselves that they can be.

-And always, thank you to my **Mom** and **Dad**, who are the curators of my heart and soul and continually keep me walking forward with my head held high, no matter what falls in my path.

Visit NicoleSharpWrites.com for more entertainment.

Want to read more by Nicole Sharp?

Try an Italian holiday

or

get started on

The **Simply** TROUBLE *Series*

Legend has it that Nicole Sharp was born to hippies during an ice storm in Stone Mountain, Georgia. While confirmation of said events cannot be agreed upon, one fact is for certain, it was a Tuesday.

By age twelve, Nicole was sure of two things: 1) She wanted to be a writer and 2) She wanted to travel. She begged her parents to allow her to voyage alone to exotic lands. They permitted her to go from California to Boise, Idaho to visit a great-grandmother.

After muddling through her college years, Nicole graduated with a Bachelors in History (think Greeks and Romans). Why not study English if she wanted to be a writer? There were better stories in history class.

Nicole is Italian. According to Ancestry.com it's a rather low percentage, but she feels she is at least 51% Italian. She's visited the homeland a handful of times, studied the language and loves the Italian cappuccino.

Nicole's first concert was to see the bluegrass group The Seldom Scene when she was a fifteen-year-old, thanks to her parent's bluegrass phase. However, she never admits it, and instead tells everyone that They Might Be Giants, whom she saw in college, was her first real concert.

Her first car was a yellow Chevy Celebrity and her favorite job was working as a docent at a museum in an old Colorado mining town. She has written extensively about both.

Visit NicoleSharpWrites.com for more entertainment.